Praise for *Life After Life*

"The line between life and death is never so powerfully ambiguous. A powerful gift for dialogue has always animated Jill McCorkle's fiction, and here, in her first novel in 17 years, we hear some astonishing voices . . . As readers, we feel honored to witness their passages."

—*The Boston Globe*

"McCorkle captures the essence of each with love, insight and an ever present sense of humor. You will fall in love with her characters."

—Rona Brinlee, NPR's *Morning Edition*

"Who knew death, regret, and lengthy ruminations about days past could add up to a novel this vibrant, hopeful, and compelling? . . . Gorgeously written . . . McCorkle's greatest gift is in illuminating the countless tiny moments that make up our time on Earth."

—*O: The Oprah Magazine*

"The elderly residents of Pine Haven live and yearn and challenge one another with an exuberance that jumps off the page."

—*The New York Times*

"Clever, bighearted, and wise." —*Vanity Fair*

"I recommend this novel to anyone looking for a beautiful, heartfelt, funny, warm and smart story. *Life After Life,* people. It's a rare delight."

—Elizabeth Gilbert, ElizabethGilbert.com,
author of *Eat, Pray, Love*

"I have always loved Jill McCorkle's books: her characters are such characters! But in *Life After Life,* she has outdone herself . . . There's talk about magic in this wonderful novel, and McCorkle displays her own sleight of hand in delivering a powerful message in such a subtle and beautiful way."

—Elizabeth Berg, author of *The Day I Ate Whatever I Wanted*

"Great . . . A vividly voiced round-robin of interlocking stories set in and around a North Carolina retirement home . . . Sharply real."

—*Entertainment Weekly*

"McCorkle shows that even when death is just a few breaths away, surprising new connections and beginnings can occur through the magic of memories and love. McCorkle has crafted a story and characters that readers won't soon forget." —*Minneapolis Star Tribune*

"Can imagination, and love, hold even death in abeyance? This question is at the center of Jill McCorkle's wondrous new novel. Like Flannery O'Connor, McCorkle's genius is to give us both philosophical speculation and a riveting narrative filled with unforgettable characters. Great writing, poignancy, humor, wisdom—all are in abundance here. Jill McCorkle is one of the South's greatest writers; she is also one of America's." —Ron Rash, author *The Cove* and *Nothing Gold Can Stay*

"It's important to have empathy, wisdom and humor, and McCorkle shows hers on every page of *Life After Life*. But it requires a consummate skill to make those qualities sing. And this book sings. It might leave you contemplating the wonder of your own existence." —*Independent Weekly*

"A narrative that brims with voices, humor, honesty and heartbreak . . . The chapters' alternating perspectives yield layer after layer of wisdom . . . *Life After Life* offers a steady gaze at people's flaws and merits, without apology and without tidy conclusions." —*The Raleigh News and Observer*

"Leave it to McCorkle to plumb the ultimate new beginning in this down-home, Southern-style Book of the Dead. Illuminating, reassuring, and enlarging our understanding of the crossing from this world to the next, her novel sings with the mystical, the magical and the fragility of this thing called life." —*The Atlanta Journal-Constitution*

"Her characters crackle with personality and her ear for dialogue is spectacular . . . Another work of art." —*The Fayetteville (NC) Observer*

"Funny and painful, *Life After Life* explores not dying, but rather the mysteries of living—the second chances, the human connection, the love. The result is an impressive and poignant interweaving of vibrant characters; overlapping tales create a whole that is greater than the separate parts. McCorkle returns to the novel with a deeper wisdom and moral intensity. With a Southern flair, she invites the reader to muse on what matters most in the days we are given."

—*Richmond Times-Dispatch*

"Thoughtful and moving."

—*AARP Blog*

"McCorkle's writing is tender and warm and funny."

—"Printer's Row," *Chicago Tribune*

"*Life After Life* should enjoy broad readership because of its life-and-death narrative, not despite it . . . In McCorkle's characters, we see ourselves and those we know—their pathos, humor, regrets, joys, and sorrows, the parts and the wholes that each of us becomes. That's the strength of the stories throughout *Life After Life*: our interconnectedness."

—*ForeWord Reviews*

"Echoing its title, this book and its characters will linger with you long after the initial reading."

—*Real South Magazine*

"A painfully funny, wonderful book about the end of life."

—*Yakima Herald Republic*

"It takes a skillful author to write a book about death that leaves the reader feeling uplifted, and McCorkle (*Going Away Shoes*) is such an author . . . [An] excellent novel."

—*Library Journal*

"Jill is going to break your heart but along the way make you glad you went with her. She has written a book that will haunt me for a long time—in the best way. She has given me people to populate my dreams."

—Dorothy Allison, author of *Cavedweller*

LIFE AFTER LIFE

Also by JILL McCORKLE

Life *After* Life

———— A NOVEL ————

JILL McCORKLE

A Shannon Ravenel Book

ALGONQUIN BOOKS OF CHAPEL HILL 2013

ℝ

A Shannon Ravenel Book

Published by
ALGONQUIN BOOKS OF CHAPEL HILL
Post Office Box 2225
Chapel Hill, North Carolina 27515-2225

a division of
Workman Publishing
225 Varick Street
New York, New York 10014

First paperback edition, Algonquin Books of Chapel Hill, November 2013.
Originally published in hardcover by Algonquin Books of Chapel Hill in 2013.
Printed in the United States of America.
Published simultaneously in Canada by Thomas Allen & Son Limited.

This is a work of fiction. While, as in all fiction, the literary perceptions and insights are based on experience, all names, characters, places, and incidents either are products of the author's imagination or are used fictitiously. No reference to any real person is intended or should be inferred.

Library of Congress Cataloging-in-Publication Data
McCorkle, Jill, [date]
Life after life : a novel / by Jill McCorkle.—1st ed.
p. cm.
ISBN 978-1-56512-255-0 (HC)
1. Older people—Fiction.   2. Retirement communities—Fiction.
3. City and town life—North Carolina—Fiction.   I. Title.
PS3563.C3444L54 2013
813'.54—dc23   2012023445

ISBN 978-1-61620-322-1 (PB)

10 9 8 7 6 5 4 3 2 1
First Paperback Edition

For my children
and for their grandparents
and their great-grandparents
and so on

There is a land of the living and a land of the dead and the bridge is love, the only survival, the only meaning.

—THORNTON WILDER

LIFE AFTER LIFE

Joanna

Now Joanna is holding the hand of someone waiting for her daughter to arrive. Only months ago, this woman—Lois Flowers—was one of the regulars in Pine Haven's dining room where the residents often linger long after the meal for some form of entertainment or another. She was a woman who kept her hair dyed black and never left her room without her hair and makeup and outfit just right. She had her color chart done in 1981 and kept the little swatches like paint chips in the zippered section of her purse. She told Joanna that having your colors done was one of the best investments a woman could ever make. "I'm a winter," she said. "It's why turquoise looks so good on me." She loved to sing and some nights she could convince several people to join in; other nights she simply stood in one corner and swayed back and forth like she might have been in Las Vegas singing everything she knew of Doris Day and Rosemary Clooney and Judy Garland. She loved anything Irving Berlin had ever written. Now she has forgotten everything except the face of her daughter, random lyrics, and that your shoes and purse should always match. Joanna has watched the daughter night after night leaning into her mother's ear to sing—first upbeat (*clang, clang, clang went the trolley*). She always ends with one of her very favorites like "It Could Happen to You" or "Over the Rainbow" or "What'll I Do?" Joanna—as ordered by Luke's many rules—keeps a notebook with an entry on each of the people she sits with. She has to do an official one to turn over to the nurse who oversees her work, but this is a different, personal notebook she writes just after someone has died. It's a notebook she bought and showed Luke to prove to him that she was taking his assignments seriously—a bright yellow college-ruled spiral-bound notebook, which was all she could find at the Thrifty Market there close to Luke's house. It was near the end for him so she didn't venture far. "This is my page," he told her. "Everybody should get at least a page." She writes what she knows: their names and birthplaces and favorite things. Sometimes she asks questions: What is your first memory? Your favorite time of day or holiday or teacher or article of clothing? How would you describe your marriage? Was there something you learned in your life that surprised you? She records the weather and season and last words if there are any. Luke said that *this* would be her religion, the last words and memories of the dying her litany. She should read and reread the entries regularly like devotionals. *Keep us close*, he said. *Keep us alive. Don't ever let us disappear.*

THE LONGEST AND *most expensive journey you will ever make is the one to yourself.* Joanna's life is blip blip blip like images on an old film projector that keeps sticking and burning. She's been spliced a lot of times over the years, but finally she feels free—not perfect, not problem free, just free. No one likes to talk about the positive parts of getting older and aging into orphan-hood, how with your parents you often bury a lot of things you were never able to confront or fix or let go of.

She has spent long hours discussing this with C.J., a girl most likely *not* to be Joanna's best friend, and yet she is. C.J. is half her age, punk and pierced and tattooed with a baby boy whose father she won't discuss—not yet at least. C.J. is beautiful and so unaware of it, long legs and hazel eyes and a beautiful dark complexion that leaves people perplexed and wondering about her ethnicity. It seems she might even be perplexed herself and cam-ouflages herself with tattoos and loose clothing and colors of hair dyes that are not natural to any race.

C.J. claims to have lots of secrets, lots of ghosts, and she says she writes down all the bad stuff in her journal, which she calls Pandora's Box, and hides it there in the best security safe of all. She said she made a special trip to Costco to buy her "safe de-posit box"—a mega-sized box of Kotex, which she then positioned at the back of her linen closet with "the sentry" placed in front: Monistat and Vagisil and all kinds of douches. She said it was a security system easily tested in the checkout line, the man next to her going from way too warm to icy cold in minutes. She said if there were any doubt, a good scratch in the right place would really get rid of someone you weren't interested in.

"If something ever happens to me," she once told Joanna, "ev-erything you need to know is in the journal in the giant Kotex box at the back of the linen closet and you can have everything I own, even Kurt—especially Kurt." Joanna told her that if anything ever happened to *her*, she had a fake book, *Darwin's Descent of Man*, that opens and holds important papers. She also has a fake can of Campbell's tomato soup. The bottom screws off and someday when she makes lots of money, that's where she plans to keep some for security. "You can have *that* and the Dog House," Joanna told her.

Like Joanna, C.J. has done a lot of different things. She has cleaned houses and read palms and groomed dogs and now grooms the elderly—hair, hands, toes—at Pine Haven and leads them in a few activities and exercises. She rents the little apartment over the Dog House and in exchange for sometimes opening or closing, Joanna babysits her son, Kurt. Joanna's only rule as a landlord is no candles since she herself has had a couple of house fires as a result of purification rituals. "That would do it," C.J. said, and laughed when the rule was explained and adjusted her lip ring, which she always removes before going to work. "I'll come up with another way to *purify*."

Joanna wasn't there for her mother, but she was there for her dad and seeing him through those last days allowed her to let go herself. Being there may prove to be the greatest gift of her life. And of course none of that would have happened without Luke and Tammy.

In her work, Joanna has learned the importance of making peace. She sees it all the time, the stubborn child who won't come to the bedside and so the parent lasts far longer than should be asked of anyone. It is painful to watch, and for this reason she feels lucky to have journeyed her way back to this place. Her dad wanted her to promise to keep the the Dog House running and now she is doing her best, opening and closing and hiring responsible people to work the place, so she can devote herself to the volunteer hospice hours she gives over in Pine Haven's nursing wing.

"Make their exits as gentle and loving as possible," Luke had said. "Tell them how good it will be, even if you don't believe it yourself. You're southern, you know how to do that." And now family members greet and embrace her like she is one of them. Lung. Brain. Breast. Uterus. Pancreas. Bone. The families discuss and explain the symptoms and diagnoses for her as if they have never been heard of before, have never happened to anyone else, and she listens. Mistakes are made in the telling and she does not correct them. It is important to remain separate, to allow them to claim the disease, claim their grief. It is important not to get too attached or personally involved. Sometimes, when family members are naming the tests and the symptoms and prognosis, she allows herself to imagine her mother, getting the news and then driving home. Actively deciding what to do next but *not* calling her. But Joanna can go only so far with that or she'll undermine her purpose in the present. She is there, compassionate and listening, guiding the patients to talk and tell their stories if inclined but knowing when to step back into the shadows of the drapes or a closet door so family members get their time. She knows how to disappear.

Relatives show her all the old photos and letters; they tell her of accomplishments and regrets and then afterward, they drift away, her presence like something from an old dream, a reminder of their grief and loss. Sometimes they see her in the grocery or hardware store or when they drive up to the Dog House, and they can't help themselves, their eyes well up and words get choked. Like Pavlov's dogs, they react to her presence. It makes her think of poor Harley, the docile old orange cat at Pine Haven with enough poundage to warm even the coldest circulation-free feet, only now all of the residents are terrified of him because of the story in a recent news broadcast about a cat who chose to curl up beside whoever was most likely to die. The reports speculated how the cat knew. Did he sense something? Did he smell some chemical release of a body shutting down? His track record was convincing enough that the people who worked in that particular place paid attention to where he spent his time and the story told was convincing enough to ruin poor Harley's life there at Pine Haven. Once he was the most beloved and coveted creature in the place, and now he is greeted by shrieks and screams—slippers and plastic cups tossed his way. He is just a reminder of what is coming, a feline representation of Joanna herself, the one who appears bedside at the end and massages their cold darkening feet.

Now Lois Flowers's daughter, Kathryn, comes rushing into the room, a look of relief to find her mother still there. She is wearing her name tag from Bank of America where she is a teller. She nods at Joanna, no need for words. Joanna has already told her there isn't much time. Lois Flowers has not opened her eyes in eighteen hours, but her breathing does change when Kathryn's cheek is pressed against hers. "She's listening," Joanna says. "She knows you're here."

Before Lois stopped talking, she always asked Kathryn how school was and did she have homework. Joanna offers her seat and goes to stand by the window. It is important to be present and also allow people space and privacy. Outside the sun is shining and the roses are in full bloom. Mr. Stanley Stone and his son, Ned, are sitting on a bench talking. They were the first family Joanna worked with when she moved back. Mrs. Stone was dying and everyone in the family remained separate and distant. They lived up to the family name, though these days, the son, Ned, always says hello and acts like he wants to say more to her. Ned was several years ahead of her in school and then went to military school so she never really knew him. She's heard all the sad stories people think of when they see him, though, and now add his father's dementia on top of everything else. Mr. Stone walks the halls of Pine Haven, often insulting those who make eye contact. Now Ned Stone is leaning forward, his head in his hands while his dad stands in front of him shaking his fist.

"Mama? Mama, it's me," Kathryn says. "It's Kathryn."

Kathryn strokes the hair back from her mother's face and leans in close. She tells her mother how much she loves her and what a good mother she has been. She tells her about a new pair of shoes she just bought and how she got them for half price and what a beautiful June day it is. "Clang, clang, clang went the trolley," she sings, and then stops, closes her eyes, and presses her cheek against her mother's. She sits smoothing her mother's hair, shaking her head in disbelief that she is *here* in this moment. *How can it be?* her expression seems to ask. It's an ordinary Friday morning and Joanna cannot help but imagine what it would have been like if she had had the chance to be with her own mother, to lean in close and whisper good-bye, and in that moment there is a change in the air, and in that moment, they all come back to her, all the last days and last words and last breaths. Kathryn whispers the words, *What'll I do—when—you* . . . and then it is time; without a word, everything changes and they know that it is time.

Notes about: Lois Elizabeth Malcolm Flowers
Born: July 14, 1929   **Died:** Friday, June 7, 2010, at approximately 10:35 a.m.
Pine Haven Retirement Facility   Fulton, North Carolina

It was a warm sunny day, drapes fully opened to let all the light in, just as Lois Flowers always requested. The room was comfortable; somehow in spite of all the stark nursing apparatus, the room was as warm and welcoming as Lois herself. On the very first day, she invited me in and told me how lovely it was to have me there. *Not the ideal situation,* she said, *but still lovely to see you.* She said she had not known my parents well but sure did like those hot dogs my dad made, especially the Chihuahua because whoever heard of putting hot salsa on a plain old hot dog? Lois Flowers loved music and she loved fashion. She had a subscription to *Vogue* that had never lapsed in over forty years. "You could never get away with outfits like that here in Fulton," she said. "But it is important to know what folks are wearing elsewhere." She loved turquoise and the way people complimented her when she wore it. "I'm a winter," she liked to say, and referred often to a folder labeled "Personal Color Harmony" and all the little color samples within. She never went shopping for clothes or lipstick without it. Her favorite holiday was Halloween because she loved to see children having so much fun, but mainly because she liked a good excuse to wear orange even though her chart said that winters *do not wear orange well.* She decided that even if she looked horrid, *so what? It was Halloween, but,* she said, *I looked quite striking in an orange alpaca sweater and black gabardine slacks. It's the one time the chart got it wrong.* She still had the orange sweater and insisted that I take it and promise to wear it every October 31. She gave her daughter, Kathryn, the newer Halloween sweater, a honey-colored cashmere with black cat and witch hat buttons. *Kathryn is a true autumn and that sweater is perfect for her,* she said. *You can see why I want every-thing perfect for her.* She suggested I rethink the way I wear my hair and then put a hand to her mouth and apologized for such a rude remark. "This is all new," she told me. "This way I say things I don't mean to say," and I was able to assure her that I completely understood and that I am reconsidering what to do with my hair. She smiled and blew me a kiss. She said, how about some golden highlights and something layered to give body?

She had matchbooks from every nice restaurant she had ever gone to. Her favorites were Tavern on the Green and Windows on the World. She said she loved eating in New York City. She said her husband teased her that all it took for her to love a restaurant was for it to be in New York City and have lots of windows and a preposition in the name. She told Kathryn she needed to get back there, that they should take a trip and see a show. When told that both restaurants were gone, she held a firm position that she *still* needed to go there. "And so do you!" she said, always pulling me into the conversation. "And if there's not a young man in your life" (she asked me often if I had met anyone interesting), she said that I should just go alone. "Women do that now," she said. "A woman can go wherever she wants right by herself."

Once, while her husband and Kathryn were out at the County Fair, Lois Flowers burned her Maidenform bra in a hibachi in their backyard.

When her husband asked *what's that smell?* she said she had no earthly idea. She said it made her feel connected to something big and important, that she stood there in the backyard and pretended she was at a rally in New York City. She never told him what she had done, even when she saw him studying the ashes and what looked like a scrap of nylon. She had never even told anyone about it until that day; she said, *I have always felt liberated.*

Her last words were to Kathryn, spoken two days before she died. "Honey, do you have homework?" She had asked that question hundreds of times over the years and if Kathryn did *not* have homework, the two of them went shopping. Lois Flowers loved her daughter and she loved to shop. Kathryn said that all of their important conversations took place during those little shopping trips. What to expect when you start your period. Why you got that bad grade. Why a sassy mouth is not a good thing. How your reputation is your most prized possession. Why you should always do your best. Why good hygiene is a must. What boys do and do not have good sense about or control over. These topics were often whispered over the lunch counter at Wood's Dimestore where Kathryn got a cherry Coke or a milkshake and Lois got a cup of black coffee, her red lipstick staining the fat lip of the heavy white mug. Sometimes they ate pie or got a hot dog and always they were flanked with a bag or two of things they had found to buy over at Belk or the Fashion Bar or Smart Shop. "I can't wait to get home and see what all we got," Lois would say many times, and Kathryn said that once home, her mother kept the excitement going for many more hours with a fashion show and then talk of all the places Kathryn would go to wear the new things and all the wonderful things that would happen as a result. "Her predictions were not often right," Kathryn said. "But she was sincere."

I hugged my orange alpaca sweater close as I waited there with Kathryn. I wanted to tell her how lucky she was to have had such a relationship with her mother, but it was clear that she knew this. She held firmly to her mother's hand for as long as she was able, and then when the men came to take her mother away, she reached for my hand as we followed them out. I will miss them both very much.

[from Joanna's notebook]

Lois Flowers

The best table is over by the window, a big glass window and you can see the whole city just like a bird soaring in the sky. White linen and candles and yes, just a little champagne. Knives and forks and ice in crystal and a crystal ash tray, too, the filter smudged with her latest color—Claret, a perfect color, one of her reds. All of the colors on the chart (every chip!) may be taken a little darker or a little lighter. You can match clothing, makeup, accessories, and interior decor to colors on your chart. Don't ever remove the tags until you check your purchase in natural daylight as well as artificial light. Daylight. She can feel the daylight, and even this high up and behind all that glass she can hear the birds and some music. There is lovely music and a bathroom attendant, too, they shake hands and brush cheeks, what'll I do when you, oh thank you ever so much, thank you for your as-sistance. A plaid should always have at least two of your colors. The second eye color catches the glints, streaks, and flecks in your eyes. Her daughter has green flecks like her father; she is an autumn. Beautiful rusts and greens and golds and new shoes and homework. Do you have homework, honey? Daylight and Chanel No. 5, cheek to cheek, so lovely, too, and there is music and there are lots of little goodies over there on a big silver tray, over there by the big window, all shapes and sizes of beautiful and delicious canapés and the light fixtures are exquisite and there's music, always there is music, and colors and colors and beautiful colors. Just the right colors for a busy woman on the go, high heels click click click on that polished marble floor, and if she stands perfectly still, she can feel the building sway, the whole city below her is so bright and beautiful it leaves her light-headed and she feels the building sway, back and forth like a song, like a slow and easy swaying song.

C.J.
(Carolina Jessamine)

S PEAKING OF THINGS NEVER to tell your kids: How about where you were fucking at the time of conception? How about *that*? Or how about what everything costs? It costs this to feed you and that to clothe you. I wish I could send you to summer camp, but it costs too much and so does a bike and so does a house that looks worth a shit. Even the best intentions (the shitty day camp through the recreation department and the jeans that are the copy of what everybody else is wearing) still leaves you feeling like an undesirable—an unwanted thing to be put in the next room while all the Mr. Wrongs come and go, like anybody even believes there is a Mr. Right. Her mom once had a date with a Mr. Wright and what a joke that was. Yeah, whatever. Fuck your brains out. She didn't say it but that's what she was thinking.

Her name is Carolina Jessamine, named for a native vine—close kin to Confederate jasmine, both hardy thriving plants that will take over a structure in no time at all. You want to hide something ugly, just plant jasmine and then watch the ugly thing disappear. Her name is beautiful or so people say but maybe they wouldn't say that or think it if they knew how she got it—one of those things she shouldn't know, but her mother was too stupid or too unaware or something to know better. Her mother was fucking in the arboretum, right over there where C.J. goes out to smoke every day on her break. Her mother is buried just beyond the very spot—talk about never going anywhere, talk about a really small and limited life. Her mother told her that the whole time she was making love in the arboretum, she was staring up at that beautiful lush vine and the little silver tag that named it: Carolina Jessamine.

Wow, thanks, Mom. If her father—unknown creature that he is—had only flipped her over and fucked her from behind, C.J. might be named Splitbeard Bluestem or Hairgrass or Common Phlox. Talk about too much information. And did her mother even tell her about the plants beyond that? The purpose the splitbeard bluestem serves to control erosion, the silvery seed heads bursting to hold on and take root and never leave or the brackish-loving hairgrass on underground runners, popping up unexpectedly like a bad nosy neighbor. It made her think of what it must look like down below, the moles and voles tunneling along; it made her think of learning all about the Underground Railroad, people escaping, disappearing, resurfacing into a whole new place and life. It makes her inhale a long deep breath just to even imagine it. Now the crossvine is in bloom, orange and red trumpets straining for sunlight. She takes one of those good cleansing breaths Toby talks about when they try to get people to do yoga and it is peaceful, a whole roomful of old folks breathing deeply and chanting— one sounding like a sewing machine and another a squirrel.

One billion angels could come and save her soul. She loves that song and might have it tattooed around her wrist when she saves some money. Then later she could add: *Please, don't leave me here* around her ankle.

But her mother did leave her. She didn't give a shit. And the longer C.J. lives, the more amazed she is at how little of a shit so many people really give beyond their own little orbits. It makes her laugh to think of Stanley Stone who just the other day suggested to Marge Walker that she give everybody a break and come stare into his navel for a while instead of her own. These old guys are crazy, but there are some good ones. Better than what she had in a mother.

And Joanna is a good friend for sure. There's somebody who lived to tell the tale, turned it all around. Her mother could have done that, too, but of course she didn't. She didn't have the courage. It is hard to even think about her mother, to picture her. Once upon a time she was beautiful and the pictures of her as a young girl would have surpassed anyone in this town, but it doesn't take long to age when you're poor and abuse your body. You can go from young and beautiful to looking like shit, like that dried-up potato chip Toby is always talking about. That was C.J.'s mom, the dried-up undesirable chip at the bottom of the bag, and by killing herself she made sure C.J. wouldn't have it any better or would have to work like hell to even get a chance. And now here she is, twenty-six years old, and she has done just about everything there is you can do without any college education. She has waited tables and scrubbed houses and washed the old flaky, filthy hair of the elderly. She cuts their old hard nails and doesn't say a word about skin so dry and hard it could cut you and old yellowed nails you need a chainsaw to get through. "Does that feel good, sweetie?" she will ask while rubbing lotion into their old worn-out feet. Some call them Pat and Mike. Some call them the old dogs. One calls them her little tootsies.

"Does that feel good?" She has asked that question often enough. An easy thing to do, and there was a time when she did it to get what she needed and wanted. Some people might call it prostitution or whoring, but she figured it was no different from what a lot of women are doing right there in their little married houses. Hmmmm, I really want to go on that trip, so let's fuck him good and hard tomorrow night between *Lost* and the late news. That'll be good for something. She has worked as assistant to a local caterer and so she has heard plenty. The girls in the black pants and white tops are invisible as they reach and fill the glasses, especially a girl like her whose skin color is questionable. *What are you?* people want to ask. *Are you part Indian? Are you Hispanic?* Her tattoos don't show in the long sleeves and she wore no earrings or bracelets to those events, her hair pulled back in a tight ponytail. After a few passes of the glasses on silver trays, she was totally invisible, nothing more than a hand there to serve.

"What did you have to do to get him to buy you that?" one woman asked, her voice shrill and girlish and they all leaned in close.

"He gets a blow job on his birthday and that's it." *Giggles. Acknowledgment. Amen.*

"What about Valentine's? I do birthday and Valentine's Day."

And what they don't know is how the men *do* notice when you fill the glasses. Some mumble so you have to step close, but take note. They don't mumble with other men. They don't mumble with their wives. One followed her to the kitchen and down the basement stairs where the wine was kept. "I've never made love in a wine cellar to a beautiful young woman," he slurred, and she told him that today wasn't looking so fucking good either and she pushed him aside and got herself back into daylight and fresh air as quickly as possible.

Sometimes at cleaning jobs, she turned on the TV for company. This was before she got pregnant with Kurt and she was all alone. She liked the Spanish channel. She doesn't know a word of Spanish other than *hola,* but it was easy to know what was happening. You'd be an idiot not to get it. She was taking a break and watching that Spanish soap opera, the man meeting his mistress while the wife was in a coma in the hospital. And then the *real* man was right there in the *real* house looking at her, and his wife was not in a coma at the hospital but shopping for their upcoming tropical vacation. And she could see right through *that* window. She had felt him watching her before and finally she ended up saying, *I don't do windows, but I can do you.* The beginning. And actually it was a good beginning, or it seemed good. It felt good, and she even let herself imagine such a life, to imagine the safe draping warmth of someone who gives a shit, a suitcase packed for a tropical vacation.

She worked for a living. She worked to live. And what scrutiny of her performance. Her performance was discussed openly, her name and number passed along from hand to hand, the same hands holding their glasses out for a refill from the faceless no name with the bottle. She's real good, they say. Who's your girl? they ask. Who do you use? The key word is *use,* isn't it? So often that's the key word. But once they decide a girl is good, then she is invisible and she can scrutinize them. They sit at their computers or in front of their mirrors and leave little notes before dashing off to the next stop.

And then the girl is left to look and plunder their things. How open their lives are. The box of condoms that never gets touched, week after week after week there in his top drawer, which is always left open for you to close. The thousands of tubes of things that promise to make her look better. The shoes heaped in the closet and invitations crowding the fridge—so many addresses she recognized where she had also knelt before the great porcelain altar and scrubbed their shit and piss and vomit, swept free all those loose hairs.

Real clean people are often overcompensating for some really bad shit and really dirty people just don't care. Which is worse? Flip a coin.

One thing she learned is that there are a lot of men who made it a point to swing by the house while she was there. Some of them remembered her mother. Some of them complimented her. They said how she knew their houses better than their wives did. One said how she knew his body much better than his wife did. She knew their secrets. It wasn't hard. On that soap opera, the mistress was scorned. That was not hard to do at all and it was also not smart to do. Now that man was scared. He was thinking: I can't win. *Ding, ding, ding—you are absolutely correct, Bob, you can't fucking win.* He won when his wife hired her. He won the first time he ever ripped her clothes off and threw her there on the master bedroom bed and fucked the living daylights out of her. *Oh yes, does that feel good?* He never had it so good. She was a tool— his favorite tool—right in there with his putter and Weed Eater and espresso maker, the high-tech blender for the margaritas she never got offered. *So sure, go ahead, bring your scrawny white ass on and fuck me; it won't mean one goddamned thing.*

The perfect affair is kind of like the perfect murder. Unlikely. There are always telltale signs. There are always bread crumbs— even the most minuscule—leading to the main event. Sometimes she cleaned everything up and sometimes she didn't. Or *doesn't.* Sometimes she doesn't.

Nothing is free. That's what she likes to say and truth is she is a real good deal compared to what they've got and are paying for. She watched one woman coming and going, so curious as to how she could be so unaware, slinking about in leggings designed for a teenager—a woman way too old to be sporting camel toe—but there she was doing it and maybe that was what first hooked him, cheap pussy, though not cheap for long. Get that ring and slip of paper and then nothing is free, is it? It'll cost later. It costs a big-ass house somebody else needs to clean and two snotty kids, an expensive car and a trip to wherever and that's just the beginning. This was why C.J. wanted out of the business; she didn't want the life of a trumped-up whore, call it whatever you please. She was never standing on street corners or in clubs over near the military base. She was in a motel waiting for some very well-respected white-collar big deal about town. She was known for her discretion and for a period of time, her trademark costumes. She could do a schoolgirl because she was young and she could do a dominatrix—in fact she liked that one because if their old clammy hands were tied, they couldn't put them on her. She could look like a young boy, slick her hair back, no makeup, a thin cotton tank hanging loosely, small breasts bound in a tight tube top so they weren't even noticeable. One man, the one people would rise up shocked to hear, brought her grapes from his garden in the summer and liked to watch her put them in a galvanized tub and step and mash them, just enough to fill a pewter goblet and raise it to his thin gray lips. He fancied himself a man of God, and in the eyes of the town he *was* a man of God—but he was also a man of kink, which she sometimes whispered just as he came, eyes rolled back in whatever part of the deal he found ecstatic. He had once read about a priest in Boston who had offered his hardened self as a sacrament, demanding the young man at his mercy to suck away his sins. *Eat, drink,* that kind of shit, and he said that kind of shit, too, his big beefy hands clutching the sides of her face. There, too, it was like she was invisible, a helpless tool. How foolish to think he might offer up his salty unleavened cock and get away with it, but he did, and she took his offering and paid her bills and enrolled herself in a course at the community college, and she wrote down everything that happened. Every night she ever performed—schoolgirl and bad girl and timid boy and black girl and Indian girl—such a repertoire; she recorded it all. The who, the when, and the where. It was her security. It was that simple. And if she ever needed to use it, she would. She would open Pandora's Box and let loose the varmints and vile diseases. She will do whatever she has to do to give Kurt a better life than the one she was given.

"How wet can you get for a trip to Myrtle Beach?" that same asshole who had followed her into the basement asked at a different event. Myrtle Beach. Get real. Even if she thought there was anything that might make him worthwhile, Myrtle Beach?

"For you?" she cooed back in his stinking face. "I am nothing but the Sahara Desert." So many of them just assume you might want it, that you can easily be bought and rung up for this or that. If so-and-so fucked you, then I have to as well. But that's their own ugly reflection, isn't it? Never satisfied. Staring up at the sun and blinding themselves while they step in shit and on land mines. She believes in watching her feet step by step by step—see the snake before it sees you. See the cliff face, the hole, the man with the knife or crazy wife or misguided dick.

Parental law: *do unto others what was done to you.* That's just fucking wrong. In this way, C.J. has thought maybe her orphanhood was a blessing. With her mother's death, she knew that she never wanted to do anything to Kurt like what was done to her.

Her mother did leave a note: *Please forgive me. I can't take it anymore.*

The only thing interesting her mother ever told her was about how long ago when people gave up their babies, they often sewed little trinkets of things into the clothes they wore or the blanket that wrapped them so that someday, if the parents changed their minds, they could find and reclaim their children. Her mother said she had learned this from a nun who once filled in as a substitute teacher, a kind woman who tried to teach the children manners. C.J.'s mom got a good glimpse of Catholicism while she herself got a creepy pervert. No wonder people can't agree on religion. But still, stupidly, after her mother died, C.J. had sat and felt the pockets and hemline of everything her mother owned looking for a message or something she might find hopeful there in the worn musty heap of her belongings.

Once when she really wanted camp, the money suddenly appeared. One day it was impossible, her mother's shoulders slumped forward as she delivered the news without making eye contact, and then the next day there was laughter and excitement and she had an ink stamp with her name on it, a footlocker, and directions to Camp Ton-A-Wandah.

Weren't you ashamed? she asked her mother later when she figured out what was going on. Good things always coinciding with the smells and sounds of sex.

"Yes," her mother said. "I was ashamed. But I have always been ashamed so what's the difference. I don't want that to be your story."

Her mom said it was impossible to cross lines, to have people see you and accept you in a whole new light. She said that the one girl who was nice to her growing up had lived in the house by the cemetery; she was a plain simple girl with a huge birthmark that made her very shy.

Her mom had told her that it does get easier. Eventually they see you with a look of recognition, but then it's too late. You've got a bad husband or two and kids and an addiction or all of the above. The simple rule: some get saved, but most don't. The choices are important before the years begin to go so very fast.

Who was her father? It was a mystery. And the only thing her mother left her was a pile of worthless shit and a lot of broken promises. C.J. likes to think she will keep her promises to Kurt and that she'll be smart enough not to promise things that will never come true. She wants to be a good mother. She wants him to be proud of her.

Lately—because of all of Joanna's questions—she has been trying to think of some things she could appreciate about her mom. It was hard at first, but then she was able to get a few. She had a beautiful singing voice and C.J. remembers sitting outside the bathroom door with her ear pressed against the wood to hear. The

Supremes and the Jackson 5 were her favorites and sometimes at bedtime her mother would sing "I'll Be There" or "Can't Hurry Love." Kurt's big brown eyes are shaped like her mother's eyes and her mother had beautiful handwriting, small and delicate cursive, scraps of which C.J. has saved. Sometimes she writes her mother notes and tells her things. Asks her things. Didn't anyone ever try to help you? Was there anyone you really loved? In this great big world, did anyone ever give a shit about Perri Loomis? Black chicks and poor white girls go missing or get raped and murdered all the time, but let them be white and blond and beautiful or rich and see where it goes. Once upon a time her mother was beautiful, but that was all. And that was not enough to save her life.

Sadie

S ADIE RANDOLPH HAS ALWAYS seen the sunnier side of life and she's not sure why that is, just that it is. People criticize it. A lot of people don't like looking at a half-full glass, but she has spent her life doing just that and feels now that she is eighty-five and bound to a wheelchair, she wouldn't have chosen to live any other way. Even now, there are things to be happy about. She was born to good people. She got to go to school and become a schoolteacher when many of the people she grew up with were not so fortunate. She married a nice boy from right there in the county she had known her whole life and he continued to run the hardware store and feed and grain sales, just like his father and grandfather before him. They had three fine children, all college educated and now with families of their own, lived in a two-story brick house across the street from the Methodist church they attended and she taught the third grade for forty years. Horace died young, a sudden heart attack while playing football on Thanksgiving afternoon. It was what he and their sons did every Thanksgiving, a town pickup game known for years as the Giblet Gravy

Bowl. He dropped dead and he could not help that. He looked to be in great shape and there was no warning whatsoever. And of course she was angry and scared at first and then so heartbroken and disappointed, but he couldn't help it; she had to keep going. At the funeral she told people she felt lucky and blessed to have ever had him at all. She feels the same about her mother who also died young; she would never trade a minute she had with them. The pain of losing people you love is the price of the ticket for getting to know them at all. Horace once told her that if something ever happened to him, she should *go, find somebody,* but she was sure he didn't really mean that, especially when he added, *But they better be every bit as good as I am.*

"Well, then that's impossible, isn't it?" she had said. It was eight years before he died, a plain old night in the winter of 1963, the whole world so focused on the young Jackie Kennedy and what on earth she would do now. Sadie almost asked what he would do if she were the one to die young, but she didn't want to go there. She doesn't even like to go there now with her eighty-five and him dead nearly forty years. Of course he would have found someone else, but ultimately it was she left behind and she didn't want to think about any of it. When she doesn't want to think about something sad or hurtful, she does what she instructed her own children and those she taught to do: Close your eyes and go somewhere safe and good. Picture something good. One child even made up a big sign with what he thought were the rules to being happy: PRETEND YOU AIN'T DIRTY FROM PLAYING EVEN IF YOU ARE, THINK GOOD THOUGHTS, THINK ABOUT AN ANIMAL YOU WOULD LIKE TO HAVE. She hung the rules in the front of her classroom and they stayed there for years. Now the boy who wrote them is very rich and owns a horse farm in Montana. Sadie has gotten a Christmas card from him every single year except the one time he was getting a divorce. He always says his work keeps him very dirty, but it never gets in the way of his happiness. He always tells her thank you.

Sadie herself had always wanted a little dog that would follow her from room to room like a shadow and that is exactly what she got after Horace died. She loved the big yellow Labradors they had always had as a family: Honey and Goldie and Spitz, after the swimmer who won all those gold medals, but Rudy was all hers, a little Pekingese she misses to this day, but sometimes if she lays her sweater just right at the foot of her bed, it looks just like him, and sometimes she can even get to a place in her mind where she can hear him snore. She loves when Harley comes meowing at her door and spends some time purring on her lap. Bless poor Harley, the way he is treated these days. She wants to tell those who are so mean to him that the one they should really fear coming and sitting beside them is little Joanna Lamb; she's the one who comes to usher out those ready to go. She is the real sweet angel of death and, Sadie suspects, is very good at what she does. She was always a fine student even though she had some trouble finding her way. She liked to do jobs like beat the erasers or straighten up the cloakroom and Sadie assigned her these things often in hopes it would build some confidence. Her parents were fine hardworking people, but they were hard on her to succeed, maybe too hard. Some children just can't take that; some just don't have the makeup and they need to be handled in a gentler way. Joanna was one of those who always looked like she needed a hug and Sadie was big on hugging. Now they have all kinds of rules about hugging and touching. What on earth would you do with the boys like Bennie Palmer who wanted to hug and kiss everybody? Children used to baaaa when Joanna came in the classroom and there were some who wanted to make her always sit beside Bo Henderson, a tiny boy with a terrible stutter, who some of the children who had not grown out of being mean called Bbbbo Ppppeep. He turned out fine, too—went to a school that broke down and rebuilt his voice, grew to be over six feet tall, started selling high end real estate and now could buy and sell most every one of those who were cruel to him. People say Joanna has been married too many times to count, but Sadie does not like idle gossip and never has, besides, what does it really matter. She knows how Joanna treats her and that is all the business of hers it is. Some people struggle harder than others and that has always been true. Take a classroom of eight-year-olds. Some will be good readers and not mind a bit standing and performing. Others cannot put any expression into it because they are having to concentrate so hard on the pronunciation of each and every word. Then some *could* be fine readers but are so frightened to be looked at and on and on. "Each child moves in his own way," she often told parents. "My job is to help that child find his natural speed and not to pit him against another."

She tried to teach her children to be positive—to dream but to also do it with their feet on the ground. If you let loose that balloon, you will lose sight of it, she said. The best way to enjoy it is to hold tight to the string and plant your feet on a good solid path. She thinks now that maybe part of why she was so happy and positive is because she saw so much that was not good. She got to be quite good at figuring out which children were neglected at home, but then she was never sure what to do with that information except to love them a little more, hold them close whenever the opportunity allowed. Sometimes it was hard to be cordial to parents she suspected of misdeeds, and it was hard not to quiz the children a little too much. People think it's a problem of economics, but that is not always true at all. There can be just as much neglect and abuse in a big fine house with professional parents as out in the trailer park. Alcohol is alcohol and meanness is meanness. An eight-year-old heart is just an innocent eight-year-old heart—fragile and wanting.

In the classroom, she often told stories about her own household and she painted pictures of all that *should* happen in a home, the good things people should strive to possess. Eight is a good age for this. They are bright-eyed and know so much, but they are still such babies in so many ways. She told how she apologized to her son after falsely accusing him of eating the last cookie. It was eaten by the plumber, who happened to mention it, or she might have forever thought her son was lying and he would have thought she falsely accused him, teaching him a terrible lesson way too young in life. Old-fashioned stories with little morals were great in the classroom. She got tired of all the younger teachers coming through and saying how old-fashioned she was because she still believed in dictionaries and manners. And she didn't like the shift away from just good old pencils and paper and regular spelling tests. She hated this creative spelling mess. She loved cursive and phonics. For years her favorite thing was the lessons in cursive—taking children from a world of boxy print letters to beautiful script. It was like teaching a language and suddenly notes home and envelopes in their mailboxes didn't seem so foreign and foreboding. Learning and facing language teaches children to learn and face other things as well, and no, she didn't learn the computer with only one more year before her retirement. The typewriter and overhead projector were just fine to get her to the finish line of a long and lovely race.

Of course, who writes anymore? She has a whole box of letters from her husband, each a little masterpiece, at least to her it is. She taught her own children the importance of a handwritten note or tried to. And she loved spending time on manners. Those boys busting to be first in line. *Slow down!* she would say. *There's no fire!* But it was like they couldn't help themselves, like those jumping-bean bodies were on fire and she was constantly needing to remind them to use their indoor voices as opposed to the outdoor voices. She said that all the time and still does. There are people here at Pine Haven who constantly need to be told to use their indoor voices, not to touch or invade the space of their neighbors and to please slow down. *Where is the fire?* she asks Stanley Stone all the time when he goes tearing down the hall to be first at the cafeteria. *Please, just tell me where's the fire.* Of course, poor Stanley is not the best example since his mind is so far gone. But at least he is on foot. It's those in wheelchairs, like herself, who are so dangerous when they pick up speed. *Please use your manners,* she often says. *Were you raised in a barn?*

There was a time when a child who squirmed too much in class was thought to have worms, but now they call it ADD.

"Worms?" little Abby asked one day when Sadie told this, and Toby had to tell the full tale of how childrens' bottoms had to get checked at night with a flashlight to see if they had the pinworms.

"Not in Boston, they didn't," Rachel Silverman said, and that tickled everybody good. Someone Sadie worked with in the schools used to say to children right there before the others, *You need to have your bottom checked,* and you know that child was likely embarrassed to death. Even an overly confident child would have to find that humiliating. Sadie told the woman that she thought that was a very unkind way to handle the problem. She was the same woman who taught what an improper fraction was by first making the smallest boy in the class, Edward Tyner, sit on her lap, and she would say "proper" and then she'd turn and sit on top of him and say "improper." The children, of course, thought it was hilarious, yet Edward never did do very well in life and Sadie has always thought this was likely a factor in that. Sadie has always tried to observe a code of ethics and manners.

Mom, her youngest son, Paul, had said years ago, *please fart just once so we know you aren't an alien.* They were in the kitchen; he was working on homework and she was frying country-style steak. He was so full of himself and got away with so much because he was the baby. Horace would have been home any minute and she would have heard his car and seen Honey go running. Oh, she would love to see his face and feel him beside her; that is the most wonderful thing that could happen. Sometimes, she *can* feel him there. Sometimes when she is almost asleep she will feel his head heavy on her shoulder and his breath on her neck.

Who said aliens don't also break wind? she asked, and Paul screamed with laughter. They called her Ann Landers because she often referred to some bit of good common sense of advice she had read there. "Wonder if Ann Landers farts," Paul said. It is hard to believe a boy so obsessed with body sounds and what he could mine in his nose has grown up to be an ophthalmologist, but he has, and she has his picture right there on her dresser with his wife, Phoebe, and their beautiful babies. They live on the West Coast, which is where Phoebe is from, and they always send her lots and lots of pictures. One time they sent a package that got wet, and when she opened it one picture had stuck to another, and when she carefully pulled them apart it was like a double exposure. The picture of her youngest grandson had somehow wound up there in a picture of Paul and Phoebe on their anniversary trip to Europe. He had stayed with her right there in Fulton, North Carolina, but the picture said he was in Paris, France. And there is such power in what you see that way. She said, *Look, he's in Paris with his mom and dad* and that is what—all these years later—gave her the whole idea for her business, which she calls Exposure. It was so hard not to believe what she saw right there before her eyes.

The business was suggested to her by Joanna, who sometimes comes to visit after she has left the nursing wing where she has helped someone cross over. She has told Sadie that some days— especially with those she has grown close to—she has to reenter life slowly, like someone coming up from a deep dive slowly so she won't get the bends. "I get it," Sadie was able to say. "I know what you mean." Lord, the bends. She has learned so much from that crazy Paul that she wouldn't know otherwise. He loves to scuba dive and he has jumped from a plane, too, which scares her to this minute to imagine so she never thinks about that, and if her mind tries to, she conjures up little Rudy with his scruffy flat face and maybe sings a song in her head. Lots of times all she can think is those instrumental songs from that album Stanley Stone plays all day long each and every day, an album that was popular back when her kids were little, Herb somebody or another, loud drum beats and lots of horns. It gets stuck in your head and won't go away—catchy songs that make her want to sip a highball or smoke a cigarette—things she has only done a couple of times in her whole life.

Stanley Stone suggested Sadie call her business *Indecent* Exposure, and of course she politely told him she would do no such thing. It is hard to watch him decline so and she goes the extra mile to be kind and courteous. She has known him her whole adult life—a highly intelligent and respectable man—who now late in his life says all kinds of things—ugly things—the kinds of things you would hear teaching junior high school, which she did once in 1965 and then went running and begging to be placed back with her third graders.

"There's a lot in this place that *is* indecent and *needs* to be exposed," Stanley said one day when they heard that one of the Barker sisters had been drugged so she didn't wake up for eighteen hours. "And I am not talking about old breasts and asses. I'm talking about laziness, negligence, and incompetence." He sounded just like a lawyer and then all of a sudden he looked at his poor son, Ned, who has had enough troubles of his own, and threatened to expose himself right there in the dining room. The only person who laughed was Toby Tyler, but she laughs at just about everything. Toby taught school her whole adult life, too, so often they talk about the classroom even though Toby taught high school English and coached field hockey as well as drove an activity bus. Toby grew up in South Carolina but chose to retire here because she threw a dart at a map of Georgia and the Carolinas with the idea she would go wherever it said. Her given name was not Toby, but she gave it to herself because she said that as a child she always wished she could just run off and join the circus. She said at first she just pretended she was related to the real Toby Tyler since they shared a last name, but then one day she thought, *Why don't I just be him?* She said as soon as she changed her name, she felt so much better.

Sadie told her that's what her business is all about. She invites people to bring in their photographs and make a wish, maybe talk about something that might've happened but didn't or a place someone might've visited but hadn't. There is a power in what you see. Seeing is believing. Bennie Palmer, who without a doubt is her very favorite student from all of her years teaching, still comes to see her and they talk about such things. He is a skillful magician and has been since he was a child and he also works as manager of the movie theater even though his wife is eager for him to do otherwise. He was in the same class as Joanna Lamb and he was as loud and cute as a button as she was quiet and kind of lost. Now he seems lost and she is confident, though neither of them fully memorized the opening of the Gettysburg Address as they were supposed to do. Only two children in all her years mastered that whole first part. One is a bank president in Omaha, Nebraska, and came to see her when in town for his mother's funeral, and the other was a girl who got pregnant and dropped out in the tenth grade, a beautiful girl who just never had a chance coming out of the kind of squalor she lived in. It would break your heart to see and know what some children come from. Bennie, or Ben they call him now, has a daughter, Abby, who also visits all the time. She is an angel, looks just like him and is such a nice girl. It's hard to say the same for his wife. The wife is that kind of girl who will cheat on a test or steal something from another child's desk and then act very haughty if she gets caught, no sense of right or wrong or moral guilt. It is clear that Bennie is not very happy and he needs to talk about it more than he does, but that's a boy for you; a boy will hold in so much bad stuff sometimes until it makes him sick to his stomach, and Sadie believes wholeheartedly that our society is to blame for that. If people would let little boys spend more time with the dress-up clothes and doll babies, it would help, but even Horace was funny about all that, not really enjoying when Paul used to like to wear an apron and rock his sister's Betsy Wetsy.

Sometimes she and Bennie talk about the things that happened about a hundred years ago when he was in the third grade, but usually they just talk about how they both create illusions and how this can make a person who is feeling sad feel a little better. Sadie believes that this is the conversation that might lead him to open up his heart one of these days soon.

This is her craft and it is the craft she started when everyone else was doing scrapbooks. The most famous scrapbook at Pine Haven is that of Mrs. Marge Walker who keeps a murder and crime scrapbook. Her husband was a judge for years and years and so it all comes natural to her she says, just like Lorice Boone believes she is the best haircutter because her father was a barber. Lorice had a booming business among those who are out of touch with reality until management confiscated her scissors. Rachel Silverman is the one who reported her after seeing her snip away the waist-length braids of someone on the nursing wing without asking. Sadie wanted to ask why Rachel was even way over there in that part of the building, but she hasn't yet. Rachel is very secretive about her comings and goings and has to be treated with great care. There was always at least one child in class who needed this kind of extra attention. They appear so strong and tough and yet you know there is a tender place just aching to be healed—so tenderhearted you could tap with a knife and it would fall right off the bone.

"You have to stop her," Rachel said when reporting Lorice. "Otherwise this place is going to look like Auschwitz."

Stanley Stone said he'd never heard of Auschwitz and asked was that the new grocery store out on Highway 211, and Rachel Silverman raised her open hand like she might slap him and then said something about him being a g-d demented idiot, marched into her apartment, and slammed the door so hard that the plaque with her name on it fell off.

"I did a good thing," Lorice told management when they came to take her scissors. "She looks a sight better with a haircut." Lorice pointed to the woman who was dozing in the solarium, not a hair on her head longer than a half an inch. If the woman had family that ever visited, Sadie suspects they'd be upset, but as far as she knows, no one has visited that woman in years. Lorice said the sisters, especially Vanessa, had never minded if she cut their hair, especially if she gave them cookies. Rachel Silverman had made Daisy, the other sister, cry one day, saying she did not want to crochet or buy or eat a g-d cookie, and then Sadie explained to her that the sisters are sweet as can be, would never hurt a flea, which is why they allow Lorice to do their hair in the first place, and so now Rachel is so good to them, always buying those crocheted Oreos and Fig Newtons and then slipping them back into Daisy's bag when she's not looking so she can sell them again.

Rachel Silverman says she has no family either, which makes it easy to make all kinds of big decisions. Sadie is getting closer to her, no doubt about it, like luring a stray cat or dog into your home. Rachel is not very trusting and you can see it. People get old, but in the eyes they might as well be eight—always they are about eight—and so Sadie is well versed in eight-year-old fear. She knows the heart of eight-year-olds and believes when all is said and done and hard times come, that's how old we are in the heart—forever eight years old. She used to love to set up the abacus at the front of the room and have children tell what they know of their lives one bead at a time. Holding to the little round wooden bead gave them confidence as they spoke the facts of their lives. I was born in Hamlet. I have a sister and a dog. I love grits. I hate mayonnaise. Things like that. They loved seeing the beads accumulate, transferring over to the ten spot. It was a lesson in math and English. It was a lesson in socializing.

Marge Walker is the only person Sadie has difficulty socializing with. Marge is lately fixated on the way people are stealing copper wiring out of air-conditioning units, most recently a church in town, and she is quite certain the Mexicans have done it. Mexicans or coloreds. She says all this loud as the PA system at school and there sits any number of people of different races from different places.

"How stupid is that?" Rachel asked in a loud voice, and Sadie was the only one who returned her gaze. She allowed eye contact, which said, *I am listening to you. I am hearing what you say and I am in agreement.* Sadie bets it won't be anytime at all before Rachel shows up with a picture or two, and if it turns out she doesn't have photos either, it's no problem at all. For those who have no pictures—as sad as that is, it is sometimes true—well, Sadie has a Polaroid camera her oldest son sent her and so she takes the photo herself and then puts the person on a backdrop of a particular place. She put the woman who got all her hair cut off (before it all got cut off) out on the grandstrand on a beautiful sunny day pictured in *Southern Living*. She used her Sharpies to turn the wheelchair into a beautiful red beach chair and then added a little yellow sand pail as if the woman might get up and go hunt for shells any minute.

Paul said to slow down on the film, it's getting hard to replace and thus very expensive. He says he will teach her how to "do digital and print," which she has no idea about, but Abby does. Twelve years old and the child knows all about digital and print and all sorts of other things you might plug in that Sadie has never heard of. *What will you do when the power goes out?* Sadie has asked her, but nobody seems too worried about that. Sadie's children all send her travel magazines and such and call so many times during the week she can't keep up with it all. Paul wants her to move to where he is, but *no,* she keeps saying *no;* she says Horace is next door and this is her home. She did not tell them where to move and live and they owe her the same consideration. Paul is stubborn and keeps trying, but in the meantime he just reads every word of her monthly bill from Pine Haven, makes phone calls and asks lots of questions as she taught him to do and, of course, best of all, sends pictures of the children and all the brochures from conventions and retreats for ophthalmologists so she can send a customer anywhere in the world. There was even one trip advertised to go down the Amazon and she pulled it out to show Benjamin and Abby just the other day because he knows that *The African Queen* is one of her very favorite movies and he has promised to bring a copy for her to watch someday soon. Toby saw that photo and claimed it immediately because her whole room is decorated with her travels around the world, compliments of Exposure and Sadie's skill as an illusionist, which is what Ben calls her. Just yesterday she took Stanley Stone's photo and put him in the ring with a wrestler man he called the Undertaker, a horrible-looking big man with long stringy hair and ghoulish eyes. His picture was in a wrestling magazine Stanley's son, Ned, had brought to him hidden in a bag. She doesn't blame him a bit for hiding it.

"Stanley, how is Ned doing?" she asked while cutting and gluing.

"Okay, I guess. He's teaching at your old school—weren't you at Sandhills Elementary?"

"I was indeed except that one year they sent me to junior high. Forty years at Sandhills," she said, so relieved to feel like the old Stanley was back. He was relaxed in the chair, his eyes closed. "You know, isn't it funny how in life our paths didn't cross too much. I mean if you needed a hammer, you went to our store, and I suspect if we'd needed your kind of legal advice we would have gone to you." She had to pause to carefully cut out the Undertaker, who was so ugly it was frightening. He was one who might be served well to run into Lorice with her scissors, that stringy old mess of hair and Stanley is starting to look a little unkempt himself, though she is not quite ready to tell him that. "But we went to different churches and between my teaching and doing all I did at home, I didn't venture very far so I really never knew Martha at all except to say hello at the store. I didn't get to teach Ned; he was in Renee Bingham's class, but I recall all the children saying how he made everybody laugh."

"He was definitely the class clown. He had a hard time in those early years." Stanley opened an eye and then it was like a switch flipped and something blew into him, and he sat up and started talking about the wrestling event he was going to have right there in the common room. He shook his fist and all signs of nice Stanley were gone. "I'm gonna take somebody out," he said, and she waved her hand, tried to see if she couldn't lure him back to where he had been. It just breaks her heart to see him this way. Sadie grew up with Stanley's older sister, but he was several years younger so they ran in different circles. Still he was a person people heard about. "I remember when people were talking about you getting married. First in your law school class and marrying a beautiful girl from northern Virginia. People said how lucky Martha was to meet such a smart and handsome fellow and they hoped she was good enough for you." Sadie hates when people say such things, but they really did say that at the time and she thought he would like to hear such a fine compliment about himself. "You were the golden prize of this town, Stanley. They said you were Phi Beta Kappa and the best dancer in your fraternity house."

"I danced the hootchie kootchie nekked every chance I got," he said. "And the girls sure did like that." He stood and acted like he might unbuckle his pants, but Sadie held one hand up and shielded her eyes with the other. She used her best teacher voice and told him to sit down and behave that very instant or he would be sent home and not allowed to return. When she looked up he was seated again and staring down at his fists.

"What I was saying is how I was thinking that we're neighbors all over again but this time we seem to speak and talk more than we ever did in our other lives."

"Yes." He was calm again and so Sadie waited a long time as he sat and seemed to relax. Her ceiling fan clicked and clacked and sometimes what she hears it say is *I think I can, I think I can* just like the Little Engine That Could. Now that is a powerful message for children to hear and learn. Where do people think the president got it in the first place? *Yes we can* is just another way to say what the little engine said a long long time ago. Most everything worth saying has already been said so the trick is to make it sound new, something a child will find interesting or funny.

"I miss my other life," she told Stanley, and worked to arrange the Undertaker's hands so it looks like he's choking Stanley, which is what Stanley requested. "I miss my kitchen and my black-and-white linoleum floor. My children liked to play hopscotch there. Roger would get a beach towel and throw it over a chair to make himself a little Indian tepee and he would always sit cross-legged and run his Matchbox cars round and round it while making cute little sounds and talking to himself. Do you remember your little Ned at that age? The way a child will make all sorts of sounds with their teeth and their tongues, sounds that nobody else is following."

"I do."

"I move room to room through my old house. I see the brightness of a late afternoon. I hear the rumble of the air-conditioning there in the window in the den, what these days they call a family room, which sounds nice, too. I see the hollyhocks at my window, tall and staked upright with their big powder-puff blooms and then just as suddenly I might smell the fire in the fireplace and hear Horace chopping wood. Do it, Stanley. Close your eyes and start wandering." She waited until he closed his eyes and then she continued; she couldn't wait to get back. "You will be amazed at what all you can see, how the seasons change, the light and temperature and then people come into the room and you hear the sweet voices of your young children or I smell the cologne I wore for almost twenty years—a gift from Horace every Christmas—Shalimar—just the word made me feel important. One day when a little girl—Susie Otis there in bright-colored dungarees—told me I smelled so good, I had the whole room say Shalimar. *Shalimar,* and they waved their hands like they held magic wands. I can smell the grilled cheese sandwiches my kids loved for me to make. I cut them in the shape of stars and hearts and I let Goldie wolf down the scraps.

"Sometimes it snows. It gets so quiet and beautiful in the snow. Horace is always there when it snows.

"And sometimes I hear Horace clear his throat. I see him pat his chest for heartburn. He said it was just a little heartburn. Oh, why didn't I know? So many people get the heartburn and especially at Thanksgiving with all that food. Oh, why didn't I know it? I have to get past that, I have to tiptoe past him, I have to get back to a good place and oh my goodness, there is that silly, silly Paul wearing a costume I made him one Halloween. He's a sea monkey. All he wanted to be was a sea monkey and I made him a funny merman looking suit complete with a scepter and a crown, and there I am right there in front of Horace's mother's old upright piano. I am holding his little hand and telling him that he is the best little sea monkey there ever was. *Yes you are, oh yes you are, sweetheart.* Lord, would you look at what shoes I'm wearing! I haven't thought of those in years. Bandolinos. Everybody thought it was something to have an Italian shoe being sold right here in Fulton and they had little different-colored straps trimming them out, otherwise it would have just been another plain old Mary Jane. They were soft. Mine were black with red straps and I always wore them when I had cafeteria duty because they were so comfortable and I could slip up on somebody doing something he ought not to be, like dotting his milk straw into his beets so he could shoot out little purple cubes at the girl beside him. Oh, Lordy, what a mess. I need to get back home and there I am back in the den and our little breakfast nook. A lot of people don't like pine paneling, but I do. I love it. My children saw all kinds of things there in the knotholes—so creative. There was a deer and a little elf. I'm not sure why, but our daughter, Lynnette, always called that elf Doo-Doo and she was scared of him and would say at almost every meal for about a year, "Doo-Doo is watching me." Sadie paused, remembering where she really is—Pine Haven, wheelchair, Stanley Stone across from her. This has started to happen more and more. It takes a minute to know where she is. She opened her eyes, expecting him to roar out some nasty expletive as he often does in the dining room if anyone mentions anything to do with body functions. But instead his eyes were filled with tears, his mouth opened in a silent cry. "Oh, Stanley, I'm so sorry." She has always known how to comfort others, but she didn't know what to do with somebody like Stanley—an intelligent, prosperous, and independent man who probably never cried in front of others in his whole life.

"I had an ugly brown car Ned called Doo-Doo," he said, and they both laughed, Sadie relieved that the word hadn't taken him off in the wrong direction and that she wouldn't need to find a way to give him a hug or a comforting pat. "And remember that guy they called Doo-Doo Pendergraft? Ran the Gulf station?" She did indeed. Doo-Doo was in her class in school and so was Boobs Walters and Goat Baumgarten. She laughed to say all those names, to imagine what somebody from out of town, like Rachel, would think.

"I miss my toolshed," Stanley said. "That's where I went when you started talking and asked me to imagine. Ned once painted the walls without asking, he painted his name and he painted an airplane." He sat forward and put his face in his hands. "He loved when we played airplane. I'd lie on my back and he'd hold my hands and press his stomach against my feet, and then up, up, I'd lift and he'd hold out his arms and make engine sounds."

"Children love to paint," Sadie said. "And they all love to fly."

"I made him scrub the walls of my shed and then paint it all white," he says. "I'm pretty sure I took a belt to him for not asking."

"But he turned out really fine, Stanley. A fine boy." She watched him slump forward again, his face hidden and shoulders shaking. "He hit a rough patch, but most of us do." She was rolling toward him, her hand outstretched, but then he sat up so fast with an awful glare on his face that it made her drop her glue stick.

"But not as fine as the goddamned Undertaker," he said. "This ain't the Sistine Chapel, woman, get the lead out."

"I take my art seriously," Sadie said, her hand to her chest, still catching her breath. "I don't do cheap and sloppy work and I never have, so if you are feeling impatient, perhaps you should take a recess and let me get back to you." She pointed to her glue stick where it had rolled under a table. "And pick that up before you excuse yourself."

"Hell, you got a whole line of people in the hall waiting for some idiot picture."

"And I will see them all and I will do so with polite kindness."

"Don't you get tired of this shit? Don't you want something for yourself?"

"Of course I do. I have a whole scrapbook of me." She reached her hand for him to hand her the glue stick and then carefully went back to work, applying a thin line and then gently blending it. She blew to help dry the glue and then handed him his picture much sooner than she normally would. "Hold the edges or you'll ruin it. I could show you sometime—my pictures."

"Yeah, all right, whatever."

"The first one I ever did was to put myself with my mother. She died when I was four. I only have a few pictures of her so she looks just the same every single time, but I keep getting older and bigger until now, there I am with my beautiful mother and I look like her grandmother. Isn't that funny? I always try to fix it so we're holding hands." She looks up, but he is gone and the clock on the wall says it is ten o'clock, which is milk break at school. It costs three cents a carton and she keeps a jar on her desk to pay for those who forget their money. The note on the wall says not to forget to go to lunch. *Do not forget. Do not forget.* But Stanley left and then there was Toby wearing those cute puffy boots she loves to wear. She is traveling the world and already has pictures of herself in Rome and London and Paris and Tel Aviv and of course the Amazon and the Taj Mahal and she has even been on the moon with Neil Armstrong. This one is tricky, though. Toby warns Sadie that her new request is likely to be hard. She is taking a break from traveling and wants to do all kinds of different sports. Today she wants to be a jockey. She has brought beautiful pictures of horses, but the real trick will be taking the Polaroid with her legs all pulled up close and her arms holding the reins. She might need to get up on the footstool or daybed to get the right angle. "How many others do I have in line?" Sadie asks, thinking she might need to make Toby last even though Toby is her very best customer.

"Three."

Sadie asks them in and their requests are pretty simple and ones she can accept and work on later in the day. One wants to go back to the Ocean Forest Hotel at Myrtle Beach like she did as a child, which will require the assistance of Abby, who can print old things off the computer. She is pretty sure that the Ocean Forest got torn down ages ago, but they will find it or something very similar. Another wants to be in the family portrait of her husband's family. "It was when his mama turned eighty," she says, "And it was the best day of my life, but I volunteered to take the picture so it looks like I'm not there and I *was* there and I want to be back there on the back row between my husband and his brother, Buddy."

"That's a tough angle," Sadie tells her, "could you be on the other side?"

"No. I never got along with his sister and don't want to stand near her."

That poor child, Millie, is there, but all she wants is change so Sadie tells her to take what's there in a little bowl by the door. That's why the change is there in the first place, but of course she doesn't tell her that or it would be a constant thing. She handled candy and colored paper clips this same way in her classroom. And then there's Abby, who says she just wants to curl up in the chair or at the foot of her bed and talk. She loves that child dearly and she loves Benjamin and clearly things at home are getting worse. Clearly his illusions just are not working, and she plans to call him this very day to say that he needs to take better care of his child. You need to put her first, she plans to tell him and she plans to use poor Stanley Stone as an example of a father who did not do a good job and is lucky that Ned got through the trouble alive and is now a kind and prosperous man. She will tell Benjamin how one look on the girl's face can tell you everything you need to know and she is even older than eight! She is twelve—almost a teenager—and old enough to start hiding behind makeup and music and acting silly and she is doing none of those things. She will tell him it might be now or never.

"I'll be quiet while you work," Abby says. Her hair needs to be washed and is yanked back in a lopsided ponytail and the T-shirt she's wearing is big enough for two people. She is carrying some of those flyers with her lost puppy.

"Of course, sweetie," she says, and motions over to her bed or the big velvet chair beside it—Horace's chair. On a good day when she lets her room get a little too warm and humid, she can smell his pipe smoke in the fabric. There are some pistachio shells and an old ballpoint pen down under the cushion that she has not been able to throw away. If only she had found them when he was alive, she would have. But she found them late one night with Rudy on her lap and Johnny Carson on the television and she let them be—relics, touchstones, and even now she will reach and grip the pen or rub the smooth pink shells and the clickety clack of *I think I can I think I can* becomes Sadie? Sadie? Are you awake?

"Sadie?" Toby waves her plump hand back and forth. "Yoo-hoo, Earth calling Sadie." She looks over at Abby and they both start laughing. "I can come back later if you're needing a nap."

"Heavens no!" she says. "I have never been a napper! I was just thinking about the best way to capture your wish." She turns to the girl. "And actually I have some work for you if you're up for it. I need a picture of the Ocean Forest Hotel if you can find it. And if you can't, just find some big brick building, like in Charleston or Savannah, and we'll make do. And I need a good picture of what was called the Old Man of the Mountain as a surprise for Joanna Lamb, who mentioned that not too long ago, I think she's the one said it. It was somewhere way up north and the rock jutted out just like a man's profile, and it, too, is no longer there."

"He lost face," Toby says, and claps her hands; honestly, she has the loudest laugh Sadie has ever heard, could nearly wake those over there in Whispering Pines. "I read about that. Face fell right off the cliff."

"Oh, and hang the closed sign on the door," Sadie tells the girl. This is the right thing for now, keep her busy and they can have a little heart to heart talk when it is just the two of them. The cloakroom was always a good place to have a little talk in confidence, sweaters and jackets falling to either side and muffling the words so others couldn't hear. She once bought a cross-stitch sampler with a quote the real Mama from *Little Women* liked to say: HOPE AND KEEP BUSY and that was good advice. In fact, she bought it on the same trip when she herself saw the Old Man of the Mountain. The children were little and Horace was alive. She is thinking that she'd like to go back, she'd like to take her mother there, and perhaps if she can go back to that place, with her mother present, she might be able to explain what she was feeling there. *Hope and Keep Busy!* It was not an easy time and she has not wanted to look at it.

"And then can we talk?" Abby whispers. She looks like she's been crying.

"Sure, honey." She watches Abby walk away, each foot in a tile like hopscotch. They will solve this problem and if she has to place a call to the parents she will. She has done this before when it was clear a child needed more than he or she was getting at home. Sometimes she made the principal aware, but other times she did not and just handled it herself.

"How 'bout this?" Toby is squatted up on the footstool and looks every bit like a little gargoyle. She screws up her brow like she's concentrating and raises her arm where she says Sadie can draw in the little crop with a Sharpie. "Giddyap."

"Perfect," Sadie says, and the camera whirrs and out pops Toby squatting on the stool. "This is going to take a while if you need to go do anything."

"I always have plenty to do," Toby says. "Yessir, I am one busy woman."

"Don't you ever get tired of this shit?" Stanley had asked her. "Don't you ever want something for yourself?"

How odd what that made her remember. Once, years ago, she went into Fowler's Grocery. It got torn down a long time ago and Food Lion has been there ever since. Fowler's had those old dark green linoleum floor tiles and poles with clamps they used to reach things way up on the top shelves. The back area, where the butcher worked, was exposed with a sloping concrete floor covered in sawdust, the smell of which she always associated with Fowler's, and there was Grover Fowler whom she had known since childhood—tired butcher with bloody hands and a good kind heart. One kind exchange and the shared memory of how they stood side by side in their fourth-grade chapel program made her heart beat faster and something in it all made him flush a deep red and lean down closer to the work he was doing. He was a sweet boy from a hard, rough home, but there on the stage his hair was slicked back and he wore a nice dress shirt and together they sang "You Are My Sunshine" and got a standing ovation from the school. Sadie told this; she didn't mean to. But there was Toby wide-eyed and listening and Abby was there and Rachel, too.

"Sadie had an affair in the grocery store," Toby announced, and Sadie said she did no such thing ever in her entire life.

"We did not do anything," she said. "He was a good boy with a sweet wife who also was in my class."

"Lusting in your heart," Toby said, and Rachel added that Jimmy Carter would be proud of her. "You never had to worry about Horace catting around, did you?" Toby asked. The question surprised Sadie, though it shouldn't by now. If Toby thinks something, she says it.

"I have never allowed myself to imagine such a thing," she said, and she hoped there was nothing there. If he ever did go up some stairs or into a room he shouldn't, she would rather not know, especially now. She had wondered once, but then it seemed to pass and so she just let it go and held on to what was good.

"I was the other woman once," Rachel whispered, and there was a long pause of silence. She looked directly at Sadie and Sadie didn't dare look away. It's no different from the child who finally reaches out to hold your hand.

"I would never cast stones," Sadie said. "You are a fine person."

"Well, I cast stones," Toby said, and there was heavy silence again. "But not at you. And not for that!" She nudged Rachel and laughed. "Marge might now."

"I hope I have to respond to a higher power," Rachel said.

"Higher IQ, anyway," Toby laughed, and put something in her mouth up against her gum, snuff no doubt. "I say bless the stupid."

Sadie pulled Abby up close and hugged her. There was so much she would need to explain to her when all the others went home. Adults do things—even good adults who do not always show good judgment. Now she opens her eyes and Abby is standing there with a sprig of rosemary from Horace. He is so dear and likely will be calling soon.

"It's getting worse," Abby tells her. "And Dollbaby still hasn't come home." The child leans into Sadie and then is sobbing, her shoulders jerking while Sadie pats her back and tries to get her to calm down. They sit side by side on the sofa and watch television, *The Price Is Right,* which has been on for centuries, it seems. Her eyes are heavy and now that Abby has calmed down she lets them close for just a minute and then when she wakes, one of those programs where everybody has to endure terrible things—lost babies and evil twins and tuberculosis and such—is on and Abby is gone. It is almost time to go to lunch. Sadie is tired, but she doesn't have time to stop, not yet; the others need her. *I do not have time to die,* she once heard Lois Flowers say, *not today,* and they all laughed. Abby has left a crumpled piece of paper on the table along with a sprig of rosemary from Horace. It is a note written on the back of a Food Lion receipt. Somebody bought some Budweiser and some trash bags, some milk and some Clorox, paper towels. On the back there is a note: *You better answer me soon!* it says. Terrible penmanship. Cursive, yes, but not done well at all. Sadie never would have allowed such cursive without a slant and the esses so misshapen and there's Harley, big sweet Harley slinking down the hall. She reaches her hand out and calls to him: *Big sweet kitty, big sweet purr.* Horace and the kids are going to love him. They will be so surprised. Her mother will love him, too.

Joanna

*D*O YOU BELIEVE IN *ghosts? Do you believe in the power of magic? Do you believe that a normal ordinary girl can disappear right before your eyes?*

Joanna had run the words through her mind many times over the years, picturing her childhood friend Ben waving his wand and directing her in and out of boxes first in his garage and then on the school auditorium stage, pulling from his sleeves coins and lengths of scarves and puny bouquets picked from neighborhood yards when the neighbors weren't looking. He said they were partners for life, bound by their secrets and knowledge; it was a vow, a pact, a solemn oath of loyalty. Now that she's back home, thirty years and a million miles and a lot of mistakes and lessons behind her, she's aware of it all as never before: the ghosts, the magic, all the ways a person might disappear.

The longest and most expensive journey you will ever make is the one to yourself. This is Joanna's current mantra, in her head since a day four years ago when Luke stepped in and changed her life. He said it first. He said he would love nothing better than to purchase the ticket that would upgrade and jump-start her trip. He said so many things during the brief time they were together, things that are now dog-eared in her mind so that she thinks of them, repeats them, relies on them every day. Without him she could never have found her way back to this place, back to her father's side in time to make amends, back to the flat, swampy land that has been home even in the years she spent elsewhere. All those years and miles away, and still she often fell asleep conjuring images of the Saxon River, that cold dark water winding its way through the Green Swamp and on down to the Carolina coast, the wide sandy shore and the white hot light of summer. Her parents had owned a modest cottage there, not on the ocean but with a view of the marsh, and coming back she'd decided it would be worth the forty-minute drive from town to live there, to wake to the briny ocean air she associated with freedom. She loved the glaze of salt that covered the windows, like ice in another lifetime and she had had so many—like a cat and, like a cat, she had returned home. *The Incredible Journey,* Luke called it; he shared her love for all the dog books and movies, would have loved her new business. She'd been left the beach cottage, her parents' home, which she quickly sold, and the Dog House, a drive-through hot-dog franchise her dad had bought two years before he died, which she kept.

"It was an investment," he told her. "If I'd known you would ever grace us, well, now just *me,* with a return home, maybe I would have gone in for hair or nails or tans, but I like a good hot dog and your mother liked a good hot dog and they aren't easy to come by." He said this before they knew he was dying, and so there was still plenty of time and room for the sarcasm and innuendo that had long forced them apart. And the hot dogs *are* good, no doubt about it, and the place is very popular with the kids from town looking for some place to go on their way to the beach. People love the way they can drive up and order something off the cute menu like, "I'll have a Puppy, two Old Yellers, and a Chihuahua."

"Never been much on hair and tans," she told him, her skin so white from years spent in Chicago and then Maine and New Hampshire, her unruly hair a shaggy cropped cut she often did herself, coloring in the gray of her temples with a Sharpie.

"True," he had said. He had shown her where everything was within the tiny structure. The young man he'd hired to manage the place was off in the corner chopping onions and filling the sauerkraut bin for the German shepherd, trying to pretend he wasn't listening. "It would have made your mother so happy if you had ever taken her advice about anything—men, school, clothes, your hair, but no, that was just too hard, wasn't it?"

"It was if I wanted to have any—hair, that is," she tried to make a joke, resisting the big barbed hook he kept dangling in front of her. "Mom loved the Twiggy look. Skinny bodies and pixie cuts." If she were in a therapy session, she might have said, *What was that all about, you guess? Whose hair is it anyway?* But she laughed again and shook her head in that way that said, *No big deal, so long ago.* "Mom wanted a little Jack Russell for a daughter and I was the plump mangy retriever who wanted to be an afghan hound." She reminded her dad how they had both loved that photograph of a man on a park bench with a long-haired blonde—or so it appeared from behind—only it was really his afghan hound; she had clipped the picture from *Life* magazine and put it on her bulletin board beside the many dandelions magician Ben had pulled from behind her ear and ribbons she had won on the junior high swim team. "But," she added, "I've always been in the Dog House."

Her dad finally laughed and said her mother had said the same thing. The thought of her mother and the fact they had never made up hung in the air around them, as thick and heavy as she had told Luke it would, and her promise to him to *be* here, to *stay* here, was the only thing holding her in place. "I will haunt you if you break your word to me," he said, still incredibly handsome and able to smile right up to the end. "I will make your life more miserable than it has ever been."

"Whoa," she had said, and stepped back from his bed. "That's a tall order." She waited for him to say something else, but he didn't. "A mean order," she added, leaning forward with the word *mean* and still nothing.

"Your mother said you *chose* to be in the doghouse," her dad had said, but he did not add the sentence that had so often come out of one of her parents' mouths: *You made your bed, now lie in it.* Or when she ran from what appeared to them a perfectly good life with a man she was lucky to marry to a relationship as quick and damaging as an electrical storm: *Lie down with dogs and get up with fleas.* "Yes, you chose the doghouse," he said, the air reeking of onions. His old white apron—one her mother had once worn—was splotched with condiments, and she noticed how tired he looked and how his hands were smaller than she had remembered. "You did it all by yourself."

When she was twenty, she would have argued with him; she would have yelled that they were rigid ignorant people who only cared about what everybody else thought—the neighbors, the relatives, the people at church—who gave a damn? Why couldn't they just care about *her*? Why, when she got ninety-nine out of a hundred correct, were they so quick to study and scrutinize the one little failure, so much attention given to what was wrong instead of what was *right,* and when she was thirty she still would have gotten angry but would have just slammed the door or the phone receiver and taken it out on whatever poor soul was with her at the time, whatever they were doing in that moment—eating a holiday dinner, making love, planting trees—ruined and lost to that cavernous black hole. She would have had an extra drink or two and blamed her parents for the excess, but in her midforties, after life with Luke, she was finally able to see her father for what he was: a worn-out man who had worked very hard and lived the only way he knew how, rigid and unforgiving from his own upbringing, too scared to have ever ventured beyond that knowledge, frightened by the thought of death, ashamed of his weak nakedness, and in need of love with no sense of how to ask for it.

"Those are the ones who will need you the most," Luke had pointed out, and sure enough, early in her training as a hospice volunteer, this became all too evident. Now it's a scene she sees often as she sits bedside by those who have reached their final destination. It is a very simple equation that comes at the end, a focus on what they *have* and what they *don't have*—a glass half full or empty—a weighing of one against the other. Sometimes the focus is just the magnification of what has always been there. But always, they are waiting for something: a face, a word, an apology, permission, a touch. Bics flicking with a frenzied vengeance at the great rock concert of life for just one more. One more song, word, sip of water. Some have many hands reaching from the bedside and others have none, and yet in that final moment, the air heavy and laden as molecules regroup and reshape in preparation for the exit, it is all the same. It is like the moment when a snake enters the yard and the birds fall silent. The silence begs your attention; it's time to go. The journey is over.

"It's okay," she told her dad and ran an ice chip around his dry lips, his mouth turning toward the touch like a newborn seeking milk. "All my experience in the doghouse will help me run the family business."

"Family business," he mumbled, and laughed. He was too weak to say much. It was the end and she whispered to him what she had learned to whisper with great confidence—*It's okay to let go*—only with him she had the desire to keep him just a little bit longer. She had never given up the idea that he might say he loved her. Each time she had said the words, he only smiled. This time he said, *You are my little girl.* They were in the house where she had grown up, a small brick ranch on a corner lot, flat yard full of spindly pine trees and bee-filled azaleas. The hospital bed filled what had once been her bedroom, his choice. He wanted to die where his wife had died, and she—in her illness—had chosen that room in order to keep their room intact, so that he could go to bed in a normal way as she lay dying at the other end of the house. "It worked for a while," he had told Joanna. "There were some mornings I woke and for just a second would not remember. I would just think she had gotten up early like she always did and was washing clothes or something."

Joanna held his hand and resisted asking the question she had asked so many times before: *Why didn't you call me?* He always said *she* should have called *them* and then it all happened so fast. Her mother had back pain, that was all, and then they were told nothing could be done and she was dead in a month. "If she had asked me to call you, I would have," he said. "But she didn't and I didn't want to cause her any more pain than she was already in."

Joanna allowed herself to imagine that her mother *had* wanted to see her, that if she had been able, she would have said something, sent a message. Luke had told her she had to let it go, let it go along with her realization that the night her mother died coincided with her own one-night stand with someone whose name she could not even remember, a journalist from somewhere in the Midwest who had a passion for Russian literature and talked about his ex-wife all night, just another lonely heart who stayed at a boring party too long. *Why don't I just go throw myself in front of a train?* she said when she woke up in his strange hotel bed to hear him leaving sloppy messages on his wife's answering machine. *Let it go.*

She stared out the high narrow windows of what had once been her bedroom; as a child she had needed to stand on her bed or a chair to see out. Cars were passing the way they would on any normal Tuesday morning and the azaleas were blooming as they did every spring. A row of daffodils lining the concrete walk came up just as they had since she planted them at age five, her mother addressing the bulbs by their formal name—King Alfred—as she oversaw Joanna's work, the depth of the hole, the teaspoon of bonemeal in each one. The years had left them spindly and bloomless, but there they were; in spite of everything, there they were. And that was when he died. She was thinking of those daffodils—King Alfred withered to a pauper—and the air in the room changed as it always does–sparked, clear, sudden—and with a last long sigh, he was gone.

The longest and most expensive journey is the one to yourself. Luke liked to add that some people never even purchase a ticket, some only get halfway, some stand like Moses glimpsing the Promised Land, which he maintained was, for all practical purposes, about as good as getting there. *Clear vision,* he said, and then added, "like Visine or Vaseline or Clearasil," so pumped with morphine by the end that his language was like some haystack of non sequiturs filled with golden needles, fragile bits of truth and wisdom she needed to collect. For a long time her mantra had been *Fuck you from the bottom of my fucked-up heart,* so clearly she had come some distance. California, New York, Chicago, New England. She did it all, but what she learned is that sooner or later you have to stop running, and when you do, the baggage comes slamming into you at freight train speed. She stopped running in New Hampshire four years ago, when she fell asleep assuming she'd be dead within the hour and then woke to the warm hand of a stranger and the distant wail of a siren. Only then was she able to slowly pull it all together. Only then did she buy the ticket.

Now when Joanna thinks about dying, she thinks of the day she almost did, the careful planning, the way the light looked there in the late-afternoon sky. It was only four but already nearing dark. It was her favorite kind of day and she had come to New Hampshire seeking it, seeking some resolution to what felt like a really lousy story. There was wood smoke in the air, birds rustling in the leaves, her breath visible as she stared at the distant outline of the White Mountains. There was a Chinese dogwood—bright red stems against the backdrop of snow—and it occurred to her that if she were staying, she would cut some and put them in a vase.

The hot tub on the deck was almost as big as the rented cottage and set inground like a pool. The rental person, a middle-aged soft-bodied guy who smelled like Febreze and chicken soup, told her the heater was busted and he hoped she wasn't disappointed. "It's got these powerful jets and holds up to ten men," he said, clearly well versed in hot tubs and their potential, and she told him a big vat of poached men was the last thing she cared to think about at the moment, in fact it left her feeling nauseated. If he had meant to be flirting, and he may have been—she had always had such a hard time telling—that cooled it all. He handed her the key and a free DVD rental and she drove straight to the liquor store and then down the long wooded dirt drive to the small somewhat rundown cottage. Nothing worked quite right—burned-out porch light, two of the gas burners not working, the bed soft as pudding and stale-smelling—but what did it matter? She poured a glass of vodka and went outside. The giant ten-man hot tub with jets should have been covered, a light snow already falling, but it wasn't her job. She was just a weekend renter, someone on a shitty vacation, a dog looking for a place to die. She took pills so it would all be an accident, just the right amount for a distracted insomniac to accidentally take. She had even practiced a couple of times. This is *the right amount,* sloppy notes told her, scrawled as she passed out. *Fuck you from the bottom of your fucked-up heart.*

She closed her eyes and imagined the ocean, the rhythmic sound of her childhood, the rocking motion of waves against sand like the lava-wave lamp Ben had in his dorm room all those years ago—back and forth, back and forth, steady as a pendulum. He had not been expecting her visit and it was awkward in a way she would never have thought possible. They were partners, after all, best friends bound by the secret oath, she reminded him, and so he canceled his plans—clearly a date—and they ended up having a night together that pretty much finished the friendship if, in fact, anything had been left. He treated her no differently than he would've the girl who got stood up or probably any other average ordinary girl. He treated her like nothing. Now you see her, now you don't.

She imagined a plug pulled from the ocean, sucking and swirling and spiraling downward, until all that was left visible there on the sandy floor was shell and rock and glass and bone. She felt the ice cold water—puzzling the irony of it being a hot tub—and she felt how heavy her boots were, full and heavy; she was thinking how people have drowned in little bowls of water and she was thinking of her childhood, the magic shows, the way Ben had her tie his hands and then his legs together before he jumped from the small bridge over the river where they used to all gather to swim. She had learned slipknots and they had practiced often; still, she held her breath as she watched him below the murky brown water, twisting and writhing like a snake. Those standing there would begin to count, and then there was nervous laughter, one boy already stripped of his shirt and ready to dive in and then poof! Ben broke the surface, grinning and twirling the ropes over his head.

He had been Houdini and she was his loyal assistant.

Ladies and gentlemen. Now I will make this normal ordinary girl disappear.

To disappear was her wish that night in New Hampshire. The night in Ben's dorm room had meant nothing to him; it vanished into thin air and yet it haunted and weighed her down like a concrete sack of shit slung around her neck. She lay awake so many nights revisiting his hands on her body, his mouth grazing her skin, the words he half mumbled as he came and then collapsed, the warm wet weight of his body on hers. The haunting continued even as he ran ahead and never looked back.

So she got married. It was just that easy to set off in the wrong direction. It was like finding a seat on the train—leg room and a place for your baggage—the comfort of knowing a stranger wouldn't plop down beside you. Done. Finis. One door slammed. And the china and flowers are all a great distraction, the best sleight of hand.

"Escape by matrimony," Luke had said. "A very common vehicle in our society." But the same can be accomplished with a job or a religion or a hobby, he added, and those things are easier to leave and change. People marry to change class, geography, luck, but when they stretch out at the end of the day, it's still the same heavy hearts thudding along at their centers.

She was such a liar—a bad liar—and a bad friend, not to mention a horrible wife, and when that felt too wrong to think about anymore she left their home near Stanford where he was a graduate student. She had never fit in in California and she had never been good at breaking up with people. She couldn't even change her hairstylist or mechanic for fear of hurting their feelings. So she just left, the kind of abandonment that makes those left relieved to be done with her, and once the pattern was established it was easy to continue: a sociopathic actor who burned himself out before he even got started, like a dud firework smoldering in its base, temp jobs and temp relationships, whatever blew her way. She got a divorce by proxy and told him to keep all the things since it was such bad luck that he had married her in the first place. Enjoy the fondue pot and wok; hock the silver. Then she got the call that her mother died and everything really spiraled out of control. Someone she worked with talked her into attending a grief circle and that's when, like magic, she met a real person— a really great guy—widowed with a two-year-old daughter and a newborn. She wasn't *in love* with him, either, but by then she believed she was someone who would never be *in* love—what did that even mean?—and should just hope for the best; she trusted him and he was certainly the kind of person you *should* love— easy to love, in fact—and wouldn't she grow to fall in love with him, and if not, wasn't just plain old love enough? It worked for a while, too, long enough that she had begun to relax with it all, long enough that she called her dad and said she couldn't wait to see him. "Grandkids," she told him. "Poof! You have grandkids!" He listened, and it seemed the sealed tomb was starting to open only for her to then have to slam it closed again. She made a mistake that had hurt someone and now someone else's mistake would hurt her. It was logical enough, but it didn't feel very logical that afternoon in late October when he sat, head in hands and crying the same way he had done in those earliest meetings when he talked about his wife. Joanna knew what was coming even before she heard the words. She could smell the end. He said that she had been so wonderful, such a good friend and lifesaver to them all. He said he knew that she couldn't possibly understand and yet she did. She stood there in the center of that kitchen they had just redone and pressed her palms against the cool granite island top. She had always wanted a kitchen like this, new appliances and yellow walls and a big window over the sink where she hung a finger painting from preschool. She had imagined family vacations to Disney and trips into the city to go to shows; she had even imagined the kids all grown when she would tell them the long and winding road that had brought her to them. They called her *Mama* and she had tuned her mind to the Parent Channel and was well versed in Mr. Rogers and the Muppets and Raffi. She bought healthy food and drove the nicest, safest car she had ever driven, a used Volvo he insisted she keep; she had gotten her hair shaped and highlighted in a high-end salon, and for the first time since leaving she had been looking forward to returning home, proud of who she had become.

She assured him that she did understand. She told him that people do a lot of things in the name of grief. And then he asked the very hardest thing of her, that perhaps after a little weaning time, she let the kids go, she let this woman he was in love with be their mother. "I think it will be so much easier on them," he said. "They're so young. They'll forget." And she nodded mutely, the world thankfully fogged from her view of kids in the next room screaming and laughing. *Mommy, Mommy.* He promised to send her pictures of them. He promised to send her money. And she promised herself that she would get in the car and drive whatever way the wind blew. She didn't want his money. There was no one expecting her. Why not just disappear?

MOMMY, MOMMY, SHE thought there in the cold icy water. *I don't want to go to Europe. Shut up and keep swimming. Mommy, Mommy, I don't want to see Daddy. Shut up and keep digging.* She had never liked those jokes. And yet there they were.

THE LAST GUY, always good for his word, had sent her a letter with photos just last year after she wrote to tell him where she was living and what she was doing, that if he ever headed southeast and wanted a really good hot dog to give her a call. It was the least she could do—unhook any regret he might feel. He, after all, had done her a favor; he had given her a glimpse of what a good life could look like. But she threw away the photos without looking, too hard, though she did like to think there might be a day in the future when some slight memory might come to the little daughter, materializing out of a smell or a fabric, perhaps something like her pink cashmere scarf the child loved to finger and rub against her cheek as she dozed off. She was wearing the scarf that night in New Hampshire, fingering the wet weight around her throat, and all she could think about is how worthless she felt and how she wondered what it would feel like to know you had lost two mothers. She had one photo in her wallet, one of those awful department store photos with the baby boy propped up like a sack of potatoes, his sister's arms around him. She also had a photo she had carried in her wallet since junior high. It looks like a screen door—old-timey with crisscrossed panels—a broom propped in the corner near the latch. Ben is behind the door. She was waiting for him to practice their show and he paused before coming back out into daylight and she snapped it; all you can see is the shadow of someone, darkness beyond the door, but she knew he was there all the same.

"And now I will make this normal ordinary girl disappear," he said, and gestured to where she sat in the school auditorium. She came up on the stage wearing the clothes he had told her to wear, a navy scooter skirt and white Hang Ten T-shirt and plain Keds; her hair was in braided pigtails. *Nothing loose that might snag,* he had said. She was aware of all the students watching and waiting as she walked over to the chamber—a box in a box, one side cut away but carefully hidden. He turned it just right. He always knew how to turn it just right. He winked at her and she felt the great power of their friendship, the secrecy of their act. *Abracadabra. Now you see her, now you don't.*

The water was cold and her clothes heavy, boots filling; there was a crack along the bottom of the hot tub like a broken highway to nowhere. Ben's best trick had always been to make her disappear and that's what she had done. He even tried to get in touch with her a few times, saying he wanted her to meet his wife, he had a baby daughter, he was so sorry her mother died, but she had already long disappeared. She was old news, bits of gossip her parents and then her dad had attempted to sweep from the stoop. She was reaching her hand out to trace that crack, no ropes, no cuffs, letting the key to the cottage drop from her hand, when something grabbed her hard; there was a sharp pain in her shoulder, deep and throbbing, and her mouth filled with water and that was all she remembered.

Later she would get a tattoo to remind her. A big purple blob of a tattoo—horseshoe-shaped—to replicate the bite of a huge dog. She later kept thinking of that old hymn, "Love Lifted Me," love in the monstrous form of Tammy, 150 pounds of fur and jowls and drool. She would later learn that Tammy didn't like for anyone to be in the water, always assuming they needed to be saved. Luke had taken her in when the young family she belonged to couldn't break her of pulling their kids from the lake every time they tried to learn how to swim. The kids, bruised and tormented, got agitated when they saw her coming, and she read their agitation as trouble and fear and got to work, her big webbed paws propelling her to their rescue. Those kids had named her Nana after the dog in Peter Pan, but Luke decided to rename her in case she had any problems connected to all the times her name had been shrieked in anger. They were in the emergency room, and he told Joanna he had named her after a song he loved as a kid, "Tammy," by Debbie Reynolds. He said that he played his old 45 every night and sang along in a way he hoped would soothe her.

"You have a turntable?" she asked, clearly impressed, or so he told her later.

"Tammy has a real missionary complex," Luke said. "She wants to save everyone." He was bone thin with a shaved head and big dark eyes, either a manic runner or a cancer patient. She didn't mean to say that aloud, but she did because he told her he was both—not cancer per se, but he *was* dying and he had been a runner since the late seventies when he discovered that a good hard run could just about always make you feel better. She nodded. She knew this as well. She said *run run fast as you can.* He stood by her gurney and extended an equally bony hand—no ring, no watch. "Tammy and I have a lot of the same problems," he said. "Fortunately she's not dying and I don't shit in the front yard."

Joanna learned so much about him in the hours he sat there with her. He had grown up near Boston but spent his summers on Lake Winnipesaukee. He preferred the politics of Massachusetts and Vermont, but New Hampshire was backdrop for the best memories of his childhood, and he was convinced that if he claimed all the parts he really loved he would be able to make peace with everything else. "Too many people throw the baby out with the bath water," he said, and she nodded, yes, the forgotten baby. She knew where that saying came from, too, though she felt too heavy to answer, the part about when spring came and the family needed to be clean and fresh, so the man bathed first and then the wife and then the children from oldest on down and by the time the baby got there the water was dark and filthy, the baby too hard to see. It was hard for her to see, too hard to open her eyes so she listened to all that he loved about New Hampshire. He loved Clark's Trading Post, a family operation with trained bears and a photo shop where you could have your picture taken in old timey clothes. He loved the Flume and the Old Man of the Mountain; he had even helped raise money when there was still hope of saving the stone structure. He loved the mountains and he loved the lakes. He had once as a teenager worked part-time at Story Land where he ran the Polar Coaster. He came from a very conservative family who never accepted who he was even though his wild years in San Francisco were long behind him and he was in love for real for the first time in his whole life. Then he talked about David and she knew as she lay there listening that *that* is what love is supposed to sound like. She couldn't see it, but she recognized it. It was all so clear.

After it was all over, she thanked him for saving her and he said that really Tammy saved her. All he did was let the giant dog out to pee. He said there were two kinds of creatures in the world— there are those in dresses fighting for the lifeboats and there are those making sure that others are okay, like the man in the footage of that plane crash in the Potomac who passed the life rope so many times he didn't make it himself. "No doubt," Luke said, "I love the feel of a skirt, especially something in crepe or silk, but the honest truth is that I really want to be a rope passer. I like to believe that's what I'd do." He pulled Tammy in close and kissed her big head. "Tammy is a rope passer. Tammy is a big voluptuous angel from heaven."

Luke believed in a lot of things Joanna had always thought were bullshit—angels and spirits—and yet how could she doubt him there at the end when he reached his hand forward to those he said were waiting for him. "They're here," he said, and pointed to the darkened hallway. "They're here." He told her that there was a time when he believed nothing; the older he got, the less he believed and then the less he believed the more capable he was of believing. "Such a cool paradox," he said.

"What?" she had asked, needing to hold on to his every word, and that's when he talked about clarity and how it is impossible to see in the midst of chaos.

"Cool and calm," he said, and pointed again. "It's very calm over there in the hallway."

After the rescue, Luke made her go to classes and to therapy. He said the price of a saved life was educating herself, healing herself, loving herself. It was impossible to get too angry once she knew the situation of his life. He really was dying and she felt foolish to have wanted to throw away what he wanted so desperately. "It's always the way," he said. "If you've got curly hair, you want it straight."

She tried to explain that it was all an accident. She didn't want to hurt anyone. She just wanted it all to be a quiet accident, just another mistake; that's what she imagined her dad or Ben and others back home would say—so unlucky in love and in life, such a fuckup, an accident waiting to happen. All she had wanted was to slip from the earth with as little trace as possible. She wanted to disappear. She had thought there could be something at the bottom of the hot tub luring her to lean in close and look—what could she toss in? She thought of her wedding band and engagement ring, something to flash and glitter against the cracked blue bottom, but she knew that would be wrong, placing too much weight on the loss behind her. Her recent husband would never have gotten over that. Her rolling in needed to be an accident—a necessary accident. The keys to the cottage would be good. She would have wandered onto the deck to see this giant ten-man hot tub and accidentally tripped and dropped her keys, leaned and reached and fallen in, maybe she hit her head, so many possibilities.

Luke said that this was exactly why she had needed to live. "There is a need for detail people like you," he said. "A need for those with one eye on minutiae and one eye on the big picture. Besides," he added, "*we* need you." And then he made the offer. He wanted David to get everything he owned and he knew that his family would not let that happen. So, Joanna would marry him. She would nurse him while taking classes and getting some good therapy so she would be fit to go out into the world with a practical satisfying skill and start over. She would be his project and he would be hers. He said she would be their Eliza Doolittle. He said he and David would continue life as they had for almost two years and she would share the guest room with Tammy. "By the time I die," he told her, "you are going to be a whole new person." Ever the lawyer, he typed it all up, how at his death she would receive enough to begin her new life and she would sign everything else, including big Tammy, over to David.

THE FIRST NIGHT after the hospital, she sat on his couch wrapped in an old worn-out quilt like a *washed-out ghost*. That's how he described her on the phone to David as he unwrapped a beef bone the size of her thigh for Tammy. *You owe her,* he said, and pointed to the massive furry beast with the large kind eyes. *In the old Eastern tradition, you owe her your life.* Tammy sat and drooled on her leg while waiting for the reward, the weight and warmth of her big heavy head a wonderful comfort. Hard to believe she was also responsible for the tight soreness through her shoulder, the sutures and doses of antibiotics.

"She bit the hell out of me."

"Tammy doesn't have hands," he said. "If she did, she wouldn't have needed to use her teeth." He paused and laughed, waved the magic wand of a bone. "Of course, if she had hands, she wouldn't have to rely on me at all and likely wouldn't be living here. She would have her own apartment and job and drive a car."

"And she wouldn't give a shit."

"Oh, I think she would." He roughed up the fur along her big neck and delivered the bone to that cavernous mouth. "Tammy is all about love, aren't you, girl? Tammy is a rope passer. Tammy *is* Love. There's a sampler I'd like to embroider except I don't think I have enough time, so we're going to have her portrait painted instead." He had slipped into a higher singsong voice reserved for Tammy. "Yes we are. Oh, yes we are." The portrait was already commissioned and there were several times in weeks to come where Joanna wore a big fake fur coat that made her the right bulk and heft and sat in for Tammy while the artist worked on the backdrop of what Luke loved so much—the White Mountains and Lake Winnipesaukee. When the portrait was finished, they had a special unveiling and Tammy ate a ribeye, and when Luke and Joanna got married Tammy was there with a pink tulle collar and a bone even bigger than the one of the rescue night.

"What number husband will I be?" Luke asked. "Three? Four?"

"I think I'm up to five in my hometown," she told him. "I hear they call me the Liz Taylor of Fulton only without the money, talent, and looks." It surprised her that she was finally able to start laughing at things she had never imagined she could. Luke and Tammy were magic.

As they spoke their vows out on the deck, the hot tub next door in full view, Luke's face was flushed, his eyes never leaving those of David who stood right behind Joanna with Tammy beside him. Then they ate and danced with a handful of locals down at Cleary's, a local spot known for their clam rolls and homemade beer. That night, Joanna lay with big Tammy snoring beside her and fell asleep to the excited whispers of David and Luke in the next room. Legally, she was the bride, but spiritually everyone present knew otherwise. Spiritually, she had never had such a feeling of peace. "Who wears the garter in this family?" she had asked before going to bed. "Because I do not want to catch it."

"You owe her big-time," Luke said that first night, and pointed to Tammy. "We never would have heard a thing, just found you frozen and floating." And this was when he began hatching the plan of what she would do with her life. If she didn't value her life any more than that, then he would value it for her and tell her exactly what to do. "You are a gift to us!" he said. "You are our gift from God."

"There's something I've never heard said."

"So I'll say it again. You are a gift—a messenger from God."

"I'm a doped-up suicidal woman who is never wanted by the people she wants. What does any of that have to do with God?"

"Redemption," Luke said, and reached for David's hand. "We are witnessing redemption. She's our project—our own little fucked-up Eliza Doolittle."

"Better than a smokehouse, I think," David said. He was handsome and outdoorsy, his hair thinning at his temples the only indication that he was older than twenty. He was a local New Hampshire boy who had grown up ten miles away and was always delivering the commentary of his life: My school bus stopped there. That's where I played Little League. That's where a man ran a stop sign and totaled my Nova. He often rode by where his dad was buried in a small church cemetery and the house where he had grown up. His mother still lived there, but he only saw her at Christmas when she announced to all the relatives visiting from elsewhere that he was going to locate the perfect wife any day now. He was someone content in that small parcel of the world, even as an outsider within his own family, and she admired and aspired to his level of comfort.

"Better than a smokehouse," Luke said. "Our final project. We will make her *reappear*," he said the word very carefully. He told her how she had mumbled *disappear* over and over in the ambulance ride. *Where did Ben go?* She had asked the question so many times that Luke worried in the beginning that someone else had been there when she fell in the hot tub.

"Repeat the mantra." Luke said. "I will reappear."

Do you believe in ghosts?

Do you believe in the power of magic?

Do you believe this girl, this normal ordinary girl, can disappear?

I do, I do, I do.

Now the day Tammy saved her seems light years away, many many miles behind her, and yet she wakes to it and falls asleep to it. The touchstone. Tammy's portrait, which David insisted she take, hangs over the mantel in her cottage, and several times a year she sends Tammy a gift and something for David, too—bones and CDs and a heavy wool scarf she knitted sitting bedside at Pine Haven. Tammy is getting old for her breed so David is talking about getting a puppy. "The big ones like Tammy don't live long," Luke had told her. "They have to cram a lot in." David has been seeing someone who came to work at one of the resorts over the summer and then never left. He says he is happy and that he's surprised by that. He thought he never would be again. And to think that now he could get married if he chose to do so.

In the summer when Joanna is wearing something sleeveless, some unknowing, kind person will often rush forward to ask what happened, hands held a safe distance from the big purple dog bite.

"It's a tattoo," she says, and sometimes she adds, without explanation, that it is meant to simulate a great big dog bite. It's Tammy's Teeth—something akin to Rosebud or Zuzu's petals or whatever it is in life that reminds you that you are alive.

Notes about my Dad: Curtis Edward Lamb
Born: February 28, 1920   **Died:** March 15, 2008, 8:10 a.m.
Fulton, North Carolina

He loved the ocean and fishing and hot dogs.

It was a sunny spring day, daffodils blooming—some so old they were only green sprigs. King Alfred gone to a pauper. It was normal traffic for a normal morning. We were in the room where I had spent my childhood, the crack in the ceiling I used to trace in the near darkness still there, and it seemed in that moment that it might all crash in. I held my hand out to the crack, shocked at how like my mother's hand it was. He said it first years ago, *You have your mother's hands and you have your mother's eyes,* and I couldn't help but wonder all these years later if that changed the way I saw things, changed the way I touched things. "You are my little girl," he said. These were his last words. I told him that I was sorry, but he seemed not to hear. I held his hand until the very end and with that last breath, the world lightened in a way that left me feeling sadder than I have ever felt.

"I'm so sorry," I said, and I was. I was so sorry not to have done things differently, so sorry I couldn't be the one to blink and break the stubborn stance that kept me from my mother. And for the first time I saw him for what he really was, a bridge between two places—the past and the present—the before and the after. The world I shared with my parents and the one I have all alone. I kept thinking of the draw bridge that used to separate Ferris Beach from the mainland, an old rough-hewn bridge that a single man, alone in a little tower, swung outward when a boat was too large to pass under. It swung and creaked and took forever. It was not ideal, but it was all there was.

[from Joanna's notebook]

Curtis Edward Lamb

Doris is at the other end of the house and he has to move that way to find her, but when he gets there it is his daughter's room and Doris isn't there, nobody is there, just walls in need of paint and a closet full of Joanna's old board games and rag dolls nobody has touched in years. So throw them out, he told Doris, but she couldn't, she said she could not bear to throw them out. So call her, let's call her, but no, she said, no. Joanna made her bed and she needs to lie in it. After all the sacrifices we made for her, the least she can do is lead a decent life. We do not owe her. She owes us. But she is our little girl, he said, and he says it again when he holds her hand. You are my little girl, and she squeezes tight while they wait in the hot-dog line. The Ferris wheel is all she can talk about and he has promised her that he will go with her, turning and turning and turning, the lights so bright and buzzing in the distance he has to look away.

Abby

ABBY PALMER BELIEVES THAT you should never have to wear church clothes on a weekday, especially in the summer, and that really you should never have to go to church, especially if your parents don't go themselves but just drop you off on the curb, which is what hers usually do. Her dad said he did his time years ago. Her mom says an Episcopalian is a good thing to be. You should never have to do chores or any kind of work on your birthday and you shouldn't *have* to have a birthday party if you don't want one, especially a stupid suck-hole party like what her mom has planned: impersonators of famous First Ladies telling their stupid stories while the girls make bracelets out of stupid junk like old mahjongg and Scrabble tiles—when what you really want is a magic show and tarot card and palm readings. You should always be allowed to keep an animal who turns up on your doorstep looking for a home and that animal should never get lost or leave you. You should pick your own friends and not the ones your mother thinks are the right friends for you, and if you want friends who are a hundred years old, that is *your* business. Liking Lady Gaga is *your* business and so is eating a Slim Jim and some Yodels if that is what *you* want to eat. You should not have to listen to your parents fighting night after night or pretend the next morning that you didn't hear anything so they can feel good about their own stinking selves. You should never leave home because bad things happen when you do, like the way her bedroom got redone while she was at camp last summer, turning a perfectly nice place into something white and starched and frilly in a way she is *not* or, worse, the way her dog, Dollbaby, vanished when she went with her dad to Wilmington to buy all the materials for their magic act. He is building a disappearing chamber for her party because that is what *she* wants even though her mom screamed and pitched a bitch and said that was a terrible idea and that her dad was doing it just for spite and to compete with her. "He is jealous of everything I do," she yelled, which, looking at her stupid painting of Hillary Clinton, is hard to believe. Who would be jealous of *that*? Hillary Clinton should sue her for that.

Abby's dad keeps telling her that there is no connection between their plan to have a disappearing chamber and Dollbaby being missing, but that is hard to believe, too. She can't help but feel like she made it happen and now she would do anything to get her back.

Dollbaby is her best friend; she is the baby sister she has begged for and never gotten. Dollbaby has brown eyes and a bushy fox tail and a nose that often leads her away for hours. But still she has always come home and Abby's dad always tells funny stories about where she has been: the dentist to get her teeth sharpened, the Dog House for a "Puppy to go," the cemetery to look for bones. It's like Dollbaby has a whole other life. She is on several mailing lists and has gotten free panty hose, tampons, toothpaste, and once was even asked to sign up for her own Visa card. No one is sure how Dollbaby got on the lists in the first place but she did, and Abby takes great care keeping up with it all; she has put all of Dollbaby's mail inside the same jewelry box where she keeps the notes she has started finding in the cemetery next door: *The time has come* and *Better late than never* and *I am with you even when you think I'm not.* Creepy.

ABBY WISHES HER mother would wear mom pants, some nice high-waisted stretch denim mom pants. But no, her mom wears low rise. Her mom wears whatever the seventeen year old sitter wears. Molly once left her swimsuit at their house and Abby saw her mom trying it on, turning from side to side and sucking in so that her ribs stuck out. She didn't see Abby see her, but she did later accuse Abby's dad of looking at the babysitter in a way he shouldn't. "You were flirting with a child," her mother said, which was just gross-out gross and left Abby feeling sick. She liked Molly, too; she was nice enough and, most important, was actually nice to Abby and took an interest in Dollbaby and all that Abby knows about the cemetery next door and who is buried where, but now her parents had ruined it all. Molly would never be able to babysit again without her mother saying all those things. I *saw how you looked at her little butt cheeks,* and there was more but Abby started screaming so she couldn't hear any more of it.

"Shut up," she screamed. "Shut up, shut up, shut the hell damn fuck up."

It was right after that she went for her first session with Dr. Owens and that was kind of good. Her mother insisted on taking

her, of course, and waiting there the whole time, complimenting the doctor on the *decor* of the office and the *prestige* of her
degrees and any other bullshit thing that could be said. Abby just
liked the white noise and the soft chairs and the knowledge that
the next fifty minutes were only about her. Dr. Owens looked like
an ordinary person, too, which was good. She could just as easily
have been one of the cafeteria women at school or the soft round
nurse in her old elementary school. It wasn't as good as being with
Sadie who lives next door at Pine Haven, but it was still worth
going because for a little while anyway it had reduced the fighting
to those times late at night when they thought she couldn't hear.

But still, her mom kept calling Molly if she needed a sitter no
matter how many times Abby begged to be left alone or over at
Pine Haven where she knew everybody. Or, she had suggested,
they could call Dorro from down the street. Dorro was middle-
aged and overweight and there wouldn't have been anything to
fight about, but no, she kept hauling in Molly until Molly must
have figured it out and stopped coming. The last time she was
there, Abby's mom had insisted that her dad drive Molly home
and that, no, Abby could not ride with them. "Don't worry, Moll,"
Abby's mother said, like the two of them might have been friends.
"You can trust him to be a gentleman, and if he isn't, well, you
know who to come to." She patted her chest and laughed and
Abby slipped out of the house and into the cemetery before her
dad returned because she knew there would be a fight. Dr. Owens
listened, her brow wrinkled. It was clear that if she had a kid *she*
wouldn't be doing it that way and that was a good thing for Abby
to know.

And as if life isn't bad enough all the way around, now her mom is planning Abby's birthday party like it's her own stupid party. She wants something educational so all the other mothers will say how wonderful she is to "combine fun and education." She says crap like that all the time, too. In celebration of First Ladies. What a lame and stupid idea from her lame and stupid mother. A party featuring the First Ladies and idiot shitty actors coming in to pretend to be them. The invitation says: *Ladies First* and then lots of crap about First Ladies, and it will be at the country club, which is a stupid place anyway unless it's a pool party. Her mother is going to have a little table with knock-off purses for the mothers (who also are invited) to peruse and they all also will get their nails done and have make-overs.

"If we have to do that, then at least let C.J. be the person," she had said, and reminded her mother who C.J. is, the woman who does nails and exercise classes over at Pine Haven and has the cute little baby named Kurt.

"You have got to be kidding," her mother said. "The slutty mixed-race one with all the tattoos? Your dad might think that's okay, but I do not. It is certainly not very First Lady–like." She laughed at her own stupid joke.

Yeah, Eleanor Roosevelt was all about pedicures, Abby had told her dad later that night. *What's-her-face Carter in the cotton coat and all those designer purses.* Her dad had held a finger up to his lips and then shook his head, let his tongue roll out to the side like a strangled victim as if to mime tolerating her mother's whims.

"It's humiliating," she screamed, near crying, and not caring what her stupid mother heard. "It's like it's her party."

"She said you love the First Ladies."

"I wrote one shitty report last year in sixth grade because I had to. That's all," she said. "That was over a year ago. She doesn't even know me."

"It'll be over soon," he said, and stretched out across the foot of her bed. He was in the same spot where Dollbaby had slept for the past two years and she knew her dad thought of it, too, because he patted the place as if the dog were still there. Neither of them had gotten over her disappearance. They were only gone for five hours. Her mother said Dollbaby dug her way out of the yard and ran away. Her mother said that she had called every vet and every rescue place in this county and two over and not a trace. "I suspect something bad has happened to her," her mother said. "Maybe it will be easier to just accept she's gone."

"I don't even want a party," she told her dad. "I want Dollbaby."

"Me, too," he said. "But you don't turn thirteen every day."

The only reason Abby was even having a big party was to compete with all the bat and bar mitzvahs she'd attended all through seventh grade. Everything was a competition for her mother, whether Abby felt the desire to compete or not. Her dad had grown up here, but her mother had not and it was very important that she establish herself in her own way and right. People should like and respect her for who she is and not because they remember when *cute little Bennie* was the fastest kid on the track team or won a prize one Halloween for being the solar system. Abby had heard it all so many times she could recite it back.

Her mother is like a topsy-turvy doll, one minute funny and happy and the life of the party and the next, somber and bleak and angry. She can't even enjoy when her mom seems good because she has to get ready for what she knows is coming. Abby has often thought how wonderful it would be to have a sturdy mother who stays the same, dependable and comfortable with some meat on her body. A mother who doesn't *want* to wear what is in the junior department at Macy's, a mother who loves wearing some big stretchy mom pants. Her one friend, Richie Henderson, has been through divorce and predicted as much for Abby's future, and after many sad and burdened months thinking about it, Abby has come to look forward to the announcement and the life that will follow. Richie says a lot of parents are much better alone. They try harder. They stop lying about everything.

"They're all pretty stupid," Richie said. "Even the smart ones are stupid assholes." His mother teaches math and science and his dad is a doctor so it makes sense that he would know the truth. "You'll see, Abby, it'll be so much better when they're apart." And so she is wishing for that, wishing for separate homes and two different bedrooms, clothes for each house, a dog at her dad's. When she blows out her candles, she'll wish for Dollbaby to come home and then she'll wish for a divorce. A big fat divorce.

If someone asked her what is the best part of her life, she would say first Dollbaby, which she can't say anymore, and then story time with her dad and then all of her friends at Pine Haven and then Richie who only thinks about skateboards and science things. For as long as she can remember her dad either read or told a story at bedtime and even though she knows she's too old, she has begged him to continue. He ends his stories with a magic trick from his old days as an amateur street magician. Her best birthday parties have been the ones where he performed tricks and then people just split a piñata and ate lots of candy and ran around the house and yard until someone got hurt or threw up or both and her mother made them calm down and sit out on the porch until their rides came. But those days are gone and she hates the way her mother is constantly wondering if she has started her period. *No.*

Her dad has told her that he is only doing one big trick for the party but promises that it will be his best ever. He has worked for weeks on the disappearing chamber, even when her mother begged that he just pull a rabbit out of a hat or something easy. "It's a masterpiece," he had told her, and then whispered so her mother couldn't hear. "I am going to make all the First Ladies disappear."

Her favorite tricks are the ones he calls sleight of hand, and even though she knows how he palms things and uses his sleeves to hide things, it is still really amazing.

Her parents met because of the magic tricks. Her mom was in college and he has said that he was sort of in college and she stopped on the corner with a crowd of sorority sisters to watch him doing magic. They had told Abby the story for as long as she could remember so their lines of dialogue were firmly etched on her mind, the way her mom described him as "that cute hippie-looking guy" and her dad said that her mom was the prettiest of these very pretty girls all decked out with straw bags and high heels and everything monogrammed, little gold pearl necklaces, which her dad said made them all look like a pack of hunting dogs marked by some lucky owner.

"Thanks a lot," her mom would say, inserting correct descriptions like add-a-bead and espadrilles and Capezio, and then go on to describe her dad's dirty bare feet and near-dead flowers strewn in with the few dollars and bits of change tossed in front of the dove's cage. He owned Hawk long after his performance days. "He had quite a scene of groupies," her mom said. "They all looked like girls who did things a good girl wouldn't be doing."

"Like what?" Abby asked numerous times, but clearly the conversation had nothing to do with her except to act as a bit of brain washing. It was more designed as one of those things to remind her dad how lucky he was to meet her when he did. She claimed to have saved him from being a street person, that she was amazed when she discovered he was prelaw. He once confessed in a fight that he was never prelaw and only said that because one of the "dirty girls" had told him that's all it would take for him to get a date with one of the uppity girls. The promise of a career and good money was all you needed.

Then when they started dating, he did a trick a day for her. Flowers appearing out of his sleeve; Hawk materializing from his empty hat. Abby once heard her dad tell Sadie that he had a marriage founded on tricks and it changed the way she looked at everything. It is one of those things she plans to ask him about some night soon when he is near dozing at the foot of her bed. She will also ask him about a friend of his from childhood, Joanna, who owns the Dog House and sometimes works at Pine Haven. "Joanna and I were a lot like you and Richie," he had said. "Best friends all through elementary school." He said that she had always been a good loyal friend. True blue, he said. "And she could do everything I could do except pee standing up. A real tomboy."

"Some would say butch." Abby's mother didn't know she heard her say that, but she did. "Though she's been married how many times? Four? Five. Clearly there's something wrong with her. "

When Abby outgrew regular bedtime stories, her dad started telling her about what the town used to be like. How once upon a time she might have looked out her bedroom window and seen into the cemetery because the hedge of myrtle wasn't there and the tall pine trees were just saplings. This was before the retirement home was built on the other side of the cemetery and before the row of modest split-levels across the street from them were plowed down and replaced with gigantic brick homes with cathedral windows, enormous garages, and no yards. A mathematician had once lived in their house and her dad had found all kinds of numbers and scribbles on the wall in what had been his study but now is their guest room. Abby had the girl's room, roses on the old wallpaper her mother fussed about for weeks, steaming and peeling every little scrap. The girl drove an old Checker cab painted dark green and last he heard was living and teaching somewhere in the Northeast.

He told how once in the cemetery there was a grave with a playhouse over it, how in 1940—almost twenty years before he was even born—the grief-stricken parents had the ten-year-old's playhouse moved there, the grave within looking like a little bed, the grave of the baby they had lost in the early 1930s there beside her. And he promised to take her there and show it to her, which he did. The playhouse rotted and fell down years ago, but he could find the grave, and he also showed her the statue of Lydia, a beautiful young woman who was rumored to try to hold on to you if you sat on her stone rose-petal-covered lap. And now Abby goes there every day and speaks to them all by name. When her dad was a child there was a grown-up-sized rocking chair inside the playhouse and he and Joanna had thought that maybe the chair was for the father to come and sit at night so he could cry there by the graves of his children without anyone seeing him. They always hoped they might see him there or hear the rocker. It chills Abby to think about that, especially as she is passing down the path where the playhouse used to be.

She isn't supposed to play in the cemetery. Her mother freaks out and says that's where people go to do drugs and homeless people sleep. One woman's purse got stolen out of her car while she was putting flowers on her husband's grave. Those things may be true, but Abby hasn't seen anything scary. She had been there that very day, in fact, and she finds lots of things but nothing like what her mother says. In the far corner where you can just barely see the brick of Pine Haven through the arboretum, there is a tiny area for Jewish people, rocks left on the various headstones like little notes to the dead. She arranges the rocks in circles and patterns, careful never to step on the graves. She visits Mary Young and her baby brother and Lydia, where there is a little stone off to the left under a bush marked JACK, our loyal friend. She knows that there had once been a statue of a German shepherd to go with the girl, but someone had stolen it years ago. Now there is just the flat stone.

LATELY AT NIGHT, before his magic trick and when he can't think of any more town stories, her dad talks about historical events he finds interesting, many of them about disasters and the lessons people could have learned from them. Floods and hurricanes and fires, that amazing molasses story in Boston, people drowned in the hot thick syrup. Cheap and faulty construction and lies told, scrimping on things that would have made all the difference. The Cocoanut Grove fire in Boston and the chicken factory right nearby in Hamlet. Locked doors and bad codes.

People locked in. She didn't want to think about it but she did, and sometimes she couldn't stop. Out on the interstate where she sometimes bikes on the service road, there is a billboard that says ARE YOU PREPARED TO MEET YOUR MAKER? Her dad always says, *Not today, thank you.* He says if you could read your life like a book, that you would be able to see what's coming. Like a well-planned magic trick, it might seem spontaneous and random, but really things line up in a way that is logical. He said that everything has a purpose.

"So what's the purpose of you and Mom screaming at each other?" Abby asked. "What is the purpose of Dollbaby getting lost?"

"And where does survival of the fittest come in?" her mother asked when she overheard that. "Tell me that one, Houdini."

"It's a puzzle," he said. "A friend of mine has a theory that if survival of the fittest is all about the guys most likely to get to spread the most seed and populate, then the prize would actually go to the sociopaths of the world—those slick player types who bed anything that might breathe. Do you believe that?" They locked down in one of those awful stares that made Abby want to run from the room screaming, made her wish they would drown in hot molasses and shut up.

"So what friend do you have who actually talks philosophical thoughts? The hot-dog heiress?"

Her mother thought it was sick to talk about historical tragedies and threatened to take it up with the Abby's *therapist,* whom she now refers to often, but her dad said people are most afraid of the unknown. It's always best to *know,* he argued. "It's why I believe in regular check-ups and asking lots of questions."

Abby's mom walked from the room and slammed the door. Her

dad once said that she has two channels with no choices in between. There is "The Zany Madcap Adventures of Me" and there
is "Nobody Loves Me, Everybody Hates and/or Is Jealous of Me."
He said the common denominator, of course, is *me*. Me, me, me.
"I am so goddamned sick of it I could die," he said, and now that
is what she thinks as she passes through the stones and vines. *I
am so goddamned sick of it I could die.*

"Everyone needs a mantra," C.J. had told the residents of Pine
Haven when they went to meditation class, which is something
Sadie never misses. It is best when you use sounds that blank your
mind. Sadie asked if it was okay if she imitated her old Singer
sewing machine because it was her greatest meditation device
for years. Absolutely, C.J. said, and so Sadie hums and Mr. Stone
makes what he calls squirrel chatter, which annoys everyone and
most just do the ordinary *om,* which Abby tries to do, but it almost
always turns into a curse or what a crash would sound like if there
was a twenty-car pileup on the interstate like that one in Tennessee
when everyone was suddenly caught in a cloud of fog with no
warning whatsoever. Could you see that coming? Her dad would
say yes, you could. He would say that the makings of such weather
and the traffic conditions could have been predicted. "You have
to keep your eyes open at all times," he said, but looked at her
mother as he said it. "You don't want to be caught unaware."

Her favorites of her dad's tricks are the ones he calls torn-and-
restored, where it always ends with him saying, *No worry, good
as new.* Abby wishes he would use it on himself. *Good as new,* he
says. A pony prancing from a pile of crap, the phoenix rising from
ashes, Jesus sprung from the tomb, the old dude we saw at the
mall slapped with paddles and brought back to life.

DOLLBABY WAS A stray and though Abby's mother tried and tried to get her to look at all the pictures in the newspaper from breeders, Abby held firm that this was the one she wanted. It was clear, after all, that Dollbaby had chosen *her*. Of all the kids, in this whole town, *she* was the one Dollbaby followed from the school where she had spent several days curled up outside the cafeteria doorway hoping for food. Who knew what Dollbaby actually was—a little of this and a little of that—the vet had said but she most resembled a Sheltie with her sharp little nose and bushy fox tail. The nose of a beagle, her dad had said the first time she ever picked up a scent and took off. She had clearly been abused and cowered at the sight of most adults and brooms and mops. She had the occasional accident in the house, but as Abby often pointed out to her parents, this was a temporary thing and would get better as Dollbaby got older and more used to living there. That was two years ago, when Abby was in fifth grade and before her parents started holding their late-night screaming matches. Now Abby is about to turn thirteen and Dollbaby has left as quickly as she came, likely gone for good, her mother had said because she had looked everywhere with no luck. Her mother said someone probably thought she was a stray and took her home.

"But she has a collar and a name tag!" Abby screamed, and her mother said her tag might have gotten lost.

"But I put pictures of her all over town!"

Her mother said the people could have come from out of town, that maybe Dollbaby ventured over toward Cracker Barrel off on the service road. "She did that another time, remember?" her mother asked. Abby's dad was there beside her mother, holding her hand like everything was okay and like *she* was the one who had lost something. Like Abby wouldn't remember Dollbaby at the Cracker Barrel? Like she wouldn't have been terrified to imagine Dollbaby crossing the interstate all by herself. But that time, someone called, a woman from New Jersey and the woman sat right there in a big rocking chair with Dollbaby on her lap until they got there to pick her up. Abby's dad offered the woman some money, but she said no thanks, she was just happy to have helped and for them to use the money, to buy something for Dollbaby, so they rode all the way out to the Dog House and got her an Old Yeller and sat and watched her lick the waxy paper clean.

"You are quite the dog, Dollbaby," Abby's dad said. "Playing Monopoly, going to the Cracker Barrel, eating at the Dog House." The mention of Monopoly made them both laugh. Several months before, Dollbaby had eaten the race car and Abby's dad made it their mission to find the car when it came out the other end. Finally, there it was, not a bit damaged, and they boiled it and then returned it to the box with the top hat and little dog and battleship. Her mother said it was outrageous and that someone with a real job wouldn't have so much time to spend searching through dog shit. Her dad said it was fascinating and educational to imagine the journey the little race car took, like Jonah in the belly of the whale or Gepetto looking for Pinocchio. He said he had always gotten those two stories mixed up and now was eager to show Pinocchio on the big screen. He had reopened the old movie theater downtown and always ran kid movies on Saturday mornings. There was a time when this alone made people at school want to be friends with her, but those days were long gone.

Just earlier today, Abby's mother said that *if,* and then she paused with the word, *if* Dollbaby is dead, they may never know.

They will only know if someone takes the time to turn in the body. "I have left messages all over town," her mother said. "So if they take the body to a vet or a shelter, we will hear. But I think for all practical purposes, we should probably assume she is dead."

That's when Abby got madder than she has ever been. "Never," she screamed. "I will *never* stop looking for her!" She grabbed another stack of the posters she had made and went outside, slamming the door behind her. If only she had stayed home and helped her mother plan the stupid party, it might not have happened. Dollbaby would never have left if Abby had been out there in the yard or walking through the cemetery to Pine Haven. If only her parents would stop being so stupid. Dollbaby hates yelling and fighting. And Abby's parents are stupid. Sometimes she hates both of them, something she only has the nerve to tell Dollbaby, who listens to every word. Her parents don't allow sweets or sodas or TV unless it is educational, which isn't the reason she hates them but it helps, and it is a big part of the reason why she started spending so many afternoons over at Pine Haven in the first place.

It is an easy walk through the cemetery and then the arboretum. She loves the cool shadiness of the cemetery, the huge trees, and old headstones to read along the way: *Greetings stranger passing by, you are now as once was I*; there is where the little playhouse used to be and the tall stone angel—*MCKEITHAN*—who once was vandalized and now stands with only one wing intact. There is a tiny lamb on top of a dark mossy stone: *Thou hast won the victory without fighting the battle, hast gained the cross without having to bear the crown.* It was a boy named Isaac Abbott who was born in 1832 and died a year later. She likes the old parts of the cemetery the best, though some of the stones are hard to read.

The far corner, which is all overgrown, is where she had been told they buried slaves and suicides and unclaimed bodies like that guy called Spaghetti over in Laurinburg. They called him the Carny Mummy and her dad had once seen him preserved over there in a glass box. She wanted to go to Laurinburg to see him, but now he was buried; they even poured concrete in on top so nobody could dig him back up, that's how famous he is. Somebody from the North had sent money to bury him sixty years after the fact because he thought it was disrespectful to Italian people. They said his name was Cancetto Farmica and not *Carny Mummy* and certainly not *Spaghetti*.

When she is way back under the dogwoods and pines and willows, she can't see anything beyond the tip top eaves of her house. There is no street and no Pine Haven, no cars. Sometimes she and Dollbaby pretend that it is 1833 and they have come to bury Isaac. They say what a sweet boy he was and how sad he died so young. Abby has always been able to make herself cry and often she has enjoyed that, but it was a mistake to bring Haley White out here in the fifth grade and let her in on the game. Haley acted like she understood and also really respected and loved these people and then she went to school and announced to the whole class that all Abby's friends were either really old or dead. Dollbaby growled the first time she saw Haley, and Abby should have paid attention to that. One day Dollbaby was sniffing and chasing something, probably a rabbit, and led Abby to a little section closed in by shrubs at least six feet tall where Stars of David are on the stones and little rocks are left like calling cards. Abby is especially drawn to the grave of Esther Cohen who not only has the most rocks but lately is the one who often has notes neatly folded inside the urn attached to her headstone. Clearly, Esther is the most popular and Abby feels both resentment and admiration since she herself is one of those girls who has always gotten the assigned class number of Valentine's and none with anything really written to her except the ones she got from Dollbaby, which her dad had made—big loopy words with backward letters—where Dollbaby professed her great love and adoration and promised not to pee on the living room rug anymore.

"I'M SORRY, HONEY," her dad had said with the news of Dollbaby's disappearance. He pulled her close and hugged her. He shook and cried as well, but it seemed he was crying about more than Dollbaby, and she almost screamed out her anger and hatred when she heard them again late that night, their voices filling the house even as they stupidly thought they were being quiet. *You have no respect,* she wanted to scream. It was what her mother had said to her when she got on that new white spread knowing her Nikes were covered in mud and maybe, hopefully, even some dog shit. You have to have respect, they both had said when she got in trouble for arguing with one of her teachers who mispronounced a lot of words like when he was talking about herbs until she quizzed him on why they were talking about *herbs* in history class and he said. "Erbs, girl!" he said, and then spelled, "A-R-A-B-S. *Erbs!*" The same teacher talked about the nigger river and said that evolution was the talk of the devil. Certainly, she didn't respect *that* and she doesn't respect her stupid idiot parents either.

This morning Esther has a lot of mail. The note that was there yesterday written in sloppy blue ink—*See you soon*—is still there. It has a smudged blot of lipstick—sealed with a kiss—and someone wrote *WHEN?* in all capital letters. The *when* looks angry, like it should be shouted. *WHEN?* Now there is a new one on the back of a Food Lion receipt. *I can't keep waiting. I deserve something better!* Abby often stops to read the notes and then to sit up under the tendrils of the weeping willow growing closeby. Usually Dollbaby joins her and everything is fine, but today, she feels Dollbaby's absence in a way that makes her feel a little scared, like the person who is writing these notes might be watching her from a tree or the Methodist steeple like that sniper she saw on television. Usually when she is out here, she thinks of all these dead people as neighbors you might call out and speak to, but it's clear she is not the only person who comes out here. It could be Haley or some of those mean girls trying to play a trick on her and so she isn't about to say a word to anybody except Dollbaby if she would just come home. Usually she would keep moving through the old part where the first family ever buried here—the Wilkins—have their own little iron fence with a gate, or she might climb up into a magnolia tree, lean and sling her leg up and over the big stone horse monument over General Fulton who founded this town and ride along for a while, or go sit on the lap of the lovely Lydia Edwards who died so young and now sits and stares in the direction of the newer graves and the arboretum. People say she once had eyes made of emeralds but somebody stole them and so now she is always watching whoever passes by to recognize the thief. "It's just me, Lydia," she used to always say until Haley went to school and told and then everybody started saying it back to her, *It's just me, Lydia,* so now she just says it in her head, which Lydia totally gets if she gets anything. But now without Dollbaby, she can't stand to be there all by herself and she feels like she needs to run as fast as she can. She puts the Food Lion note in her back pocket and takes off. She will collect the others later on her way back. She pats her leg for Dollbaby to follow out of habit and wills herself not to cry. She tries to whistle and sing so it won't be so quiet. She sings her favorite Lady Gaga song, "Telephone." She is passing the newer section now—graves without all the trees and vines. Newer stones with fancy-colored photographs of the dead people. Taco Bell in full view in the distance. Her favorite belongs to some people who lived in her house when her dad was a kid— Fred and Cleva Burns and their stone is cut to look like a giant ship: *Break, break, break,* it reads. Back when she talked aloud to everybody and not just in her head, she told Fred and Cleva how she had found some of their things and kept them in a special box. She has found bobby pins, which her mother would never use, and an old dried-up ink cartridge she didn't even know what it was. She found a token from the Ferris Beach pavilion wedged in a crack in her windowsill and her dad said that place had been torn down for over twenty years.

Abby's best friend, Sadie Randolph, has a beautiful pink granite stone with her husband Horace's name and dates on one side and hers on the other. "All they'll have to do is put in that final date," she has said, which always makes Abby sad to even imagine. When she was still able to come out here, Sadie planted rosemary— for remembrance—and now it is huge and bushy, growing up between their names. Abby always breaks off a little and takes it with her. Sadie likes that.

The arboretum is lush and green, gravel paths and flowers and trees all carefully labeled. There are all kinds of fruit and flowering trees, lots of magnolias blooming. Abby's favorite part is the long arbor that stretches the full length of the cemetery, built there, her dad had said, so that the people over at Pine Haven wouldn't have to look out and see the cemetery. Now they just see a screen of Confederate jasmine and cross vines and wisteria. All the plant names are right there to read on little gold-etched tags that remind her of Dollbaby's name tag that she had made at Petco while her mother still tried to talk her into a different dog— a brand-new teacup-sized this or that puppy with Dollbaby sitting right there to hear every single word. She had said she would take a puppy as well, that it could be Dollbaby's pet, and with that her stupid mother finally shut up.

Some call the arboretum the tunnel of love, but Abby thinks of it as the tunnel of life from the dark shade of the cemetery, through the labeled vines and then out into the bright sunlight and wide flat asphalt parking lot of Pine Haven—the perfect place for roller skating or skateboarding, which she loves to do. She can skateboard as good as Richie Hendricks and sometimes the two of them do that for hours. He has always liked Dollbaby and she likes him because of that.

Sadie is always waiting for her with a Hershey's bar or a big Whitman's Sampler and a crisp dollar bill for the soda machine down the hall. The sodas only cost seventy-five cents so she always gives the returned change to Millie, a plump long-term resident with spiky hair who guards the machine all day long and begs for change. Millie has a pink and white blanket she carries around and calls it her *African*. "Don't you touch my *African*," she says, "not unless I say to touch it." Sadie says she means to say *afghan* but that people who didn't get enough school often make this mistake. One of the residents called Millie a Mongoloid, and the new woman who lives across from Sadie, Mrs. Silverman, who is from the North said, "Oh my God, where on earth have I landed? Is anyone here educated?"

Abby has been told that Millie is at least forty even though she looks and acts like a big kid and that no one ever comes to see her, that she has kind of been adopted by all the residents and workers just like Harley, the huge orange cat who prowls the grounds and who used to lead Dollbaby on some good chases through the cemetery. Used to everybody loved Harley, but now they're afraid he will make them die so they scream and throw things when they see him coming. Sadie told Abby that was nonsense, and if they'd let her, she would keep Harley full-time with her so he wouldn't have to mess with all the others being mean to him. "Harley has been falsely persecuted," she said, and stroked his big fat head. She also told Abby that grown-ups often say things they don't mean, like that they hate someone or that they wish someone had never been born, the kind of thing a kid would get in big trouble for at school.

Sadie really does know everyone who has ever lived in this town, even the old shriveled-up Indian woman who reaches and whines and tries to play with Abby's hair when she passes. "Come heren right now, baby," the woman says, her tongue moving and twisting like it can't be still. "Come on come on come on." Sadie says that Lottie has been off since an accident that gave her a bad hit to the head years before. Lottie lives in the part of the building set aside for those less fortunate with no family and nowhere to go, like Millie. Sadie says that part of the building is the last car on the train—the end of the line.

Sadie knew Abby's dad when he was a boy in this town. She

taught him in third grade as she did most everyone who grew up there, but she had taken a special interest in him when his mother died so young. Her mother had also died young so she said they needed to stick together and now Abby's dad likes to tell anyone interested that they have done just that for over forty years. Sadie sometimes tells others who live at Pine Haven that Abby is her granddaughter.

Abby was afraid of Sadie's new neighbor, Rachel Silverman, in the beginning, but now she likes her and spends a lot of afternoons curled up in the big common living room where people sometimes gather to talk. There are only a couple of men living at Pine Haven. Sadie says men just don't keep very well and Rachel laughed and said Sadie talked about men like they might be a head of lettuce or loaf of bread. "Well, look around," Sadie said, "only a few here," and so it would be hard not to notice Mr. Stanley Stone who used to be a lawyer but now spends lots of time watching and reading about wrestling. People say he needs a haircut and a shave, but he says they should mind their own goddamned business. He says he likes to think of what he'd call himself if he ever got in the ring: Stony or Rocky or the Marble Man. "Get it?" he asked and struck a cowboy pose with his legs bowed out and his arm lassoing the air. "I'm mixing me some metaphors for you intellectuals. Marble like stone and Marlboro like a well-hung cowboy stud." He looked at Mrs. Silverman when he said that, but she ignored him. Toby, who wears winter boots all year long and a fanny pack stashed with all kinds of things she is always eager to share repeated what he said and laughed until she cried. "Well hung," she repeated. "Don't listen, Abby." But of course Abby did listen. She listens to everything they say.

Mr. Stone's son teaches at her school and so it's weird to see him there with his crazy old dad acting as bad as Todd Reynolds who got in trouble in fifth grade for unzipping his pants and mooning everybody on the field trip bus.

Abby often tells her mother that she is at a friend's house and that is true. These are her friends and Sadie's suite is like a house, with her big overstuffed velvet chairs with doilies on the back and lots of needlework filling the walls. It even smells like Sadie's old house where Abby once visited with her dad.

"Whose house?" her mother always asks. "Which friend? Is it someone you'd like to ask to sleep over?"

It is clear her mother doesn't believe her. She spends a lot of time pushing Abby to call up or be friends with girls whose mothers Abby's mom wants to be friends with. That's what's really going on. Now that she has lied about all those girls from time to time, there has been no choice but to invite them to her party. She cornered the one nice girl in that group in the bathroom the last week of school and confessed her situation. She figured the worst thing that happened would just be that the girl turned on her and she'd be even more of an unnoticed outcast than she already is. So once an outcast, who cares? It's like Mrs. Silverman said to someone who wanted to convert her one day. "Surely whoever is in charge, if in fact there is an afterlife, is smart enough to know when people say they believe something at the last minute in hopes of a pass," she said. "If there is a smart person in charge, then he or she will respect where I stand. And if that's not the case, then why should I even care?"

"There *is* a heaven," the woman said. "And there *are* rules for getting in."

"Do they lobotomize you at the gate?" Mrs. Silverman asked, which made Toby laugh even harder. Sadie explained to Abby what that meant, going in and scrambling part of the brain so people will forget the parts that make them sad. It made Abby cringe.

Mr. Stone said, "I'd rather have a bottle in front of me than a frontal lobotomy," and Mrs. Silverman said that that joke was so old she was riding a dinosaur the first time she heard it. He turned pink and Abby felt kind of sorry for him until he raised his middle finger, another thing that would get a kid sent to detention for days. If Mr. Stone was in his son's class, he'd be suspended. Abby could not stop thinking about the lobotomy, though, like the thought made her need to squeeze her eyes shut. It made her picture something like an ice pick. It was a terrible word to think about but one she could definitely use later on her parents or some of the mean kids. "Go get a lobotomy," she will say, and then, "Oh, I forgot, you already did that." If those girls turn on her at the party tomorrow she might use it just like she did in elementary school when she told Laurie Monroe, one of the meanest girls of all, that she had *ancestors,* that her *epidermis* was showing, that her mother is a *thespian and performs in public* and that she *slumbered* in her sleep. Her dad had taught her all of those; he said they worked when he was a kid and probably still would.

"Of course no such thing happens in heaven," Mrs. Marge Walker had shouted. "They don't want you all scarred up in heaven. They want you looking your best."

"So what about her?" Sadie pointed to Lottie, but Lottie didn't notice, just kept working that tongue in and out of her mouth like it had a life all its own. "I believe Lottie will be in heaven."

"We don't know that for sure," Mrs. Walker said, a stack of

pamphlets on her lap. "We have no idea what the scorecard of her soul looks like or what the rules are in *her* heaven."

"Ah, segregation," Mr. Stone said, and that time Mrs. Silverman turned and nodded in his direction like she was with him. He smiled at Mrs. Silverman, but she didn't look at him, probably afraid he'd be mean again.

"Good, better, best," Mrs. Walker continued. "I didn't create the system. That's just the way it is."

"Well," Mrs. Silverman said, "I think that *if* there *is* a heaven, then it has to be a socialist society; otherwise it wouldn't be *heaven* but just more of the kind of unjust hell you're always describing." No one, not even Mr. Stone, said anything after that and Abby decided she would try to use everything she learned from watching Mrs. Silverman—hands on hips, one eyebrow raised, little words like *if* made to sound big and powerful.

ABBY HAD STARED out the big bathroom window as she described the situation she was in to the girl at school, Elise Conway, a girl whose dad was a doctor in town and who had more Girl Scout badges than anyone had ever had at her age in their town. The girl was really no better looking than Abby; in fact they kind of looked alike—both a little plump but still not really needing a bra. Elise also had freckles over her nose and her ears stuck out enough that Abby once had heard a boy call her Dumbo. Abby could see the car-pool line already forming and focused on the steeple of the Methodist church while she waited for the girl to respond. She felt that heavy sick feeling as she waited, similar to hearing the news about Dollbaby but not as bad. Nothing is as bad as that, she told herself.

"Is your dad really a magician?" Elise asked. "And can he really let people in the movies anytime he wants like you said?"

"He's the best magician," Abby said, scaring herself with the realization that this would soon be put to the test. "And he practically owns the theater. I can go anytime I want day or night and I can just take whatever I want from the candy counter." That was not an entire lie. She could take stuff, she just had to pay for it.

"And do you really know someone who reads palms and tells the future?"

"Yes," Abby said, and put her hands on her hips. "And *if* you help me, I can take you to meet them." And of course she was thinking of that young woman C.J. with all the tattoos and nose and lip rings, who did all the old peoples' hair and nails. Abby saw her shuffling a deck of tarot cards one day and she also said she loved the Ouija board even if it does only conjure the slowest most stupid spirits. "They deserve to talk, too, right?" C.J. had asked Abby. "Likely my relatives would be there with them, which is why I do it." She laughed and then looked at Abby's palm, studied it for a long time and then looked her right in the eyes in a way that was kind of creepy but cool. "You are very lucky," she said. "You may not see it for a long time, but trust that your good luck will come." The memory gave Abby a rush of courage so she continued.

"I'll take you to meet them if you'll come to my party and act like we're friends. Maybe get some of the other people to come, too." She turned from the window and made eye contact. "I have fifty dollars saved and I'll use it all to buy Girl Scout cookies or whatever it is you're selling."

Abby gave most of the cookies to Sadie and some of the others so her parents wouldn't know what she did. She went door to door, leaving them with a note that said to have a nice day. All the girls accepted the invitation to her party and now all she has to do is show up tomorrow and get it over with, hope it all can just happen and be over, and then she can go back to searching for Dollbaby. That's the worst thing of all. Even if the party sucks and people have a terrible time and call her lame and stupid, it won't be nearly as bad as not having Dollbaby. She stands at the end of the arbor and squints out at the bright parking lot. "Here's to a long and happy cookie-filled life," Stanley Stone said when she gave him two boxes of Thin Mints, and for just a second he seemed normal, like who you would want to be your grandfather, but then, when he saw Toby and Sadie, added that sex was the real secret to long life. Sadie asked that he please hush and not say such things with Abby present, but he just shrugged and stared at Mrs. Silverman who said puhhleeeze. Then she said that *sanity* was the real secret.

Toby said that sanity is good, but she thinks the secret to long life is water, water, and more water. Drink water all day long to keep your body all flushed out. "May your pee always run clear and carry no trace of a scent except when you go somewhere fancy and eat asparagus." She said that a person should be able to hide, go underground at any second, and not be detected.

"That's why animals don't eat asparagus," Mr. Stone told Abby, like he might be teaching a class.

"Yes, that would be one reason," Mrs. Silverman said, and raised a pretend gun to her head. Ever since then, though, Abby drinks enough water to have clear pee. She is almost as obsessive about clear pee as she is touching all of her favorite stones and monuments in the cemetery and checking the notes in Esther Cohen's urn.

SOMETIMES LATE AT night, Abby sneaks out through the cemetery and the arboretum and stands outside Sadie's window. Sadie once got her to listen to a song playing on the radio about a man in a nursing home who had the bed by the window and spent the day describing the world out there to his roommate only there wasn't anything there at all. When the man in the song died and his roommate got a turn by the window, he saw nothing but a brick wall, but he continued what had been started and described a pretty world for the new person just brought in. "That's what I do, Abby," she said. "I try to paint a pretty picture."

"What about my parents?" she asked. "Can you paint a pretty picture of them?"

Sadie pulled her close and whispered in her ear. "I am going to try, sweetheart. I promise you I will try."

The morning sun is bright and Abby can hear strains of music or television coming from different windows. She hears the sound of Richie's skateboard even before she sees him. She waits for him to lift his hand first before she waves. He has built a really good ramp and is able to clear several feet before landing. He has his hair pulled back in a ponytail and a big scab on his knee. His Billabong T-shirt is orange and blue. Some people think he's a loser, too, and maybe that's why she likes him. Even if he is a loser, he went and got his bike and rode all over town putting up pictures of Dollbaby. REWARD, it said with a picture of Dollbaby she took last Christmas: Dollbaby with a rawhide chew shaped like a stocking. Abby promised that there would be a big reward even though she had spent all of her money so people would show up at her stupid party, trusting that her parents would give her whatever she needed if they were lucky enough to get a happy call. Every time the phone rings she freezes and in her mind she repeats the words she needs to hear, the same words the woman from New Jersey at Cracker Barrel said. *I have your little Dollbaby. I'll hold her until you get here.*

Abby needs her own phone and is supposed to get one for her birthday. She is about the only kid without one, not that anyone will ever call her, but at least she can look like she's busy, hold it up to her ear in the cafeteria or at the bus stop so she won't just be standing there trying to think of something to say or what to do with her hands. She will act like she's talking to a friend and maybe her nosy mother will leave her alone. That would be easy enough: *Oh my God! You've got to be kidding. Like don't I know that!* That would make her mother so happy, just like it made her so happy when she found Michelle Obama goody bags to give everybody. Abby has to be home for lunch to finish filling them, but until then she can just visit Sadie and then keep looking for Dollbaby. She holds her hand up to her ear to practice talking. She pretends it's the woman at the Cracker Barrel saying she will sit right there and hold that sweet Dollbaby until they can pick her up. Richie has stopped skating and is shielding his eyes against the sun, waiting for her to walk over. She can tell he thinks she really has a phone, so she eases her hand down and into her back pocket. *Call all you want, but there's no one home.* When she starts walking, he starts skating again. She will sit on the curb and watch him for at least ten minutes or so before she goes inside to visit Sadie. He will ask how things are and she will stick out her tongue and hold a fake gun to her head like she saw Mrs. Silverman do. She will tell him that there's no news about Dollbaby and he'll say, "That sucks," and then she'll tell him how her parents were at it again late last night, she could hear them through the hole around the base of the radiator in her room, and he'll say, "They're so fucked up," which always makes her feel good even though it makes her feel kind of sick, too, and then when she thinks she might start crying, she thinks about Sadie and the way she will be waiting with a dollar bill and a big box of candy and how she can curl up on the daybed and just listen to Sadie talk or watch whatever is on the television. She does this every day.

Notes about: Gregory Luke Wishart
Born: October 14, 1957 **Died:** February 12, 2007, 12:25 p.m.
Lake Winnipesaukee, New Hampshire

The day was dark and rainy, trees and roads glazed in ice, one of those days when it would be impossible to look out and know the time; morning could just as easily have been nightfall. The ropes on an empty flagpole at the school across the street clanged in the wind. He did not want anyone there other than David and Tammy and me, of course. He said I had to be there to take notes, that it was my job and we had made a bargain. He said this would be my test run for what I will do in the future. He said that I needed to describe the black silk nightshirt he was wearing and tell how sophisticated it looked, that I should always remember him looking so sophisticated and elegant in both life and death. His favorite color was green, the shade of moss, and his favorite food was cherry cobbler. He asked to hear Debbie Reynolds singing "Tammy" and he sang along, lips barely moving, *I hear the cottonwoods whispering above,* and otherwise wanted only classical—no words to get tangled up in. He said it was odd how he had loved that character Tammy, and why? "A rundown houseboat in the middle of some godforsaken bumfuck southern locale." He laughed. "What was that about?" He said that he must have been southern in a previous life and that I should definitely include that mysterious detail in my notes. He said that Eddie never should have left Debbie. What was he thinking? Sure, Liz was hot, but Debbie was *Debbie,* the good girl, the girl next door, the girl who would be a good mother and a good wife and a dear and loyal friend. He loved Debbie as Molly Brown, too. *Unsinkable,* he said, and pointed at me, *just like you, thanks to Tammy,* and he asked to hear the song just one more time, that scratchy 45 he remembered his parents buying and slow dancing to when he was a kid, and he sang along, eyes closing with the drift of that solo violin at the end. He pointed to the corner just beyond his grandmother's old braided rug he treasured and said that it was very calm over there—cool and calm. But then eighteen hours passed and he said nothing at all, just reached out as if plucking feathers from the air, his eyes wide open and staring. It seemed his breathing was a little bit faster whenever David leaned close and twice he moved his finger along my wrist where a watch would be if I wore one. He always said I needed to wear one so that I will never ever miss anything again, but I will always miss him. Every day I will speak to him. Every day I will remember.

[from Joanna's notebook]

Luke Wishart

The light on the lake skips and shimmers like glass he can walk over, slick cool shiny glass, and his body tingles and moves without him, slick and cool and there is barking and singing and lapping, lapping, lapping, waves on the beach, and there is the clanging of the boat rocking in its slip while he waits in the warm water with the light whispering above. His grandparents are there at the outdoor sink, scaling and cleaning the fish they caught, and his parents are inside dancing, feet turning slowly on that worn braided rug, and when it gets dark they will all squeeze onto the bench at the end of the dock and watch the lights over the lake—the stars and fireworks and distant island, the glowing face of his father's watch he reaches and holds as he leans in close and closes his eyes.

Rachel

RACHEL SILVERMAN IS IN the South—God only knows what she was thinking—and yet she thought it and she chose it and now she's here in the middle of nowhere, the land of quilts and doilies, yes ma'am and no sir, *Don't mind me, I'll just take a little piece of chicken, I love the neck or a wing,* please and goddamned thank you, hot as hell and surrounded by some sweet-tea-soaked idiots she'd just as soon slap as listen to. Thank God, they're not all that way—goobers and hee-haw and Judgment Day—but there are enough that are so she sticks close to her neighbor, Sadie Randolph, in the suite across the hall and the little lesbian from South Carolina who loves tobacco products. They were both schoolteachers, both still capable of and interested in reading the newspaper, and they don't judge their neighbors, or if they do, it's a judgment Rachel absolutely agrees with like the other day when Toby bit off the end of a cigar and announced she was tired of people trying to save her soul. *It's insulting,* she said. *They don't know my soul from a cat's ass.*

So Rachel is *here,* as the big X on the map in the front hall tells her. She is *here,* Pine Haven Estates—retirement village and assisted living—Fulton, North Carolina, not far from the ocean and minutes from Interstate 95, just seven hundred miles from where she spent her whole life in Massachusetts, which was also just an hour from the ocean and minutes from the same highway. She is here, her last adventure. She has come to see the hometown of her one great love—a man who was not her husband and who likely never would have been. She had three glorious months with him in the summer of 1970, which was the year she turned thirty-nine. Imagine, turning thirty-nine at a time when people still made reference to Jack Benny and found humor in a person never admitting he had turned forty. Now you'd be hard-pressed to find a young person who had ever even heard of Jack Benny and now thirty-nine sounds like someone barely living, still wet behind the ears, their muscles capable of doing all kinds of things they take for granted.

They met during one wonderful summer on the Cape, both there alone, and then after that there were occasional afternoons and odd Saturday mornings—some stretches of time more generous and giving than others—until the winter of 1976 when he was out of her life forever. Still, it seemed she talked more in those stolen hours than she ever had and likely the only comparable thing she has known (aside from friends of her girlhood) is her time with Sadie, a polite kinship growing each afternoon and evening to longer conversations and confessions.

Sadie is from this town and is well versed in the history and the natives and yet also seems somehow removed from it all—perhaps by her active reading life or maybe by her many years living alone. *Solitude can do good things for a person,* she has said. *The interior life is sometimes the only life*. Rachel could not agree more. It's how people have survived adverse conditions through the ages, and though one might long for a physical touch, it's not a bad way to go. Certainly there are far worse ways to go. *I am never lonely*, Sadie said just the other night, and Rachel realized that she and Toby both leaned in closer, as if about to hear some great wisdom passed their way.

His name was Joe, a simple, easy name for a seemingly easy man, but he was far more complex than what appeared on the surface and he made Rachel's life complex for a very long time, the difficulties far outnumbering the comfort, and yet still she chose to continue. Several times he even said: "So just stop. Just end it." But she never did. Now life is simple, and now she has come seeking his South, the place of his boyhood, the setting of all those stories he told her when they burrowed into the far back booth of a Duxbury deli or some small motel down on the Cape. That life was complicated and fraught. That life left her heart pounding and her sleep fitful, so afraid she might be caught, afraid she might speak his name in the darkness of the bed where her husband of so many years lay. That life involved long days at work where she was a lawyer—one of a handful of women in her firm and therefore needing to prove her value twice as hard as the men around her. That life involved dark winter days and snow shovels and raw hands and dry skin. And it involved those secret meetings—brandy-laced and delicious, the smell of wet wool and diesel fumes when standing and waiting for the train, suddenly intoxicating. Anticipation and deceit—lovemaking and lies—cases and stuffed files and somewhere in there a uterus that needed to be pulled out and tossed away, and the years of debating about adopting or not came and went, one day an obsession and the next a distant memory, the room in that first Beacon Hill apartment that would have been a nursery, stripped and shelved, a library guests asked to see, stopping and perching on the velvet-cushioned bay as she often did to glimpse the Charles River and distant spires of the Longfellow Bridge while they marveled at her impressive collection of first editions. Just before she migrated south, she had a taxi drive her back to that old apartment, and she stood on the icy sidewalk staring up at the library window. They had not lived there in years and she felt a wave of time sickness to see it, years of lost hope seeped into the cold red brick. She could almost hear their voices—her husband's, her own, the heavy black wall phone in the kitchen, the radio on top of the refrigerator, always tuned to the educational network, rattles in the windows and rainbows cast by the warped bubbled glass of the panes. When she got back into the cab, she felt she was saying good-bye to something living and breathing, a life that would continue to exist, one that she could reach back and touch if brave enough to do so.

But now life is simple. Now life is about coffee in the morning. Life is about meals and books and memories and the occasional silly television show she doesn't enjoy that much and yet finds herself drawn to all the same. She does not give a damn about who can dance and who can't, and she doesn't recognize a soul they say is a celebrity except, of course, Cloris Leachman whom Rachel saw in *South Pacific* on Broadway in 1954. Sometimes there's a good movie showing or some interesting musicians passing through. Sometimes she joins a bridge game or conversation or has that young woman with all the tattoos and piercings give her a pedicure and foot massage. She was never a pedicure type of woman, so resisting what she felt it represented in her own young womanhood—a type of woman who was not an intellectual and not a part of the workforce. And Rachel Silverman was definitely a part of the workforce. She was quite simply a force. People in the firm called her the Shark and at that time the Jewish women she knew who were all into hair and nails were of a different ilk to say the least. She was explaining this to the tattooed pedicurist who sat and listened and followed every word only to then wave a hand and say, "Aww, but that was ages ago. Everybody likes a pedicure now." The girl's own nails were charcoal gray, which she says is the latest, but Rachel chose something less corpselike, a pale pink with no frost.

"Oh, come on now, Shark," the girl said. "You can do better than *that*." She leaned in close to whisper, her breath like cinnamon and her body soaked in patchouli like Rachel had not encountered in ages. "That's what Marge Walker always gets. Come on. Where's the Shark?" Marge is the queen of all the traits that get on Rachel's nerves, a tight-girdled, self-righteous moron.

The girl persisted and now Rachel has deep burgundy toenails, the color of a nice Bordeaux. "Sexy," the girl, C.J., told her. "You're no church lady." She swatted Rachel with a rolled-up paper as she was leaving. "You're the shark."

Rachel got a little way down the hall and decided to go back and tip her a twenty. She is a child herself and raising a baby who is sometimes in there with her. She is probably making minimum wage with nobody there to help her. Rachel has seen her out in the arboretum smoking, a lonely wild-looking girl who could be beautiful by conventional standards but chooses to use dye and studs and cologne in a way that might repel some. Rachel certainly understands the impulse that would lead a person to do such a thing.

"I can't take this," the girl said, and Rachel reached and balled her hand over the girl's so all those others sitting there under the dryers wouldn't make it their business to know what was going on.

"You can give me a ride some time, take me to see some things in town."

"This town?" She wrinkled her nose and laughed then extended her hand, gray nails with little pink dots on them, all kinds of rings and bracelets jangling. "Sure, I'll take you. I might need some legal advice sometime so maybe we could do some swapping."

"It's a deal."

"Oh." The girl held on to Rachel's sleeve. "My name is C.J." She paused before continuing. "I see you sneaking out in the cemetery a lot."

"Rachel Silverman," she said in her best attorney voice. "And I've seen you out there sneaking cigarettes."

"Yes." The girl leaned in and put her forehead near Rachel's so they were eye to eye. "So we need to be good friends. I totally respect your need to get out of here."

"And I can't say I respect your addiction, but I do understand it. God knows, I smoked for twenty years and I loved every puff."

SHE AND ART smoked Kents and Joe smoked Camels, and once when Art went to her purse to look for a cigarette he pulled out a pack of Camels and looked at her in the strangest way. Her mind slowed to mush knowing the nylons she had not taken the time to put back on were in there, too, as well as a ticket stub for *The Godfather* and the pack of Milk Duds Joe had greeted her with there in the darkened theater. "Oh no," she said, "I took my client's cigarettes." She reached for her purse and pulled out the Kents, took the Camels, stuffed them in, and snapped it shut. "I'll have to confess." She did not let a beat fall but pointed out the window to the beautiful sunset and asked what he thought about eating out. She said she was starved for Italian food.

You're one good-looking feminist, Joe had said the first time he ever saw her stripped down to a nylon slip. They were out on Highway 1 near that ridiculous steak house he liked to go where it was like you were in the Wild West waiting for a stagecoach, enormous fake cows littering the grounds. "You are one hot broad canned piece of feminist." Who would believe that? And though his words made her angry, and though she felt a wave of respect and then guilt for the smart progressive-minded husband she was cheating on, she didn't say a word and instead gave in to the moment. Truth was she was a little bit flattered and when had she ever had such sex? Never in her life and when had she ever eaten such a steak? Big bloody slab filling her plate and she ate every bite like a starving pig; she was ravenous and in that moment greedy, she could not get enough. The snow was falling in big wet flakes and those fake cows stood there stupidly under the glow of neon lights. She had thought of that place not long after she moved into Pine Haven and C.J. set up a Christmas village in the entryway of the building where there was an enormous decorated tree. Rachel had always had an aversion to the gaudy blinking lights and incessant Christmas music, but she found herself drawn to that little winter street, the diner all lit and warm-looking with a tiny blinking sign asking you to come in and eat.

"Don't you just want to go in there and order something?" C.J.

had asked when she saw Rachel looking. "I'd get a grilled cheese like that one on the sign." At the time Rachel was not ready to be friendly to anyone and so she said *absolutely not*. She had just arrived and was thinking that this might have been the dumbest decision she had ever made in the eighty years of her life. Occasionally, she still wakes in the middle of the night, confused about where she is, and is shocked with the reality of it all. She woke not long ago and had a second or two when she was back in that first apartment, the morning light so familiar to another time, and it took a while to get her bearings.

And then other times, she thinks, where else would she rather be? Why wouldn't she want her final home to be here, right next door to where Joe is buried. She goes two times a day—once in the morning and then again late afternoon—and she saves up lots of things to tell him. Of course he is buried alongside his wife, which feels a little awkward; Rachel never met Rosemary and only once glimpsed a tiny snapshot in Joe's wallet, something he didn't know she had seen, so out of character for her to snoop and look and yet she had done it. That was when she knew that everything had taken a turn; she felt curious and jealous and demanding, and yet she had her *own* separate life. She knows Joe would have left Rosemary if Rachel had asked him to. Oh, it was all so complicated. You have to be young to even think about such complications and then they age you so quickly. She flew down to see where he was buried, that was all, and then she found this place, and when she inquired, there was one vacant apartment and it faced the arboretum that led right there to the cemetery and his grave. It was one of those rare times in life when it seemed an answer dropped right in her lap and she wrote a check for the deposit on the spot. Her few remaining friends were surprised, to say the least; she told her only real relative, her older brother's son who looked in on her from time to time but whose life was full and busy in New York, that she was interested in the retirement possibilities of the Carolinas—the good hospitals and all the universities—theater and ballet where you can easily get tickets—no shoveling snow, no fear of crossing the street. What was harder to explain was her venturing an hour east of the golf resorts and two hours south of the universities to a small town no one had ever heard of. It's near the beach, she had said. I can get there as fast as I could get to the Cape. And the facility is excellent, she explained, and they all trusted her and why wouldn't they? To their minds, she had never made a false move or stupid decision in her entire life.

Now she is here and ready to explore beyond the cemetery. And she has a date with C.J. for tomorrow afternoon. They will drive to the other side of town and find the house where Joe grew up. She wants to see the river he talked about so much and she wants to see the fields out from town where he worked in tobacco as a boy. The girl has even said that sometime maybe she could take the Pine Haven bus and take a few of them to the beach. Joe loved the beach and had told her she had to see it to believe it, that he couldn't wait to take her there, that the Cape couldn't compare.

"You'd have to pay of course," the girl said, her baby boy strapped to her chest like a little papoose. "But my friend, Joanna, the hospice volunteer—you've seen her if you haven't met her—owns a hot-dog stand and says I can always eat free. I live right above it." Someday Rachel will explain to Sadie and C.J. what it's all about, but for now she acts like she has come to claim her husband's childhood world. Sometimes she tells stories about Joe, things he said and did, a memory of the one-armed man who owned the old ice plant where he worked as a kid, a man known for getting women in compromising positions when he asked for favors. "I really need a hand," he would say, which came to have all kinds of meanings. Then there was a bridge out in the county said to be haunted—Heartbeat Bridge—where the heart of a woman, murdered by her jealous husband, was thrown and continues to beat. Joe and his friends used to go out there at night and sit and listen, wait for the heartbeats that would send whatever girl was sitting close by into their laps and backseats. She assigns these stories to Art, her husband of forty-five years.

"That Art was a rounder, wasn't he?" Toby asked. "Every story you tell is sex sex sex. I bet you did some singing of 'How Great Thou *Art*' or maybe 'How Great Art Art.'"

"That's not true." Rachel sat up straight but knew, even as she fixed her firmest look, that she *had* told quite a few stories that made reference to sex and then the teasing expression on Toby's face, like a fierce mischievous little gnome with cropped coarse hair, made her laugh. "I don't know Christian hymns other than 'Amazing Grace.'"

"You've gotta be kidding!" Marge said, hands on hips.

"I say I got you on that one." Toby laughed. "I see Freudian slips and leaps all the time. Should have been a shrink."

"Should have *seen* a shrink," Marge said.

"I did and he said stay away from people like you."

"I went to Heartbeat Bridge a couple of times myself." Sadie blushed, put her hand up to her mouth and giggled. Everyone else laughed except Marge who was still stuck on how Toby was sacrilegious for using the title of a hymn in such a way and they should all be ashamed for telling too much and talking about S-E-X.

"This from the one who announces bowel movements like a sporting event," Toby said, and laughed until her shoulders shook and tears filled her eyes. She said she needed to be excused and would be right back else they'd need a mop. She said she had drunk over a gallon of water that day to purify herself.

"It'll take more than that," Marge said, and turned her attention back to Rachel. "When did Art die and why are you here?"

"Art died a year and a half ago," Rachel said. "And I am here because he thought of this town as home."

Rachel has Joe's childhood address and where he went to church; she knows where his parents are buried and where there once was a pavilion over by the river where he loved to go as a child. Sadie has said that the movie theater is still there; it's the very one that Abby's daddy got back up and running not too many years ago. The old ice plant where he worked is still there, too, but it's not an ice plant anymore, just an old empty building, or was last time she was out. But that old pavilion is long gone; it flooded and rotted away years ago. She said what puzzles her is that she never in her life met a boy named Art and she has always prided herself on knowing everyone in town. How could that be? Did he use a different name? Rachel said he visited his relatives and then acted like she couldn't remember their names. Pleading to have forgotten something here at Pine Haven is well expected and accepted. But she has decided that soon she will tell Sadie that she remembered Art's cousin's name. "Art had a cousin by the name of Joe Carlyle." She practices saying it without doing all those things she has read people do when telling a lie, looking away, swallowing excessively, twisting their hands. "Yes, that's it. Joe Carlyle. Have you ever known of a Joe Carlyle? Joseph Edward Carlyle."

This is what she will tell Sadie when most people have filed off to bed and it's just the two of them there in one sitting room or the other. Sadie is in a wheelchair so she doesn't venture far. She has a business she has created where she makes old photographs come to life, and she makes things that never happened happen. She said it was a natural progression since she has been doing this in her head her whole life. She is so good at it people often believe her and those with dementia make the leap so beautifully that they sometimes look like they have been to heaven and back after a session with Sadie and what she calls her magic scissors and glue stick.

That is *wrong*! Saint Marge of the Negative Vindictive Sisterhood (or so Toby calls her) often says about Sadie leading people to indulge in fantasy, which she also thinks is sacrilegious. Marge is negative about everything, her doughy face permanently etched in a frown, every suggestion and thought negated unless it involves her relationship with Jesus who to hear her tell it, thinks *she* walks on the water. Rachel has suggested Sadie make a picture for Marge where Marge is the Madonna or maybe Marge hanging on the cross, Marge rising from the dead.

"I can make you a memory and I can make a dream come true," Sadie had said. "But I cannot make a silk purse out of a sow's ear."

"She's a sow all right," Toby had said, and gestured toward Marge, who was ushering in a whole flock of children from her Sunday school class. They had come, she said, for fun and fellowship with some senior citizens and to get credit at their schools.

They had the lovely idea that everyone should name his or her apartment or room like you might a home at the sea or a bedroom in a bed and breakfast. "For instance," Marge said, and held up her hand to get everyone's attention. She was wearing a faux-denim pantsuit with lots of swirls and paisley designs appliquéd that reminded Rachel of the one and only time she ever went to Las Vegas. Art had a business conference and won several thousand dollars. She played the slot machines and sat by the pool and complained about how garish it all was the one time she reached Joe on his work line. It was snowing in Boston and Rosemary was up for a few days. They were having a friend of his in for dinner and she couldn't help but wonder which friend. Someone she knew? It made her so jealous to hear and yet there she was in Vegas with her husband; there she was with a sack full of quarters and tickets for several shows and a heart as dry and empty as the desert. Why does she remember such things, bits of memories popping in like little commercials of another time? Why does she feel so strongly that split-screen life of gray wet snow and hot blinding desert?

"Listen now," Marge said again, louder and clearly getting annoyed at that crazy old Stanley Stone who was asking those children to feel his thin white bicep. "You will all choose a name that means something special to you. For instance, my apartment will be called—"

"The Extralarge Marge Barge," Stanley called out, and all the children laughed. "The Kingdom of Boredom."

Her face flushed a deep pink and she heaved a big sigh. "I will pray for those lacking social graces and I will name my apartment Camelot, because I have always been told that I bear a striking resemblance to Jacqueline Kennedy."

The polite people looked away when she said this, but Stanley and all the children and Toby started laughing and couldn't stop. "She was Catholic, you know," Toby said.

"But there were things to admire, too," Marge said. "I am more open-minded than you think!"

"Yeah, right. But here's some more real history for you," Toby offered. "Speaking of presidential places. FDR first called Camp David 'Shangri-La,' like in one of my favorite novels, *Lost Horizon* by James Hilton."

"Toby is one of the smartest people living here," Sadie told Rachel, and before she could say that this was quite obvious, one resident had named her suite Shangri-La and another named hers Camp David. Then one pounced on Tara and another Twelve Oaks, leaving several other unimaginative ones disappointed. The one who got Tara now spends her time striking a pose and saying things like "I'll never be hungry again!" only to have Stanley Stone reply with "That's because you eat all the goddamn time. And not even good stuff. I see you eating old mess like Twinkies." The young girl assigned to him suggested he name his place something that spoke to his legal profession, but he said his apartment is called Hell in a Cell, like what he saw on wrestling. He said he planned to invite people in for matches. He winked at Rachel when he said this and she ignored him. "My second choice is the Love Machine or A Taste of Honey after my favorite song." He winked and again she ignored him. When he heard that her given name was Rachel Naomi Gold and that she then married a Silverman, he said that she was sliding downward in the elements. "Looking for Mr. Bronze, I suspect," he said. "Third place. However, if you keep on sliding, then eventually you'll find me—the Stone."

"Thank you," she said. "The Stone Age makes sense for you."

The Barker sisters, who Sadie says never married and ran their family's laundry service for over fifty years, didn't understand the assignment and were thinking of names of candy—gumdrop, jelly bean, SweeTarts. Butterfinger, Milky Way, Snickers. Sweet and lost in their dementia, they are always sitting by the front door to greet whoever enters, the bands they wear on their wrists and ankles to keep them in the building often setting off alarms. Daisy, the younger of the two, a dainty-faced little thing with a great big bottom, crochets all different kinds of cookies and sells them for a quarter; then she gives all of the money to Millie, the one with Down syndrome, for Pepsi-Colas. The older sister, Vanessa, is overweight and nearly blind, her yellow white hair slicked back and often held with a little pink barrette. She sat dozing through most of the discussion only to pipe up at the end to say "Mounds," which is what the sign on their door says.

Back during the bicentennial when people were hot to put out plaques and name their homes, Joe said he would love to put a sign up in front of his house that said YE OLDE PIECE OF SHIT MORTGAGED TO THE MAX—so when they asked Rachel she said, "My Apartment"; she whispered to Sadie, "Piece o' Shit," and they both got a big laugh. "My Apartment or Piece o' Shit" she announced to the soured-looking girl assigned to her. "You pick."

Toby said she was was torn between the Ponderosa and the Little Chicken Farm, which was from one of her very favorite movies based on the favorite novel she had already mentioned. She said she used to always have her English classes watch the Frank Capra version of *Lost Horizon*. She chose the Little Chicken Farm, which relieved Rachel not because she gave a damn what

the name was but because Toby was able to make a quick decision. Rachel hates indecision and always has. She gets so impatient when they go back and forth and back and forth and back
and forth; some of these around here cannot make a decision or
deliver a plain simple sentence to save their lives. You ask what
they had for dinner and they have to go back to childhood to explain why they have never liked spinach and so on. It takes goddamned forever to tell one simple thing that ought to take thirty
seconds; and everybody has to talk whether they have something
worth saying or not. Rachel wants to say: *Don't call me until you
have reduced your thoughts to the lowest common denominator.
Call with something definite. If I hear you wandering and stammer-
ing and figuring while I'm sitting there, I'll shut the door or hang up
on you. Life is too short to listen to all that mess.*

"You never could've sat through a faculty meeting at my school,"
Toby told her. "You'd've blown a big gasket for sure."

The other thing that has gotten on her last nerve lately is the
way so many people say MassaTOOsetts. Joe did that, too; it was
the only thing wrong with him that she could tell. She wants to
scream MassaCHOOsetts, choo choo choo, not TOO. And now
this. Rachel never would have imagined that she would someday
be a service project for adolescent girls and then there came one
tapping on her door wanting her to make some ridiculous origami
representation of herself. "You know," Rachel told her. "The real
Christian thing would be if you children just came and visited and
listened to what we could teach you. Come because you like us
and want to spend time with us, not to get your stupid points for
school that you'll talk all about in your college-entry essay. Don't
bullshit me—I know what this is all about. I have lost some of my

physical abilities but none of my mental ones, okay? If I were the real reason you were coming, then we would be doing something I am interested in. Maybe we would read and discuss current events or we might decide to buy a lottery ticket and be creative with our number selection. Maybe we would watch something like *It Happened One Night* or read something like *The Scarlet Letter* or *The Awakening* and discuss the ever-evolving roles of womanhood in film and literature?" The child stood and glared back at her, a clipboard in her hand with all kinds of fancy origami paper. "Like that girl over with Sadie? She comes all the time. She isn't assigned to come, she just does it. And do you know why? She likes us. She likes to be with us."

"She's a loser," the girl said. "You old guys are her only friends."

"Well, she could do a lot worse," Rachel said. "And we all are crazy about her. We all think she is"—she paused, that little priss not backing down and not even blinking those big blue eyes— "better than any child who has ever entered this place."

CLOVER DEN. THERE'S a nice name. That was one of the spots they met a couple of times, a little dark hole in the wall, but it was risky, near Scollay Square, a little too close to where she might see someone she knew. But now she thinks that if she had decided to participate, she would have made a sign that said CLOVER DEN, and the picture she would love for Sadie to create is one of herself with Joe, the two of them sitting back in that dark booth on a late-winter afternoon. They were such an unlikely couple and there is such power in the relationship that never takes place in a permanent way, the "mights" romantically overwhelming all that likely would have been truth. But still you hold on.

Even now, she hears his slow, easy speech, the way it rolled like waves that pulled her in close only to then push her back, rolling with temptation and trepidation. She remembered everything he had ever said to her and was always looking for hidden messages; even now, she is looking for messages, thinking she might find something meant just for her in one of his favorite places, the same way she pored over the obituary that arrived in her mail one day—his return address in Fulton, North Carolina, but not his handwriting—a typed and copied note attached with a paper clip: *Your address was in Joe's book.* And then there he was, a photograph much younger than when she knew him. He was born and raised there. He had two children. He was survived by a wife. She heard Art coming up the front steps and so she tucked it away in a copy of *Jane Eyre* she pulled from the shelf and did not come back to it for several days. She had to wait for a good time when she knew Art would be gone and would not come in to find her there, maybe crying, who knew? The plotting to read and reread his obituary was not unlike all the times she had plotted to meet him. And then just about the same time Art got sick, another letter came from that same address; that time it was the obituary for Rosemary—a short, simple paragraph of facts—no note attached, and she couldn't help but wonder if whoever sent it knew who she was. Perhaps Rosemary had asked that it be sent to her. She had no idea just as she didn't know how much time she had left with Art, but what she did know was that now she could venture southward if she wanted. She could explore all that Joe had ever told her about and no one on the face of the earth would know who she was or why she was there.

And so she is *here*—as the sign up front tells her—here at Pine

Haven—home of lard, Jesus, sugared-up tea and enough meshuggeners to fill Fenway Park. She is here, in the land of Joe.

Sadie has said that Stanley Stone used to be one of the finest most dignified gentlemen the town had ever seen though that is hard to believe given his unkempt appearance and the hateful way he turns on people. One minute he will wink and smile at Rachel and then the next minute say something completely insulting and rude.

"He knows everybody in town," Sadie said. She told how he also grew up there, a very distinguished lawyer with a lovely wife who was known for her rose garden and the way she opened it to June brides to come and pick what they needed. He himself was in the Kiwanis and was always the chief pancake flipper for their big Pancake Supper once a year. But who would know that now? There's some cruelty for you. He's still handsome but not always together in the mind.

"Together in the mind?" Rachel said. "How about insane, crazy as a bat." She was about to recount how she heard him talking to his son like the young man might be a slave or a dog—*you don't know shit from Shinola,* he said—but then she thought better. "Did you say he grew up here?"

"Yes, and his parents before him." And then Sadie put down her scissors and glue stick so she could clap her hands. "If anybody in this town ever knew your Art, he would be the man," she said. "And every now and then he remembers. Every now and then I see a glimmer of the old Stanley Stone. And you're both lawyers. "And"—Sadie lowered her voice—"I see him watching you all the time lately. I think he has a little spark for you."

Rachel felt her face flush and it surprised her. She has certainly

noticed him ogling her but also thought he might be half blind or
something since so many of them are. Besides, no matter what
he used to be or how physically attractive he could be if he tried,
what in the hell would she do with some angered lunatic? Who
needs a lunatic? Unless, of course, he would remember Joe. And
whatever he remembers might be worth a little of her time. She
has plenty of time. "Well, maybe I'll ask him, then."

"Definitely you should," Sadie said. "Maybe it will help me remember him. I'll roll over there with you, too, but first I have
to finish Toby's picture." She waved at the door where Toby was
waiting, hands on hips, boots turned outward. Her fanny pack was
full, pieces of cellophane sticking out of the zipper. "Look, Toby,"
Sadie said. "Here you are at the Taj Mahal."

"Wow, would you look at that." Toby shook her head in awe and
motioned for Rachel to look. "Thanks to Sadie here, I have been
just about goddamn everywhere. "

"Everywhere," Sadie echoed, and laughed. Rachel has figured
out that Sadie is someone who never curses but loves to hear others do it. The two of them were waiting for her response, *here* at
Pine Haven. Pine Haven, North Carolina, right beside Whispering
Pines Cemetery where the love of her life is buried and where in
a little bit she will slip away without anyone taking note and sit on
a stump nearby and tell him all about her day. There is no snow
outside. It is summer and the sun is shining and she has left the
life she always knew to come here to Pine Haven. Sugar-filled tea
and long, slow syllables and Jesus every way you can get him.

"See?" Toby tapped the toe of her boot waiting. "That's me at
the Taj Mahal. Sadie is such a good artist, nobody would ever see
the glue that put me there. See?"

"Yes," Rachel said, and stepped closer, feeling more like a schoolgirl than she ever did when she was one. "It's the most incredible thing I have seen in years." She paused, feeling for a moment like she might cry, which she has not done since leaving Boston, looking down from the plane with the knowledge that most likely she would never see that place again. "Really, Sadie, you are a beautiful genius."

"Ha, told you," Toby said, and Sadie blushed and shook her head.

"I am so flattered. Thank you so much," she said. "I know there are people doing it all with computers. There is better work than mine, I am sure, but when I pick up my scissors and glue, I am transported to another place. It always happens to children that way. Just give them some glue and paper and crayons and they can make a whole wonderful world." Sadie said she needed a little rest after all the work and excitement and she would see them at lunch.

Now Rachel pulls her door shut to My Apartment and makes her way down the hall. She will slip out the side door and then cross the parking lot. It's earlier than usual, but whatever just stirred in her has left her feeling restless and anxious and a little bit sad. She passes the soda machine where Millie sits all day, guarding the machine and begging money. She gives her all the change in the pocket of her skirt and keeps walking. She hears the music long before she gets to Hell in a Cell. Herb Alpert and the Tijuana Brass. He plays it nonstop and it puts her in a time warp each and every time. The door is half open and she can see him sitting in his chair and staring out the window; it's unusual to see him so quiet, looking so handsome and pensive and *normal* in a way you don't notice when he's flexing his arms and talking about wrestling or acting hateful and rude. She walks fast so he won't see her and call out something obscene.

"A Taste of Honey," "Whipped Cream," "Tangerine," "Lady-fingers"—"Is this an album or a menu?" Art had asked. It was 1965 and they played that album to death. She pushes open the door and steps into the sunlight. There is a hearse parked and hidden in the shade of the tall wax-myrtle hedge; it seems there almost always is, someone leaving in a bag. It's the kind of thing Rachel never mentions to anyone else. Why mention that elephant in the room. A gangly boy with long auburn hair is on a skateboard, and their little friend, the one that terrible girl called a loser, is sitting on the curb watching him. The children don't see her and she walks quickly; she feels beckoned by the shade and damp moist undergrowth as she makes her way through the arboretum, the trumpet and cross vines in full bloom, jasmine, wisteria. It was 1965 and she and Art had attended Norman Thomas's big birth-day celebration the year before. They had sent him money for his presidential campaign. Art shook his hand and told him that his book, *Is Conscience a Crime?*, was a masterpiece. They applauded his stance on birth control, ironically since nature had taken care of that for her. They admired the way he stood against segregation long before it was even something in the news. They protested Vietnam. It was 1965, and she wore short dresses and leather boots and she had a shoulder-length fall that she clipped onto her own hair and then tied a long scarf up at her hairline. She was never into high fashion, but she did latch onto what suited her and then wore it in a way that made it all her own. Like the way she now likes to roll up her slacks in neat pedal-pusher cuffs. She did it so she wouldn't pick up twigs and burrs in the cemetery, but then she got so many compliments from people like that young pedicure girl that she kept doing it and now others are copying her. Even Marge has rolled her pants up a couple of times, which says there may be hope for everyone.

"Green Peppers." "Butterball." "Lollipops and Roses." It was 1965 and she had never even heard of Joe Carlyle. It was 1965 and life seemed easier. Her parents were alive and so was her brother; her bones were hard and strong and her vision perfect. She was a young married woman with a professional career and she thought that one day she would have it all, a career and a baby and a house on the Cape. It was 1965 and she was filled with hope, lush pots of ivy spilling from her window boxes as she leaned out late in the day to see the sunset, to smell the river, to watch her husband turn the corner as he headed home. She was so alive.

Kendra

KENDRA HAS SPENT MUCH of the day putting little white stickers on what she plans to keep, carefully placing them up under the furniture where they can't be seen. Each one has her initials and a number that makes it look like she has cataloged everything in the house. What she has cataloged, of course, are the things worth having—the expensive things—some of them things they bought from the woman who sold them the house but most from a local estate auction where the pitiful old guy was clueless about everything. "That belonged to my wife's grandmother," he would say, and then cried in a way that was shameless. Kendra tried to be kind, but it was hard the way he looked, his face all red and twisted and unattractive, and besides, she was so excited about what she was getting for practically nothing. Persian rugs and massive antique sideboards and wardrobes. The man had no idea what his belongings were worth and she was just grateful that the son he kept referring to had remained in Chicago and not come to oversee everything, unlike, of course, the daughter of the woman they bought this house from. She was all business and knew just what she was doing and of course she was someone who remembered Ben from school even though she was a little older. Everyone in the whole dump town knows who he is. "He wanted to be a magician, right?" the woman asked, and laughed. She had one of those big blotchy birthmarks on the side of her face and Kendra spent the whole time wondering why in the hell she wouldn't at least put some makeup on it to try to hide it. Who cares if she lives in Cambridge and teaches at Harvard? She was the kind of woman Kendra has a hard time being around and she certainly did not enjoy the time mother and daughter spent roaming the house and reminiscing. The daughter had paused and stood for a long time in what had been a hideous dark study and stared out the window where an old split-level used to be. Now there's a giant contemporary with a three-car garage, which is a huge improvement, though Kendra didn't say that. "We had some good times here," the woman said, her fingertips pressing the big glass window. She looked like she might cry and Kendra was relieved as hell that she didn't. She should go see a dermatologist and move on. Kendra was ready for them to get out of her house. It was that very afternoon she went to the estate sale and cleaned up. Kendra has always been lucky about being in the right place at the right time. Of course you make your luck and this is what she is in the process of doing. She is making her luck, making her own fortune happen.

She's not quite ready to drop the bomb on her husband, but this way she will be prepared when the right time comes. She likes knowing the stickers are there; she likes the secrecy of her other life and the way that it is taking root and blossoming. It makes her feel powerful. She will keep the house, of course, she'd be a fool not to, and if she could get away with it, she'd go ahead and change the locks before Ben even knows what is coming. How can he *not* know what's coming? And yet it seems he doesn't. She will keep the house and she will keep the child, though of course she is hoping he will also want her for huge chunks of time like the weekends so she can have the time she needs to herself. The judges almost always go with the mother on this and she has made sure that she has met and had some kind of witty conversation with every judge in town. Her plan is to keep this as an investment, a little B&B oasis in the rundown middle of this dried-up boring town. And then she will live in a newer place like the Meadows, where she will have access to tennis courts and golf course and pool, not that she would use them, but that's the traffic she likes to see. Of course, she does love the old Brendle mansion on the outskirts of town—a real plantation. But that will be after the more public evolution of her life with Andrew Porter once he is also divorced. Andrew is a heart surgeon. She loves to think that sentence, to say it when she is all by herself like in the shower: *And this is Andrew, Andrew is a heart surgeon.* "He brings people *back* after they really *do* disappear," she told Benjamin right after they met him. "He really *is* brilliant and really *does* have a profession." Everyone else calls him Andy but she prefers he go by Andrew. Names are important. Like she has always called Ben "Benjamin" and told him a million times how much better he would be received in the community if he went by his full name instead of Ben or, God forbid, the Bennie that some of his old redneck friends fall back on. Bennie and the Jets—that was what his pony league football team called themselves because he was the quarterback and unfortunately there are still enough of those guys hanging around this godforsaken place that they see him and call out his name. He has so many stupid nicknames she doesn't even pay attention, who cares? Kendra grew up in Charlottesville, Virginia, and she has often wished she had stayed there or ventured northward. She is someone who should be in DC or New York and always thought she would be.

Kendra Burleigh Baker. The Burleigh, of course, a play on the tobacco her family was once famous for. She has even thought lately that once she is established in her brand-new life, she might go by Burleigh or even B. Leigh, which would also be real cute. Then she would always have a reason to tell about her family history. A name is important. She called herself Kenni all through college and flirted with calling herself Dra just to go for something really different, until Ben, who then was just one of the many boys asking her out, said it would be hard not to add "ma," Dra Ma, and the whole hallway of girls in the dorm started laughing. Probably the only reason she even looked at him twice is because everybody else had a crush on him. That's how immature she was, as hard as that is to believe. All the girls were attracted to how different he was at their school, a lone kind of hippie type in a sea of starched drunken preppie boys, and he *said* he was in law school. All she really wanted was someone affluent who could whisk her off to a fine plantation and treat her like a queen.

If she had known that all Ben really was was a dopey amateur magician and a film projectionist, well, who would ever choose that? He thinks of himself as an artist but she is *so* much more the artist. Anything he has ever done, it's because she said it was a good idea. If there is a real artist in the house, she is it. It was *her* idea, after all, to have big murals painted on the dining room and living room walls, hills and sun like you might be in Tuscany, but anytime they have had a party and someone compliments how beautiful it looks, he just says, "Thanks," like it was his goddamned idea and not hers. "How hard is it to just say, 'Kenni is the artist around here.' How hard is that?" she has asked a million and one times, but of course he never hears a word she says. If it was something said by that crazy woman who was his friend a hundred years ago and now sells hot dogs and helps people die, he would listen.

"How dare you," she recently said to him after overhearing him tell Abby how much he admires the freak. "What is there to admire about her? She is plain and unattractive in all ways. People talk like it's amazing she's been married so many times, but the amazing part is that anybody ever wanted her. Who would even want to marry such a loser?" She was about to comment on her hair and how if she were sick in the bed and had to look at that mess, she would just as soon die, too, but he was out the door and in his car, saying he was going to *work*. Work, her ass. Redoing an old movie theater and getting senior citizens in once a week is hardly real work. For all she knows he spends time with that crazy woman even though she has told him that he better not. "How embarrassing would that be?" she asked, and got right up in his face. Several times she has wanted him to hit her because then she could photograph it and have some good ammo for when they get down to the real business of splitting everything up.

He's the one who grew up here but still didn't know the people they really needed to know. She told him how she could see and understand the strata of the town so much better than he could because she was an implant. Of course she meant to say *transplant,* but she said implant, and he has never let her forget that. He brings it up every time they argue, in fact, and she sees *that* as a kind of harassment, certainly something worth mentioning to her lawyer when the time comes. Of course she knew the correct word was *transplant.* She accidentally said *implant,* and he in all his smart-ass glory said: *You and all the other boobs.* She is the reason they are even on the A list in town; she got them invited to everything so they could meet all the right people. It's what she came from, after all. She had not grown up that way, but she was *supposed* to have and that was a well-known fact. She couldn't help that her grandfather lost everything in the depression. That loss did not change the blood that coursed through her veins and the long line of wealthy important people she descended from. And of course meeting Dr. Andrew Porter had changed all that. He didn't belong in that town any more than she did and yet there he was. He was originally from Raleigh with parents who had deep roots in one of the better parts of Alabama and his wife was from Pennsylvania, and though Kendra wanted to be like and possess so much about her, she also really didn't care for her. Those are the hardest friends to have. Those you just know you *should* have when really you detest them. Ben said she was jealous and that she needed to be more careful that her jealousy and coveting didn't show, which pissed her off beyond belief. She didn't speak to him for days after that. The truth was all those expensive clothes were wasted on Liz Porter. She did not have the body for designer clothes like Kendra does. Liz has the look of a rich girl but an ordinary-looking rich girl and that's where someone like Kendra comes in. She is someone who can pull off having it all.

She and Ben went to dinner at their house one night, and

everything switched just like that—a lightbulb glared in full romantic glory above her head. That night was the beginning of it
all. After that, everything in her life looked shabby and cheap. She
wants a huge bathroom with steam showers and heat lamps and
a heated floor. She wants a bathroom so huge that there would
be room for someone to come in and set up a massage table—so
much better to have them come to you than to go down to that
one dreadful place in town offering massages, the Big Chill, an
operation run by a woman who used to work as an assistant in a
smoke-out facility, which some say doubled as abortion clinic/
whorehouse. No one with a brain would go there for a massage,
and Kendra has a brain, a beautiful brain, and a good heart and
a beautiful body or so she has been told by Andrew, who actually
gives a damn, so what else matters? She would rather dive into
that awful snake-infested river than go to such a place even though
Liz Porter has been and reported back that it was a lovely little
spa—massages, facials, pedicures. The girl who did her toenails
was a darling, tattooed all over and smart as a whip. They only
play music from the sixties and seventies and they burn patchouli
incense. "It's cute," Liz Porter said. "I love retro."

Well, Kendra loves retro, too; of course she does, but only
retro that is worth her time. Like she would love to own a '68
Mustang convertible, which Andrew says she will someday. "You
have to be patient," he whispered in her ear just recently; they
were at the hospital gift store where she was pretending to buy
something for a sick friend. He followed her back to a corner
filled with cheap kid things like Beanie Babies and coloring
books and he cupped her ass with one hand and pulled her in
close for one hard second before turning back out into the world

and complimenting the ancient woman at the counter on her fine selection of pediatric gifts.

Kendra wants her own dressing room with little globe lights all around a great big mirror. Maybe she will even have a three-way mirror with a platform like at Nordstrom. She is someone who really should be in New York or Chicago or Boston instead of here where you can't even find what Oprah recommends you buy to use and wear. She is by nature, a beautiful woman, everyone tells her so. Her hair is blond and only in recent years has needed the benefit of highlights—she is a perfect size 4 and small enough that she can wear three-inch heels and still keep all the men in the room—even the shortest ones—feeling manly. Part of it is the good fortune of nature, but there is also a lot of care and maintenance that goes into it.

She picks up a rawhide bone and throws it in the trash. She keeps finding them everywhere, sick little reminders. That damn dog, pissing if she yelled at it, and she had no choice but to yell at it, so ill trained and fucked up. She has no time for dredging up all kinds of sympathy for fucked-up creatures. That's another thing she told Ben about that crazy friend of his; who even has time for fucked-up people when there are so many good ones? That stupid dog would have ruined all these wonderful rugs that came from that sad old man and there was no way that Kendra was going to let that happen. She still can't get over the good deal she got—and *she* got the good deal, *she* is the one who dealt with that pathetic guy so sick with grief to let all those nice Persian rugs go along with a huge mahogany sideboard and a baby grand piano. She said as much to Liz while doing her "Oh, do you really like this?" routine, which she has more than perfected only to see the drop in

Liz's expression, the wash of compassion, and that pissed Kendra off and made her add, "Bless his heart." Of course Liz can act all compassionate on his behalf because she has always been handed everything in life without having to do anything to get it. Kendra, on the other hand, has been robbed in life, the fortune that should have accompanied her good family name long compromised.

Kendra can't imagine any death or tragic event that would make her unaware of rugs worth thousands of dollars, that is, if they aren't coated in dog piss. The rug in the living room alone was appraised at over twenty, and when Liz Porter came over and oohed and ahhed, Kendra knew that finally *she* had something Liz wanted. Liz with her plain, plump rich girl look—and that is where money makes a huge difference. An overweight body in cheap clothes is just as hideous as it sounds, but you can take a plump girl and squeeze her into expensive clothes and it does make a difference. *Elegant pearl dripping sausages,* Kendra thinks. Nothing is going to hide what is unattractive, of course, but a person can distract and it is clear Liz has been raised and groomed to do just that. Liz even knelt right there in Kendra's living room, tasteful black skirt riding up the heft of her thighs, while she rubbed her hands over the threads, admiring the intricate patterns—she even knew about this particular kind of rug and had little boring stories to tell about the poverty-stricken people who wove them over a century ago, like anybody cared to hear that. The dog came in about then and Kendra yanked her onto the back porch and locked the door. She was not about to have that goddamned mongrel pissing around with Liz Porter in the room. Liz Porter had two King Charles spaniels, which they had driven to DC to buy, and she had also been to Fairfield Spa down in Savannah several times when her husband thought she looked tired. Of course, she can go and enjoy herself at patchouli stinkhole cheap massage; that's slumming for her. She can afford to slum *because* she is married to Andrew Porter. She has a husband who is worth a shit. She told Ben how Liz Porter went to a weeklong spa and sometimes flew to New York just to see a show and buy new clothes. "That's the kind of man she's married to," she said.

"The kind who likes to get rid of his wife?" He waved one of his stupid wands over her head and then pulled a dead rubber chicken out of his sleeve. He had a wreath of ivy on his head and was carrying a sheet he planned to wear like a toga to introduce his upcoming triple feature: *Ben Hur* and *El Cid* and *Cleopatra*.

"Oh, ha ha," she said. "He's a heart surgeon and still manages to do all that needs to be done, including being a real husband." She had said that several times but lately has had to stop saying it given what is going to happen very soon. Now she is trying to be coolly polite and only arguing back late at night when she knows Abby is asleep and he has had enough to drink that he won't fully remember. The last time she said something like that, Ben had said, "So maybe he can give you a heart, like the Tin Man." And then he laughed and laughed, fell back on the bed with his dirty shoes still on, and laughed. "Oh, that's right," he sputtered. "The Tin Man actually already *had* a heart—won't work then."

"You are just jealous," she said, but then stopped because Abby was there in the doorway with that stinking Dollbaby. Abby had tied one of Kendra's nice *retro* Vera scarves she got on eBay around the mutt's neck, and it got Kendra's attention off of her sarcastic husband and back to the dog and her daughter who never tries to do anything to improve her looks even with all of Kendra's help and suggestions.

"If we have to have a dog," she said, "at least get one I won't be ashamed to walk! One that looks like a dog."

And with that Ben mumbled that she should get a job and buy her own fucking dog.

She told him that a *job* was not in their marital agreement, that the marital agreement was that he would use that business degree he got or finish that law degree he used to get her to marry him. When she decided to marry him, he was going back to school and in the interim he was in business with his old roommate and friend, a terribly unattractive boy who had no social skills and terrible hygiene but was flat out rolling in dough. Her moment of reckoning was when she realized that Ben was not in it for what she thought. Ben talked the ugly idiot into cutting ties with his demanding (and extremely successful) father and doing his own thing.

"Hey, man," she heard Ben say. "Life is short. And if you want to work in forestry, that's your choice." The two were drinking beer out on the back stoop of their dump rental house and passing a joint. "And you sell yourself so short, man. C'mon, you think all you are is what your dad gave you? You don't see who you really are?"

The puffed-up pussy was crying by then and Kendra had wanted to take a broom and sweep them both out into the yard like the wasted strays they were.

"Look at you, man," Ben said. "You actually read *Ulysses,* and you're the only one who got an A in that class. And you knew how to rewire the sound system, remember? What about all your great ideas? You're a geek, man. The world is yours on a silver platter."

She knew then that everything she wanted had gone right down the tubes, and to make it worse, she was already pregnant with something that had not been her idea. Before she even had the chance to say she didn't want it, he had all but given out cigars, so proud of himself. She was holding a piece of Wedgewood china, a gift from one of her mother's friends, and she threw it against the wall.

They still get postcards from the old friend, long ago reunited with his dad and making a mint. "You deserve a share of that," she has said. "You need to be more assertive—like call him up and say, 'Hey? Remember me? I'm the only person who even treated you like a human and could stand to be around you,'" but he couldn't hear her.

"Hey, man, good for you," she heard him say into the phone when the guy called from some European vacation or the huge summer home he and his wife were building over on Bald Head Island. And his wife was beautiful—young and beautiful—and hadn't even had a baby yet.

"He owes you," she said, often enough that he told her she reminded him of that fairy tale where the greedy wife keeps sending the poor husband out to wish for bigger and bigger until they wind up with nothing. "Or the one where the man gets so pissed off at her nagging that he uses his last wish to wish the big sausage got stuck to her face for a nose or something like that—remember that one? I love that story. Abby would love that story."

"I am the last person to be greedy," she said. "There is not a greedy bone in my body. I just want you to be appreciated for your own part in him being the success he is. Without you he would have killed himself or something, or should have."

"Here it is." He pulled out a postcard from his drawer. "Here is what you've been searching for. It says, 'Thanks, man. You have been such a good friend to me.'" She grabbed and tore it, and he told her to produce a similar artifact from her drawer. He said, "Let's see who thinks you're nice." She could tell he was getting ready to light into her but then froze in the way he always does when Abby enters the room. And there she was, a mini carbon copy of him. Everybody said that, too, and it infuriated her. Oh, she's the spitting image of Ben. Kendra's blond hair and blue eyes were lost in the mix and so was her body. Abby has dark wiry hair and a chunky little body, and what kind of mother would she be if she didn't make her lose weight? Of course she needed a regimen for exercise. Doesn't the child see when they try on clothes in the junior department how they all fit her mom? Shouldn't that make a kid want to lose weight and improve her looks? But instead she is *his* child and as a result doesn't care *who* her friends are and doesn't care *what* she wears. She just doesn't care about anything except that goddamned dog.

And the child doesn't appreciate anything either, like this party for instance. She will go on and on about a stupid fucking disappearing chamber and doesn't even notice all the time Kendra has spent researching First Ladies and planning the party. Well, someday it will all be behind her. In fact, just the other side of the birthday party is the meeting she has been waiting for so patiently for months and after that everything else will fall right into place. Something is definitely about to happen. Tomorrow night will mark the beginning of a brand-new life.

She'll likely have to give up her gym membership so as not to run into Liz anymore, but that's okay; it has gotten so hard these days to continue being nice to her, smiling and acting like they are actually friends. Liz even whispered about what she was planning for their anniversary, and oh, won't Kendra have some fun with that one? She plans to buy the exact same nightgown and robe set that she watched Liz buy—talk about compare and contrast. Andrew won't know what hit him. As for Abby, she will come around someday, and she will see why her mother had no choice but to run away with Andrew Porter. They will probably move northward; why wouldn't they? His children are old enough to get on a plane if they want to visit, and even though they are quite a bit older, she can imagine they will make room for Abby someday. A few years of private school and personal trainers and the child will look back and think *thank God*. Then she will finally see Kendra for who she really is, a good mother and a smart woman with a plan. The one thing Kendra will not ever let her know about is the disappearance of Dollbaby and what really happened. Kendra likes to think that Abby will grow into the kind of woman who could laugh about it someday, that she will be the kind of woman who would understand why her mother had no choice but to do what she did, but that's a little trickier. It will be hard enough to successfully convince the kid her dad is a total loser (without saying a word of course). Very few people are skilled enough to handle such subtle trickery, but Kendra considers herself a professional. Ben thinks he's a magician? Oh my, just watch her make him disappear. Just watch him stand and wonder what in the hell hit him. You want to see what's up *her* sleeve? You want to see what's in *her* hat? She reaches and plants another sticker under the bench of the baby grand.

"I suspect you're someone with quite a bag of tricks," Andrew

Porter whispered in her ear that very first night they met and she told him that she was indeed and that if he was very good, she just might let him see what's up her sleeve.

"I'd rather see what's up your skirt," he whispered, a little drunk for sure but not too drunk to know what he was doing. And then Liz walked up and asked if Kendra wanted to go with her to the little girls' room. Oh, the stupid little girls' room and all the stupid little girls in there. Kendra has never liked other girls but learned early to pretend that she did so she could get closer to the boys she was interested in. She has always thought of herself as a Scarlett O'Hara type and does believe that the end always justifies the means.

She puts a sticker under the art deco lamp in the hall and nearly trips on the dog bowl that Abby has left there in hopes Dollbaby will be home any day now. Impossible, of course, and now on top of everything else, she has to deal with that. She will make up something, tell all about the phone call she got—so so sad—Dollbaby wandering way out in the county, hit by a car. If she had known the child was going to be this torn up and spend days searching, she would have just said right up front something like *Dollbaby got hit by a car*. But then it would have potentially been *her* fault instead of the way she planned it, which was to say Dollbaby got out of the fence Ben built for her. How's that for a disappearing chamber? How's that for some fucking magic?

Notes about: Willis Morgan Hall
Born: March 13, 1921 **Died:** March 14, 2007, 5:20 p.m.
Holderness, New Hampshire

Willis Hall died of throat cancer in the old farmhouse where he had spent his whole life, where every room smelled of the sweet cherry pipe tobacco he smoked for years along with cigars and, ten years prior, cigarettes. He was known in his handsome early years as the boy who would imitate the Philip Morris ads or say "Hey, good looking, got a cigarette?" and had met two of his three wives with that line. All three of his ex-wives were with him at the end. He joked that he and the king Yul Brynner played had a lot in common. They both should have quit smoking sooner and they both had lots of wives gathered at the deathbed. The only time he was ever away from home was when he was in the service. He was at the Battle of the Bulge, which he liked to say was indeed just as bad as it sounded. *Bulge is not a nice word,* he said. *Used most often for what is unattractive—eyes and stomachs—or what is pornographic, you know?* Every year some schoolchildren would pop up with questions for a history project and he gave them just enough for a story, just what they needed. The cold and the filthy conditions, the way that battle hit them worst just when they thought they were almost out of the woods.

The ground was still covered in snow though the days were just enough longer that it felt like spring was coming. One wife noted that he always said he loved this time of year when everything was thawing and muddy, the plants starting to stir and break the soil. He said he felt so sexy in the spring. "He told you that, too?" another wife asked, the youngest of the three, though they all looked about the same age and could have been sisters, and they all laughed.

"How can you not love him?" the other wife said. "Who wouldn't fall for him? Sweet as sugar, aren't you?"

"Easy to fall, but hard to keep him," another said. They all were re-married, and though he had girlfriends, two who had brought casseroles, only the wives were present that day at dusk. It was his favorite time of day, they said. He liked dusk and he liked well-made shoes and he loved Angie Dickinson especially as Pepper the Police Woman; he liked Martini and Rossi, which Angie advertised and of course she was the reason he also started eating avocados, which were often not easy to find in New Hampshire. All three wives said—at different private times—how they had wanted life with him to work but that he was stuck there, not even willing to take a vacation. Not willing for his wife to work and be gone all day. In the summer he might venture out a little bit, eat out locally, go to the occasional movie, but once the snow fell, that was it, he stayed put. "And," the third of the three had said, sadly shaking her head, "there is a lot of snow in New Hampshire in the winter."

The only photograph in the room is one of himself as a child, his mother and father on either side lifting him by the arms up and over a mound of snow as tall as he was. When asked about his parents, he said they were wonderful to him. His mother once told him that everyone loved him so much, all the girls in town loved him, how would he ever choose a wife? "It was hard," he said, and laughed. "I would love for my mother to know how wonderfully difficult that choice proved to be."

When asked to tell about the charm he seemed to have over everyone, how he had managed to have three ex-wives who love him dearly, he said his favorite power tool had always been silence. "I'm their mirror," he said. "And they always come back for one more look." Toward the end, when in and out of a deep drugged sleep, he gripped my hand with a strength that surprised me and said *stay*.

I will think of him every time I smell tobacco or peel an avocado or hear mention of Angie Dickinson or the word *bulge*. I will continue to marvel at his ability to reflect back to people what they need to see and how it seemed he needed nothing. I asked permission to take one of his many empty tobacco tins, thinking I would keep things in it, earrings, loose change, but the smell is still so powerful I keep it capped like a genie for a time I might need to conjure the memory of Willis Hall, a good-humored selfless spirit I didn't really know at all beyond what he reflected back on whoever was talking to him at the time.

[from Joanna's notebook]

Willis Hall

Smoke and snow and snow and snow. Sometimes a cigarette can keep you warm—that tiny bit of light, red glow, smoke breath warm within, or you can pretend it does. The Ardennes are not unlike the White Mountains or the Green Mountains, or you can pretend that—snow, rock, trees—but so far from home. And cold. Cold hands, warm heart, his mother said, and she said one, two, three, jump, and he was up and over a mound of snow—a mound, a bulge, a hill of heavy falling snow, and a forest so dense, too dense to see, and snowing, breath smoking. The young man beside him can't go anymore—Stay, he says—his wounded feet torn and raw so he sinks down into a burrow of roots and waits and waits and smokes when it is safe to smoke, breathes in and breathes out, and now he's cold, ice cold to the touch. Breathe in and breathe out and sometimes don't breathe at all, stay and hold his hand, wrap his feet, this identical boy in age and uniform. The safest choice is not to move but to breathe in and breathe out, breathe in and breathe out and sometimes don't breathe at all. Sweet as sugar, his mother says. Cold hands, warm heart. Cold hands, warm heart.

Stanley

STANLEY STONE CAN'T COMPLAIN. He lives in a little apartment with a good bed and good light. The windows of his bedroom face west so he sees the sun setting over the woods near the interstate. He's got two sons, one a successful software salesman in the Midwest and the younger one, Ned, a health and PE teacher at the local elementary school. Ned does a little acting with the community theater and he leases a field just outside of town and now is known for having the best pumpkin patch in the county. And it's good that he is finally known as the best in something because that is a long time coming. He was a kid who was always in trouble but had finally graduated and seemed to have gotten it all together. Once upon a time, he had a nice smart wife and was the assistant principal of a high school over in South Carolina, and then next thing they knew, she left him and he had to pay her a lot of money, got a DUI, and on and on and on, everything in his life falling apart like a house made of limp worthless cards.

He also slept in Stanley's bed for three weeks after Martha

died, and even though Stanley protested and cussed and said some pretty awful things, he found that hearing Ned's breath those nights was maybe the greatest comfort he has ever known. Stanley couldn't sleep with the emptiness, the cool sheets, the way the clock face wasn't blocked by her silhouette and glared out at him with its old glowing green face. He could not sleep with all the thoughts of all he had not done in their life together.

Not only did Ned stay, carefully turning off the lamp by the chair where Martha always read and then climbing in when he thought Stanley was already asleep, but he never told, never mentioned it, not even these times recently when Stanley has been hard on him and once again said harsh and judgmental things he doesn't really *mean* to say, an old habit that is dying hard. After his wife left him, Ned was a spiral out of control. "So you lost a baby," Stanley had said to him. "A lot of people do. You get over it." But Ned could not get over it. He was worse off than his wife and she was having a hard time of it, too. Stanley told how Martha had a miscarriage between the two boys. Such a common thing. He didn't say, *Stand up and take it like a man,* but he wanted to say that. There was a part of him thinking that was the right thing.

"It's not the same, Stanley," Martha had said, her hand on his arm feeling like the weight of a big stinking dead albatross. "Their baby was born. Their baby had a name."

"And their baby had an awful genetic disease that would have been miserable to live with and cost them more than they could ever have afforded." He tried to make her see his reason, but she wouldn't even look at him at that point. "It's called survival of the fittest. It was not meant to live."

"*It* was your grandson. *It* was your namesake."

"Foolish to name it. What were they thinking?"

"They were hoping, that's all. Hoping." Martha stood her ground on that one, and even though he told her that she needed to stay out of their lives and let them tend to it themselves, she was right there, buying the casket and arranging for the service, and yes, he felt like a shit to think it, but all he could think is how he wished it had been born dead or born too early or any number of other scenarios than what they had, a scene at a hospital where the two grown-up parents fell apart and were no better than children themselves. The girl's parents showed up and Ned let them do all the comforting and then it was done—over. The marriage was over and he was stuck with a mortgage and alimony until she got on her feet. And all that time Ned kept himself functioning just above a stupor. When confronted, he said it was the one thing he knew how to do until he slammed into a station wagon full of high school girls on their way to a pep rally. He didn't kill anyone, but he could have; everyone kept saying it was an absolute miracle that he didn't given how fast he was going. People who saw him tossed through the windshield said he seemed to bounce like rubber off onto the shoulder, that the drugs and liquor that were killing him had actually, in that moment, saved his life.

And so he did his time. Months in the hospital, a rebuilt pelvis. A plate in his head. A scar along his right eye that looks like he got in a knife fight. He got a couple of months in jail because he had been warned too many times by too many people and then a lot of community service and what Stanley now is able to laugh and say was the hardest service of all—going with Martha to church every single week. She was the one who suggested he forget about the pressures of administrative positions and think about teaching.

"You have always been good with kids," she told him. "You could coach. You could do driver's ed." As soon as she said it, she caught herself. "Maybe not driver's ed. But . . ." She paused and Stanley could tell she was choosing her words carefully. "You could do a course with kids, you know, to talk about what can happen." And that's what he did and in no time it seemed he was on the right path; he worked hard and he checked in with Martha several times a week to talk about what all he was doing. She listened about the pumpkin patch long after any normal person with a normal threshold for boredom could've stood and yet there she was, the two of them so closely knit together by then that Stanley could do as he pleased and not have to deal too much with either of them. He was working hard and getting pretty sick of it. There was very little he enjoyed and he realized this the day there was an electrical storm that blew the power out and he could not watch the evening news. The evening news. That was what he looked forward to.

Ned's older brother, Pete, had breezed through without a single problem; they see him on major holidays and Stanley gets presents along the way. Pete was easy, a no-nonsense unemotional boy, the opposite of Ned, who was the kind of tantrum-throwing child Stanley had no patience for. People always talked about how good Martha was, how sweet, and yeah, he could give her that, but what all those people didn't know was also how passive and withdrawn she was. Yes, she was *there* for Ned, and yes, dinner was almost always on the table—sometimes microwave shit in later years but there nonetheless—and the clothes did get washed and she did almost always go to church and to bridge club, but even before Martha got sick there was a low-grade despondency, a depression that Stanley was probably responsible for, too. He tried to make it better in the early years. He bought flowers every now and then. He never forgot her birthday, but still something was always missing in their life together.

People didn't go running into therapy every five minutes back then, but he suspects if they had, someone would have told him that he was a really shitty father—a really shitty man, in fact. He had done so much wrong and yet on the surface he looked like a man who had done a wonderful job with everything. When Martha complained of her weariness and fatigue, he made jokes. When someone at church had suggested that she might have Epstein-Barr, he told how he knew a fellow named Epstein in the service—Epstein's Bar and Grill—food guaranteed to slow you down so you have to take to the bed or have a blinding migraine that lets you off the hook to do pretty much anything. Sex? What in the hell was *that*?

But then she got cancer and no one denied the reality of that.

Stanley wasn't there enough. He knows that now. Truth is he knew it then but just didn't have the guts to stand up and deal with it. He was so focused on his business. He did what was expected of him. It was like standing and reciting the Pledge of Allegiance. Every now and then, you actually feel patriotic and like you might give a goddamn, but usually it's just a pain in the ass to have to stand when you've worked your ass off and feel tired. Just do what is expected in a way that numbs the world. And he stayed there, humming along, worked on a few church committees, advised the city council, did the Boy Scouts a couple of years, took a sack of toys to some poor family across the river at Christmas. When he looks back now he wishes he could recall some of the faces there waiting, but he can't. He was thinking of things like how his muffler didn't sound quite right or what in the hell was he going to buy for Martha when she didn't need another goddamned thing cluttering the space. It already drove him crazy, that wall of knickknacks that rattled when you came through the living room. Things rattled all over the house. She loved little Limoges boxes—expensive-as-hell things commemorating this or that and to this day he regrets the way he cleared a shelf with the brush of a hand, leaving everyone silent for days. He remembers that with great clarity, the landing of every splintered shard of porcelain, but he can't remember a single child receiving from his asshole hands the only Christmas gift of the year, something Martha or someone at the church had bought and wrapped. *Boy: age 8. Wants a skateboard but really needs clothes. Girl: age 6. Wants a kitten but understands she might get a Polly Pocket doll instead. Really needs shoes and a coat and underwear.* He found these slips of paper in her purse, right there with grocery lists and a coupon file—pieces carefully clipped but obviously never used.

He and Martha had not planned what they would do in their old age; like everything else, he had assumed they would deal with it when they got to it, muddle on through. There was plenty of money. He had made sure of that, but somehow he had always assumed she would be the one left to deal with everything. The day she died—that awful day he had to sit there and tell her it was okay to die—he knew he had to figure out and execute his own plan immediately. He didn't want to wait until he got sick and slapped into an old folks' home somewhere. It would be like Pete to just come get him and check him in to some really nice spot near him and then drop by once a month. But Stanley wanted to stay home. He grew up here and he has lived here for seventy-nine years and he wants to die here. The past decade has brought Ned back to life, remorseful and reformed and not willing to leave Stanley's side, but very much alive. Ned wants to be the son Stanley has always wanted him to be, though even Stanley would be hard-pressed to say what that might entail. And though Stanley would not have given anything for Ned's presence all those nights he lay there beside him, it was also his own time of reckoning. He had been a bad father and he could not let Ned feel all the responsibility himself. Ned was vowing to stay put, live with him, do things together, and that's when Stanley began hatching the idea of what he would do. What he *had* to do. He would tell his sons first that he *wanted* to live in a place like Pine Haven and then when they successfully reminded him of all the times he had said he would *never* live in such a place, he would convince them that he *needed* to be there, *needed* the assistance and the secure knowledge that someone—a medical person he would stress—is always close by. He knew not to list physical problems because that would have meant many hospital visits and tests. No, the easiest was just to create his own dementia, confess that he was having trouble remembering things and then focus on something—wrestling—in a way that was obsessive and exhausting. He has never acted a day in his life, but he took the role and has done quite well with it. The hardest part was giving up driving but small sacrifice if it buys him some time alone and forces Ned to move on. Everyone seems convinced and for the first time in years Stanley feels a real sense of solitude. People usually say *peace* and solitude but he's not there yet. The peace is yet to come and maybe it never will. Maybe a lack of peace is what comes to someone like him who never was able to give the right thing at the right time. Someday he will let Ned know the truth; someday, when Ned has more people in his life and Stanley is closer to the end, he will list his many regrets and all the ways he feels he failed as a father. "We're even," Stanley will say. "It ain't a pretty picture, but we're even. And you," he will add, "you are young and have a whole life ahead of you."

Some of those nights when Ned lay there beside him, Stanley would inch his hand close enough to feel the warmth of his son's body. How many nights could he have so easily reached for Martha's hand. Once she was diagnosed, it seemed wrong, false somehow. Though of course he did hold her hand at the end, he was so sorry that it came about because she was dying, that she would see it that way, the result of her dying. And he *did* love her. She was a good person, a kind person. She was a friend, a companion, and perhaps that's all it was. And perhaps that was all someone like him was capable of. Oh sure, trace it back to hard parents, hard living, but how awful to come to the end and see that all you've been is another goddamned link in the chain that keeps out the happiness. And Pete is just like him. Everyone thinks he's so successful and great, a chip on every square. And yet for all Stanley knows Pete could be as empty and hollow as that cheap chocolate Easter Bunny that poor weird child from next door was giving out last month along with Girl Scout cookies.

When he was a much younger man, he liked watching wrestling. It was a guilty pleasure and something he would never have wanted Martha or his colleagues to know any more than he would invite them in when he read *Playboy* and allowed his hand to satisfy in a way that Martha never had and never would. There was something in the reckless abandon in both acts that he loved and admired. He liked the way big burly men strapped themselves into nothing more than a jock, peroxided their hair or got big tattoos and then came out like animals sprung from a cage. He thought how it must feel good as hell to scream at the top of your lungs and hurl your body into somebody built like a concrete post, to breathe heavy and pound and slam and sweat. Yeah, it did have a lot in common with his sexual fantasies in those days, though the fantasies were all about women—strong, tough women. Not to diminish the sweet corn-fed-looking ones, the tea-cake service ladies and Martha was definitely one of them, but he liked the fantasy of a woman who could grip his wrists and hold him in place. He liked women like he saw on Roller Derby, but God knows that was a century ago.

It was the Saturday night after Martha died. Pete and his family had come and gone, done all the right things and all that needed doing.

"I don't need you here, Ned," he said. "What's your problem?"

"I want to be here for you." The boy's voice cracked like he might've been twelve and there he was a forty-five-year-old divorced reformed druggie schoolteacher studying to be Curly in a low-rent production of *Oklahoma,* a show Stanley thinks is only rivaled in stupidity by *Seven Brides for Seven Brothers.* Who cares what the surrey looks like or how goddamned high the corn is. Martha ate all that shit with a spoon and he was as tolerant as he could be, but a man has his limits for sure. He sure hated to see Lois Flowers decline so quickly and have to live over in the nursing wing, but he had sure as hell *not* missed those sing-alongs at dinnertime. She either sang ridiculous jazzed-up show tunes or beautiful old songs that nearly broke his heart.

"Don't pity me, Ned. It's unbecoming to both of us," Stanley had said. "And you've done your time. Use your 'get out of jail free' card and just go away." He went in his bedroom and slammed the door; he tried to read but couldn't and there wasn't a sound. He imagined Ned just stood there frozen long after the fact, like a snake will do once you startle it. Ned coiled up and ready to strike, only Stanley knew that was not true. Ned was a different man; the anger and the bitterness and the weak victim wash he'd lived in all those years, all dried up. So many nights, Stanley got himself to sleep with a tortured litany of all of his failings. He was a shitty father. Embroider it on a pillow. And he was a shitty husband. Paint it on the overpass of the interstate. And the God he prayed to on behalf of others was not someone he even knew or believed in. When Martha's hospice volunteer, a young woman he sees coming and going out of the nursing building here at Pine Haven, came to their house, she told Stanley that Martha needed his help.

"She needs you to help her go," she said. "She needs you to tell her it's okay to die."

"But it's not okay to die," he said, and he said it loud, so loud he is sure that Martha heard him even though she had been in a coma for days. Her breathing changed and there was a restless-ness, limbs twitching.

"Please," she whispered, and gripped his hand. "Help her." It was just the two of them there. Pete was with his family at the Holiday Inn and Ned had gone to the grocery store and so he went and sat down, took Martha's hand in his own. "Tell her," the woman prompted and stepped back from the doorway. Outside the birds were singing and the winter sky was a clear pale blue, the color of those little boxes she bought when the boys were born. He leaned in close to Martha's ear and whispered that he loved her and that he would miss her but that he understood it was time for her to go. And her eyes opened like something in a horror movie and that was the end. It was just like that. It was just that fast.

That stare. He tried to think of everything else in the world except that stare, but it kept coming back and waking him, shocking him out of the traces of light sleep. Regrets and regrets and then he heard the door open and then felt weight on the other side of the bed. And then Ned was there, defying him, disobeying him, stretched out in Martha's place. Stanley faked sleep, letting his breath lighten, but with Ned's presence his mind was able to wander, allowing him to step into a ring and beat the shit out of everything that he hated in his life. He would wrestle it all to the ground. He heard the announcer say so: Stanley Stone—hard as a rock, heart of granite and blood as cold as marble.

After a week of Ned lying there at night and their quiet breakfasts together that had become something Stanley looked forward to, he began thinking up his plan. He would slowly start to slip. He would ease himself into character, an actor on the stage. He would be obsessed with wrestling and just rude enough to keep people at a distance. He would not shave every morning and get a regular haircut as he had done for the past fifty years. He would convince his sons he couldn't remember things like cholesterol medication or taking a shower; he would make them believe with great conviction that he needed to live in one of those retirement places and then everyone would be on his own, and if Ned had any chance of making it in life, he'd have the freedom to do so. It was a project that took many months, but it was successful. At first they were amused by their dad watching television. Other than the news and occasional major sport events, he had never watched television even when Martha begged him to join her. He learned a lot from watching television and he also had Ned drive him to Raleigh when the Wrestling Federation came to town, busloads of people screaming and cheering for the Undertaker and the Hardy Boys. He bought himself an Undertaker T-shirt and started wearing really short shorts around the house. He liked the way the Undertaker looked like Johnny Cash on steroids and so that's what he thought of himself. He was Johnny back from the dead. He was the Undertaker dressed all in black.

It worked. He convinced them, and here he is—a nice little apartment with a great big bathroom designed for if and when he needs a wheelchair; three good meals a day, great cable television. What's not to like? Ned still comes every day to check on him so Stanley makes sure to do something that keeps Ned at a distance and believing that this is the right and best choice. When Ned is around he always says rude things, which means he has to do it when Ned is not around as well, which is harder to do but necessary to keep everyone fooled. He has thought that if he had to, he could begin to dress like a wrestler—tight shorts and tank tops and such—but he is hoping he won't have to go there. It has been hard enough for him to get used to doing and saying things that make people uncomfortable; occasionally, he has enjoyed it, but usually it just wears him out. He points to women with oxygen tanks and tells how he is responsible for their tragic circumstances, how he took their breath away. He burps the alphabet at the dinner table about once every two weeks, usually right after grace has been said over the PA system, which leaves some of the more confused ones staring up as if God himself had said, Eat.

"How far can you get?" Toby asked one night, saying she once burped her way to *m* but it made her throw up so she hadn't tried it since. "Z, of course," he said, and he told her he is a man who always finishes what he starts.

"We got some new mares in the stable," he told Ned recently, and waved his arm around the dining room, his pointed finger stopping to rest on that woman from Boston—Rachel Silverman. "There's a tough broad," he said, and resisted when Ned tried to shush him. "We got 'em all here on the ranch. A couple of high-stepping ponies, a hell of a lot of nags gone to glue, but that new one's got some fire in her, haunches like a sack mule, but you can't have it all now, can you?"

"Dad, let's go to your room," Ned whispered, and though Stanley would have liked nothing better, so aware of the young woman who had been Martha's hospice volunteer in the doorway, to have shown reason at a time like that would have possibly undone too much hard work. He saw Ned and the young woman exchange embarrassed smiles; she knew who he was, but who knew if Ned would remember her. Ned was sobbing like a baby the afternoon Martha died.

"That's the one I'm planning to mount," Stanley said, and whispered to Ned, "Here I am, big Billygoat Gruff ready for some action." He pumped his hips and surveyed the reaction around the room. The young food attendants giggled, something they would probably get in trouble for later. Most of the women just blushed and glared at him, Marge Walker rising from her chair like she was going to take action. Toby was the one who laughed. She was puffing on a fake cigarette and was standing close enough to hear what he had said.

"My money says she'll throw you right off," Toby said, and puffed harder, flicked the holder like there might be ashes on the end. She looked at Ned. "This your old man?" Ned nodded. "He's a hoot." She turned to Rachel who was wearing what looked like a black business suit with pink tennis shoes; it was her first month there. "Did you hear that, umm, what's your name again?"

"Rachel. Rachel Silverman," she said. "And I would most definitely throw him. I would throw him *away*."

"You hear that, Rocky? She'll throw your old white ass to the mat."

"I love nothing better than a good bucking." He winked at her, feeling so self-conscious and ridiculous he had to fall back on something he had planned to do at awkward times, which was to raise his arms and imitate that silly dance people used to do to that song "YMCA." He could not count the number of times in his life when he had watched grown intelligent people do the alphabet to that stupid song and look like a bunch of silly idiots.

"Me, too," Toby said, and laughed great big, kept puffing. "Buck away."

"Dad, really." Ned pulled Stanley on toward his apartment and Toby followed. "Yesterday he said he wanted to do a wrestling demo," she said. "He says if he does I can be his manager. Name's Toby. Toby Tyler." She put her hand out and went back down the hall. Clearly she is his best audience member, not to mention a really good person.

"That's one of my good friends," he told Ned. "They say she's queer but who knows and who cares? You know the Village People were queer. Remember that dance I was just doing?"

"Yes, Dad." Ned said, and gripped his arm tighter.

"You aren't queer, are you, son?" Stanley asked. "Been a long time since I've heard of you gettin a piece." He knew he had gone too far, but sometimes he had no choice but to make him leave. "I'll be damned. My son is a queer."

"Would it matter?"

"Not if you're happy. Mighty slim pickings in this town, though."

"I'm not gay, Dad. I was married, remember?"

"Lots of gay people get married," he said, and stopped to adjust his belt, avoiding going into his apartment. The show is so much harder to pull off when it is just the two of them. "They call it a beard."

"I like women. I just haven't met one." Ned's vein in his right cheek was showing, always a good sign that he would have to leave very soon or else lose his temper, which it seemed he had made some kind of pact or oath not to do.

"Well, there's a cute one works here. Go on over there and find her. She's the one who came when your mom died."

Ned turned and Stanley realized he had sounded way too sane. "She tries every day to get me to fuck her and I keep telling her that I'm only interested in old pussy."

"Dad."

"Really. Someday when you get to be old you'll understand, but what I have told her is that I got a young son who I bet would like to pin her to the mat. Oh shit, look at the time. It's time for the rumble. I taped it. The Royal Rumble so either you got to go now or you have to promise to sit and not speak for the whole time." Stanley stopped making eye contact and turned on the television as loud as it would go. Ned stood in the doorway a few more minutes and then finally said he would be back later. "I love you, Dad," he said, and closed the door. And every day is the same. Same show. Same ending. He will have to do it again later this afternoon, but at least it is getting easier and it seems Ned does talk to more people these days; he's a little more outgoing and one day the hospice girl even asked Stanley how his son was doing.

Stanley is glad Ned has finally bought his own place, a little house on the way to the beach. Still, he knows that the boy's real idea of home is locked up in that house on the corner of Fifteenth and Winthrop. His heart is locked there, too, even though that house is gone as of a year ago, a Food Lion in its place. The boys were furious at him for selling so quickly and everyone lectured him about how he knew better than anyone how a person shouldn't make major decisions like that in the aftermath of death, but he knew he couldn't stand to look at it; he knew it would make it even harder for Ned to find his way, that he'd be like some old alley cat making his way back to the door again and again and again. The place felt terrible after Martha died, like he couldn't even breathe, so he did everything quickly. He had her prize rosebushes lifted and given away, her favorite planted at her grave, which he has not visited since going there with Ned to plant it. But now, ever since Sadie Randolph invited Stanley to close his eyes and wander his own home, he has not been able to stop the journey. There is not a night to pass that Stanley doesn't make his way through that house, the afghan and television and peace lilies. Martha always wanted a greenhouse, an expanse of light and glass to brighten the dark hallway. When she got sick he almost did it but then didn't. *Why bother now?* he could imagine her saying, and wouldn't that have been an awful ending? *Why bother now that I won't live through winter, now that we need all the money for this awful oxygen machine and the morphine that keeps me looped and reaching for things nobody else can see.*

But now he lets himself imagine the joy he might have seen if he'd surprised her with what she really wanted, unasked, just given—a gift.

"Oh, Stanley, it's beautiful," she says. "It's what I've always wanted." And the sound of her voice in his head is more painful than anything he has ever allowed himself to imagine. He winces and is glad to open his eyes and find Ned gone. He doesn't want Ned to get to the end and feel bad, sorry for all that he missed in life. He wants him in there with the thick of it—swimming, diving, claiming his own life and giving to it with all the gusto he has. Ned has done his time. He has more than earned a new life.

Stanley turns down the dark hallway where the greenhouse would have been and he stands in the doorway. There is the dog he promised and never got. The notebooks of numbers that would say when they could afford to do this or that—the stack of travel books on Martha's bedside table, carefully marked with a Post-it to remind him of all the places they never went. Bermuda. She just wanted to go to *Bermuda*; you can practically see Bermuda from here and yet they never got there.

Just yesterday Toby knocked and popped her head in, Rachel

Silverman right there behind her. "Stanley? Where are you? Outer space?" Toby is one of those people who is always cheerful and he can't help but wonder when she breaks. What does it take to bring that old girl down? He knows there is something. You can't live this many years and not know the weight, the pull of some regret.

"Yes. Outer space," he said, too tired for the show. Just too damn tired.

"You look sad." Her voice was so level and calm—a depth that sounded so good to his ear. The last thing he wanted was for someone to see him cry, to blow his hard-earned cover.

"Of course I'm sad," he said, and went to open his bathroom door. He stepped in and took a deep breath. "I'm sad there's no guns in this goddamned place so I could pick off some old assholes who need a mercy killing." He left the door open while he peed.

"I told you he's testy," Toby said. "But I still like him. We'll come back another day, though. Sadie says if anybody in town can answer all your questions, Stanley is the man."

"We'll see," Rachel said. "He's not very dependable and not very nice and truth be told, I've probably had enough drama for one life."

He had his hand on the knob to steady himself. He likes her. He doesn't want to like her, but he really does.

"Well, I don't have many friends here," Toby said. "So I figure if I get the people I like to get to know and like each other maybe we can have a movie group or a book club other than that shitty book club they have here on Thursday night. I taught English literature for forty years and I am sick and tired of reading romantic sagas and inspirational how-to mess. Break out the good stuff."

Rachel laughed and Stanley leaned just a little to the left so he could see them in his mirror, still waiting politely in the doorway. "I would love to join your club," she said. "You and Sadie are the only sane people here as far as I can tell."

"Don't I know it?" Toby asked. "Do you ever chew or dip?"

"Chew or dip *what?*"

"Snuff, cigar. Sometimes I take a little dip or a chew, get a good buzz. I know it's not very popular or ladylike, but I used to smoke like a stack—three packs a day and I still love to get something going in my system, you know?"

"Actually, I do know," Rachel said. "I smoked a hundred years ago."

Stanley wanted to open the door and say, *You've come a long way baby,* but even he was tired of his own show, so he just flushed and waited for them to leave. He eased the door shut and turned on the radio. He likes to listen to NPR. He likes the news and Garrison Keillor and he likes listening to classical music, the notes swaddling his mind without words, sopping up all that haunts him as he eases his tired aching body into his chair. And now he's here again. Rachel Silverman passed by earlier going wherever it is she goes every single morning and every late afternoon. He watches her move across the parking lot and then dip into the shade of the arbor. He watches until he can't see a trace of her and then he closes his eyes and allows himself to enter the house on Fifteenth and Winthrop. He walks down the carpeted hall to Ned's room, pale blue walls and the heavy pine furniture Martha picked out for the boys; he finds Ned in there studying and tells him he should take a break, they should do something fun, something they've never done before. And when they pass by his toolshed and Stanley sees where Ned has painted an airplane and written his name, he says: *Wow, would you look at that?* And he doesn't get angry at all. Really, when you back up and take a good hard look at it, there is nothing to get angry *about* and the way Ned looks at him from inside that soft kid body—a cowlick in his sweaty boy hair and a laugh that shows his teeth growing in at all angles— breaks what is left of Stanley's heart.

Notes about: Mary Grace Robertson
Born: November 19, 1912   **Died:** April 1, 2007, 7:45 p.m.
Watts Nursing Home   Holderness, New Hampshire

It was a cool and rainy week, with no promise of spring anywhere to be seen, the yard of the low-budget home void of any life—a mud field with only a few tire tracks leading in. I sat with her every now and then, nothing formal, my own need to find those Luke had requested I seek out—those he called *the lost and forgotten*. I had asked to be called when they thought she was near the end, and she clearly was, her extremeties mottled and cool to the touch. Her roommate, separated by a curtain, cried incessantly. Her belongings included a large unopened tin of Poppycock popcorn, a Christmas bow still on the top of the can, and a crocheted throw made by a group at the local Unitarian Church. Her dentures were wrapped in tissue and in her drawer, along with an old family Bible. Her name is scrawled almost illegibly in the family tree at the beginning. Mary Grace Robertson. Daughter of William and Elizabeth. Born in Portland, Maine. And there was a wallet-sized school photo—in color but clearly of another time, perhaps the seventies, given the bushy cut of his red hair and the tinted aviator glasses. On the back someone had written: *Pete age 15.* No one working there knew who he was or anything about her, other than she was a charity case, someone abandoned to a clinic like a baby left at an orphanage, years ago, her mental state never any clearer or more reactive than it was at the time of her death. Her eyes opened only once during my last visit, first filling with what seemed recognition and then closing with a long sigh. After a day of trying to hold her hand, she finally clasped her fingers around mine and squeezed and then when the roommate fell asleep and the room was silent, she died. *Think how many people die all alone,* Luke had said when listing the many rules and guidelines he wanted me to follow. *Never forget that single fact. Never forget how important it is to be there. Never forget those people.* So what is there to remember? Charity gifts. Her full given name in that nearly illegible scrawl, cool gnarled fingers like roots holding on, the kind of night that can almost convince you spring will never come again. But it will. Once upon a time there was Mary Grace Robertson—daughter of William and Elizabeth—born into this world on November 19, 1912, in Portland, Maine.

[from Joanna's notebook]

Mary Robertson

She is running and running, the field outside the window, running and running. He says, Shut up and put this in your mouth, hold these rags, idiot. Kerosene is shiny, poured like liquor out the bottle and into the ditch, where he pushes her down and says, Hold these rags, Hold these rags. She says it's Christmas, but he says it's not. She says she has a family but he says not anymore. He says hold these rags and then the field burns blue and gold, blue and gold. Somebody spoke to her once, a boy from the school came and spoke to her and left his picture. He said his momma used to know her way back, way way back when the field was just the field and her father was out in it, when the field was just a field and before all the blue and gold and nothing, just nothing when she closes her eyes and closes her ears and stops running; he reaches his hand out and she takes it. He's a boy from the school and he says, It's okay, it's okay, because he is there to help her.

Toby

TOBY TYLER CAME TO Pine Haven because she didn't have anywhere better to go. She tells people how she pinned up a map and then threw a dart to see where it landed and that is entirely true. What she doesn't tell is that she followed four darts before she got to this one, each time almost signing a lease in some retirement village and then getting cold feet. The fifth dart brought her here and just when she was having doubts she met Sadie who told how she had sent children to the library to check out *Toby Tyler* for years and years. *I love* Toby Tyler, Sadie had said, and just hearing those magic words sealed the deal. Toby had hoped for a sign and what could possibly be better than that? Not to mention the cigarette prices out there along I-95 were the cheapest she'd seen in a while.

For the most part, her life in Columbia had been good, but it was time to leave. It was getting too hard to keep up the little yard she had loved and tended for so long. The yellow maple she had planted and watched mature over a stretch of thirty years was as beautiful as ever, but she had come to dread the raking and the bagging; she feared slipping and falling even though she is still in pretty good physical shape. She goes over to the exercise room every single day and walks on the treadmill. She takes the chair exercise class even though it's pretty slow and boring for someone like her. Still, she does it, all the while doing the different kind of breathing exercises she had learned in her old yoga class where she was the oldest member by at least twenty years. She could tell it made that cute little instructor nervous every time she reared back and tried to do a camel pose to the point she finally offered to sign a piece a paper that would remove all liability if she fell out dead on the floor. This made everybody in the class laugh and then they relaxed. They threw her a going-away party after she announced the next week would be her last class and she left thinking how odd that that was the first time she learned several of their names and yet she could have called on any one of them in a crisis. If she saw them in the grocery store or pumping gas, she liked to hold her palms together in front of her heart and say *Namaste*. Everybody found that hilarious, but it was honest, too. She did honor them and that place deep within where the whole universe resides, where you let go of all those bad things that can weigh you down.

But she feared a crisis, always has, and wanted to be prepared before anything happened. Toby Tyler has always lived by the rule of wanting to see trouble before it sees her. If she can see it coming, then she is smart enough and strong enough to come up with a solution. It might not be enough to save her life or change the world, but she could come up with something. She has kept framed and hanging on her wall something given to her when her mother was dying several years ago. Toby was good to her mother, always within an hour's drive to do things for her, and somehow her mother knew not to quiz her personal life. At some point they turned a corner when her mother no longer asked if Toby had met someone or if she thought she might one day have babies. It was sweet that way, sweet the way her mother there at the end told her she loved her just the way she is, that in fact she couldn't imagine Toby any other way than just who she is. Of course her mother called her Annabelle, a beautiful name to have been given in life but not one that ever suited her. And her mother loved to talk about how they used to love *The Original Amateur Hour* with Ted Mack on Sunday nights sponsored by the Geritol wannabe—Serutan—which they always told you was *natures spelled back-wards.* Ted Mack was the first real *American Idol* and that was back when Toby had all kinds of notions in her head, one of them being that she fancied herself a singer and a dancer, kind of a Dale Evans/Gene Kelly thing she had worked out—*the tapping cowgirl,* they called her in her head. Sometimes she practiced her drishti while sitting with her mother, focusing her gaze loosely on some distant spot so that she could keep breathing and not lose her balance while slowly letting go.

She had long dreaded the day when she would not have her mother there to visit. Some of the teachers she worked with—the few she was closest to—knew she was struggling. The new kid, there to teach history while he was taking courses to get his master's degree over at USC, left something in her mailbox, the story of a rabbi hearing the world was about to be flooded and every bit of life as it had been known would be submerged, changed, gone. And then he said to his people, and Toby could just picture this all so well—she gave him a hat and long beard and inflection in his voice—he said: *Okay, my people, listen up. We have only twenty-four hours to learn how to live underwater.*

Somehow, standing there in that crowded little mailroom back of the school office, something lifted from her and she kept thinking of all the things she had already learned to live with. And maybe this was the moment she had been building up to; like the real Toby Tyler running off to join the circus, she could go anywhere and do anything. And the plan she hatched was to step down as they'd asked and to keep seeing her mother as much as she could in those final weeks, and when the time came, she would just sell her wonderful little house she loved so much and head out into the new world. It would be just like in *Lost Horizon*. She might find her own Shangri-La or that's what she told the yoga class. "I am moving north in search of paradise." They all thought that was hilarious especially when she showed them the brochure for Pine Haven with a picture of what her little cottage would look like. Now she is here, and she does love it for the most part. She thought naming their spaces was kind of silly, too, but she immediately knew what hers would be. She said the Ponderosa to make people laugh, but she always knew it would be the Little Chicken Farm, which is right there at the begin-ning of the movie version of *Lost Horizon*, which that nice boy from next door who runs the movie house said he might screen here in the recreation hall. Toby had quoted the opening to him just like she did his kid who is always hanging out with Sadie and who had been assigned to her for the naming of spaces. *In these days of wars and rumors of wars—haven't you ever dreamed of a place where there was peace and security, where living was not a struggle but a lasting delight? Of course you have. So has every man since Time began. Always the same dream. Sometimes he calls it Utopia—sometimes the Fountain of Youth—sometimes merely "that little chicken farm."*

That little girl was so amazed at how Toby had it all memorized so well because the girl herself had had a terrible time having to learn lines for a school play and she hated in Sunday school when they made you quote things from memory. She said she had been assigned something from Psalms, the one about how your anger should only endure for a moment because Joy comes in the morning, one that for some reason Toby always confused with a verse of Wordsworth's "Intimations on Immortality," much of which she could also quote. She told the girl that her recitation of the chicken farm was just the beginning. She could do the witches from *Macbeth* and Lady Macbeth, Juliet's balcony scene, the ending of *The Glass Menagerie,* several sonnets, and a truckload of Emily Dickinson. She also knew several Charlie McCarthy routines and was practiced at doing both voices; she used to have a dummy she was pretty good with, but then he started scaring her at night so she sold him when she moved. The girl laughed at that but said she could understand. She was once scared of a doll, too, and she wasn't sure why that one and not the others.

"It's just like people," Toby said. "There is something in a face that can let you know all you need to know. Or the aura, you know? I have some experience with seeing the auras. Like I once knew this really nasty fella who was short, but people thought he was even shorter than he was because he had *no* aura at all. He had a sub-aura. People would hear that fella's name and their hands would drop knee height like he might be a dwarf or a gnome." This made the child laugh. "I kid you not," Toby said.

"I'm telling you that you can look at a person and most likely see all you need to know."

"You think?" The girl was in the throes of an acne outbreak and boy did Toby remember *that;* who doesn't, other than those lucky enough not to have been there? All those injected hormones out in the world are forcing children to cycle through things way too fast.

"Yeah, like in your face, I see a beautiful soul with great capabilities of memorization." And then she went on to teach the girl how to memorize, how you can sing just about all of Emily Dickinson to "The Yellow Rose of Texas" and Bible verses are much easier when you understand in clear contemporary English what is really being said. For instance, her verse was kind of like "Don't get mad, get Glad" (like the commercial)—you're crying your fanny off right now but tomorrow it'll all be behind you. *Let the sun shine.* Toby waved her arms and sang like she was in the cast of *Hair.*

"Joy in the Morning," Toby told her was used for the title of a book and then there was a movie of the same title starring Dr. Kildaire and Yvette Mimieux. "I had the biggest crush on her," Toby told the girl, and then added, "You know what I mean; I wanted to look like her."

"Yeah, I want to look like Lady Gaga," Abby said, and laughed; she was surprised that Toby knows who that is. But you can't just go from years of living with kids to then knowing nothing at all. It would be too much of a shock to the system. She has a television; she reads magazines. She cares what is going on out there even when it's not very pretty. Toby told Abby to slap some pork chops on her head and wrap herself in beef jerky and she'd be a dead ringer. By the end of that day, the child had her verse memorized and also could sing *I died for beauty but was scarce / Adjusted in the Tomb / When One who died for truth was lain / In an adjoining room.*

"Aren't you kinda young to live here?" Abby asked.

"I'm the youngest of the oldest, that's true," she said. "But I have always been a little ahead of the others my age, you know?"

Now she takes a stroll over to the main building to find some of the others. It's a high-class joint in many ways. She never in her life stopped what she was doing for formal meals and for tea in the afternoon, but now she absolutely loves it. It ends up getting kind of heated sometimes, which is what she loves best. People fight over chairs, things like that, things they taught you not to do in kindergarten, and yet everybody has circled right back around to it. *I want to sit with so-and-so. That's my chair. You're in my chair. Wah-wah.* Marge Walker always gets there early and plants her dressed-to-the-nines fanny in the big red leather wingback like she's the queen. Often Marge is on a rant about how she's tired of prisoners being treated like vacationers with hardworking taxpayers footing the bill, how those prisoners get to eat three meals a day and watch television and how she is also sick and tired of the foreigners taking up space in the produce section.

"The people?" Toby once asked.

"No. I mean all that mess that comes from Mexico or wherever, ten kinds of peppers nobody ever heard of," her whole mouth twisted bitterly with the words. "Who wants that old mess?"

"Maybe I would," one of the women who is on the kitchen staff said, and introduced herself as Mrs. Lopez. Toby told her not to be offended, Marge was someone who had been surprised that Lois Flowers had still not lost weight even with cancer.

Today Marge is saying how she isn't going to sign a thing that turns anything over to her children. She said if they want to circle in like vultures for her money, so be it, but she plans to spend every single cent to stay alive as long as she possibly can. "I'm going to live so long they'll be sorry."

Toby asks Joanna, the hospice woman, what got Marge going and apparently it was that one of her sons was wanting power of attorney. Marge overheard and turned to Toby.

"He is in financial trouble himself," she says. "He's wanting his piece of the pie early. Now I do not mind helping my children. That is what my husband and I agreed on many years ago, but trying to take over my kingdom is not the way to go about it. "

"Good for you," Toby says.

"If I start feeling like somebody is pushing me out before it's time for me to leave, it makes me mad as hell and I will plant my feet and say I am *not* going."

Sadie laughs to hear Marge cuss; they all do.

"I'm gonna live as long as I possibly can just to spite him. I want everything artificial that can be given to me for as long as there's a pulse. Breath, food, the works. Mr. Walker and I worked hard all those years and I'll be"—she paused, sputtering and stumbling over the *d* at the tip of her tongue—"durned if I let them hover like vultures."

"I do not want to linger," Sadie says.

"Well, that's because you don't have greedy, stingy children. I sat up just last night adding up what I saved them in babysitting hours and meals eaten and clothes washed."

"You go, girl," Toby waves to Abby, who is sitting there beside Sadie. Poor child's dog is still missing and she is heartbroken so this laughing is good. "But damn, Marge, slow it all down, okay? 'Cause you're making me want to like you."

"Well, I don't know if I want *you* to like me." Marge opens her scrapbook, an amazing document for sure, every murder committed in the county for the past decade followed to a tee. She said it had begun as a way to keep up with her husband's career and then her son's. Her husband had a huge murder case nearly thirty years ago in which he sent a man to the chair for butchering his wife and child. *He showed him who was in charge,* Marge liked to say, and she had many times held the group spellbound with the horrible details of that case and how brave Judge Henry Walker had always been, not the least bit worried or intimidated by threats. *Henry Walker had a reputation unlike anyone else in this area,* she said. *Henry Walker was a moral man unlike his son who seems a little bit too interested in my purse.* Now she turns to a page about an awful murder out in the county where a man drove out to his girlfriend's mama's trailer and killed everybody there, even the dog. She points to the mug shot of the boyfriend who did the killing. "My son is representing him." She looks up. "All the more reason not to give him any money."

"That's his job," Stanley Stone says. "He's the defense attorney and a damn good one, it seems." Stanley is a total mystery—sometimes clear as a bell and then off the rail and mean as a snake like the other day. "Toby, why don't you do something so she'll shut up."

"Do a recitation," Abby says.

"Or tell us what makes you mad," Marge says, and flips the page to a big headline that says MURDER SUICIDE IN SOUTH CAROLINA. "What makes someone *like you* angry."

"Cat fight," Stanley says. "Go put on your bikinis and let's get muddy."

"There's a lot that makes me mad. Like I have an aversion to the moochers and leachers, the seekers and glommers of your soul," Toby says, and Sadie says that sounds a little like the Sermon on the Mount. "And"—Toby pauses and takes a deep breath—"people like you make me mad, but right now I'd rather talk about something I think is worth talking about. How about that? Like I can tell you things about my life as a teacher—a damn good teacher, too—and how I told those young girls, don't let me hear you complaining about your periods anymore 'cause if you're not having one it means one of two things. Either some boy's been parking overtime where he should've pulled out or you're up to no good with your own precious bodies, starving and vomiting and messing up nature's beautiful patterns." She stops and goes to adjust the tubes leading to Lorice Boone's oxygen tank. She tells Lorice that's the payment for all those years smoking, that she herself might need oxygen one of these days because she also smoked like a fiend for many years. Yes, that was the price for having looked so sexy with a fag hanging from her lips while coaching the girls' tennis team. "And, yes, I said *fag* 'cause it used to just mean a cigarette." She looks at Abby and pretends to take a deep draw and exhale like she might be Bette Davis. "And there's something else that gets my blood boiling, I'm so goddamned tired of all the words getting taken and twisted—what is that all about? I found that I was having a harder and harder time keeping up with the new slang the kids were using—*bad* and *sick* for good—things like that."

"And the use of *dig* made such good sense way back when,"

Rachel Silverman pipes up. She has dirt and straw all over the back of her pants like she might've been stretched out on the ground. "And *bread, dough.*" That Rachel is as tough and cynical as they come. Toby adores her and would love nothing better than to be her best friend.

"What about *dish,*" Stanley says and eyes Rachel's body up and down. "Or *puss.*"

"What about *pop?*" Rachel aims an imaginary gun at him.

"That would make me"—he pauses—"*stiff.*" He blows a kiss her way.

"I am going to report this X-rated mess and a child sitting here in your presence." Marge slams her scrapbook shut and stands up. "You all are damned to hell as far as I can tell except those two." She points at the sisters, one crocheting and the other snoozing. "Blessed are the sweet and simple."

"Wait, Marge, before I completely don't like you again," Toby says. "I can translate. He pointed to her face and she acted like she was going to kill him and then that would make him dead."

"Hey, that's cool," Abby says. "That's what you did with the Bible verse."

"She what?" Marge says, but Stanley interrupts with *croak* and *hooch* and *keister.*

"I'm partial to *groovy* myself." Stanley's hair is standing all out from his head like he might have stuck his finger in a socket and his shirt is buttoned wrong so one side is hanging longer than the other. He has the cover of that Herb Alpert and the Tijuana Brass album he plays nonstop and asks who would like to be the lucky *damsel* to wear a whipped-cream *frock* like the one on the cover.

"Damsel! Frock!" Sadie laughs and wheezes. "Those are some

ancient words. Have you ever even heard those words, sweetie?" She pats Abby's hand and holds on tight, and when the room quiets down from Stanley's mess, Toby continues.

"I told those girls, someday you'll be wishing for your period and I don't just mean to make sure you aren't pregnant—*knocked up*—and they looked at me with their mouths all screwed up like I was stupid and what could I possibly mean.

"I said when you get old like *moi* here"—she slaps her chest and grimaces, pulls her pants leg up over the top of her boots to show a white scaly-looking leg—"I told 'em, I said, everything stops—the faucet goes off. It's like the scene in *Lost Horizon* that I had them watch in English class after reading the novel. I said, you want some fantasy? A real stretch of the imagination and yet something that still is real in all the right ways? I had them read *Spoon River Anthology* and *The Glass Menagerie* and *Our Town* because they could read the parts aloud and pretend they were there. At first they were silly and awkward, but the ones who got it *got it*. They are still young enough that sometimes you can snag one or two and set them on a new course before they dive back into those flimsy old paperbacks modeled after some silly television show or, most recently—like the past several years—something with wizards and trolls and vampires. But I made them remember that one scene in the movie where the beautiful woman is taken from Shangri-La and, poof, dries up to an old brown potato chip like what you used to find down in the bottom of the bag. Lays and most of them have corrected this, which is a shame because it was that old brown crunchy one there at the bottom that made me enjoy all the others more, you know? Like I pointed out to them you need to enjoy those smooth, pretty faces and natural-colored thick hair and breasts that are healthy and cancer free and don't pull you down to Hades when you stand up, or as Emily Dickinson might say, *I like a look of Agony / Because I know it's true*. True! Real!"

"You were some teacher," Rachel says, and nods to Abby who is sitting there soaking it all up like a sponge. "I hope you have some teachers as good as she was. Good for you, Toby. I'm surprised they let you retire."

"She was forced to retire," Marge says. "And her name's not Toby. She made that up when she moved in out here and everybody knows it."

"Well, I don't know it," Rachel says. "All I know is what I learned when I met her and I learned her name is Toby. And I still say she must have been some kind of wonderful teacher, the kind of teacher children would benefit from having."

"The jury's still out on that," Toby says. "Though yes, I think I did a fine job. I think I was a really great teacher."

"And you're so modest," Marge says. "And no telling what you were *teaching* there in the locker room with those young girls."

"I smell a cat fight," Stanley says.

"You know what? You can't hurt me anymore than I have already been hurt in life so just give it up. You're ignorant and I'd rather be who I am and smart than who you are and ignorant."

"Who you are is a sin."

"Well, it's nobody's goddamned business who I am, Marge, and it's official—I am back to not liking you at all. And you better watch out is what I'm saying to you." Toby pats her fanny pack like there is something in it and then points her finger like a gun, says *pow, pop,* and then blows the tip of her finger. "You better watch out 'cause what have I got to lose? I didn't *have* to come live here like you. I can still drive, still do pretty much anything I want to do, which is why I'm in an independent cottage and not over here in the next tier of living." She puts her hand up to her mouth and then apologizes to Stanley, Rachel, and Sadie. "No offense."

"None taken." Stanley acts like he's shaking something, either a martini or a can of Reddi-wip since he's so focused on that picture of a woman with a whipped-cream dress. "We all know we're has-beens."

"Speak for yourself," Rachel says.

"I got all kinds of rules for good living and she doesn't match any of them," Toby says. "For instance, I say you should be kind to others. I say 'tis better to remain silent and be thought a fool than to open one's mouth and remove all doubt.' I say your pee should always run clear, which means you got to drink a lot throughout the whole day to keep yourself pure and cleansed."

"The question is *what* you drink," Marge says, and gets several laughs from the peanut gallery. She has settled back into her big chair, scared to death someone else will sit there, and reopened her scrapbook. No doubt about it, she's done some fine documenting of all the mayhem and murder in the county. She has a real talent, a real eye for the macabre, which Toby does admire, but that doesn't mean she has to like her.

"Always take the stairs," Toby says because Marge is always using the elevator, and then turns to Sadie. "Unless you can't, of course. Let's see. Stretch your spine each day like you're wringing out a sponge—just sit in a chair and go from side to side like this." She demonstrates and they hear her back pop. "And think of at least one thing that makes you laugh loud and long."

"For me it's just an orgasm a day," Stanley says, and Sadie immediately puts a finger up to her lips since Abby is sitting there so he lowers his voice and whispers, which makes the girl laugh. "Rain or shine. Every day."

"There you go," Toby says. "That's the kind of laughing I mean, but none of us want to dwell too long on that image, do we? No sirree, we sure don't. But I'll tell you, I was a good teacher and it only started getting hard for me when everything changed. Like one day I was a normal teacher . . ."

Marge sighs and shifts around in her seat until Stanley asks does she have to use the bathroom or does she have Saint Vitus? Sadie whispers something about worms and needing to check her bottom, which makes several people giggle and makes Marge rise up like a cobra, but Toby can't even stop to laugh.

"Then next thing I knew the children were coming in with names like Bandana and Eurasia and Montpelier. And I said, those are things and places, children, and you are people. What on earth is going on? And there were names I couldn't even pronounce and I can guaran-damn-tee you that you don't readily go calling names you can't say—I'm looking for the Johns and Bills and Toms and they just weren't there anymore. I had Lucaramel and Tahitia only it was pronounced Ta-HI-shee-Ah. I had to write a phonetic spelling alongside almost every child's name by the time I retired."

"Got fired," Marge says. "But I was a teacher long ago, too, and I so know what you are talking about. I hated multiculturalism."

"That's not what I said," Toby says. "I don't hate multiculturalism. You are worse than FOX News."

"I think you do."

"It was the white ones, too. It was equal opportunity weird names. I'd hear mommas calling them in and it sounded like they were hawkers for a law firm: Parker, Ramsey, and Tate! Parker, Ramsey, and Tate! And next thing you know up run three little towheads like dandelion puffs, all decked out in little sailor suits."

"You are describing my grandchildren who were just here," Marge says. "How dare you use their names."

"I did it because their daddy is trying to get you to die early so he can have all your money. He wants to buy those children a boat to go with their outfits."

"You did it because you are the word that means a female dog." Marge is red in the face, jowls quivering. "People like you are always frustrated now, aren't you?"

"Only by *people like you*—the judges and the juries. Nothing about me has slipped. I just decided to move on in here early and get a good hard look at where I'm headed." She unzips her fanny pack but doesn't reach in. She has got a little tin of Skoal in there and cannot wait to get a bit of it up against her gum. She will be buzzing like a cowgirl riding the range and she cannot wait. *Welcome home tapping cowgirl, where have you been?* "And when I look at *some* of you, I can tell it ain't a pretty sight," she says. Her hands are shaking and she feels like she might cry, which makes her furious.

"Be sure your sins will reveal themselves."

"Good," Toby says. "I hope so. I am so tired of people like you—snowflake, lily white, holy roller"—she pauses looking over at Abby but then deciding to go for broke—"*asshole*—who hear I did a little coaching and want to stick a great big stereotype on me, that I'm a certain way. You going to point to Rachel there and say she's stingy or something about her *beezer*, her *schnoz* because that's a stereotype or are you going to point over there at Suzie Mitchell and Mr. McIntyre and say they must be eating some fried chicken and watermelon all day while waiting on a welfare check? And Lottie there and Mrs. Locklear better stay away from the fire water. Mr. McIntyre has a tail and Rachel Silverman has horns on her head."

"I would find that immensely attractive," Stanley Stone says. "Her horns, that is, not his tail. No offense." He nods at Mr. McIntyre who says none taken, all the while reaching his hand to rub the base of his spine to make certain there is nothing there.

"Well, first I am a person," Toby continues. "I am a human, a woman; I was an English teacher and a bit of an amateur writer myself, but I'll tell you things went so far off course I just didn't even know where I was anymore. I think it was the beginning of the end, too. What once was generous compassion for high school students with all their angst and crap going on turned into pure agitation and fury. I didn't get frustrated by who I am; I got frustrated by what they were reading and wanting to write about. I said, you're too smart for all this shit. Dwarves and wizards and gnomes and vampires—big blue aliens with tails like monkeys. I said what I wouldn't give for a good old-fashioned story about somebody losing his or her virginity or getting an abortion— Grandma died and for the first time I knew I was mortal or what about the one where the boy doesn't want to kill a deer, but Granddaddy makes him so he can be a man. I was wanting to write something myself and it was dying to get out of my head but couldn't find the door it was all so plugged up with that malarkey."

"*Malarkey* is a fine old word," Stanley says. "I want to know the derivation of malarkey."

"I think of my head as my apartment," Toby says because she is on a roll now, oh yeah; full speed ahead and that Abby soaking it up like a sponge and that is good. She won't hear any of this in school, which is a disgrace. "I have lived up here in my head my whole life. I climb those steps every day and there is always a little voice saying, *Welcome home, Toby. Come on in girl, you made it one more day.*"

"I do something very similar," Sadie says, and Rachel nods. "You know I do. Why Stanley and I were doing it just recently, weren't we?" She nods and finally Stanley looks up and nods back, smiles at her and then at Rachel. They look at each other a little longer than normal until he grins, which makes her turn away. There is some chemistry between those two and Toby is hoping to stir it even if he is demented much of the time.

"Which is why"—she glares at Marge—"it doesn't really matter where I live. The building and walls where I stay is just the foyer to where I really live."

"Foy *ay*," Marge corrects. "Some English teacher."

"Whatever, look it up. I say foy *yer*. But I didn't want to have to give it all up. I had worked so hard and all I was longing for was some whining little boy who didn't want to kill a deer. I was craving one in fact, would've loved him and given him an instant A. Where did all the orphans go? Jane and Oliver and Pip? It's an honorable and very dramatic position. And the girl who is upset to have a period. Where did she go? Or the one all torn up about losing her virginity? Where did she go? If they're still out there, they're keeping a low profile and hiding from all those getting boobs for Christmas and graduation and making themselves up to look thirty."

"Yes," Abby says. "That's all some girls talk about. That's all they want, too, boobs and a boyfriend."

"Well, I'll tell you what I wanted. I wanted dead deers and dead grandparents and busted condoms. I wanted anything other than a zombie or a shape-shifting demon wolf coyote bullshit. What am I to do with a bunch of aliens at Armageddon?

"I'd run like hell," Mr. McIntyre said, and the sisters laughed and laughed, said they would run, too.

"Toby? Honey, I think you might need to settle down," Sadie says. "This is not good for you. It's in the past, remember? And now you are traveling all over the world on vacation and riding horses and such. Remember? And it's recess now. Sit up straight and sip your tea." Sadie is sweet and Toby loves her to death, but she still can't stop. She has thought these things for a long long time and now it feels so good like opening Pandora's box and getting rid of all that bad stuff.

"Some of them said about their papers, *I meant to be vague,* like that might excuse something that didn't make a goddamned bit of sense. Or the one who said I just didn't *get* what he was doing because it's so brilliant. The aliens are from *Erewhon,* get it? And I said, Oh yeah, I get it and so did Samuel Butler who named a novel that over a hundred years ago and I suspect might have known how to write a sentence, too. Read and if you aren't going to read at least do your Googling and maybe try to at least read *about* what has actually been written! I took my work seriously and where did it get me? Where? Where?"

"Fired would be my guess."

"Yes, that's right," she turns, and steps toward Marge, Stanley meowing in the background. "Fired. There I was asking for a little reality and who wouldn't be after Columbine? What teacher on the planet after Virginia Tech didn't study her classroom windows and doors and the desk arrangements and hatch some plan for how she would protect all those young bodies, even the ones that got on her last goddamned nerve!"

"And then this one boy, meaning to push my button, this one boy named something like Montreal Fedora offered up some literary criticism on the death of Julius Caesar. He said and I quote: 'Them dudes was mean as shit, weren't they?'"

"And I said '*Those* dudes *were* mean as shit.' That is what I got in trouble for. Some kid in there, probably Parker, Ramsey, or Tate went home and tattled, *not* about what was being discussed in class but that the teacher said *shit.* 'Ms. Tyler, come to the office, please,'" she mimics. "'Ms. Tyler, please come to the office.'"

"This had happened many times. I made a notch on my desk in fact every time it happened and one whole side looked like a fine-tooth comb. My principal was about fourteen and had never read Shakespeare. How do I know? I asked him one day. In that moment when I needed him on my side, I almost wished that I had not done that or that I had been a teacher who did not argue against prayer in my class, which I had done for years, or did not allow hats, but what in the hell did I care if they wore hats? Some of them might have been sporting bad haircuts they were ashamed of or keeping their lice locked in, what did I care? I didn't tell on kids who refused to stand for the Pledge of Allegiance either. I figured we'd have plenty of battles to fight and I needed to choose the most important. I mean these are humans growing up and witnessing the Uterus as a competitive sporting arena. Who would've ever thought that? Irresponsible birth control will get you a TV show and a magazine cover. Octo, Sexto, Moron. Goddamn."

"You should've been fired a century ago."

"*Et tu,* Marge? I said to my principal, the boy king, I asked him, If I retire like you say I have to, who will teach these children? Who will guard the gate? Who can promise me they'll tell the boys to keep their trousers zipped and tell the girls not to go promising things they do not intend to deliver. Who will teach birth control? Who will teach the value of literature? I said, Who will tell them nobody gives a shit about how dwarves and trolls have sex? If they had, the Brothers Grimm would have figured it out and already done it. They had every opportunity."

"What I wouldn't have given for a stained soul. One good stained soul story. Murder, suicide, adultery, a simple lie or betrayal. I wanted a stain or a tear in a soul and I wanted a vivid description of some place in the world that leaves me feeling like I was there. Like when Sadie tells us about her kitchen or when she takes us to places like India and Scotland. I mean we can all think of a place and we all have stains on our souls."

"Speak for yourself."

"I am. I am speaking for myself and you know what? I am proud to say that I have done so for most of my life. It might not have amounted to much, but I did my best. And these children with their new words and crazy names, God help them and love them, they are the next frontier and we have to trust that something good will happen. That someone like Abby there will remember me on this day and all that I have said."

"I promise and swear that I will," Abby says, and raises her pure sweet hand. It makes Toby feel like she might cry and she is already running short on breath and needs to pee like a racehorse.

"Thank you sweetheart," she says. "You can save this world, Abby. You can make a difference." She heads off to her room before anybody can see her cry. She waves her hand over her head, a signal that it ain't over. She hears Marge say *good riddance.* She hears Stanley say, *I love a woman with a good set of horns.*

"Parents have also questioned your *character,*" the boy principal said that day in his office. He chose his word very carefully and he could not make eye contact.

"Oh really."

"Yes."

"And what is it they question? All these years and this is what I come to?" She stood still, waiting, and he still did not look up at her. She could hear students jumping up to peek in the high window of the door; she could hear bus duty announcements on the PA system and still he did not look up, his hand resting on a typewritten letter, a file folder with her name on it.

"A student reported you looked at her inappropriately."

"Who said that?"

"I'd rather not say just yet," he said to the blotter on his desk. "Does anything come to mind you'd like to say?"

"Sure. I say a lot of things and give them a lot of looks and who wouldn't? Bare butt cracks with underwear that's nothing more than a piece of floss running through. You want me to act like it's okay for a young educated woman to squat and give a show? Is that what you would do? Sit there and watch while the young men are so torn, some looking away in embarrassment and others filling their eyeballs and then their pockets. All I did was say, *Where is your self-respect, honey?* Is it because I said *honey?* Was I wrong to call her *honey?* If so, let's blame the South; let's blame generations of sweet talk and euphemism."

PEOPLE LIKE YOU, Marge had said. *People like you.* Like anyone even knows who she really is. No, the only thing she agrees with Marge about is the business about living as long as you can. Sometimes your only chance to beat out a prejudice is to outlive it. And she may not be able to live long enough for everything to be fixed and accepted, but she has already lived to see so much good change. And when all is said and done, that's all that really matters, that's all that is really important. She was a good teacher. She was a good daughter. She has some good friends and once upon a time she even knew real love. She drinks lots of water every day and she can recite important literature at the drop of a hat. She can climb the stairs of her head and give a recitation at any time of day or night. She has a good strong pulse and a heart like a V-8 engine. She has found the secret to living underwater. She has found her own Little Chicken Farm and if she had the chance to do it all over again, she would not ask for a different life at all. She has loved her life. But what she would ask is to be born into a different world; she would ask for an honest and accepting world. *This is my letter to the world / That never wrote to me.* Damn right, Emily, damn right.

Notes about: Suzanne O'Toole Sullivan
Born: June 09, 1966   **Died:** April 29, 2007   5:22 pm
Holderness, New Hampshire

Her house was filled with pink—ribbons and hats and sashes—and she faithfully wore the Red Sox cap her son gave her when she first got sick. She talked nonstop—telling stories and laughing or belting out a song—so that everyone in the room was put at ease. She had two young children and her bedroom was filled with their cards and drawings. She said that her husband didn't know what to do, was not able to talk to her, and could only hold her hand in the most courteous way. He kissed her head as he did those of their children. They had not made love since her diagnosis and she suspected they never would again. Instead he brought her flowers every day and her first request when I arrived was that I please remove the dead and wilted ones. "I wish he could be himself again," she said.

She grew up just an hour away and was a speech pathologist. She said she loved her work and had missed it. She grew up in a big family—the baby of six—and so she was used to lots of noise. Noise and sound were a comfort to her, but every now and then she liked to be all alone. She liked to be underwater—loved to scuba dive—and as a kid she had loved to hop bareback on her horse, Charlie, and ride and ride until all she was hearing was hooves and her own heart. She said her own children have no speech problems that she had heard but that her husband was someone who always tripped on *R*s with a *W* sound if he talked too fast, which lately—ever since she got sick—he had done constantly.

On this day, as soon as Michael (four) and Clarissa (seven) left the room, she began to let go. I reached for the phone to call her husband—it was time for him to get home—but she put her hand on mine and shook her head no. We could hear Bugs Bunny in the next room and she smiled when Elmer Fudd said "you wascal wabbit." Her eyebrows lifted as she listened, the cartoon, the laughter, and finally there was the sound of the front door and a chorus of the kids running to greet her husband.

"I'm home," he called. "I'm here," and with the sound of him rushing to her, and the shrill laughter of their children, she let go.

And I let go in a way we are not supposed to do. I was so aware of myself as an outsider as I watched the three of them hover beside her, the children studying me the way they might an animal at the zoo. I was so aware of how this experience separated them from the rest of the world in a way that could not be touched. It just had to be sealed and, when possible, set aside in a very safe place. And heaven help the bighearted soul in their future who might be able to come in and fill the space and be a part of their lives. That's what I was thinking. I was thinking too much about myself and so I failed the assignment. I broke so many rules. I got personal. I got attached. And what's more, Suzanne Sullivan knew this; she was the person in control the whole while. She was the one protecting the rest of us. Bugs Bunny will always remind me. Bugs Bunny and red roosters and the high-pitched squeals of excited children, and if I ever again make love in a way that means something to me, I will be so grateful. I will not take it for granted.

[from Joanna's notebook]

Suzanne Sullivan

Eh, what's up, Doc? You wotten wabbit you. She doesn't want to go. She does not want to go. She thinks of the sound waves words and laughter out of the television, through the doorway and down the hall, bending around the corner and into her room where the woman sits so fearfully you can smell her anxiety, you can hear it, a dull dreading, a dull thumping, rhythmic and deep like music. She hears the Beatles and Vivaldi and the Sesame Street *song, jump rope rhymes and hymns and wind against the chimes hanging on their porch. Their porch. This is their house and they have children and a dog and Bugs Bunny has been there her whole life, never aging, never letting Elmer win, always fading out in that circle at the end of the show. The red rooster ran down the road. The wed woosta wan and wan and wan, birds and wings and keys and hooves, thumping and pounding, Charlie's body wet beneath her as she races home, that glorious horse smell rising up, lingering when she leans forward and hugs his big strong neck, and all she can see is the green of the fields and the wide open sky and all she can hear is the pounding of hooves, galloping and galloping and galloping.*

Rachel

RACHEL SILVERMAN HIT A point in her marriage when she knew that it was her only chance to leave. It was that clear to her, a passageway closing like an artery constricting or a door swinging and locking in place. It was only a matter of time before age and retirement, illness and diagnosis and necessary care, would shift the whole world like those here at Pine Haven who get moved into another building or wing—from living to assisted living to nursing care or the memory unit where they wander within the safety of a confined space. All of life builds and grows and then you hit the peak—often unaware that you have reached it—and then you start thinking about downsizing, down down down. One day you are independent and thriving and then you are bedridden and surrounded by the smells and sounds of those who will never venture outside again and all that falls between the two blurs like the view from a passing train. It's why she wanders down the halls of the nursing unit every day, responding to the hands that reach for her, the cloudy tearful eyes, the cries and murmurs of nonsense, the stench of what's left in a body and the sounds of medical equipment, bells and buzzers. This is also life. She comes and walks these halls to remind herself. This is life.

One day she was leaning out that apartment window, smooth young arms waving to acquaintances on the street below, and then there was an emptiness that she filled with Joe—years when she felt on the verge of leaving, changing, starting over—but then didn't. She had missed her chance; one minute it seemed like there was plenty of time to decide and then there wasn't.

She and Art were in the city, picking up groceries, getting things from the cleaners, chores they had done together for years and she saw it there in his stooped profile and sluggish turn. It was coming—something was coming—and her thoughts of how she would someday slip away and into another life were gone. Joe was already in her past; life had taken him back to his wife and children and there was no room for her. They had promised that they would keep meeting, stay in touch, but of course that was not possible.

But that day in the grocery, she glimpsed the end. It was one of those times in life when everything comes clear like a spotlight turning on. Art was not healthy, and though they had not made love in years, she did love him as a friend and as a human. She was a lot of things, but unkind was not one of them, and how could you leave someone in a weakened state. And sure enough she was right and then she was there—the doctors' appointments and procedures and medicines, a long slow decline into those final days when it occurred to her that the window was about to fly open again. She had forgotten it could or that it ever would again and as people came to tell Art good-bye, cars lining the blocks surrounding their home in Lexington, the thought started to burn and glow every time someone whispered, "What will she do? Where will she go?" Interesting what feels like home. Nothing had felt right since that very first apartment in the city, and when Sadie suggests that they imagine themselves back in a place they used to inhabit, this is where Rachel goes first. She opens the windows of that front bay, hears the noises in the street, smells the river.

So the window was about to fly open again and then she knew. When Art died, she would leave and move as close to Joe as she could get. She wouldn't care what anyone chose to do with her body or ashes at the other end, it was now that mattered, and when Art died, it was already decided what she would do next. He told her she had been a good wife and of course she resisted the urge to confess all the ways she had not. He told her he was sorry they never had children, sorry to leave her alone with no family whatsoever, and she didn't scream about adoption as she had so many times through the years, didn't remind him that *he* was the one who prevented a child coming into their lives. The fights and resentments of their whole marriage went away then, as if dissolving in the air around her, and she did feel the air change, just as the young woman who often sits bedside with the dying told her it does. Though Rachel would never tell a living soul, she booked her flight to North Carolina that very same day.

She went out for coffee and all the rest she would need to sit shiva and while she was out walked right into a travel agent's office and made a reservation. It was a crazy thing and it made her feel both guilty and wonderful, but she's sure to this day that was when her spine began shifting and dissolving, osteoporosis settling in. Punishment for her hurry? Punishment for not waiting until after his burial when she had carried out his last requests?

He had told her very specifically what he wanted—the briefest time of shiva but within that time full observance of those rituals his parents and grandparents had honored. She draped the mirrors and removed her shoes. She left the door unlocked for friends and neighbors to come and go without knocking. Art had talked about how historically the death of someone presented a new way of telling time, a before and after; it was a time to catalog that life and ponder emotions like *guilt or shame or regret or anger.* It had been hard to look him in the eye as he said those words and it was even hard to recall them without flinching because already everything had shifted even though she cautioned and reminded herself how foolish it was to feel this way. After all, Joe was dead, too, yet in her mind it was like he would be there to greet her, that somehow the light and air of his childhood world would once again let her see and touch him. And though she also would hate to cave to superstition, it was hard for her not to believe that some foul joke had been played on her, weakening her spine in such a way that in a few more years she would likely be misshapen like so many others, left bent and staring into her own heart. All her life she was independent and proud of it, standing tall with her head held up high, and now she is rapidly being forced inward. For all of her outspokenness she had lived a lie and still is.

And now she is here: Fulton, North Carolina, and sitting beside his grave. He's in the newer part and except for morning and late afternoon, his grave bakes in the summer sun, the grass around him and Rosemary all scorched and dry. When she arrived last fall, mere days after the unveiling of Art's stone and the closing on their house, there was a plastic pot of yellow chrysanthemums that dried up and then sat there dead all through Christmas and spring. She finally moved the pot and hid it up under a big shrub, but she didn't feel she could replace it with something pretty, not yet. One day soon, she will, though. She even has a fantasy of sooner or later running into one of his children and explaining that she is an old friend of his and would love to help tend his grave if that is okay with them.

It was hard to talk in the beginning because Rosemary was present, too, but then Rachel finally decided that if indeed Joe and Rosemary are out there watching and listening, they know that she is here with the best of intentions and with genuine love. Joe had told her that he'd like to be cremated and half of him—she remembers his very words—*put in the Saxon River down at Mulligan's Beach where that old pavilion had been and the other half taken and thrown off the end of Johnnie Mercer's Pier down at Wrightsville Beach where I once caught an enormous cobia, so big they took my photo and put it in the paper.* But he is here, under the hard-baked dirt, with a very modest headstone beside the wife *loving and devoted.* Rachel has noticed that people get lazy about death and the wishes of their loved ones. A standard routine run of the mill funeral instead of all the sorts of special requests like those Toby and Sadie talk and laugh about many evenings. Sadie wants everyone to sing "We Gather Together" because it reminds her of the last time she stood beside Horace and held his hand. They were standing in the same church where they got married and the only difference, Sadie said, is that the church had gone modern with big new furniture and some suspended microphones. "But Horace looked exactly the same," she said. "He needed to trim some fuzz around his ears, but otherwise he looked exactly the same."

Toby said she wants everyone to recite a line from a piece of literature they love and that fool Stanley said he would be quoting some erotica. "In fact," he'd said, "why don't I begin practicing by reading a little to some choice damsels this very night."

"Whoa, now," Toby had said. "You aren't getting rid of me that fast! Hold your horses there, big fella. Besides, good chance I'll be the one burying you."

He said that in that case she could read erotica for him. It made Rachel laugh in spite of herself. She tries to ignore him, but it's hard to do a lot of the time. Such a fool. Handsome and still quite fit but an absolute fool.

Now Rachel tells Rosemary she's sorry if she ever hurt her. "I was like a trapped bird in those days," she says. "I was beating my wings and the window was closing, you know? I didn't realize how panicked I was until I met Joe that summer and everything changed. I had gotten used to living in the dark when suddenly the drapes swung back and I felt young again. I did think of you and I felt guilty, just not enough to sacrifice and give up what I was finally feeling. It's a terrible admission, but there it is. I hope you had a secret, too, Rosemary. I like to think you did. I wish we could zoom from our lives and see the great big picture. It might make more sense.

"I was foolish in many ways though I thought I was so smart and sophisticated. I fancied myself a Katharine Graham type. That's the kind of woman I aspired to, which my husband appreciated. He admired strong, intelligent women. And then, Joe, well, you know Joe. He was a wave of testosterone, something I had never encountered. In fact, I was ashamed that I found him so attractive.

"A big change I notice in myself now is that I have no fear and it feels good. It is comforting. It is as close to religion as I likely have ever been. This readiness, this satisfaction, this love. Dear God, sweetheart, look at me, sitting in the cemetery talking like we were back in our dark corner in the Clover Den. I doubt if Rosemary ever went there—she was in Boston for such a short time, but I suspect you would have liked it, Rosemary. I suspect I would have liked you and you, me. Isn't that odd to imagine? And you both would have liked Art. He was a fine man. I think what makes me so unafraid is that most everyone I have cared about is gone. My parents died long ago and my brother has been gone for over a decade. So many of my colleagues are gone. In many ways, I am more with the dead than I am with the living. It's why I need to hold their hands and seek their eyes. And yes, it smells awful and the equipment noise is a cacophony that sticks in your head and makes you want to scream. But I am so drawn to them, drawn to the descriptions I used to hear young doctors joke about—their bodies reverting back to fetus position, mouths permanently fixed in an O, their feces-stained hands curled into fists as they call out names of those lost to them. Art and I had several young doctor friends who talked about those *circling the drain*. I laughed along with the others. But I don't laugh now. Now I try to uncurl their stained fists and rest my hands there; I try to make contact, and the times I do, I am filled with a sense of love and purpose. I am a sister, a mother, a child. I am someone who cares.

"You know more than anyone, Joe, that I have never been religious. The closest I came to religion was my brother's bar mitzvah—they didn't do that for girls like they do now. He practiced and practiced, and by way of that, I memorized his parts, too.

Remember, Joe? I did it for you one night when we drove down to Gloucester? I had to teach you how to say it—*Glosstah.* I could do my brother's whole *haftorah,* though I'm not sure I could do it these days. There is a lot lost in my head that I can't locate, but it was from the scripture about Miriam getting leprosy as a punishment for asking questions and I remember being disgusted by the way the men always got the good parts like taking dictation from God and parting the Red Sea while the woman gets leprosy for being curious and seeking justice. Still, my brother did a good job and my parents were very proud and we feasted afterward. I had a new dress for the services, navy voile with a white lace collar."

She stretches her legs out and leans against a neighboring headstone so dark with mildew it's hard to read the name. She tells him how she can't wait to see his childhood home, how like an archaeologist she is hoping to find a trace of him. She is telling how glad she is to have moved near him when she looks up and sees the pedicure girl, C.J., standing there watching her.

"Hey." The girl blows a stream of smoke off to the side.

"Hey yourself."

"Were you talking to those people?" she asks, and Rachel shrugs. C.J. steps closer, tosses her cigarette and grinds it out with the toe of her big clunky boot. Eighty degrees and she's wearing what look like combat boots. "You know, Shark, you're different from all the others here."

"Is that so?"

"Yeah. You're not so polite." She pauses and then laughs. "I mean that as a big compliment—I think that polite and hypocritical often go together."

"Well, then compliment taken."

"It's a southern thing." She pulls another cigarette out from the pocket of her baggy jeans. "'Why, thank you, *sugah pie*,' you might say, even if what you really mean is 'go to hell.'"

"It *is* southern," Rachel says, finally recovering from the surprise, aware that there's a part of her still believing Joe and Rosemary might join the conversation. "But it's also a human thing. Just more noticeable here because everybody talks too *goddamned* much and wants to be sweet." She lets her voice get loud so as to reclaim her dignity.

"Ha, be sweet," C.J. says. "My mom always said that." She nods her head in the direction of deep shade, a hedge of wax myrtle shading another, older section of graves.

"Where is your mom?"

"Right over there in the low-rent district," she points. "You know a long time ago they used to always throw the suicides in a far corner. Suicides, slaves, Jewish people like yourself."

"*Is* that what happened?" Rachel asks. "Your mother, I mean."

"Yep—the ultimate fuck you. No offense," she says, and then while still looking over to the shade, mumbles, "Thanks, Mom."

"I'm so sorry—was she sick?"

"Isn't anyone who does that?"

"A lot of answers to that question I suppose and all very complicated."

"I still come see her." She shrugs. "When my son is older, I'll bring him over here."

"Where is your son?"

"Day care. My friend, Joanna, who works as a volunteer here made that happen. She's like my fairy godmother—jobs when I need them, a garage apartment. Free babysitting."

"Your dad?"

"Now there's a long story."

"All I've got is time," Rachel says. She watches C.J. staring off at a sound in the undergrowth—a bird or squirrel. She's a pretty girl under all that dark makeup, especially pretty when she smiles. "Are you still up for taking me for a ride around town? Tomorrow, maybe?" Rachel asks. "I'll pay the big bucks."

"Sure. I can do that if you don't mind a baby in a car seat and a rotten muffler." She steps so close Rachel can smell the patchouli as she leans in to read. "So who are these people, Joe and Rosemary Carlyle?"

"He was a friend years ago. " She pauses. "A friend of my husband's really. I never knew the wife."

"But you talk to them."

"Sometimes."

"That's cool. No different from writing in a journal really or talking in the mirror like this one woman over in nursing does all day long. I mean I write letters to my mom sometimes and I tell my baby all kinds of things, you know? It's probably why a lot of people have pets."

"Maybe so."

"Well, that's my break. I'll find you before I get off to figure out a time for tomorrow." She turns to go and then pauses. "Listen, I don't want you to get the wrong idea about me. I might look like a druggie or that I'm irresponsible or something, but I'm not. I smoke cigarettes, but otherwise I'm pretty damn virginal. I work hard and I take good care of my son."

"Is his name Jesus?"

"What?" She stops, laughs. "Oh, I get it. Ha. I'm not *that* virginal.

No, his name is Kurt after a really cool guy who *also* offed himself. I really like talking to you. See ya." The girl doesn't even wait for Rachel to reply, just turns and moves away as quietly as she appeared. Rachel sits and waits, takes a deep breath. She wishes she could start talking again, but something is different; something leaves her turned inward and speaking to the Joe there. *Good-bye sweetheart,* she says, *I'll be back later,* and to Rosemary she says, *I am sorry. I truly am sorry.* There is a warm breeze, tendrils of ivy and vines swinging like a curtain over the passage back into the open daylight and parking lot and there is a mockingbird doing a car alarm—over and over and over again, just another sound trapped and repeated with no sense of time or meaning.

Kendra

KENDRA HAS FINISHED PLACING stickers on everything worth having and now is trying to decide what she will wear to Abby's party tomorrow. It has to be something that really showcases her figure in the sexiest way possible. She is determined to leave Ben Palmer on his knees and begging just because he deserves it after all the ways he has misled and disappointed her. She will probably wear that short Boho miniskirt that leaves people amazed that she is over forty and has a child, and her hot pink Juicy halter top. She loves shopping in the teen department when Abby needs something. There aren't too many women her age who could do this. Flat stomach and abs. She was so glad when Ben stopped begging for a second child and left her alone. She didn't *want* another one; he wasn't the one who had to go through absolute torture and feeling like an elephant. And he wasn't the one who had to get up in the middle of the night to feed her that first month she actually tried to nurse. To this day when she tells people what a difficult time she had, how she just was not someone able to nurse, he has an expression that suggests otherwise, that she didn't want to nurse and therefore was not a good mother like all those people he held up to her as good examples. Some people just can't nurse. It isn't meant to be, and if this weren't a truth, there never would have been such a thing as a wet nurse.

Truth be told, she had not been ready to have a baby—it was a total accident—but of course she would never say that to Abby or how she spent a lot of time crying and saying she didn't want a baby at all since she was practically a baby herself and had never gotten to spend a whole summer in Europe the way she had told him she wanted to. And now of course she does want Abby and wouldn't trade her for anything under the sun, but at the time what she had really wanted was a career and a body that made people stop and look. She had been hired to do the local traffic report over at WSPR and it was just the beginning. She knows that had she not left when she did, replaced by someone who could not even hold a candle to her, she would likely have made it right into an anchor chair and God knows where she'd be. Oprah started that way. They all did. But, no, thanks to dear unambitious Ben, she was knocked up too soon and the rest is history. Of course people do still stop and look.

She has always been able to do that, always been proud of how foolish some men look when she saunters by, a swish of her hips at just the right time. She once even sawed the heel off one shoe just a fraction like Marilyn Monroe had famously done and it really does work. Kendra can also still wear things that cling, thanks to Pilates and a good genetic composition. She loves that most of the women she gets put with on various committees and things at Abby's school are so much younger than she is and still there is not a single one of them that can compete with her. Of course, they really can't hold her interest either, but very few people can in this shitty town. The work she does would make a lot of money in a big city where people are interested in art but around here the best you can do is an occasional craft fair where no one knows anything. People will buy doorstops that are nothing more than a brick wrapped in felt, but no one wants to see her display of miniature sushis, carefully shaped and baked and painted, fragile and delicate and no two the same. If only she lived elsewhere, but she lives here in Shitville with a husband who is as ambitious as a newt. He's smart enough to do so much, but just to spite her he doesn't. Ever since he said *I do* he's been saying *I don't. I don't like that, I don't want that,* and she knows it is out of pure spite. Well, he will see who is the best at being spiteful. When Andy watches her walk by, he all but licks his lips and she does everything she can to keep him on the line, closer and closer each time.

"Shake it, don't break it," he whispered the other day when she ran by his office on the pretense of collecting for a charity and got two seconds alone with him in a hallway. She could feel the heat coming out of him, especially when she told him how if she broke it, then she'd need to come to him to fix it. "Isn't that what you do?" she asked. "Fix people?"

"I cure the heart," he said, and laughed, though by then he was backing away from her, his neck a little flushed.

"Exactly," she said, and pushed past him so he could get a good look as she walked. She knew if he weren't so turned on, he would have been mad that she crossed the line of his workplace. She would have to make a point of telling his wife she had seen him. "Your husband works so hard," she will say. "I think you need to take him on a little vacation."

"What about he takes me?" his wife says in this version. "I deserve that." And Kendra smiles and pours the idiot some more wine. "Of course you do, dear. Bless your heart."

Kendra tried and tried to get Abby interested in some of the new looks that girls her age are wearing, but she said the only thing she wanted for her birthday was a phone and *now* all she wants is for Dollbaby to come home. "Honey," she said, and handed her some jeans. "Just try on a few things. You need some new clothes." Abby needed an eight in the same jeans Kendra got in a four and she had to spend the whole ride home reassuring her that most girls do have a little plump phase, that once she starts her period and starts growing breasts it will all get much better.

"Stop!" Abby screamed so loud Kendra almost wrecked the car. "I hate when you talk about all of that. I hate you," she screamed again when they stopped in the driveway. She jumped from the car, and instead of running up on the porch where Ben was working on that stupid disappearing chamber, she went tearing off toward the cemetery and the old folks' home where she spends way too much time.

"Why can't you just take her shopping?" Ben asked later when he came into their room where she was trying on her new things. "Why can't it ever just be about her? Buy something for her and for once leave yourself out. She is the kid, after all." Oh, how insightful. He has had just enough therapy to start to notice a few things, now.

"It is about her," she screamed. "Just because I happen to find something for myself, too, does not mean I am not a good mother. I am a good mother. I am a great goddamned mother!"

"That's what you keep saying."

"I am!" She kicked that big red rubber toy that Dollbaby used to leave in the middle of the room all dirty and slimy. No matter how many times she collects all those things and puts them on the back porch, Abby goes and gets them and scatters them back around all the different rooms, like it might bring Dollbaby back. "But she might come back," Abby had said, Ben of course agreeing with her, and Kendra wanted to scream and stomp and say *impossible*.

Ben leaned down and picked up the toy where it had bounced against the wall and set it back on the beach towel Abby had left in the corner, under a photo she had taped to the wall. Dollbaby with angel halo and wings, the first Halloween they had her.

"Just be a good mother," he said, and looked at her with those tired red eyes. Was he crying? Was he stoned? Did she give a damn? "Just do something just for her."

"This party is just for her," she said. "I am about to throw the best birthday party that any girl in her class has ever had. I can guarantee you that every mother in town will be calling me up afterward to try to get answers and copy it."

"I rest my case," he said, and she bit back what was the true and best thing to say to someone who said he was going to be a lawyer and then never got there.

What a loser. Kendra does not want a situation of till death do us part alimony. She might if there was more to get, which once upon a time she was led to believe there was. It would mean she wouldn't ever be able to get a real job (fine with her) but also that she couldn't have a live-in lover, not that she isn't crafty enough to figure all that out and get away with it—she certainly is!—but all it would take would be for Mr. Sleight of Hand to hire the right lawyer who might hire an investigator and then that would be embarrassing.

Till death do us part alimony is a great way to stick it to someone for sure, but given she's the one who is having an affair, it might be hard to do. And this is a topic that will divide a room full of women in a hurry. She heard one woman saying how such an agreement is a step back for women everywhere. That a smart woman should just get a chunk of something right up front and not live as a dependent. Well, Kendra has never been into all that feminist bullshit although she likes to appear that she is. Truth is that she is perfectly happy to be totally dependent on a man and never work at all and she is sure many women share this. Of course, they are also probably the boring housewife types she would never want anything to do with, but still.

She pretends to be a feminist just like she pretends to be compassionate when someone is struggling with her weight or blood pressure or bad permanent even though she really doesn't give a damn. But why not lie? She does it all the time. Why not lie and create a whole new history for yourself, especially if no one ever takes the time to investigate and catch the lies. She has told that she once designed a costume for Bernadette Peters and that she once had dinner with one of the Bee Gees—she can't remember which one—who insisted she stopped waitressing and join their table. He propositioned her and then sent her postcards for years that said he couldn't forget her. It is amazing what people will believe. She has told that she is a descendent of both Robert E. Lee and Ulysses Grant. *I embody the whole Civil War right here in my own little body,* she has said numerous times to great reaction and applause.

"Where are the postcards from the Bee Gee?" that awful Linda Blackmon asked. Linda is the one who copies everything Kendra ever buys and wears, and then Benjamin said "good question" and looked at her with hands up and eyebrows raised as if to say, *Well?*

"Burned, of course," she said without batting an eye. "Why tarnish his image with what was really kind of pathetic?"

"That is so considerate." Ben clapped his hands. "That's my wife, the most generous and compassionate human walking the planet."

Ben Palmer will deserve whatever he gets. He has practically ruined her life. He is the reason she has migraines and low blood sugar and likely what is called fibromyalgia. She gave him a baby and she has spent the best years of her life with him and for what? Did he ever take her on that cruise she wanted? How embarrassing was it when this one went to Rome and this one went to Hawaii and this one summers on Martha's Vineyard and drops celebrity names all the time. Kendra deserves that, too and she is goddamned going to have it. She puts a sticker on the bottom of the big heavy Victorian sofa the woman with the birthmarked daughter left behind and what does she find but another goddamned chew toy. Chew toys and screws from that goddamned box he's building. It's all a mess. And she can't wait to get out of it. She is hoping that she can keep her strength up until it is all behind her. Meanwhile, she is getting sick and tired of all the phone calls. *I think I saw your dog on the playground, but I couldn't catch her. I think I saw your dog two days ago at the Tastee Freez.* The messages keep coming. *I am so sorry to hear about Dollbaby. I hope you find her soon.*

Wouldn't she love to scream impossible! That is *impossible.*

Dollbaby is gone and never to be seen again. Dollbaby took a little nap and never woke up. Kendra spent quite a bit of money for that little naptime, including a hefty tip for the long-haired solemn-faced kid who didn't want to believe her story about why this dog *had* to be put down. "She practically bit a child's nose off," she told him. "Twenty stitches and who do you think paid for it all? We'll be lucky if they don't sue us for all we own. What do you need, the court order?" She finally convinced him even though the idiot dog was on its back and wagging its tail the whole time. "Appearances are so deceiving," she told the boy.

Now she has to practice looking sad and work some tears into her eyes, because as soon as Abby walks in she will have to tell her the sad sad news. Someone called from way out in the country— Dollbaby got hit by a car. Oh, if only that fence your father built had not been so easy to get out of. Oh, if only the dear sweet thing had not gotten out and run away from home. If we ever get another dog, we will hire someone who knows what he is doing and can build a real fence. Poor, poor Dollbaby. Let's try to picture her in heaven with a mountain of bones and beautiful fields to run through. Let's give her a Persian rug to piss on all day long.

Notes about: Jeremiah Mason Bass

Born: August 5, 1932   **Died:** June 21, 2007, 4:10 p.m.

Winthrop Nursing Facility   Laconia, New Hampshire

Mr. Bass was my last assignment in New Hampshire. Luke had instructed that I leave on a high note and clearly there will not be one
higher than this. Luke's request, other than to throw him a good funeral and make sure all legal issues were in order, was that I leave New
Hampshire when I felt healthy and confident and had had a good experience. After Suzanne Sullivan, I feared that I would not be able to
keep my word and I told the supervisor this. I had already said that I
knew I could not handle children and now I had added anyone dying
prematurely. I had dreamed of Suzanne Sullivan many times in the
weeks after her death. In the dreams she always had the long blond hair
she had in the pictures on the wall of her house and she was always
doing other things, unwrapping snacks for her kids or looking up phone
numbers. Once she was grooming a horse and she kept telling me that
there had been a mistake and she wasn't supposed to leave at all, that
I needed to speak to people and make phone calls and see if I couldn't
get this mistake fixed.

No one can change this, Luke had said, meaning his own situation.
The world is in motion.

"Can't change it," Mr. Bass said the first day I met him. He had been described by several as "colorful" and that would be a gross understatement. He said his whole life had been dictated by his name—Bigmouth Bass they call him. He said he had fished since he was big enough to hold a pole. He fished all over the United States of America and once down in Mexico when his wife won a trip for selling the most cars over at Regal Chevrolet. That was in 1976. He caught a marlin once and loved to tell the tale, what a fight it was—*the pull, the pull*—He was widowed in 1997 and has successfully gotten loose of every hook that almost caught him. *They don't call me slippery for nothing.*

He wore his white hair so slicked you could see the grooves of the fine-toothed comb he kept in his front pocket and he was missing quite a few teeth which he self-consciously hid with one hand cupping his chin and covering his mouth. "I've caught nearly everything you can catch," he said. "Fish, I mean, and people always give me fish things because of my name and my work. Ran a bait-and-tackle shop for years while my wife sold cars. She was something. Now that was my hardest catch of all, took all kinds of lures and tackle to get her to bite—you know, Aqua Velva, which I think stinks, but she liked it quite good, and a luxury automobile and steak dinners and a shiny diamond ring. They called me Bigmouth Bass and they called her the other Bigmouth Bass. Once I called her the Bigmouth Ass and I wished I hadn't done that 'cause she made me pay. I am not about to tell a decent young woman such as yourself *how* she made me pay, but just trust me that she did."

Every inch of his room was decorated with posters and photographs and lures and tackle. He had a huge stack of rods in the corner and said he had a photo of every fish he'd caught since about 1956 when his daughter was born. He's got every fish she caught and her brother, too. *Every one. Every one. I cleaned them all and ate my fair share.* He had several plaques of mounted rubber fish and he loved to press the little red buttons that made them flop and sing: "Take Me to the River," "Pretty Fishy," "Catch Us if You Can." He liked to get them all flopping and singing at once and he did that right up to the day he died.

"You know what is so strange?" he asked, just before he drifted off and stopped talking. "I love the bottom feeders. I love to catch them and I love to eat them. I love grouper and I love catfish. But"—he paused and beckoned his son, a giant boy-looking man in his big summer shorts and tennis shoes, who kept wiping his face and blowing his nose into Dunkin' Donuts napkins he kept pulling from his pocket—"I don't like them in life. Don't be a bottom feeder in life." He shook his finger. "Your mother was not a bottom feeder and she sold cars so that should tell you something."

The big boy son nodded and wiped his eyes and then looked at me and started laughing. He laughed until he wheezed and his father joined in with him. I left to get a cup of coffee when the daughter arrived, a woman built just like her brother who wore a Bass Pro Shop T-shirt and cap and placed an extra cap on her father's head. I could hear their laughter all the way down the hall and when I returned they told me that they thought he was gone, that they were singing along to Pretty Fishy, and he just stopped breathing. "We sure are gonna miss you, old man." The son leaned and kissed his father's forehead and then blew his nose into a napkin and draped his arm around his sister. "He was a good one, wasn't he?"

"A real keeper," the daughter said. "A real prize."

This was the high point Luke told me to find. *Can't change it. They don't call me slippery for nothing.* Anything about fishing will bring Jeremiah Bass to mind: lures and tackle and bait and hooks—*the pull, the pull.*

[from Joanna's notebook]

Jeremiah Mason Bass

A hand-crafted lure is valuable and it takes a lot of time and some good eyes and the still and steady hands of a surgeon and he has to get the light just right, a bright light under a magnifier and carefully loop and tie fine filament and one day he will build a ship in a bottle, maybe have a room full of ships in bottles and imagine himself a tiny little captain way down in there but Mrs. Bass says that's leisure work and leisure time, but they aren't there yet because children cost money and there needs to be food on the table and money in the bank and what better food is there than a fish, the Lord multiplied and multiplied those baskets of fish, the scales on their bodies numbered and all you need is a line and pole and some luck like a lucky lure, sparkly and shiny spinning down there below the murky surface down where it's cold and the light can't quite reach and you just sink a little lower and lower down where it's cooler and darker, a little colder, a little darker, a wavy spin of algae and roots, down and down to the soft muddy bottom.

Stanley

S TANLEY HAS BEEN READING a lot lately when he's by himself—about roses—and listening to music. He has some of
Martha's books as well as all the catalogs she used to get that still
get forwarded, his old address marked through and replaced with
a yellow sticker and this address. It amazes him—this process of
lives being forwarded, of someone like Martha, long dead, still
being asked for her support, her opinion, her use of a coupon
worth a hundred dollars if she acts now. He never realized until
he started flipping through all of Martha's magazines and books
that he had really loved her garden, too. He didn't do anything
except admire it and can't even recall if he admired it directly to
her, but he certainly accepted compliments from so many people
in town who said they often altered their driving path just to pass
by. One young woman who had worked as an intern at the court
house told him how her wedding bouquet came straight from his
yard and that she had always felt guilty because she stole them in
the middle of the night. He accepted her apology but didn't tell
her that this was something that had happened often through the

years, so often in fact, that Martha was insulted when people did *not* take roses. Sometimes she would even tie a pair of scissors to a length of rope on the fence with a note that they pick respect-fully and not touch this or that or the other, because so-and-so was planning to use those on the table of her debutante luncheon. It had not occurred to him how the garden had allowed Martha invitations to nearly every event in town and how she knew al-most everyone as a result. It was something to admire and he has come to also admire the work that went into it. He has studied the layers and soil system and the constant pruning and tending that all those finicky fancy varieties required and marvels how she had done it all herself. She might send him or Ned down to the nursery with a list, but she was the one out there in dirty pedal pushers and white Keds (just like the pink ones Rachel Silverman wears). She wore a floppy yellow straw hat she had bought at Vir-ginia Beach years before and what he has recently learned are called gauntlet gloves whose thick rubber protected her arms from the thorns.

He could imagine trying to have a garden, maybe even right outside his window there along the far side of the parking lot where he watches Rachel Silverman walk back and forth and where, unfortunately, he often sees the arrival of the funeral home car over at nursing. They try to be discreet but how impos-sible is that? Maybe some climbing roses on a trellis (like what he has marked on page 96 of one enormous catalog) would do the trick and he has found the names of many hardy climbers that he believes would take over in no time. Who knew there were roses with the growing habits and ethics of something like kudzu or bamboo, those types willing to run over whatever is in their path, like some people he has known, like himself from time to time he has to admit. And he has been just as prickly and unpredictable. What would Martha have said about that analogy? And what would Ned say? Ned would probably roll up his sleeves and show his scars; Ned can probably recall every prick and scratch of his life. Knock Outs, ramblers. Those would be Stanley's kind of roses as opposed to the pedigreed tea varieties, which remain exactly as the pedigree dictates—this height and that weight—not unlike Martha who never changed in appearance except that couple of times when she got in her head that she needed to try to be someone other than herself and dressed up in some night garb that embarrassed him. He's not sure why. Maybe it was because it wasn't what he expected and as much as he liked to fantasize on the ramblers and the Knock Outs and things like men in a ring beating the shit out of one another, it really was not his nature either. He had wanted the pedigree and the guarantee of what he was getting, like the Labrador retrievers Sadie is always talking about and the one whose breeder had guaranteed there were not hip problems in that line. But no one could have guaranteed Martha's health. No one saw it coming. God, he can't go there, but what he can do is try to start a garden that might bring people out again. It would give some of these old shut-ins something to do. He could probably get old Toby out there digging and hauling manure and no telling who else might join in. Maybe Rachel Silverman. Maybe this would be something Ned could also take an interest in and would make him feel he'd finally done enough. Maybe he could grow some vegetables, too, or have a water garden with some koi. That was something he'd said he wanted to do when he retired and Martha as a result had given him books all about it for every birthday, Christmas, and anniversary. He is reaching for the water garden catalog that comes from up around where Rachel Silverman is from, filing a note in his head to ask her if she's ever been to Paradise Gardens up in MassaTOOsetts. He hears a knock at his door and quickly stashes the catalog and turns instead to the pinup poster in his latest Wrestling magazine, a great big poster of Kurt Angle who the crowds always greet with YOU SUCK. That's what he'll say to whoever it is. Ned.

"You suck!" he says, and waves the picture at Ned who eases the door shut and comes and sits. "I thought you left already. You need more money or something?"

"No. I just hate thinking about you sitting around all day with nothing to do." Ned looks a lot like Martha—the fair skin and big blue eyes—the expression of someone who would love to laugh or scream but seems afraid to. "Why don't we go out, do something. We can go to lunch. We could go hit some golf balls."

"Since when do you golf?" Stanley asks, and quickly adds, "I thought you were more into cooking and playing with yourself."

"There's a lot you don't know about me," Ned says. "I do like to cook, but I also like to golf and read and go to the movies."

"What about date? Do you ever think about trying that?" Stanley leans forward and pushes all of his catalogs under his chair and pulls back out the Herb Alpert album cover. "You need to find someone like this—a creamy delight."

"Dad."

"Really. I've got just three words for you." He raises his fist before he considers how this was Martha's old joke with the kids.

I have three words for you, she would say in an angry loud voice that was so foreign to her mouth, and then after much clamor and question, she would scream out in the same angry tone, *I love you.*

"Just three," he says again. "Match dot com."

"No." Ned starts laughing. "God only knows what you know about Match dot com, but it's not for me, not yet, at least."

"Too good, huh?"

"No. Just not interested."

"Why don't you call your wife. She might at least be good for some sex."

"Nice thought there, but she remarried," Ned says, and Stanley can tell he's getting to him, though Ned still doesn't lash out with what would be so easy, how he has told Stanley that a million times, how he has told how she has a two-year-old and is pregnant with another. Ned cried when he told Stanley about it, maybe hoping for some sympathy, but Stanley was unable to reach his hand out and do anything. He couldn't afford to blow his cover so all he said was *good riddance, bet those are some ugly children.* Now Stanley wants to say something that isn't too mean but will still convince him to leave and stay gone at least until tomorrow.

"She wasn't right for you," he says. "Everything that happened was a blessing. Something to celebrate."

Ned takes a deep breath, face red and fists curled. "It was *not* a blessing," he says. "I don't even know why I try." He looks at the portrait of Martha as if she is the one he is talking to. Maybe he promised Martha that he would make amends, maybe this is all about some kind of deathbed promise and Ned hates it all as much as Stanley does.

"I don't know why you do either," Stanley says. "And she sure as hell doesn't know." He points to Martha. "She's as dead as a doornail. Remember? You were there."

"Nice. Thanks, Dad." He stands and pulls an envelope from his back pocket and places two tickets to an upcoming wrestling event on the table beside Stanley's magazine. "If you need someone to go with you, I'll be glad to drive," he says, no eye contact.

"You sat there and cried, remember? Cried like a two-year-old."

"Yes. I remember," Ned says, his voice a little louder, jaw clenched. "And I remember how you just *sat* there." He leaves, letting the door slam behind him, and when Stanley is absolutely sure he's gone he leans forward and cries. This plan is not working the way he had hoped it would.

Toby

WELCOME HOME, GIRL. TOBY is relieved to get back in her own space, her little cottage filled with belongings she has known her whole life: her mother's furniture and china and the big dark mantel clock that had belonged to her father's father. She pulls out her yoga bolster and eye bag and leans back to do some deep breathing, each breath a way of ridding herself of all those bad feelings Marge Walker left her with. You think you've got your skin grown nice and thick and healthy and then it starts sliding right off of you, like a snake or a burn victim, leaving you tender and exposed.

Mr. Thornton Wilder once said how people who have lived in it for years know less about love than the child who has lost a dog yesterday, or something like that, and she knows it's true. Just looking at poor Abby sitting there, she knows everyone is helpless to heal her; only time can do that. And *that* is a truth for everyone, even old large barge Marge. Everyone has a hurt. Everyone has a weakness and how humans can live with devoting time to rubbing salt in and on another, she will never ever know.

Ommmmm. Ommmmmm. She is playing a CD she bought at Walgreens called *Global Soundings* and there's all kinds of things in there, thunder and waterfalls and birds and lions. She likes to close her eyes and just follow along just like she does when she visits Sadie. Poor Sadie. It does wonders for her to have guests posing for this and that and Toby faithfully shows up to ask for something whether she really feels like it or not. Some days she just likes to read and smoke cigarettes—her little secret. It's why she won't wear the nicotine patch but opts to keep smacking on Nicorette instead. Allowing herself to cheat and smoke every now and again is one great pleasure she has in life. Inhale, exhale. Inhale, exhale. She tries to do the kind of breathing so many of the people in her old yoga class did, breathing there at the back of their throats with what almost sounds like a growl. She has trouble doing it and always has, but she likes how it sounds kind of primal and wild in there just like what she hears on *Global Soundings.*

When she lies here like this with the sun warming her patch on the floor like a raft in the midst of the cool air-conditioning and the white noise of her system, her mind floats in and out and she is always amazed by what snippets it calls up that don't have anything to do with anything. It's almost like being haunted by little past moments and what would that mean? One of hers is of being in the parking lot of her high school on a day so hot the asphalt is soft under the tread of her shoes and the underside of the maple leaves look silver. This one has recurred many times, a free-floating little particle that is detached from any sense of a particular day or event. And another is from her childhood on the sidewalk in front of a grocery store near her home and it is gray winter light, again detached and meaningless like part of a memory looking for a home. There are so many memories looking for a home like when Toby and Sally lived together while they were studying to be teachers and how it was different from all the other friendships she knew. She tried to talk to Sally about it, but it was clear she wasn't going to be able to do that and what had happened on those rare dark nights would remain there, like those free-floating snippets of memories, nothing to attach them to a particular story or cause or effect. They happened and yet they remained removed from life and all that came after. Sally got married to a man who provided her with a very comfortable and good life and she traveled all over creation and had two beautiful children. Toby is godmother to the oldest and to this day never forgets to acknowledge her: Anna Clarice Martin (now Tolar) of Mt. Pleasant who has a doctorate degree in history and now a baby of her own. Toby is almost certain that the Anna of her name came from her own Annabelle. Sally had always told her how much she loved her name even though Toby had said it had never ever fit her her whole life, like asking a muddy unruly child to step into a designer evening gown and satin high heels. Toby told Sally that she loved her and Sally always said she knew, that she loved her, too, and patted her hand the same as she did her German shepherd and, later, other women friends who went with her on her many trips. Toby went on the one to Greece and the one to Spain and they were both fun trips and both served the purpose to remind her of how distant and long ago whatever it had been was. Free-floating particles. Bits of life. She breathes in and she breathes out. It has occurred to her that someday she might ask Sally what she made of it all, if she ever thinks about it. These days so many young people experiment with who they are and it isn't the big deal it was when she was young. But she suspects they are all still very vulnerable. After all love is love. Sometimes you just have to believe that love is love and accept that it manifests in many different ways. Accept the great fortune of seeing it at all.

Notes about: Martha Marie Anderson Stone

Born: September 5, 1935   **Died:** January 2, 2008, 11:30 a.m.

Fulton, North Carolina

It was a beautiful sunny day, clear and cold. At least twelve cardinals gathered near the birdfeeder outside her window, bright red creatures in the leafless oak. She loved her birdfeeders and her rose garden and she loved her box collection. She liked to hold and look at her special boxes, a collection of tiny Limoges containers with special dates and events scripted within. The top is broken on the one to commemorate her older son's birth and she has glued where the body had split in two. "Ironic," she said as she showed them. "Ned's box is whole and Pete's is broken." She asked to see the one for her anniversary—white and gold alone on its own shelf—and pointed to where a tiny chip was missing. "But not bad," she said. "Salvageable."

She was a beautiful young woman—photos all over the house—May days and graduations, debutante parties and a large wedding portrait over the mantel in the living room. She loved to dance and she loved to garden. Her favorite time of the year was June when she opened her garden to graduates and debutantes and June brides to come and gather roses of all varieties for their little luncheons and brunches and teas. "There is nothing quite like an armload of roses," she said. Her favorites were 'Marchesa Bocchella', pink and so fragrant, and the creamy white 'Penelope' with their large pink hips come fall. She liked telling the histories of the various roses to the young women who came seeking them. She told me to please come back in June and take some. "If I'm not here"—she paused, knowing the truth and letting it sink in—"Then you just help yourself. Tell Stanley and the boys I said so."

Her sons were with her at the end, the whole handsome family pictured all over the house in photographs at various holidays and seasons like scenes from something like Ozzie and Harriet. Pete was making arrangements and writing things into a little leather-bound notebook he kept in the breast pocket of his jacket. He asked his mother what songs she wanted sung and were there scriptures she wanted read. Her look the first time he asked was one of shock, but then she came forward to answer: She wanted "Softly and Tenderly" and Psalm 23. "I know that's not very original," she said, "but neither is death." She smiled, but none of them were able to respond; they were not looking at her.

The younger son, Ned, came and sat beside her, but he always put his head down near her hand and then stayed there, shoulders shaking as she patted and comforted him. Her husband had continued to talk to her like it was an ordinary day and she would be getting up any second now so that life could resume as normal.

Toward the end, she talked about where she grew up there in downtown Richmond, and she talked about her mother and father and her girlhood friends. She named rose after rose with a vivid description, calling their names like old friends: 'Ferdinand Pichard' and 'Mabel Morrison', 'Baroness Rothschild' and 'White Wings', until finally her husband told her it was okay to let go. Her husband did not want to tell her good-bye. He did not want to tell her that it was okay to go, but she waited until he did so.

"Our whole marriage has been about me making the decisions," he said when asked to help her, to give her permission to go. "Do you really mean she can't die without me telling her to?"

This was a house full of sadness—a silent sadness broken only by that flock of cardinals with their calls of *cheer, cheer, cheer*. He went to her bedside and she died within seconds. Roses and cardinals and fragile little boxes—these were her obvious, easiest, loves, and what will always hold her in my memory.

[from Joanna's notebook]

Martha Stone

Her boys are here—such handsome boys—and Stanley. Stanley Jefferson Stone. She had their names painted in a little porcelain box when they got engaged. He could have married anyone but he married her and she carried a large bouquet of 'Cecile Brunner', "the sweetheart rose," and trailing ivy and baby's breath. He married her. Distances, distances, years make distances. She tried silly things, the negligee, the champagne, the fragrant petals shed from a 'Charles de Mills' leading to the bed where she waited in the sheer nylon gown in high heels he said cost too much. He shook his head and asked how much did they cost. They are in the back of the closet remind- ing her what not to do, what never to do again. He laughed and said she looked ridiculous and she cried the rest of the night. She was only thirty-five and that seemed so old then, but no, she was only thirty-five—the boys at a little sleepaway camp. She was trained in all the good ways to be a good wife and a hostess and a mother, but she wanted to be more, too. She wanted him to keep looking at her the way he did in those first weeks they met, the way he looked at her before the first night she undressed and waited there beneath the sheets, her heart pounding. When would she ever wear those shoes, he asked. Ah, come on now, he said. Jesus. He got quieter and kinder when he learned she was so sick, but that day, that day she stood in her new high heels and lovely sheer gown wishing she were somewhere else. There had been other boys, other paths. She had known many fine boys. Boys will be boys. She told him she didn't like him to spank their boys, she didn't believe in doing that, a lot of people don't do that anymore. Please stop. Please stop. And he never liked her collection, he said look at all the clutter, look. Right here. Right here. Here, here, here. He swept the shelf clear and her beautiful collection she had collected her whole life, went everywhere. Right here! Right here! He puts his hand on her arm and tells her it's okay for her to leave. She wants him to say stay, but he says it's okay to leave now. You can leave, Martha, it's okay. He says, Right here, right here, and here, here, here. He speaks her name because there are rose petals all over the room where she put them like it said to do in a book—here, here, here –he says and she opens her eyes to see.

C.J.

C.J. PICKS UP KURT and drives home, waving to the kid man-
ning the window of the Dog House, a seventeen-year-old
girl who makes *her* feel old with all her talk of vampires and how
she'd love to get her own teeth filed sharp. *I'm the old one in this
picture,* C.J. thinks, and it makes her laugh. That's a first and by
way of thinking about age and feeling old, she can't stop thinking
about that old shark, Rachel Silverman, out there talking to dead
people like she was on a picnic or something. One of these nights,
maybe C.J. will pull out the Ouija board and gather up a bunch
of the old guys to have a séance. She bets they'd get a kick out of
that and she'd probably hear some really crazy stuff. Hell, they
talk crazy stuff anyway so it would just be a little extra. She once
worked as a psychic so she can play all that stuff pretty good and
truth is she does believe. In what? Who knows, but she does. It's
something she and Joanna talk about often, those times when you
are so aware of not being alone, so aware of something big and
beyond this life.

And truth is she really likes Rachel Silverman and wouldn't

mind hanging out with her a little or driving her around town, though God only knows what it is she thinks she'll see. She seems smart enough and still in touch with reality so maybe she really could give some legal advice. C.J. has nothing to lose and maybe a little something to gain and what else does she have to do anyway other than hanging out with Joanna, which is fine but does get a little boring from time to time. Joanna is kind of settled in a way that's probably good but still could use a little heat or excitement. *Like maybe you're scared of guys or scared of getting hurt,* C.J. has told her. *Maybe that's why you never meet the right one.*

C.J.'s friend, Sam Lowe, keeps trying to ask her out, but she has managed so far to keep that from actually happening; why risk fucking up the one friend she has who is close to her own age and she certainly can't tell him that technically she *is* seeing someone. She has been tempted to tell Joanna about a thousand times that she does have a boyfriend—or *man*-friend whatever—but keeps chickening out. She's scared of making the wrong move and he reminds her often how they really have to be very careful and so her big worry right now is about tonight and what to wear and where to meet. All those cryptic little notes are driving her fucking crazy and today—just like yesterday—there was nothing there at all. He's a grown goddamned man. He like slices people open and saves them and shit, jump-starts their old bum hearts and he can't even pick up a telephone or leave a real note on her door at home or at work to say what he needs to say? He made her promise that she would never ever call him and she has kept her promise. He says he *has* been leaving notes, but where are they? He accuses her of taking them and not responding; he said he didn't like her fucking with him. How stupid would that be? She's the one who needs him. And how creepy is it anyway that he makes her walk that path out near where her mother is buried because anytime she is out there, it feels like she's being watched, that her mother is out there watching, and now she'll feel like those Carlyle people are watching and listening to her, too, which is really fucked up, like who wants to star in her own horror show? She certainly doesn't. She has had more than enough of her share. She even told him how she hates to go out there so it's like he keeps testing her and how mean is it that? Maybe it made sense when they first got together, but that's been a year and half ago. She loved how after they were together that first time that he immediately told his wife he thought she should give herself a break and have their house cleaned every week—maybe even twice a week—instead of every other and how he thought she should go to a spa somewhere or traveling with friends the way he knows women always like to do. Before C.J. could even blink she had a brand-new cell phone she didn't even have to pay for and a television and nights of him sneaking her in and out of his house—a huge house with a Jacuzzi and stereo speakers in the ceiling of every room.

But it scares me to walk back there, she told him when he kept insisting they leave each other notes in the cemetery. *I don't like it.*

You, he said, unzipping her jeans and reaching in, *have no choice.* She was six months pregnant and he had already given her a big roll of money for the month and that's the way it went for quite a while. He is still angry at her for moving into Joanna's little apartment over the Dog House and not needing him so much. He said that place was not nearly so discreet and it smelled bad, too, like onions and old grease. She thought he would be pleased, proud that she was working and making deals that were aboveboard and helping her to be independent. She got the job at Pine Haven all on her own by responding to a help-wanted ad and then auditioning by shampooing several residents and doing their nails. She thought he'd be pleased, but he had not been happy at all and everything has slowly gone downhill since, no matter how many times she has explained that she wants him to be proud of her. She wants to feel proud of herself.

And it really *does* scare her to walk back there. She doesn't like the dark shade and the smell of the damp undergrowth. She doesn't like the way people leave old dead flowers or, worse, ugly faded plastic ones junked up on the graves. She has had enough horror to deal with like that morning she kept yelling for her mother to get up only to finally give up and head on out to catch the school bus. When she got home and there were policemen there and everything, they asked didn't she notice her mom wasn't moving at all and she said that, yeah, she noticed, but it didn't look any different from any other day for the past five or six or seven years.

Sometimes she tries to imagine her mom's death, to walk through what happened that night with C.J. right there in the next room, painting her toenails and listening to Nirvana. Her high school art project was a sketch of Kurt Cobain and she played Lithium about a million times while she worked on getting his hands right. Sometimes she wants to give her mom the benefit of the doubt and call it accidental like that one really nice policewoman. That woman kept correcting anyone who said "suicide" like she was trailing behind with a broom, sweeping up the mess they were making. Not suicide. *Accidental overdose.*

"How about *accident waiting to happen?*" she had asked the

woman, and stared until she looked away. C.J. was a master at the game of chicken and had been for years. She could stare into the worst face or situation and not flinch. The woman was being nice to her and she would have loved to have uncurled her fists and accepted that, but she couldn't; it had been way too long. The woman wanted to open the exit door so C.J. wouldn't be trapped and locked in with the great legacy of suicide as all the shrinks and educated cops like to call it. She has thought of that term *legacy of suicide* so often. Plenty of people outlive it and when they do, they get younger like instantly being given the extra years they might have lost, like passing go and getting two hundred bucks. The thought of Monopoly makes her think of that kid Abby who is always hanging out at Pine Haven. She told how her dog ate the race car, and when it came out the other end, her dad boiled it and put it back in the box. Her dad is that old friend of Joanna's who once hit on C.J. and is married to a total bitch who C.J. is convinced tried to kill the kid's dog. Sam Lowe told her all about it, this woman in a tight miniskirt dragging in a dog and demanding that he put it to sleep on the spot. She said she would pay what was owed plus a huge tip. "Bless her heart," she said, and patted the dog's head. "She went completely mad and they say will likely do it again." He took the money and when she turned to leave—maybe she didn't know she could have demanded to watch—he asked if she wanted her cremated for pickup, but she said that would be way too painful. "It's better this way," she said. "The sooner the better, okay?"

He assured her that he would do it as soon as she left and then he sat there and kept putting it off until the end of the day when the dog had fallen asleep with her little pointed nose wedged up beside his foot. "There was nothing wrong with her," he said. "She's a great little dog so I took her home. What's one more?" He had already told her how he had grown up with many dogs—that his dad was known for taking in strays and naming them after pirates. "My dad is known as a dog-collecting weirdo who lived in a trailer in what became a pricey subdivision," Sam said. "His other claim to fame is being the son of a man who blew his head off when he was only like forty years old or something. Nice, huh?"

It was that story that had gotten C.J.'s interest and they have been friends ever since. She told him all about her own mother and how all she heard at school and from the foster parents who stepped in her senior year of high school was about her goddamned *legacy* like she might have been in line for the fucking throne or something. Sam said that when his dad got beyond the age of the suicide, it was kind of like he was born again. "Not religious stuff," he said. "I mean it was like he seemed younger and was willing to do things he hadn't ever done. Took my mom on a trip out west, encouraged her to go back to school. Finally built a real house at the beach like he'd always dreamed of doing."

C.J. had never even thought of that before, how wonderful it would feel to get past the age her mother was—only thirty-six— and in a little over ten years, she would be there. Kurt would be in junior high and it would feel like a whole new life. It could be a whole brand-new life. When she said this to Sam, he turned and hugged her, squeezing so tight she could feel his heart beating, smell the detergent of his clean shirt. She knows that Sam really does like her and he likes Kurt, too, but he seems so young to her. That's the difference in being a kid with a Mom and Dad who give a shit. It keeps a person younger. He went to college and always knew he would. Now he hopes to go to vet school in another year or so after he takes a few courses and gets his test scores up. He hopes all kinds of things and starts lots of sentences that way. *I hope I'm right about this little dog. I hope Kurt will someday know how hard you work and how much you love him. I hope you'll let me help you get that muffler fixed or at least go to a friend of mine to look at it. I hope we will always be good friends.* She would like to tell him that she hopes all of that, too. She hopes for some part of herself to be everything he could ever hope to find in a woman. *You deserve that,* she wants to tell him. *You deserve every good thing this life can give you.*

And now, even though she worries about giving him the wrong idea, she has a flyer that she plans to take out to him tomorrow, maybe while she's driving Rachel Silverman around. It's a picture of Abby's dog, Dollbaby, who without a doubt looks just like the one he rescued, and no doubt about it, the woman Sam described sounds a whole lot like Abby's bitch of a mom.

This is the kind of thing C.J. keeps in her journal in the safe. She has written how she plans to resurrect Dollbaby and leave her right out there on the front porch of their house. Of course she also wrote about that time the weird magician dad came on to her after a party she worked, complimenting her tattoos and wanting her to get into his truck. He's not bad-looking, really, for an old guy—when he's not drunk that is—but because C.J. was used to seeing his kid come and go, it changed the whole picture so she couldn't think of him as just another of those jerks who can't keep it zipped. Instead he was somebody's dad who couldn't keep it zipped. But because of the way Joanna obviously feels about him, C.J. has decided to cut the guy some slack and give him a break; blame it on alcohol as so many people do. Blame it on being married to a bitch, as so many people do. He's certainly not who Joanna thinks he is or that's C.J.'s opinion and she thinks Joanna can do a whole lot better and hopes that she will. Occasionally, when she has allowed herself to dream and imagine a secure life with someone like Mr. Jump-Start the Heart, she has immediately thought about how she could maybe introduce Joanna to somebody really cool who is smart and deserving of her. She likes to imagine that her life will be secure and happy, and that she will be someone Kurt is proud of, that he will be a boy like Sadie's son, happy and successful in his own life but never for a minute forgetting about her.

The phone rings and she picks up to a distant buzzing and finally, on her third hello, he says, *Eight p.m. at Esther Cohen's place.* He says, *And you better not be late this time,* and hangs up. She dreads the walk, but there's no other way. Kurt is in his bouncy chair and grins when she looks his way. Kurt has his father's eyes and maybe that is why she has such a hard time saying no these days. She goes in the bathroom and jots a little note in her journal: *Meeting at 8 p.m.* It sounds like he's mad, but a lot of nights have started out this way only to end with him being really sweet and offering something extra for Kurt. There's so much she wants Kurt to have and maybe it's time to ask, a savings account or something. *Kurt will need a lot of things in this life. He will need an education and the right clothes, a good dog and summer camp. Someday he will need a car.*

Even if he ever decides that he doesn't want *her* anymore, he has to help Kurt. All of this is about Kurt, though there is a part of her that still wishes for something more. It's hard not to wish for just a little bit more.

Rachel

Lunch is not something Rachel ever in her life really looked forward to or participated in. As a working woman, she almost always worked straight through or used the time in her office to catch a cat nap. There were early years when she used that lovely hour of time to stroll Charles Street, all alone, window shopping. House things. Baby things. Clothes she imagined wearing and art she imagined on the wall. And of course since everyone knew she wasn't someone who invested huge amounts of time in lunch unless there was a meeting of some sort she had to attend, then she was missing in action. This made it especially easy after she had met Joe and began meeting him in the middle of the day.

Business. Over lunch. She never liked mixing any kind of business with anything social. She is someone who likes firm boundaries. She has always wanted to be a voice in her community and someone actively participating, but what she never was able to tolerate was all the communication that went into it: who is doing what when. Where are you? What are you going to eat? What are you going to wear? Humans who get themselves all tangled up in that kind of thing must get something out of it, but she never did and so to get out on a city street all by herself where no one knew her felt wonderful. She feels the same way out in the cemetery talking to the dead. Just her and the long dead and the birds and the trees. And now C.J., of course, who scared the holy shit out of her, but she's harmless, a good kid for sure. A sad good kid, all pierced and dyed and tattooed like somebody from the carnival, who will help her go where she needs to go.

Lately, Rachel finds herself looking forward to going to lunch. The food is pretty good and they serve the big meal in the middle of the day. Dinner—or supper as so many of them call it—is at five thirty. Who in the hell wants dinner at five thirty? You don't have to be Einstein to figure out how a place like this works; a later dinner would require a later work shift for those in the kitchen and so on. It's a business. Like anything else in the world, old age has become a booming business and—like any other endeavor—there are some who put their hearts in it and do a good job and there are those who need to be fired. Rachel is someone who came in reading the fine print on everything and asking enough questions and filing enough complaints that they would know she is someone *not* to cross—*ever*. So she has completely readjusted her schedule, eating her big meal in the middle of the day, which seems a small thing if you know your laundry is taken care of and the food prepared well and someone is keeping the place clean and scrubbed. At first she would come and get her food and take it with her, but now that she is used to being with Sadie and Toby, she just stays and eats right there with them.

The people at Pine Haven know that she is interested in a low-fat healthy diet—as they all should be!—and it has taken her weeks, if at all, to convince Sadie and Toby that frying a vegetable defeats the purpose of eating a vegetable. She orders unsweetened tea, but it almost always appears at her place as something that makes her body shake with the syrupy sweetness. There will be a whole new form of diabetes attributed to just that—gritty and grainy to the taste. Pure sugar. It's a wonder that they don't all weigh even more than they do especially with the lack of exercise.

When she asked what on earth the deal is, Sadie explained tea was just always sweet and then somebody, probably a doctor or somebody, said if people were tired of looking huge and dropping dead of heart attacks and strokes, they might think of laying off the sugar and all the lard intake. "Then people began to ask for unsweetened tea," Sadie explained. "For as long as I can remember there was just *tea* and then *unsweetened tea*. If you asked for *tea,* it was sweet. I don't know when all this fuss over *sweet tea* started. Now people say it all the time."

"It's quaint," Marge Walker said. "People from the outside associate that with our homeland here in the South and I like it that way. Who here likes sweet tea?" she asked, and practically everyone raised a hand.

"I like a Long Island Iced Tea," Stanley said. "That's a northern drink. And, of course, tea is from China and I am part Chinese."

"What part?" Marge asked, and everyone immediately looked away for fear of what might happen so she immediately added, "You're about as Chinese as she is," and she pointed over at Lottie who was working her tongue in and out of her mouth and shredding a paper towel.

"I *am* Chinese. I'm a terrible driver and I abused my children. I made them study all the time and called them bad names."

"You're a bigot," Rachel said. It was one of those days when she could not put up with his ridiculous comments for one more second and didn't even care what might come back to her. "You're a racist idiot."

"Speaking of bad names," he said.

"Kindness," Sadie said. "I believe in kindness. Be ye kind one to another," and everyone got quiet as they usually do when Sadie speaks. The only one to continue was Stanley Stone who asked Rachel if she would like to come to his room for Saki and origami and she had to bite her tongue and sit on her hands so she wouldn't try to break his neck.

Now Rachel stops by Sadie's room, but Sadie is napping. Rachel almost wakes her but then changes her mind. For several days now, Sadie has been skipping lunch, taking long naps after a busy morning so that she is able to rally again late in the afternoon. The last time she came to the table, she was wearing her pajamas under a big sweater, which was not like her at all. She has also begun to talk to people who aren't there, pausing to answer the invisible switchboard off to the side of her bed that she works to plug and unplug saying, *Hello? Hello?* Toby has seen this, too, but neither of them mentioned it for a while. It doesn't happen very often and when it does, it doesn't last more than a few minutes. Sadie will shake her head, laugh, and then be back as clear as a bell. Toby said she saw no reason to tell anyone about it, that she herself was very open to all the ways a person might communicate spiritually. "Who am I to say that Sadie doesn't really have somebody on the line?" Toby asked, and Rachel nodded her agreement. Now she

stands and watches Sadie asleep with what looks like an old grocery list in her hand and Harley purring at her feet. He stares at
Rachel with big green eyes, ready to bolt if she raises her hand the
way most do when they see him so she just eases back out with a
whispered promise to come back a little later.

"Do you think anyone here likes potatoes?" Rachel asks
when seated, and looks at her little daily menu, picks up the pen-
cil to mark what she wants. "I see potato salad and baked potato
and French fries. I see sweet potato pie."

"Must you always be so critical?" Marge asks. She says that she
is offended by the way Rachel criticizes the food and therefore *the
whole South and all the southerners in it* and that she bets there
are plenty of *Jewish Yankee* foods that they could all make fun of.

"Maybe," Rachel says. "In fact, I am sure you could. However,
here's the difference. You don't hear me sitting around and talking
about it all the time or plastering it on the front of every local-
yokel rag and filling up the menu with one choice. Gefilte fish, gefilte fish. Gefilte fish salad and gefilte fish fried. My my, wouldn't I
sho love me some gefilte fish." She knows she is being mean even
as she does it and yet she can't help herself. Sadie's absence almost
always affects her this way, taking away her reason and desire to
strike a more moderate tone.

"Let's be prejudiced against unkind people," Sadie had said
when the conversation turned to stereotypes and got Toby so upset. "Let's be prejudiced against those who act ugly."

"The gefilte, now there's a monster of a fish," Stanley said. "I
caught me a gefilte one time. Big-ass fish long as my leg, fought it
for hours there on the coast of Israel."

Even Rachel has to laugh at that and it helps to swallow back the discomfort she has felt since leaving the cemetery. The two of them hold eye contact for a second before he continues with his little rant. It's not often you encounter such brazen and boisterous stupidity. And of course she has learned that anytime she makes eye contact with him and seems to have a moment of understanding, it flips him out into the most absurd place, like a kid determined to shock and steal the show. The behavior is unacceptable as hell. She watches him, waiting to see what will come next.

"At the state fair," he tells, "they had fried sweet tea and fried Coca-Cola and fried beer, which required a current ID."

"In case no one knew you were legal, right?" Toby asks, and the whole table laughs. Toby can almost always make that happen. What a gift. Just yesterday she told how that child from next door said her poor puppy once ate a monopoly piece and her Daddy boiled it clean once it came out the other end. Toby said it had a *get out of tail free* card. "Get it? Do you get it?" Toby asked, and laughed so hard she had to excuse herself to go to the ladies room. It made Rachel think of that movie, *One Flew over the Cuckoo's Nest*, which she hadn't thought of in years, the part where the Danny DeVito character keeps putting a hotel in his mouth. Nineteen seventy-five. That was one of their movies there at a little theater in Arlington. *Godfather, Exorcist, Jaws, Taxi Driver.* Not a very romantic backdrop but lots of moments that made her jump and lean in to hide her face against Joe's shoulder, his big warm hand on the back of her head pulling her close.

"Hey, cat got your tongue? Dreaming of gefilte fish?" Stanley is tapping his fork against her plate. He stares at her in a way that makes her uncomfortable, like he can read her thoughts. The

T-shirt under his rumpled half-unbuttoned dress shirt says ROYAL RUMBLE and has a picture of one of those ugly wrestlers.

"Hey, I've got a question for you, Stanley," Toby says. "Did you ever know somebody named Art Silverman?" Toby looks at Rachel and shrugs a *what have you got to lose* look.

"Is he a wrestler on the circuit?"

"No," Rachel says. "He was my husband."

"Does he live here?"

"No. He's dead." Rachel is sorry Toby brought it all up but is still trying to decide if she's ready to make the next move, to ask about Joe. Now that C.J. has heard her talking to him, the whole secret is feeling a little off kilter. "But he used to visit here in the summer when he was growing up."

"Doesn't ring a bell. Why would I know him?"

"He was quite the ladies' man," Toby says. "And you're about the same age so I figure he might have competed with you."

"I have no competition." He raises his eyebrows. "In anything." He grins at Rachel and so she looks everywhere except at him. She watches the Barker sisters off in the corner eating sweet potato pie they have decorated with M&Ms, which one of them had in her purse. "However, to the best of my knowledge, in those days there were only three Jewish families in this town." He slams his fist on the table. "Look at me when I talk to you or I'll pin you to the mat, sister." He leans in so close she can feel his breath on her face.

"Fine then." She turns to face him. "I wouldn't expect you to know a goddamned thing I'm interested in, but I will listen."

"The Cohens lived beside us and old man Berkowitz lived on the way to the beach and the Friedmans who owned that old department store lived on the corner of Seventeenth and Pine. Sadie can tell you. She knew them all very well. Lots of Jewish families now, but back then that was it."

"None of that helps me," she says, and then without allowing herself time to think and change her mind, she continues. "Art visited a cousin of his who was not Jewish," Rachel says. They all look up as if struggling to figure this out. "People do marry out of their faiths, you know."

"Not people who are saved," Marge says, and adds more sugar to her tea. "People who are not saved do all kinds of things. Commit horrible atrocious crimes. Steal from their own family members—even their mothers. What was the cousin's name? If *he* lived here, one of us will know him. My people have been here forever. My people were here way before the Civil War."

"Well, let's get it on the *hysterical* register," Toby says. "Your family is old as dirt."

Rachel swallows and takes a deep breath before she allows his name to roll from her tongue. "Art's cousin was named Joe Carlyle."

"Oh dear Lord," Marge sits back in her chair. "I sure know who he is. Everybody knows who he is. Even Sadie would tell you what a rounder he was. Cousin, huh? Well, those are *not* good lines I can tell you that. "

"Might be where Art learned all his moves," Toby says, and laughs.

"Yes, might be," Rachel says, and feels them all looking at her. She wishes she were all alone on a busy horn honking street or in Filene's Basement with women throwing clothes and bumping around or all by herself in a chair in her room. She feels like she might cry, which is something she rarely does and it surprises her.

"He went with anybody who would look at him. And that poor wife." Marge has put down her knife and fork and has her hands up to her face. "I don't believe in divorce at all, but I believe that was a case where God would have told Rosemary to go forth and get one. I don't know if she was kind of simple retarded–like or just crazy from living with him."

"Art never knew any of that," Rachel says. "He couldn't have. He visited when he was just a young man."

"Well, then he didn't know him very well." Marge looks at Stanley for confirmation. "Joe Carlyle was bad news his whole life. And you should have seen his obituary." Marge looks right at her and Rachel has to stop herself from saying she did see it, that she has a copy in a book right beside her bed.

"He clearly wrote it himself," Marge continues. "He used words like *matriculate,* which people around here just do not say, and the article said he was intelligent in three different places."

"Like in the bedroom? In the car? And where?" Stanley asks.

"Three places in the *article.*" Marge raises her voice and then squeezes her lips together, clearly wanting to call Stanley something. "He said he was intelligent three different times and we all know if you have to say it that often, then it must not be true."

"Intelligent, once, twice, or thrice, who knows, but what I do know is that he was a real son of a bitch," Stanley says. "Screwed everything in sight and never paid his bills. He always had some kind of moneymaking scheme he was in on and had enough slick charm to get a little ways with it if he were dealing with someone from out of town. People were always trying to take him to court. He was as slippery as that Jell-O they keep trying to make us eat." Stanley sounds totally sane and clear and intelligent—too sane and clear—and then all of a sudden, after long eye contact with Rachel, shifts his attention back to Marge. "Hey, Marge, did you ever have a BM to improve your mood like that visiting priest advised you to do?"

"What!" She pauses with a forkful of potatoes. "How dare you turn that ugly crazy talk on me!"

"He was right there. Didn't you see him? Shaved head, pink golf slacks? Didn't look like a priest at all, said the two of you had a baby together back in the service, an ugly-as-hell baby, too." Stanley puts his elbows on the table and sticks his tongue out at Marge; it is the kind of thing that on an ordinary day might make Rachel laugh, but right now she is feeling sick.

"You need to go away." Marge holds her knife up and shakes it. "They need to haul you off somewhere with the other crazy people. There is no priest and I never had a thing to do with Joe Carlyle, though I can tell you it wasn't for lack of trying on his part!"

"Joe or the priest?"

"I don't know what in the hell you're talking about with a priest. I have nothing to do with the Catholic church and I never have. We were talking about Joe Carlyle and that's all."

"Marge," Toby says. "That language."

"Art never said anything like this. In fact, he thought a lot of his cousin," Rachel says. "Are you sure that you're talking about the right person? He grew up on Chandler Street and went to the Methodist church."

"That's him," Stanley says. "And he was always hanging out at the river, always had several gals on the line at once. He had to marry Rosemary because she was pregnant and her daddy would've killed him otherwise. Rosemary was a good kid, quite a bit younger, who wound up in the wrong place at the wrong time."

"Then she nursed him all those years he was an invalid," Marge says. "The church practically supported them because he had burned up every cent running here and there to Boston and DC and New York and Chicago. Bunch of worthless big talking hot air. My husband, Judge Henry Walker, who never judged anybody, claimed that there was a place for the likes of Joe Carlyle."

"Not worth two cents," Stanley adds. "But his wife stood by him."

"What choice was there?" Marge asks. "She wasn't trained to do squat and had children to raise. How humiliating. If he'd been my husband, I'd've found a way to get rid of him."

"Oh yeah?" Toby asks. "What would you have done?"

"Read my scrapbook some time and you'll see," she says. "There's more than one way to skin a cat."

"Or kill a spouse." Stanley spears his baked potato and holds it up. "Remember that famous potato that looked just like Richard Nixon? Who does this look like?"

Rachel pushes back from the table and stands. "That's a sad story," she says, and turns. "That's not what Art believed at all and so I am happy he isn't here to hear all of these stories." She walks quickly, but she hears Marge continue. "Truths," Marge says. "It's all the Lord's truth. A bad seed."

Rachel walks as fast as possible, knowing someone is following her. She gets to Sadie's door and then stands there, hand on the knob. She wants to hear her reaction to Joe's name. She needs to be near someone kind.

"Hey, what's the deal?" Stanley Stone grabs her arm and holds on. "I'm sorry if we upset you. Kind of hard to talk about somebody you've known your whole life and not be honest."

"There is no deal." She pushes him away and feels the tears filling her eyes. "My husband loved him, that's all. My husband spent years of his life, loving and respecting Joe Carlyle and believing that he was a wonderful man."

"And maybe he was," Stanley says. "Maybe he was good to your husband and deserves a little credit for that."

"It's a lot to process." She turns the knob and peeks in to see that Sadie is still napping, Harley curled up under her arm, his big fat head on her chest, so she eases the door back and then turns to go to her own room.

"I'm sure," he says. "I'm really sorry." He puts his hand on her shoulder and she lets him. He kneads her collarbone, rubs and pats her, and she lets him. She takes a deep breath and lifts the hem of her shirt to dab at her nose.

"Is there anything I can do?" Stanley asks.

She turns and looks him right in the eye and he doesn't go off or anything. He pulls her collar back into place and pats her again. "Nobody is all bad. I'm sure there were good things about him."

"Yes," she says. "There would have to be." She takes a deep breath. There would have to be. She was there. She saw and knew the good. She once saw him rush to help an old woman back to her feet, picked up all of her groceries. He gave money to beggars, talked to people in a way that made them feel important. He talked about how much he loved his children and wanted them to be proud of him. He said he had never loved anyone the way he loved her. She hears a door open and sees big floral arrangements being brought in to the chapel where there will be a service for Lois Flowers tomorrow. They announced it right before lunch noting that in the chapel there is a photograph of Lois with a remembrance candle burning and a guest book for all to write notes to her children. She is about to ask Stanley if he grew up with Lois, too, but realizes he is gone, never turning back to his ridiculous statements as he usually does but hurrying way down the hall with his shirttail hanging out and then disappearing around the corner. It is like she's been robbed, that time has played a trick on her and not a funny one. There is nothing funny about what she just heard, the way that all she believed in has been called into question. It is like believing in the afterlife only to discover there is nothing there.

Joanna

WHEN JOANNA LEAVES PINE Haven, she sees Stanley
Stone's son, Ned, across the parking lot studying the
bumper sticker on her car. It's a sticker C.J. had made after Joanna
told her how she hates all those brag stickers about "My child is
an honor student" blah blah blah. Her sticker is bright orange
with black lettering and says: MY KID IS AN ASSHOLE AND I BLAME
SANDHILLS ELEMENTARY. Ned is wearing tennis shorts and flip
flops and standing with his hands on his hips.

Joanna had waited with Kathryn Flowers until the funeral di-
rector and two workers arrived to put Lois on a stretcher and carry
her away. Kathryn had continued, the whole time they waited, to
reach for her mother's hand, each time startling, as if surprised to
find the lifelessness there. Joanna has seen this many times, the
dull quiet of a room after the fact, all the energy raised to such a
pitch suddenly gone. Places always feel so empty right after someone dies, the sensation of a whole lifetime of people and memories
disappearing with that last breath, all the air sucked right out of

the scene. Kathryn was exhausted and said so, the many weeks of watching and waiting closing in on her.

"Thank you," Kathryn said, "please let's stay in touch," and Joanna nodded and said of course, hugged her close as she often had, and as always, she knew that they will not stay in touch at all. It is too hard to stay in touch, too heavily laden to revisit regularly. They will see each other from time to time, brief glimpses and greetings that last only seconds and yet pull in all that has fallen into the past four weeks and the routine they have shared while waiting for Lois to die. Joanna will be at the memorial. She said how much she is going to miss Lois and she will. How could she not? And selfishly she will miss her daily schedule and time spent in a room that allowed her to see Ben's house while sitting with a woman who seems to her to have been the perfect mother.

"So what have you got against Sandhills? You probably went there yourself once, didn't you?" Ned asks when she gets close. "And who is your kid? The *asshole* could be in my class."

"No kids," she says. "A friend of mine made that as a joke."

"Funny," he says without cracking a smile. The silence is painful as is his not making eye contact with her and not making any moves to step away from her car.

"I'm Joanna." She extends her hand. "I was the volunteer with your mother when she died."

"I know."

"She was lovely," Joanna says. "I always think of her when the roses are blooming. She knew everything there was to know about roses."

"You saw and heard it all, didn't you?" he asks. "What did she say about me?"

"She was very private. She showed me all of her little boxes."

"Her garden is gone now," he says, and finally looks up, eyes red, a vein along his temple visible. "Paved paradise and put up a parking lot, something like that."

"I know," she says. "I was sad to see that."

"And my dad is now completely demented and can't even do it quietly like so many do."

"I know."

"So what don't you know?" he asks, eyes the same piercing blue of his dad's—eyes that most have learned to avoid for fear of getting flashed or cussed out.

"There's a lot I don't know," she says, and moves to open the door.

"Did you know that I would have a kid old enough for elementary school if he'd lived?"

"Yes."

"And did you know I got a divorce and had a breakdown, nearly drank myself to death and almost went to prison?"

"Yes."

"And does it even occur to you to politely say you don't know any of this?"

"Not really. We all have stories."

"Yeah, like you, for instance. Married how many times? Seven? Eight? Always in love with the town magician who has taken my seat at all the bars in and around the county."

"Didn't know any of that," she says, her face hot with anger and embarrassment and who knows what else. "So you win. Feel good about it." She gets in and slams the door. She cranks the car and waits for the blast of air from the vents to go from hot to cold. He doesn't move so she finally inches forward and cuts the wheels enough to get out. His hand is raised, maybe to say something else, but she ignores him, resisting the urge to flip him off and to swing around like she might hit him. At least he makes it easier not to feel sorry for him.

One of the many therapy sessions Luke insisted she take involved unpacking the heart. You close your eyes and take every person and every thing taking up space in your heart out and set them on your make-believe lawn. Every grievance and relationship and project. And then when the space inside is empty and clean, you survey the goods and decide what to put back. It was Luke's favorite exercise and one that she and C.J. have talked about many times since, laughing over the notion of whole corpses exhumed and expunged, exorcised. Joanna had told Luke that her imagined yard looked like Gettysburg or like that scene in *Gone with the Wind* when the camera pulls back and there are wounded and dead bodies as far as the eye can see—enough emotional carnage to keep the buzzards feasting for centuries. And then how clear so much becomes, like pulling old unrecognizable food from the fridge. Of course you need to throw that away. It's old. It's curdled. It smells bad so why in the hell would you keep it? Why in the hell would you want to chew or swallow it?

"Did they give you a mantra to say while you unpacked?" Luke had asked. "Or like did you have a song playing in your head as you cleaned house?"

"Get the fuck away from me," she told him. "That was my mantra. That's what I said to ninety-nine percent of what I pulled from my chest. Just get the fuck away from me."

"Sounds like *Alien*," Luke said. "You know when Sigourney pulls that awful thing out of herself."

"Exactly. That's exactly what it was like." *Leave me the fuck alone.* That is what she wants to scream at Ned Stone who is still standing there. Just the other day, C.J. told her about how Toby was stretched out on the floor of the exercise room in corpse pose to meditate and yelled at several people who wheeled too close to her head. *Get the hell away,* she said. *I'm doing my savasana.* It makes Joanna laugh whenever she thinks about it and how one of the sisters put a hand up to her mouth and gasped, clearly thinking *savasana* meant something nasty. She can tell Ned Stone thinks she is laughing at him. Fine. He's a jerk. A sad jerk but still a jerk. She would have loved nothing better than to befriend him, to take the time to talk about and remember his mother, but who wants to spend time with a jerk? Leave *him* the fuck alone.

She drives and then circles, takes deep breaths. She turns and drives past Ben's house, a big, beautiful, old house, the front porch crammed with all kinds of folk art and odd chairs. There is a big silver wooden box at one end of the porch and she recognizes it immediately as the disappearing chamber. And the blue Saab in the driveway is definitely the one she has seen these recent nights. C.J. said that Ben's wife was a total bitch. "Worse than I even thought, I'll tell you someday." C.J. was always saying that, *I'll tell you someday,* and Joanna keeps a running record of all she wants to know: Who are these men who used to call her that she kept notes on and who is Kurt's father? Who is this guy Sam she has started to mention and where does she go all those nights Kurt sleeps at Joanna's house? It's clear that there is a lot C.J. keeps hidden; and it's clear that there are some very old wounds she's still nursing. If only the inner wounds really *were* visible to the eye, you'd know better than to depend on those held together with flimsy sutures or you would immediately recognize and avoid those leaking puddles of bitter bile. You would scream and beg for help when you saw someone helplessly bleeding out all over the floor.

C.J. once said that if she can find a person who would never— even at the height of anger—or the lowest low take the pulpiest part of your heart and use it against you, then she could see being in a relationship. *That is the person I want,* she said. *Otherwise, fuck 'em. Accept no subs. I want someone as true blue and faithful as the moon. That's who I will love. That's who I will let get close to Kurt.*

"Who did you want to be when you were a kid?" C.J. had asked, another game they had played. C.J. had already said that she wanted to be the Little Mermaid, but then, when she realized she was never going to have a father or red hair or a good singing voice, switched over to Judge Judy. She liked the way Judge Judy took charge and told everybody what to do. It didn't matter who you were, if Judge Judy thought you were wrong and full of shit, she said so.

Joanna had wanted to be the Scottish woman in that movie *The Three Lives of Thomasina*—a beautiful woman who lived alone in the woods and who took in stray hurt animals and was thought to be a witch. Joanna owned a copy and they watched it one night, C.J. fluctuating between saying it was *beyond cheesy* to how much she loved the cat's voice narrating and the way the cat came back, eventually pulling all of its lives together. "So be her," C.J. said. "Start taking in some creatures. My friend Sam has tons of dogs and cats nobody wants. Get some warm bodies around here." Joanna was sitting in a rocking chair with Kurt hugged against her chest while she watched C.J. eat the last of the pizza and thought, *I have.*

C.J. had said when she worked as a psychic at the county fair she learned how to look in people's eyes, noting breath and pulse. It wasn't hard to read people, wasn't hard to give the gift of hope. Sometimes when the two of them were sitting there on Joanna's porch, mini lights and candles and jazz playing, anything was possible. Kurt loved it at Joanna's house and she loved the nights C.J. left him there to sleep over.

Joanna told C.J. that if she ever marries again (she seriously doubts this but *if*) instead of getting gifts, she wants people to take things. She will throw a big barbecue and say that everyone must take something on the way out—a vase or bowl or glass, a trivet or mug or bookend—candlestick, clock, linens, a book, a plant. In fact, when C.J. comes over later, Joanna will remind her. She will say that since she will likely never remarry, C.J. should just take something now. Part of unpacking the heart is getting rid of things you no longer need. And some things are hard to let go of. For Joanna it was knowing she would never nurse a baby, never greet a partner with the exciting news that she was pregnant. She once dreamed she nursed a baby goat, grateful amber eyes seeking her own as her milk let down and she woke with a feeling of exhilaration, the tingling sensation still in her breasts.

"Gross," C.J. had said. "What does that mean? Like aren't goats the bad guys in the Bible? Like lambs are good and goats are bad? Or maybe it's because your last name is Lamb."

"Maybe it's just a dream," Joanna had said, a little sorry she brought it up because C.J. continued to interpret for days after. "Pay attention if anyone says a word like *bleat* or *cloven* to you," she said. "Maybe you're going to meet a guy named Billy." And she went from Billy to Old Goat to the abbreviated O.G., which she still uses when there's someone she thinks Joanna should meet. Now Joanna starts gathering a few things she thinks C.J. might like: a cut-crystal vase and a silver ice bucket and some bronze bookends, A and Z.

Lois Flowers gave a lot of things away. Her daughter said that her mother was famous for slipping a bracelet from her wrist or a sweater from her back to give to someone who had complimented her. "People learned to be sincere," Kathryn said. "Otherwise you just might end up with a mallard green mohair hat and my mother eager to see you wearing it!" How hard to even sum up Lois Flowers in her notebook. She brought forward more stories than anyone has since she spent those last weeks with Luke. She had helped Kathryn work on the obituary. A whole life reduced to adjectives and a list of accomplishments. They placed a book in the chapel for residents to write their thoughts. The adjectives that spring to her own mind are *vibrant* and *generous* and *fun loving.*

Joanna could only imagine what her obituary might say if she departed right now and perhaps that is what haunts Ned Stone. He believes who he is based on all that is said *about* him. Joanna should have told him that she is considered the Patron Saint of Divorce. People talk about her. They have ever since she returned. You look exactly the same, they say, or almost the same. Your hair is the same—like it might still be 1975—and not too much gray at all. People talk and she doesn't care. If she had cared she never would have been able to come back and she wanted to come back, she needed to come back. Luke helped her get to a place where she *could* come back. People say she is the ship that keeps sinking, the tire that keeps going flat, the wine that turns straight to vinegar. She is a matrimonial nightmare, but all of those titles are so much easier to handle than having them know the truth, how long it has taken to get herself back, how her marriage to Luke, as unconventional as it was, was the greatest expression of love she has ever known. Why they are so interested is the real curiosity and so now she has decided to answer back in all honesty and then some. She can give them more than their money's worth. In a nutshell, she first married a really nice and conscientious person her parents were crazy about only to realize she shouldn't have. Her parents were thrilled and even told people how he was the best thing to ever happen to their family. Then her mother never forgave her. It was embarrassing. Who gets married and leaves in a year? She had wanted to answer that by saying it's the person who knew even as she said *I do* that she *didn't,* that's who. But at the time it seemed easier to get married than to have to face the town and return everything, all those gifts and the china and the shit nobody ever uses. Then she was off and running in all the wrong directions for all the wrong reasons. Running is rarely the best choice and running without thinking most likely a disaster.

"This is why I'm so proud of you for being a single mom," she told C.J. "Don't ever get married unless you are madly in love and know it is the best thing for your life."

"You assume I had a choice there," C.J. said, and then batted away all the questions that immediately sprang to mind. "Another day," she said. "A lot more wine and another day and maybe I'll tell the whole story."

"I hope so," Joanna had said, the weight of Kurt sleeping on her own chest feeling so good. C.J. had revealed nothing about who the father was or even if he knew about the child. But she did say she wrote everything down in case Kurt might need to know things someday. She said she writes and writes and deposits it in the special *safe* in her bathroom.

"So finish the marriage story," C.J. said. "How many and how many men in between? I'm still counting."

And she told all, one thread at a time, unraveling and unraveling the people who moved in and out of her life like waves until she married the man whose wife had died young, leaving two sweet babies she helped raise for over a year until he fell in love with someone else. And then, finally, hopeless and fed up with herself, she drove to New Hampshire, overmedicated, and fell in the busted hot tub and got rescued by Tammy and married Luke and then Luke died and she came home just in time to patch things up with her dad and here she is.

"That's some trip," C.J. said. "Damn. You could have a reality show. People in town say you broke up two homes. Married a lawyer. Married a queer. Married somebody dying just to get his money."

"Oh yeah," Joanna said, and reminded how just the other day at Pine Haven she had told someone. "And don't forget the one in prison or the dentist in Pasadena. Don't forget the one who eats fire in the carnival and the orthopedist in Denver."

"An orthopedist?" one woman who normally was hard of hearing screamed. "And you left him?"

"I bet if you took better care of your hair and clothes you wouldn't have lost so many husbands," Marge Walker said.

"Or if you stayed trim," another woman—very overweight and out of breath—added.

"Or if you learned to tell busybodies to shut up," Rachel Silverman said.

"Amen," Stanley Stone said. "I second the attractive Yankee-accented broad with the slight stoop in her posture."

"Trust me," Joanna liked to say. "I was married to a doctor. And a lawyer and an Indian chief. A butcher and baker and a candlestick maker."

"And a queer, too," Stanley said.

"Yes, and a gigolo," Joanna added, and then said, "I have always been loved by children, the elderly, dogs, and the mentally handicapped."

"Probably not the best announcement to make if you want to get a date," C.J. said.

When Joanna first came back to town, she said this sort of sarcastic thing often when someone began to quiz her. It provided an imaginary shield and now, she realizes, is not unlike C.J.'s piercings and tattoos and the harsh makeup she wears. "I've lived on communes and on ranches and worked as a maid in a topless resort," she once said in the checkout line at Food Lion. What she wanted to say was that returning to this place was likely the most masochistic thing she could possibly do but she had made a promise to her last husband that she would return and build a good life for herself and she is true to her word.

"Why do you do that to them?" her dad asked, one of those last days when his mind was clear and he wanted to explain to her the importance of keeping the Dog House a simple enterprise—no burgers or sandwiches of any kind—just hot dogs. The dog and bun are a given; the creativity and choice is all in the condiments.

"I'm just tired of their questions. Tired of their looks. One human makes one mistake—"

"One?" He held up one finger and cocked his head to the side, eyes tired but kind.

"More, many! But that's what I mean, one mistake that is never forgiven or forgotten leads straight to the next and the next and the next. What I learned is how to forgive myself and what I learned is I don't give a damn if anyone else ever forgives me or cares about me. That kind of caring is what ruined me."

"Your mother felt blamed."

"Because I blamed her. I did. But now I have let it all go. Please let it all go. I loved her, Dad, and I love you."

All of my husbands have been very nice people. That's another line she likes to use when being quizzed. First of all, people don't like when you say they were all nice because they are hoping for some dirt and second they want to ask *how many* but then decide not to; you can hear the gears of their brains clicking, smell the wood burning, and then someone won't be able to stand it any longer.

"Damn! How many times have you been married?" old Mr. Stone has asked numerous times.

"In which decade?" she asked. He thought this was hilarious and opened his magazine to a centerfold poster of one of those awful-looking wrestlers. He told her *this* was good husband material—a real man with the real goods. *How about that package?* he asked. It was hard to believe this was the same man she had had to coax to his dying wife's bedside, and no wonder his son was such an angry asshole.

"Do you have kids from all those husbands?" Toby asked, her

fanny pack stuffed with candy and tobacco products. Mr. Stone stopped to listen and unfortunately so did his son who had just arrived. She said she had a stepdaughter named Tammy in New Hampshire and two stepchildren in Chicago. She said she loved the children very much, but it was not a good match, which would almost always be true if your husband falls in love with someone else. Mr. Stone guffawed again and slapped his son on the back. Ned's face flushed with embarrassment, but they were both rescued by the continuation of Mr. Stone's actions as he snapped his fingers and then extended his open palm to Toby who unzipped her pack and put what looked like a piece of Nicorette into his hand.

"You're right!" he said chewing away. "I'm a lawyer and I know these things. Why would you expect an institution to remain constant? Jobs don't, laws don't. What's right for you in 1972 might not be right for you in 1974 and so on." He paused and held his hand to Toby again and this time she gave him a stick of Dentyne, which he sneered at but still put in his mouth. "What year is this? How do you and your ex-husband get along?"

"Which one?" she asked, and he bent over laughing, Toby and several others joining in.

WHAT SHE HAD longed for that night in New Hampshire was to just disappear—Beam me up, Scotty—she wanted to be erased, an unnoticed mark like that one *Twilight Zone* episode where the astronauts disappeared. When their pictures dissolved from the newspaper, all memory of their existence dissolved, too. That night she wanted the impossible, to have never existed at all. *Do you believe in ghosts? Do you believe in the power of magic? Do you believe that a normal ordinary girl can disappear?*

She did. But now each morning brings her the knowledge and relief that—thanks to Tammy—she failed. A cup of coffee, a walk, the weather. There is always something on the horizon. The people like Lois Flowers keep her feeling aware and alive just as Luke said they would.

She would have married David, too, if necessary, but it all worked out just fine. His recent letters are all about his smoke-house and his mother who still sends women to his door on a regular basis and someone he met who was working there for the summer and plays in a bluegrass band. He writes about his morning walks with Tammy who swims every day regardless of the weather. He said he plans to get a puppy in preparation for Tammy's old age and Joanna sent him a copy of her menu and circled the Puppy—plain with ketchup or mustard.

"So four times you've been married or three?" C.J. asked.

"Three. But keep my secret. Some people, like Marge Walker who was my Sunday school teacher a hundred years ago, have it up to seven."

"I hate her," C.J. says. "it's bad karma to hate I know, but it's hard. She has the worst feet. It's like her soul is represented there, you know?"

She and C.J. agree on just about everything—except of course on pedicures and wax jobs. Joanna does not understand a French pedicure. Why, she asked C.J. would you want to look like you were growing out your toenails like Howard Hughes. C.J. said she didn't know who he was and Joanna told her a rich eccentric who wound up at the end of his life eating ice cream and growing out his hair and nails.

"Sounds like most of the people at Pine Haven," C.J. said,

"except of course the rich part." Now C.J. will routinely say she has a date with *Howard Hughes* when on her way to soak feet and clip toenails and it makes them both laugh every time.

"But," Joanna told her, "what I really don't understand is the Brazilian wax job. Why would you want to look prepubescent? And worse, what kind of guy finds this attractive?"

"Yuck," C.J. said. "I never really thought of it that way and now I'm really sorry I did." C.J. said she really needed to meditate on this and would have to get back to her.

The box on Ben's front porch is a far cry from what they had used—old pasteboard television or air-conditioner boxes they got down at Western Auto and then spray painted or covered in pictures from magazines. Joanna was in charge of decorating their props and she spent hours working on everything, always so hopeful he would notice every sequin and feather. *And now ladies and gentlemen,* Ben announced, *I will make this normal ordinary girl disappear.* Joanna crawled into the damp pasteboard box too many times to count and then she waited, humid breath trapped and held within. Her heart raced when she heard his voice: *Ladies and gentlemen . . .* In the photo, he stood behind the screen. In the photo, he exists but there is no way to read him, no way to predict what is about to come.

She circles again and now his wife is out on the porch in short shorts and holding a legal pad. And then Ben is there behind her for just a second before he steps back inside. She imagines he is waiting there behind the screen, watching her, taking note of *her* passing by *his* house just as he has passed by hers. Or maybe he doesn't notice her at all. *Now you see her, now you don't.*

Notes about: Judge Henry Morton Walker
Born: October 4, 1922   **Died:** July 10, 2008, approximately 1:30 a.m.
Fulton, North Carolina

Judge Walker was an elderly courtly man well known and respected in the community; he was smart, confident, handsome. He knew how to put everyone at ease, especially his wife, Marge, who stayed busy measuring his intake of fluids and excretion of urine and taking his temperature and telling everyone what to do. He called her *the little general.* He called her Bossy and Bully. But usually he called her *sweetheart,* and when he did, it was like the wind went out of her and for just a second she hung there like a limp spent balloon until she could refill herself, inflating with upset and agitation about how whoever made his bed didn't do it very well: *And what kind of nurse was that woman who was just there? It took her forever to find a vein in his hand.* And she appreciated the Sunday school class coming to sing him a song, *but haven't they ever heard of something called the telephone, which a polite person should use prior to just showing up and ringing the doorbell?*

"Come sit with me, honey," he said. "Come rest for a minute and calm down." But she could not stop cooking and cleaning and making corrections on everything that had been done. He told me that she had always been a busy little thing, but it had been worse during crises. He said that when their son was in Vietnam, she polished the silver weekly and berated every paper boy so badly that finally the editor who lived down the street hand delivered their copy every day. "She means well," he told me. "And I could not have had a better wife." Every now and then, when Marge thought they were all alone, she leaned in and kissed him in a way that surprised me. It went against everything you might have thought and maybe explained his great affection a little bit better. "You're something, Marge," I heard him say on more than one occasion. "You sure are something." I never heard him complain or raise his voice. His one serious moment was when he told his son he wanted to give him a name to remember. This was a man he had sent to the chair twenty-five years before, and though all the evidence seemed conclusive, there was something that had always bothered him. "You may hear of the case," he said. "He was found guilty for the deaths of his wife and baby." And then on another day, he told me that he felt lucky to get to see the end coming, get things in order, be aware. He said he had seen so many tragedies and sudden deaths, those whose lives were stolen without any warning, that to get to be present and have time to say things and get your papers in order seemed like a real gift. He said he needed as much time with Marge as he could get—to say good-bye, to prepare her for all she would need to know. He said the pain in his spine was such that he could not roll over onto his left side to read as he had done nearly every night before sleeping since he was a teenager. He said there were so many things to miss, but there were also many things to be grateful for. "We appreciate all that you and your supervisors and the doctors have done," he said to me. "Marge thanks you, too, even if she forgets to say it." He told his children to leave and get some rest and he told me the

same. He said he would see everyone bright and early in the morning
and then he waited until Marge had fallen asleep in the chair beside his
bed and he died.

Marge called as soon as she woke and found him there. She was furious that he did not wake her up before leaving and even angrier at the
way the funeral home people made a mark on her living room wall with
that stretcher. "I called and told them they could just come right back
over and take care of it, too," she said. "I could do it myself with a Mr.
Clean sponge, but I didn't put it there. How irresponsible can you be?
Pick up the dead and ruin a freshly painted wall. Well, I have had it and
they have not heard the last of me." And then she went into her room
and did not come out for several hours. Judge Henry Walker had once
referred to his wife as Hurricane Marge—lovingly adding that she was
a force, a beauty, something to behold and someone you'd better clear
a path for. And he was the eye of that storm, a lesson in calm patience
and control and dignity.

[from Joanna's notebook]

Henry Morton Walker

Guilty or innocent. Guilty or innocent. Knox Godwin, lanky and lazy with a permanent smirk and a record as long as any in the county, but did he do what they said he did? Did they really prove it? Did he really stab his wife that many times and why so many? Why so many with her clearly dead—no human on this earth capable of surviving that infliction. Testimony said she was most certainly dead by the thirteenth stab and then to deliver eleven more? And then to do the same to the three-year-old watching. Knox Godwin, please rise, and he never looks up; even when ordered to look up he looks up and over as if staring at a spot on the wall as if his eyes won't focus or maybe he is seeing what he said happened, that he came home from hunting and found the dog shaking in the yard, paws covered in blood and he ran in and cradled his wife and baby girl and screamed and screamed. Weren't nothing I could do, he said, weren't nothing I could do. But the jury finds you guilty—guilty as charged. I did not do it, he said. I love my wife. I love my baby. I did not do it. And there was a similar case several counties over and another several counties over from that, murders that seemed to happen randomly or did they and he didn't push to know what if any connections there were. He didn't want to think about it and the more time that passed, he really didn't want to think about it. He wanted to trust the system. He was not God. He could not know. He upheld the system as best he knew how and he was there when they sat him in the chair and fastened him in and that's when Knox Godwin looked at him and that's when Knox Godwin said just wait until it's your wife, your baby. Then you'll see. Then you'll know and that's when he felt something ice cold and heavy weighing him so low all he could think was how he could not wait to get home, could not wait to see Marge there with everything watched over and organized; she would fuss about something so insignificant and he would hold her and comfort her and tell her not to worry, it would all be okay, it would all be just fine, their life at home a refuge far removed from the hatred and violence he witnessed day after day and Knox Godwin called his name: Judge Walker, hey, Henry Walker, and the lights flickered and dimmed as they always do—such current, such pulse, the burning smell leaving him feeling so cold and heavy and guilty, holding his breath, shielding his eyes and nose and mouth, sparks of light on his inner lids, bloodred lights.

Abby

ABBY WANTED SADIE TO stay awake, but she said she couldn't; she said she was so tired, she could not hold her eyes open and would Abby please come back later. *Everything will be better later, honey,* she said. *Everyone always feels better after lunch and recess and story time.*

Everything will be better later. Now she repeats this again and again and has since leaving Sadie's room and venturing back into the parking lot where she sat on the curb and watched the big black limousine parked there. She had waited until they wheeled out a stretcher—the person all covered and zipped into a bag. A woman in a navy suit stood there with her hand on the body until one of the men took her hand and led her off to the side. They closed the doors and off they went. She circles back by Esther Cohen's on her way home, the dark trails of vines clinging as she pushes her way back through to the old section. There's a cigarette butt rubbed out on the headstone and the other notes are gone. She stands, listening—squirrels in the leaves, birds singing, cars in the distance. This has never happened before and she reaches into her back pocket for the note she found earlier, but it's not there, probably left at Sadie's. She hears a dog barking but knows it's not Dollbaby. She is about to leave when she sees the little folded scrap under the urn. *Time's up. Fuck you.* She holds her breath waiting. It could be a trick, a trap; there could be people watching her, wanting to see her get all scared or cry and run toward home. She takes a deep breath and waits for her heart to stop racing. She hears rustling in the leaves behind her; she hears a distant car and then very slowly turns and begins walking, the note clutched in her fist. *Everything will be better. Everything will be better.*

When she comes out of the other side of the cemetery, her mother is out on the front porch, bending and looking under the big wicker sofa. When her mother stands and calls out to her, Abby knows that it's not good. It's the voice her mother always uses when something is not good. Abby is shaking her head and crying before her mother even says all the words—how she got a phone call and how Dollbaby was way out in the country, hit by a car, a nice old farmer took the time to move her off the road and read her tag and then he buried her.

"Why did he bury her?" Abby screams. "She's mine. She's my dog and I want to bury her."

"Honey," her mom says. "He thought he was being helpful."

"Well, he's not. He's not being helpful." Abby runs upstairs and into her prissy white room and rips the covers from the bed; she pulls the sheets off and bundles them all in the center of the room. Then she opens all of her drawers and dumps them out. She kicks and throws and tangles until her heart is pounding and she is all sobbed out, her eyes swollen and face splotchy. She cries until she dozes off that way, imagining Dollbaby is there, trying not to imagine how she looked there by the side of the road. She does not move when her parents come into her room, first her mother and then later her dad. He puts his hand on her back and holds it there, says he is so sorry. He wishes he had built a better fence. He promises a new dog when she's ready and then she hears him go back downstairs and onto the porch where he is working on the chamber—the final touches, he had said and held out shiny brass handles that she saw through barely opened eyes. She keeps the covers pulled over her head to block the afternoon sun and imagines that Dollbaby is coming home. She hears her nails on the hardwood stairs, the kerplunk when she flops down right beside Abby's bed. The next time she opens her eyes, the room is darker, past when Sadie usually eats dinner, and she begins putting everything back where it belongs, slowly folding and remaking and smoothing. The last thing she wants is a stupid birthday party. She is thinking of all the ways she might be able to get out of it when she hears her parents, the angry sounding whispers that will keep getting louder.

"They're all so stupid," Richie had told her. "They're all so full of shit."

She writes that on a piece of paper she plans to leave where they will see it. *You are full of shit and I hate you.* She stuffs a couple of T-shirts and her cheap MP3 player into her backpack. She's supposed to get a real iPod for her birthday and she's supposed to get a phone, but who cares? She's not going to that stupid party. She's going back to Sadie's and ask if she can sleep over.

"It's your fault," her mother says. "You should have built a better fence."

"Oh great, nice," he says. "Be sure you tell everybody I killed the dog. Be sure you spin it so I'm the bad guy again. Be sure to call Andy and Liz so they'll feel so sorry for you and want to take you to dinner or something since of course it's all about *you*."

Abby stands out in the front hall, but they don't see her there.

"Maybe I will call them. Always nice to speak to an adult."

"Price tag on your ass." He points to a round white sticker on her mother's pants. "I hear the price is up, though the value is down."

"Fuck you."

"Obviously not your job these days, but I do know you're working somewhere."

"You don't know anything."

"Don't be a fool," he says. "I know all I need to know."

They aren't even interested in Dollbaby. They've already forgotten all about her and they've forgotten about Abby, too. Nobody said, *Let's drive and get her.* Nobody said, *What can I do for you, sweetheart,* the way that Sadie will do when she gets back over there. Sadie will know what to do because she cares. Her parents don't care. They are just like Richie said. So fuck them. When they look for her there will be no one home. *Time's up. Fuck you.* She moves quietly through the hall and out the front door, then pauses at the opening of the cemetery. She almost takes the long way, on the sidewalk and around the big block, but she doesn't want anyone to see her. The streetlights aren't on yet, but they will be soon. She steps in and waits, listens until she hears the door slam. Her dad gets in his car and drives away and then she watches as the kitchen light comes on and then the one on the stairs. She is going to count to ten and then she is going to run as fast as she can. She will not stop anywhere near Esther Cohen's grave but will run straight through to the other side and she will first go to Sadie's room to see if she's still awake, and if she is, she will ask if she can come in and talk. And if Sadie is sleeping, then she will just sit right there near her bed and wait. The shadows are long, the passage dark up ahead. Sometimes she counts the bats that fly out of the eaves of the long abandoned caretaker's cottage over near Esther Cohen's grave, but not now. Not today. Now she quickens her steps, her feet moving to the rhythm of Dollbaby, Dollbaby, Dollbaby. She tries not to think about what she looked like there by the side of the road. *Dollbaby, Dollbaby, Dollbaby.* She hears rustling beyond the shrubs as she passes and tries not to think. Don't think, don't think. *Dollbaby, Dollbaby, Dollbaby.* She walks as quickly as she can, eyes on the ground so she won't trip and fall. *Dollbaby, Dollbaby, almost there, almost there.*

Stanley

S TANLEY IS TIRED OF his game, tired of pretending he doesn't notice what is really going on; the way it is so clear Sadie is fading away, the way Rachel Silverman clearly had more connection to Joe Carlyle than she let on, the way Ned, for all the pushing, is still not out there actively seeking a new life and company better than his flaky old man. After dinner he goes and sits in the chapel and stares at all the photos of Lois Flowers. He had known her for years. Some people thought she was a little uppity and overdressed for these city limits, but he admired the way she went her own way, or at least seemed to. He closes his eyes and pictures her swaying there in the dining hall, jet black hair fixed just so. He liked the way she could make her voice gruff and then come right back and hit every high note. She will be missed around here. She leaves a big empty hole.

He looks up and there is Rachel Silverman. She sits in the pew across from him, also looking straight ahead at Lois, a young Lois on a city street, a war bride, a young mother, mother of the bride, grandmother.

He's so tired, but he has to say something, especially after being so serious earlier. He had hoped to sit with her at dinner, but she didn't come and neither did Sadie. He sat with Toby who spent the whole time talking about how it just wasn't the same without Sadie and Rachel. The silence is unbearable and he knows he has to break it. "This ain't no synagogue, sister."

"It's interfaith." She spits and then softens and points at the photographs. "I used to wear my hair just like that. In fact, I also had a sweater just like that, too. What a lovely person she was."

"Lois was always known for her clothes. I've known her my whole life." He feels a catch in his throat and has to say something else, quick, one of those stupid things he thinks up just for these occasions. "And speaking of clothes, why do they call a cheap little part of a turtleneck a "dickey"? Why not a neckey?" He can smell her cologne, can see the dirt on the side of her hot pink shoe. "A dickey should fit on something else, right? And where'd you get those shoes anyway? They make me think of jokes my sons used to tell when they were young and ridiculous."

"I bought them."

"I know how it went. Why did the elephant wear red tennis shoes? And then it was something like to hide in a strawberry patch or a bag of M&Ms or some other stupid place."

"Are you calling me an elephant?"

"No, no way. I know not to tell women such things."

"Shhhh." Marge and a whole army of church women with walkers come in and sit right behind him. "This is a place of worship and respect."

"You're right," Rachel says, and turns back toward the front and then in a few minutes she gets up and heads back out in the hall.

Stanley waits until he hears the door close and then he follows, runs, in fact, to catch up with her. He gets right up behind her and asks if she'd like to come to his room to listen to Herb Alpert and drink martinis.

"Not this time," she says sarcastically.

"You can pretend I'm *Joe Carlyle*." He speaks the name in a way that makes it sound like it's dripping in disgust. He walks ahead of her, self-consciously aware of how disheveled and demented he must seem to her. He is almost to his hall when she comes up behind him. She presses in close and whispers in his ear. "First of all, I do *not* have haunches like a sack mule as you said several months ago and I do *not* have horns, and secondly, I am on to you. If you would ever like to have a real conversation with me sans whipped cream and martinis and other malarkey bullshit, I am here, otherwise, just stay the hell away from me. This is hurtful. All that you are doing is hurtful."

"What do you mean you're on to me?" He can't look at her.

"The act. I watch you. I'm no fool. You need to join the theater. You might actually be appreciated there."

"What act?"

"Oh, come on. I spent years in a courtroom and I know how to study a face," she says. He knows she is within a foot of him, but he still doesn't turn around. He can smell her cologne. "You have nice eyes, in fact, and a captivating face when you aren't behaving like some goddamned imbecile." She says this last part with gritted teeth. "Earlier today, for instance, there was a moment."

"Are you saying you find me attractive?" he interrupts.

"No. But I am saying that for a few minutes there you acted like a human being, and a kind one at that."

"That's sad."

"What's sad? Being kind to someone? That I know you're faking, though God only knows why? That I thought you might be someone, like Toby or Sadie, who I could actually have a real conversation with? We were both lawyers. We both live in this"—she pauses—"this home for the aged. We both clearly have things we're hiding from."

"Oh boy."

"I rest my case." She steps around and bends forward to make eye contact. "So why?"

Stanley sighs and opens the door to his apartment, motions for her to come in and she surprises him and does, leaving him suddenly worried about the way it looks or what he might have lying about that she might latch onto. She walks straight and picks up a copy of *Wrestlemania* under which is a copy of the *New Yorker* and *Harper's,* a stack of *Wall Street Journals* and all of his gardening catalogs. And under Herb Alpert she finds Frank Sinatra and Louis Prima and Cab Calloway and a whole library of classical. "What's the deal?"

"My son. He wouldn't leave me alone, said he was going to move in with me. I just want him to have a life." He pauses, realizing how stupid it all sounds as he says it, recognizes how he has avoided dealing with all the barriers standing between the two of them, barriers that have been in place for as long as he can remember. "He thinks I saved him and that he's forever indebted to me or some such crap and I want him to break off and have his own life."

"But isn't this kind of extreme?"

"Yes, but it's such a long tiring story." He waits, giving her the

chance to bail, but instead she sits and makes herself comfortable and motions that he continue. "He fucked up early in life—
always in trouble—one of those kids who always got caught, then
it looked like he was on a path and was going to be okay but no
such luck. Too vulnerable. I want him to have a life. Kids need
to live their own lives." He takes out the Herb Alpert album and
puts it on the stereo. "It keeps people from bothering me." They
both laugh. "In the beginning, people would come by and want to
hear it, say things like, *I haven't thought of this in years,* but after a
while, it got old. Even Toby is sick of it."

"But surely there's an easier way to do this with your son," she
says. "I mean, think of what you're missing by not having a *real*
relationship with him."

"We've never had a relationship," he says, and the weight of the
words hit him. He sits down, shocked by how sad and stupid it all
is. "Oh God. We really have never had a relationship." He puts his
head in his hands and takes several deep breaths. "Me telling him
what to do. That's it. That's all." He feels her hand on his shoulder,
patting and then held there. "Enough about me," he finally says.
"Tell me about you. Tell me about Joe Carlyle."

She begins talking and he listens. In fact, he can't believe how
open and honest she is, her voice rising and falling in a way that he
finds mesmerizing. She is able to describe in a few simple words
the loneliness she felt in her life, the kind of loneliness that others
don't really see because everything looks so good and full from the
outside. *An inner loneliness.* She said it was something she always
thought would go away and then she thought, no, you just learn
to live with it. Then she met Joe Carlyle at the height of loneliness and it felt like the whole world shifted. She was almost forty

and was suddenly aware of all the doors that were going to begin closing—childbirth and career pursuits, even the geography of what you call home, family members and friends aging and dying and leaving new empty spaces to fill.

"Sounds pretty depressing, doesn't it?" she asks, and smiles at him in a way he has never seen her smile. She is relaxed, leaning on the arm of his sofa, fingers toying with a piece of needlework thrown over the arm that Martha had always kept there and that Ned had reverently placed just so when he helped Stanley move into this place. Martha had done the work as a young woman and now Rachel Silverman's sturdy ringless hand strokes the fine threads in a way that is tender and admiring. "But it feels good to talk." She nods at him. "It does. It feels like I'm alive again. Which is what I felt that summer I met Joe. We live days and weeks and months and years with so little awareness of life. We wait for the bad things that wake us up and shock our systems. But every now and then, on the most average day, it occurs to you that this is it. This is all there is."

"I do know this," he says. "I know what you're saying."

"And Joe, whatever else he was, was a talker and a wonderful storyteller. Oh, he could make you feel like you were there. He talked about that Saxon River all the time, the dark brown water like tea, the low hanging branches, the moccasins zigzagging from bank to bank. I hung on his every word. I'll confess I found him very attractive. Up until that moment, I wasn't even aware that I had a libido." She pauses, as if testing, checking to see if he registers a look of shock or surprise, so he is careful to keep his face as blank as possible and nod in a knowing way. He spent enough time in court to know how to do a few things, too. He nods again and motions his hand for her to continue and she does. "Well, I had one. It had been dormant my whole life and then all of a sudden there it was!"

Stanley is about to say Joe Carlyle affected a lot of women that way, but he stops himself and instead studies his own hands, the hair on his knuckles, his wedding band so loose lately he worries he might lose it. It also occurs to him how lucky Joe Carlyle was on that day—a man in the right place at the right time even if he was a son of a bitch.

"And so there I was as Art was dying looking ahead to the last chapter of my life and wondering how I wanted to spend it. I don't have children to depend on or them on me. There it was, the ultimate freedom. Did I want to go to Europe? Go to some island somewhere? Take lots of trips and cruises with Elderhostel? Retire where I'd spent my whole life and just watch winter after winter come and go until I broke a hip and slid on downhill? Then I thought why not see the world Joe had made come so alive for me? The small-town life, the river beach and old pavilion. I wanted to see where he had been a child; I wanted to see where his heart developed. And of course I believed it to be a good heart; I still want to believe it was a good heart, that some part of what I had with him was real and worth protecting."

"I'm sure it was," he says without looking up.

"No you aren't," she says. "But I do appreciate your saying so. It's kind of you, Stanley, and I need the kindness."

"You will have it, then." His voice shakes as he says this and it makes him cough. "I've really missed conversation. Never thought I would, but I do."

"You know"—she reaches and puts her hand on his bare

arm—"even if all he did was wake me up, that would be something good, wouldn't it?"

"Yes, I think so."

"And the way he described life around here sounded like a life I would love to have had. It was so different from anything I had ever known."

"I'm sure about *that*." He laughs and asks if she wants a glass of sweet tea before or after she accepts Jesus Christ as her Lord and Savior. "But what about your heart," Stanley says, unable to look at her as he says it, so aware of the portrait of Martha staring out at him from over the mantel, a bouquet of roses Ned brought earlier in the day, there in her favorite cut-glass vase. "Tell me about your heart."

"Late. My heart came so very late. Little glimmers early on. The other day I was thinking maybe only now has my heart fully come to be. I sit and listen to Sadie talk and I close my eyes and roam to all the places I loved. And I didn't even know how much I loved them, which is sad but better late than never." She slides her hand along his arm, plays with the band of his watch before lacing her fingers with his. "She has opened something in me that probably should have been opened when I was eight. Right? Isn't that what she always says. We're all just eight years old. My parents were immigrants and they were terrified that at any moment someone in authority might show up and deport them. They lived like they were living by way of some mistake. My brother and I were their great hopes. First my brother because he was the oldest and of course because he was a boy. He became a doctor, which thrilled them and then I became a lawyer because I knew they would have to be proud of that, too."

"Hmmmm." He feels his face flush. "I'm sure they were proud of you. Not many broads our age doing that."

"I didn't want to be afraid like my parents had always been," she said, "and of course the irony is that I was anyway. Foolishly, I had convinced myself I had no fear at all. In fact, I felt that way this very morning only to have it all unravel. At lunch today, I felt absolute terror to hear the truth and I also realized that without the stability I had in my life with Art, I would have always *been* afraid, I might never have done anything at all. Art's presence kept me from being afraid and I never gave him credit for that."

"Until now."

"Yes, until now."

"I had something similar, I think," he says, so aware of not glancing at Martha's portrait.

She leans her head back and closes her eyes. "Thank you for listening." She pauses and he squeezes her hand in response, so aware of every particle in the room, the filigreed doily under her fingertips, the crack of the bedroom door where he can see the foot of his bed where one of Martha's prize quilts is spread.

"I went back to my room after lunch," she says, "and I thought of all the things I might do, everything from heading back to Boston to closing my eyes and pointing at a map, but then I started thinking that maybe there's something good to find in it all. In the school of Sadie, we'd start looking for the positive things that might have led me here."

"Did you come up with anything?" he asks. "You know, other than Jesus and lard and the Confederate statue and the fact that our winters are so much easier than those in MassaTOOsetts."

"Meeting Sadie and Toby," she says, and then adds "and you" as what seems an afterthought. "Watching someone like Lois leave the earth with such great style and grace."

"Let's go back to the part about me."

"Okay. Meeting you here, and working so hard to figure you out. You've made me furious and you've made me laugh at ridiculous asinine things I couldn't imagine laughing at and the process has sharpened and renewed all of my senses."

"Nothing dull about you, that's for sure. You're the sharpest tool I've met here."

"Thanks," she says. "Though not the world's greatest feat in this particular establishment."

"You know," he says, "I've got to tell you that I'm really feeling the need to put some better clothes on. Let you see how I'm supposed to look. You know I'm really capable of driving and doing all sorts of things. I still have my license and a car. If I tell Ned the truth, I can get my keys back. I can, hell, I can go and do anything I want. I'm only seventy-nine. They say my heart is that of a sixty-year-old."

"You do have a good heart," she says. "I would not have thought so a month—even a day—ago, but I think you do. And I think your son deserves to know that."

"I hope so," he says, and automatically switches channels as he has done for so long. "The heart is a tough old organ, you know? Like the liver, the kidneys, the lungs, the brain . . ."

"I think I see where this is going."

"Really?" He pauses. "I'd love to know what you're thinking. I was going to say *spleen* and *thyroid,* but here's what I'll tell you instead. I ain't dead. I clearly ain't what I used to be, but I also am not dead."

"I see."

"I'm putting on good clothes and shaving so you can see what I'm supposed to look like." He pats her hand and rushes to his bedroom door. "Promise me you won't leave."

"I promise," she says, and raises her hand. "Besides, where would I go?"

"Wherever you go every day. I watch you." He raises his voice as he dashes to his closet to pull out a pair of pressed khakis and a starched pale blue dress shirt. "I see you going off into the woods twice a day."

There is silence and at first he's afraid she left without telling him. He waits, staring in the mirror, smoothing back his hair. "I go talk to Joe," she says. "And Rosemary. I talk to her, too."

"How about you talk to the living for a while? How about you talk to me? Come see me instead and we can talk. We can dance. I'm an excellent dancer, or used to be." He slathers up and shaves, looks in the mirror once more, then checks his breath. He is old, but he's not dead. She is standing and staring at Martha's portrait when he comes out.

"Your wife was beautiful," she says, and he nods, uncomfortable with the way she has conjured Martha into the room, disrupting what he thought might be a romantic moment.

"She was a good person, too," he says. "I don't think I ever realized how good either."

"Yes, same with Art," she says. "And Joe. You know I really don't want to let go of what I had with Joe."

"So don't. Besides, he probably was different with you. Don't beat yourself up about it. Do like Sadie, cut out the part you like and stick it elsewhere."

She laughs. "I'm too much of a realist for that, always have been. I'll get it all put in perspective. I'm very good at that sort of thing. It just takes time."

"Yeah, I'm a realist, too," he says, and she mouths *right* and lifts up a wrestling magazine from the coffee table.

"So tell me about Art," he says, and she does. Practical and hardworking lawyer. Liberal thinker. Active in local politics.

"My God," he says. "I think you were married to me."

"I left my whole life behind me," she says as if shocked by the realization.

"So did I. Except for Ned, of course."

"And I'm supposed to go see everything tomorrow. The house where Joe grew up and the place on the river he loved so much. The road through the thick piney marshland where there are herons and mosquitoes almost as big." She laughs. Joe always said they had two kinds of mosquitoes where he was from: the no-see-ums that can eat you alive without ever being seen and those big enough to open the door and walk on in. He told her that when they were stretched out on the sand and he kept wiggling his fingers in between the buttons of her blouse to give her a pinch.

"It's a beautiful drive through there," Stanley says. "And you can stop and get a hot dog right there at the halfway point. It's just about all there is."

"That's what the girl told me. The girl who does hair and nails is taking me."

"The one with all the metal in her ears and nose?"

"Yes. I like her," Rachel says, and again lifts the magazine from the coffee table and opens it to a centerfold of the one they call the Undertaker. "She uses her metal and tattoos like *some* people use other things."

"Tough life she's had," Stanley says. "She's done pretty well given the hand she was dealt. A lot of sadness." He lets his arm drop around her shoulders and is surprised at how easily she relaxes and leans into him. "I can drive you all those places," he says, and without allowing himself a moment to think or reconsider, he leans in close with the idea he wants to kiss Rachel Silverman right on the lips, but she sees him coming and raises a hand between them.

"Isn't this a little fast?" she asks.

"Maybe, but I'm thinking we'd be foolish to wait."

"That may be."

"In fact, I don't think we should waste a minute, do you?"

"No. No, I suppose you're right."

He goes to pull the blinds and sees that strange little girl from next door running across the parking lot. He doesn't know how Sadie can stand the way she runs in and out all day long, but it doesn't seem to bother her. The sun has dropped out of sight, and there are just a few lingering streaks of violet light out there near the cemetery. He turns on the stereo—Herb Alpert. "A Taste of Honey." "We can listen to something else," he says. "But I can promise that when this is on, no one comes to visit."

"So, then, leave it," she says and walks over to him. "We can dance to this one. We can pretend it's 1965."

Rosemary Sewell Carlyle
Born: December 3, 1933   **Died:** September 15, 2008, 2:20 p.m.
Fulton, North Carolina

The small brick ranch baked in the treeless yard, dried overgrown azaleas the only adornment. A rotten canoe with her name in white stenciled letters leaned against the chain-link fence along with an assortment of paddles and a rusty bike. Inside, the drapes were pulled and stacks of magazines covered every surface of the bedroom where she lay in bed. The house was drenched in tobacco residue, the smell so strong that I never wore anything that couldn't immediately be put in the washing machine; I often stripped my clothes off on the back porch as soon as I got home. When I asked about the photo on her dresser, she said it was the day she wed down in Dillon, South Carolina—*not but fifteen*. She was going to have a baby and had decided that might be okay because how else would a girl like her get a man like Joe Carlyle. *Live and learn,* she said. *Live and learn.* She dozed, in and out with the rhythmic flow of the mechanical breaths that prolonged her life. What to take? What to save from this one? Loss? Sadness? Her children were rarely in touch; she didn't even know where her son lived. "They'll be here when they think there's something they can take," she said. "They'll all show up when I'm gone to get this little bit of nothing."

When I asked if she had always lived in this county, she nodded. "I went to the North one time for a visit," she said. "I rode a train and was so scared I didn't get out of my seat for nearly fifteen hours." She closed her eyes as if trying to see herself there, shuddered. "I was scared to death."

When I asked about the canoe with her name on it, she said *happier times*. She said when she was a young girl the river was the place to be. Long ago that was the place to be—music and dancing on a summer night—but now who even remembered and who cared. *That was a lifetime ago.* She was quiet most of the time. She liked for the television to be on and turned up loud. She said she watched *All My Children* and the one that came on right before it even though she didn't care about any of them or what happened to them. When I asked if there was anything I could do for her, she showed me her address book and asked that I make sure the people with red checks by their names get the news of her death. There were about a dozen addresses, all women in other towns, half in other states. She died during a commercial break while I was rubbing her feet, that address book open and on her lap.

[from Joanna's notebook]

Rosemary Carlyle

She found all kinds of things in his pockets. Who goes to a movie right by himself in the middle of the day? And what business did he have traveling to work in places so far off anyway? Collecting addresses like you might collect green stamps. She hated getting hauled around and wouldn't have gone even if he'd wanted her to. She never trusted him once they were married and why would she? She felt sorry for him there at the end—paralyzed and unable to talk—diapers and everything he would have hated to know. He never even changed a diaper for their children and then he had to wear them. He deserved that. She thought it served him right. She had come to hate him by then and hate will eat you up. It's why she can't open her eyes even as she feels the sun moving across the room. The river was nice but so long ago. What is a favorite day? that girl asks. Questions and questions she don't know the answer to. Is there one? Can you go there? Think about it, but if there was one she forgot it. If there was one, it was a hundred miles away because her wedding day was hot and sticky and she felt sick as a dog and it was downhill from there on. But that lotion on her feet feels good. It smells good. Maybe this is the best day. Maybe this is it.

Sadie

I T IS HARD TO stay awake with Harley there purring like a fat little motorbike. He is so darling. Sadie loves him too good to talk about and she loves sweet little snorting Rudy and she loves Abby so much. Oh, and she loves her children and they are all so wonderful about calling and checking in on her. Paul wants her to come live closer to him, Lynnette wants that, too, but of course she has told them that she likes living right there where she has always lived. Horace is right next door and she has so many friends. She has too many friends to name and of course she has her own mother to think about. She has spent some time today cutting out a picture of herself that someone took just recently and now she and her mother are going up to New Hampshire where someone was talking about some time yesterday or today. Toby, maybe. Toby is so funny; it is like it is her job to make everybody laugh. And that Benjamin, she is so upset about him it makes her chest ache, what he is doing to that precious sweet child of his. A child is to be treasured. A child should always come before everything else.

Abby was here just a minute ago and she said something about her mother's pants. She said she wished her mother would wear pants like other mothers. "High-waisted stretch pants and not cut to her crack like what a teenager would wear." Sadie told her she couldn't even imagine that and Toby said well she could. "And underwear up the crack like dental floss." That Toby is something and it made Sadie laugh even though she didn't want Abby to see her laugh. She told Toby she needed some time alone with Abby and that's when they just sat side by side and watched some television.

"My sweet mother," she told Abby. "I could have taught her so much." She held Abby's hand and squeezed it. She loves the feel of a child's hand in her own; there is nothing better than that. "You might have to teach your mother," she said, but then when Abby asked *how* she realized she had no idea at all.

"I was in a school show one time," Sadie told her, and then she told all about being in a show with Grover Fowler and they laughed and laughed. She always really liked Grover Fowler but she didn't tell that part. Harley feels good there on her lap and he likes to put his nose up against hers and kind of bump. Yes, the children want her to move, but she can't move. She has a whole business and people who would be so disappointed if they couldn't come see her and have her make them up a picture. And Horace. When Horace was gone, she slept on his side of the bed so that instead of missing him, she was only missing herself and where she used to be. And she misses her bathtub, too. She might say she never knew until lately just what a comfort a good hot bath could be, but that would not be true. She knew as soon as she was without Horace that nothing could be taken for granted. She loved to lie there in the heat—her body not young but certainly younger than it is now—and she watched the light and in it the mimosa tree in the sideyard. Some call that a trash tree, but she said a trashy beauty with its little pink puffs and long seedpods she liked to shell as a child pretending she was shelling butter beans like she remembers seeing her mother doing. She heard kids and skates and car radios and yard sprinklers like a beautiful symphony. Call it July. And there could be a recording of each and every month and each and every day and that would be so nice, recording the days. She always wanted some day of the week underwear, but that seemed so extravagant, especially for someone who was married and taught school. But then she got Lynnette some and Lynnette never wore the right day at the right time, but that was okay. Lynnette was a child who hears that different drummer and Sadie is proud of the fact that she never tried to change what the child was hearing but instead encouraged her to do her best and be happy. In the middle of a dark night she liked to plant her open palm on Horace's back and draw in the heat and then she would move her hand in slow steady circles. He will call soon. He always calls and she is always right ready to answer.

When it was time to go, Goldie just went. Goldie was old and blind and diabetic and she waited for them to go to the lake for the afternoon and then she took a little vacation, too. She wandered way up under the house to a cool spot and just drifted away. They searched everywhere, made calls and put up signs like little Abby did, and then Horace found her; he smelled her, of course, and it was hard to get her out from under there, but no one got upset with her about how she did it. They all knew that she had made her choice and done the very best she could. She was such a good girl and so was the one before her named for that young man who won all those Olympic medals. All of her children are good swimmers and it was important to her that they learned how. All children need to know how to swim. It is very important especially if you grow up in a place with a river and being so near to the ocean. She thinks she hears the children right outside the window there but she can't say and she can't quite open her eyes. They love to play kick the can and tag this time of day and when the streetlights come on, Horace goes out and cups his hands around his mouth and calls for them to come on inside. *Supper, children, supper.* That music is trapped in her head and she can't get rid of it. It's not unpleasant but she's tired of it. She's tired and maybe will take a little nap before whatever is supposed to happen next happens before Horace comes by.

"Goldie, dear, I think it's time to go," she says, and there's scruffy little Rudy there at her feet and there's Harley, sweet purring Harley, and his eyes are as green as Horace's. Horace has beautiful eyes—sometimes green and sometimes gray and he always sends her a sprig of rosemary so she will remember him. She laughs, so silly, to think that she could ever in her life forget him. They have been together for years and they plan to marry in the summer. They both want children. He has left a message for her right there by the switchboard and she strains to read it. She needs her glasses. She needs to write back and let him know she is going now. She is going to find her mother because she has the grocery list of all they need: Clorox and paper towels and trash bags and some milk. He says, Oh honey, you can relax. I'll go to the store so you can just stretch out there and relax and so she does. She does relax and there is someone at the door but it is way past her bedtime so she lets her mother answer the door. Her mother tiptoes and says shhhhhh. *Hush, she says, hush, now, my baby is sleeping. And her mother sits down beside her and holds her hand; she says sweet dreams, my baby, sweet dreams—she says Sadie? Sadie?—and she says it's suppertime—supper, children, supper—and there's money in the jar if a child should need some, there always is.*

C.J.

C.J. HAS THAT WEIRD feeling that she's being watched or like someone has been here in her space. She goes and checks in the bathroom where she keeps her journal and then in her top drawer where she keeps cash. Nothing is out of place and so she tries to relax, to think about how she can turn this night with Andy into a good one, get them back where they were in the very beginning when he was so generous and called her several times a day. She puts Kurt on his back and watches him play with the soft stuffed dog Joanna gave him last week. Joanna calls herself his fairy godmother, but the truth is that she is fairy godmother to C.J. as well and lately C.J. is trying to figure out some ways she might begin to pay her back for all the help and favors. She could give Joanna a manicure and pedicure—and *not* a French one, she would add. Or she could clean her house. She could fill in more at the Dog House—cleaning and refilling all the condiment bins after hours, which is something Joanna often does herself. Andy keeps asking if she has ever told Joanna about him, pressing to make sure that she has not broken her promise to him. "Who does she think you're with all these nights?" he has asked, and "Isn't she the least bit curious?" And of course, Joanna is curious and has asked a million questions but C.J. still has not told her anything even though there have been many times she has wanted to. She has even tried to imagine the look of shock Joanna would have with the news and then her asking, *How? How did you wind up with him?* And of course that would be the hardest part, telling her how she used to be—fucking old creeps for peanuts and doing things that now make her shudder—and how he hit on her knowing it would be an easy hit and then how he kept coming back and how then he really seemed to care, especially once Kurt was born.

"You'll tell her when the time is right," Andy had told her. "You'll tell her when everything is out in the open and our news won't hurt anyone." By *anyone* he meant his own children, one of them not much younger than C.J., and his wife who C.J. has nothing against and so doesn't like to think about. She reminds herself how he has said the marriage was over ages ago—she was not his first affair—but now she is his only and the longest and certainly the only one with a baby. She likes the sound of *our* news—*our news* like a couple, like a family.

But they're not there yet and now she is starting to worry that they might *not* get there; she is nervous about how pissy he has seemed lately. She's worried that he might have changed his mind about her or found somebody new. They haven't slept together in several weeks and his messages have been so weird the past several days. In the beginning he just talked about how much he wanted her, how he wanted to build a perfect little world and keep her there, dress her in expensive clothes just so he could rip them off and fuck her morning noon and night. "When Kurt is asleep, of course," she had added, and he laughed and said *of course*. He said he loved what a good mother she is to Kurt and how he hoped they'd have another one just like him. She could go to school if she wanted. Hell, she could do anything she wanted. And now she wants to get back to all of that, back to the good parts.

She makes sure there is nothing in the playpen Kurt might find and put in his mouth and goes to take a shower, leaving the door open so she can hear him in there making those cute little squeaking sounds. The bathroom window is open to let out the steam and she can hear the voices and laughter of people in line at the Dog House. It has become a regular hangout for a lot of teenagers, especially now that that girl who is all into vampires works there. She practices how she will approach Andy, practices how she will try to get things back to the way they had been. She decides to wear the white silk blouse he gave her for her birthday even though it is not her style at all; the price tag was still on it when he gave it to her and she almost said how she wished she could have the money instead, that she could get about ten shirts she liked and still have lots of grocery money, but it seemed to make him happy when he thought he was teaching her something so she laughed and said how beautiful it was and that it cost almost as much as her car.

The kids crowding the picnic tables outside the Dog House all turn and wave when she straps Kurt into his child seat and leaves; though they all seem like nice enough kids, something gives her the creeps. She has had the weird worry lately that one of them or some of them have gone in and out of her apartment when she's not there even though she keeps the door locked. Why else does she keep having that feeling? The linen closet door wasn't closed all the way, but lately she has had so many thoughts about what she wants to do for Kurt that she is in and out of there all the time adding to the list she keeps in her journal, for instance one of the nurses at Pine Haven had told her about a book she should read about child development and she had written down the title. Even if someone had been in there, there wasn't anything worth stealing. Now that they know that, there would be no reason to go back unless they wanted a place to smoke pot or have sex and surely she would know if they had done either of those. She would definitely know and they wouldn't do that. That would be stupid and she is being stupid, the whole thought of having to go back out into the cemetery giving her the creeps, but that's stupid, too.

Kurt is asleep when she gets to Joanna's house and so she carries the whole car seat inside. Joanna's kitchen looks like a yard sale is happening, the counter covered with all kinds of pots and vases and junk.

"Whoa, look at you," Joanna whispers. "I've never seen you so dressed up. And so conservative-looking. What on earth happened to C.J.?"

"Not a biggie," C.J. says, and tiptoes into Joanna's room to avoid looking at her. "I'm putting in an application at Macy's, hoping to maybe work the cosmetic counter and thought I should look good."

"Work? When? You've got a job and our deal is that you help me."

"Oh, I know, this wouldn't mess that up." She places the car seat down in the corner where she can still see Kurt from the kitchen.

"I thought you had a date."

"Oh, I do. And I'm meeting him there at the mall. He works at the Olive Garden." She talks fast, all the answers she prepared for all the questions she knew Joanna would ask. "What's with all the junk, are you having a yard sale?"

"No." Joanna reaches and fingers the silk blouse and raises a questioning eyebrow. "I told you I want you to take something. Every time you come over you can just take something."

"I thought that's what we were going to do at your wedding."

"Yeah, right. The *wedding*. Well, I'm impatient," Joanna says, and holds up a giant white vase. "How about this beauty and I can throw in a never before used knife sharpener and colander?" She laughs. "Seriously, C.J., who is this guy and why are you being so secretive? Do you need money because I can loan you—"

"No. It's just that I don't want to jinx it," she says. "But I promise to tell you soon. Either way, I will tell you soon."

"What does that mean *either* way?" Joanna steps closer. "And why do you look like you're about to cry?"

"I don't know. I really don't. I'm nervous and you're making me *more* nervous."

"About?"

"It's stupid. It's as stupid as you giving away all of your junk." She blots the corners of her eyes and forces a laugh. "Really. I should be quizzing you like you're not planning to off yourself or something are you?"

"What do you mean?" Joanna turns and the look on her face is one C.J. has never seen, clearly very upset. She puts the vase down. "That isn't funny. I told you my story and you told me yours and neither one is a joke. I would never do such a thing and I can't believe you'd even joke about it."

"Good," C.J. says, " I'm sorry. I didn't mean anything by it. Jesus. And I do mean *good*. Kurt needs you."

"And I need him." Joanna starts putting things back in the cabinets. "Do you even *know* this person you have a date with?"

"Yes, Mother," C.J. says. "We were in high school together. And by the way, I need you, too."

"Yes, I know you do which is why I *do* ask all these questions. I worry. You're so secretive lately and I don't understand why you feel you can't trust me."

"It's not that and you really need to trust *me*. I worry, too. Like I think you need to get all dressed up and go on a date. And I worry because Kurt is starting to roll all over the place and you have to watch him every second and your house is full of crap everywhere." She points to the floor as if he is there rolling and turns quickly to leave. She hates if anything ever makes her cry; she hates how ugly crying makes a person, the way your face gets all twisted and ugly and fucks your whole face up.

"Honey," Joanna says, for a minute sounding so much like C.J.'s real fucking mother she can't stand it. "What is it? Do you need money? Are you in trouble?"

She paws the air and then fans her face so her mascara won't run. "No! Nothing like that. I'm just PMS or maybe I'm just all fucked up. Maybe I'm nervous about having a date. Who wants to date someone with a six-month-old?"

"Lots of people would," Joanna says. "Look at you. He's lucky and he better treat you that way."

"How'd you learn to say all those mom things?"

"I don't know. Maybe I know all the things I wish someone had said to me long before I *did* try to vacate the planet Earth." Joanna pats her shoulder and pushes her toward the door. "No reason for you to have to wait to learn all those things, right? So go and have fun and when you come back first thing in the morning, we'll start all over again with you selecting a fine piece of kitchen or glassware to claim as your very own."

"It's a deal," she says, and leans to the side once more so she can see Kurt sleeping, his head leaned to the right, pacifier still in his mouth. "You sure you want him to sleep over?"

"Instead of you waking me up at one or two? Um, yeah, I think so." Joanna paused. "And if you decide to go home early, just call and swing by."

"Okay. If you're sure," C.J. says, and takes a good deep breath— a cleansing breath, Toby would say. She is feeling better. She is feeling hopeful. "It'll be early because I promised Rachel Silverman I'd ride her around tomorrow and give her a tour of the town. She's pretty cool. You'd like talking to her some time when you're over with the living ones."

"I'll keep that in mind. Now go, have fun. Kurt's fine and I'm fine and you're fine," Joanna stands in the doorway and waves. "And take good notes so that someday when you actually decide to let me in on what is happening in your life, you won't forget a thing."

"I do trust you. I do want to tell you."

"Whenever you're ready."

"You know me," she says, and sticks out her tongue. "Always something up my sleeve." C.J. waves and takes another deep breath. She starts the car and notices Kurt's new stuffed dog there on the seat beside her, but she decides not to go back in; she's afraid she would tell everything if she did and for now it's best to keep the secret. She will hope for the best and even if the best doesn't happen, she still has plenty of good stuff going on. She has Kurt and she has a job and a place to live and who knows what could happen with Sam Lowe and actually that big white vase isn't so bad at all. In fact, she can imagine filling it with something like peacock feathers or sunflowers and tacking little lights up along the ceiling of every room. She's already thought how she wants to paint Kurt's room so it looks like he lives in a castle; she wants him to always feel like he has a good home. A family and a home. The parking lot at Pine Haven is empty and she's twenty minutes early so she lets herself in the side door and goes to the beauty parlor to check her hair and makeup and make sure she doesn't have mascara or baby spit on that new blouse. This place is like a tomb after about seven, faint buzzings of televisions behind apartment doors and of course that goddamned music Mr. Stone can't get enough of. If it was this quiet during the daytime hours, she would have to beg him to listen to something else because it would drive her crazy but in the daytime, she has her own music going and lots of hair dryers and nail dryers and a bunch of people who can't hear anyway and have to scream at each other. She takes out her lip and nose rings and brushes the spikiness from her hair, wipes the smudge of burgundy lipstick from her mouth. It surprises her lately how much she looks like her mother. Some nights before bed—her face stripped clean of all makeup and studs—she can't even bear to look.

Abby

THE SIDE DOOR OF Pine Haven is still open and so Abby is able to slip inside without setting off an alarm or having to ring a doorbell. Usually things are all locked up by now so she is relieved. They feed people at five thirty or six and then a lot of them go on to bed or to their own rooms to watch television. Rachel Silverman says she does not like that *made-for-preschool children* schedule one damn bit, but Sadie says she doesn't mind because she likes to watch *Jeopardy* in her pajamas. She sees C.J. all dressed up in front of the big mirror in the beauty parlor. Normally she would love nothing better than to find C.J. there alone; she would ask her to read her palm or do those fortune cards, but Abby is not up for anything tonight. Nothing sounds good. There is not a person at the desk so Abby runs past without having to check in. She knocks lightly and then opens Sadie's door and moves into the room. It's almost completely dark, just the faint light from her bathroom window and the nightlights by her bed that come on when it gets dark. Harley jumps when she comes in but then comes when she calls him. Sadie is still sleeping, the piece of paper Abby had forgotten earlier in the day in her hand.

Sadie, Sadie? She shakes but Sadie doesn't stir so she decides she'll just curl up and wait. She turns the television on and the volume way down. Sadie has slept right through *Jeopardy* because the television is on the Weather Channel where she keeps it the rest of the day, so Abby leaves it there and closes her eyes. The thought of Dollbaby getting hit and then left in the middle of the road makes her cry all over again. She hates whoever hit her and the farmer who buried her. She hates her dad because he built a shitty fence and her mom for never being nice to Dollbaby in the first place. She's sick of them, sick of everybody. I'm so sick of it I could die. That's what her dad said that time about her mom. *I'm so goddamned sick of it I could die.*

"Sadie?" she whispers. "Sadie?" She will let her sleep a while longer and then she'll wake her and tell her the bad news about Dollbaby and about how her parents didn't even try to do anything about it. *You might have to teach your mother some things,* Sadie had said, but what did that mean? She wishes it were last night when she was still hoping Dollbaby was okay, when her dad pulled a big ostrich feather from his sleeve and gave it to her, promising more where that came from at her party, and when she asked him if he thought there was a chance Dollbaby was still alive he said, of course he did. "There's always a chance," he said even though most of his stories were about no chances at all, like the one the other night—a train wreck in this very county in 1943 where over seventy people died, most of them soldiers trying to get home for Christmas. Sadie said she remembered it well; she was Abby's age when it happened and the whole county was *devastated by the disaster.* She said she has never seen a train since that she didn't think of it. "Some mistakes were made," her dad said like he always did. "They should have seen it coming."

"Why do you fill her head up with all that awful stuff?" her mother said, one of those times she didn't know Abby was listening. "You're going to make her so weird."

But now she's glad it's all in her head—the brakes and screams and all those loud sounds that can keep her from thinking. *Why do you fill her head up with all that awful stuff? You're making her weird. Mistakes were made. They should have seen it coming.*

"Sadie?" she whispers. "Sadie? Are you awake? Please wake up."

Kendra

THE HOUSE IS QUIET and now, finally, she can call Andy. No answer. No answer. No goddamned answer. It's been like this all day long. She kicks at a loose bolt Ben has dropped there in the front hall—bolts and screws everywhere and for what? A stupid disappearing chamber when *he* is who she wishes would disappear. Let him disappear and all this shit he leaves around for that stupid theater like anybody in town even gives a shit. Who would notice if he stopped it all other than a handful of ancients from next door and whatever kids he can coax in to watch things like Jerry Lewis movies and stupid westerns. She will go take a nice long hot shower, relieved that Ben left and went wherever it is he goes with his loser self. She has just turned the water on when her cell phone starts ringing and she races to pick it up. It was him so she hits dial back. It's his house phone, but she is feeling brave; if something screws up and Liz answers, she will act like she was calling *her*.

Liz's voice is cool, suspicious. She knows something. Then without any waiting or beating around the bush she says it: she knows he's been having an affair.

Is it a trick? Kendra doesn't know what to say so she opts for nothing. She says, *Oh,* and then nothing, but Liz keeps talking. She says it's all over and they are going away to figure it all out. Going away. *A day, a week, forever?*

"Do you hear me?" Liz asks.

"Yes." Kendra stands there in a towel, aware of the water running in the shower and of how dark it is outside the window, no moon and the streetlight on their corner burned out.

"And?" Liz asks.

"I don't know what to say."

"Neither do I." Liz hangs up and Kendra is left in silence with no idea what to do. She almost dials his cell phone but then stops. It is so rare for her not to know what to do, but she has no idea and something in the stillness of the house completely unnerves her. The little white sticker she had put under the table on Ben's side of the bed is visible and she rushes over to remove it. She's not used to the silence. She's not used to being alone. It's not supposed to happen this way. She's not supposed to be alone. She's afraid to be alone.

Joanna

AT FIRST IT SOUNDS like a shutter has blown loose again and is whining against the wind, a creaking strain, open and closed, but then it is too rhythmic for the wind, too measured. It's the hammock. Someone is on her porch. She looks out the kitchen window to see Ben's car parked in her driveway. It *has* been his car these recent nights, circling, stopping. She goes and cracks open the front door.

"Hello?"

"Hey."

"Who's there?"

"Guess."

"What are you doing here?" She still stands behind the screen door, latch in place.

"I come here a lot. Sometimes I fish, sometimes I sit." He tilts a bottle up to his mouth, then offers it out. "C'mon, join me." He sits, legs hanging off the side and pushing against the floorboards. "It's like old times."

"You come here? To my house?"

"Yeah, amazed you haven't noticed before. Come on." She goes and brings Kurt's carrier closer. He'll be waking soon and she likes to reach him as close to that first cry as she can make it. "Are you there?"

"Yes. I'm here." She shushes him, tells him she's babysitting and to keep his voice down, and then he immediately starts talking about his kid. "You've met her," he says, and Joanna nods yes, says she sees her often over at Pine Haven. "Well, it would suck to be her right about now," he says. He reaches for Joanna's arm and pulls her there beside him then drops his arm around her shoulders and squeezes. "Been a long time since we sat this close, hasn't it?" he asks, and she nods, aware of his thumb circling her bare arm, the smell of him exactly the same though she never could have described it in a million years except it was his smell; it was his childhood home, any jacket or shirt or magic show prop he had ever tossed her way.

"I know Abby's dog is missing," she says, and takes a deep breath, uncertain of where any of this might go and afraid to even wonder.

"Not just missing. *Dead*." He says the word in a low whisper, dragging out its hard ugly sound. "And a dead dog is just the beginning."

She turns, waiting for him to continue and there in the dark of the porch, he looks very much the way he always did, the night erasing just enough years that he could be that boy; it could be that time.

"I mean it all sucks. Marriage is like a job and some people love what they do and some people hate it. Some stay because they feel like they have to and some just say fuck it. I mean we all have people in our lives we have to tolerate, right? They're selfish or hateful or narcissistic, but goddamn, it really sucks to marry one of those." He laughs and hugs her close again. "Now you never lingered, did you? You're the one who can just say *fuck it* and walk right off."

"No, that's not true," she says. She takes the bottle from him and drinks, some kind of whiskey that nearly turns her inside out, and then she quizzes him, what had made him want such a girl in the first place—was it all about *appearances?* Did he need drama? Want drama? What would possess someone to go there unless he thought he was rescuing her—poor little thing, but was he so blind? Was he so stupid? "Once upon a time you had a pretty good brain," she says, and twists out from under his arm. "In fact, there was a time when I thought you were really smart." She pauses. "And nice. I used to think you were nice."

"You're one to talk. You're the charity bride, right?" He drains the bottle and throws it off the porch into the shrubs. "Married a million times. Married a gay dude. That's pretty desperate, isn't it? Bet that was a fun honeymoon."

"Actually, it was."

"And then the widower. Talk about a pity party."

"Must be it. So glad you cared enough to keep up with me."

"Well, I felt responsible. You see." He grips her shoulders and forces his forehead against her own. "I made you disappear."

"You don't have that power," she says, voice shaking but determined not to let him get the best of her. "I'm more like Mary Poppins. I go where I'm needed and then the wind shifts and I'm needed elsewhere."

"Oh yeah. So what brought you back?"

"My dad."

"I thought maybe it was me. I thought maybe you were once again seeking true love."

"I gave up on that a long time ago."

"Ouch. Because of me?"

"You give yourself an awful lot of credit, don't you?" she says, and he sighs and leans back, one arm hiding his face. "You can come and go like the wind until you have kids and even though they weren't my blood, they felt like mine. I was helping to raise them. But it didn't work."

"Yeah? So where does that leave you other than alone?"

"I don't know." She reaches and pulls his arm from his eyes, waits until he is looking at her. "Being with someone isn't as important as it once was. I'm alone, but I'm never lonely. How's that? I've got a life, people I care about, work I find very satisfying."

"So, is it too late for us? Are we too old?"

"No, but you are married."

"Oh yeah." He laughs, leans back and pulls another bottle he'd obviously stashed in the dark corner, takes a drink and passes it to her. She just sits holding it for a long while, their feet pushing off the floor, the sound of the ocean in the distance. He talks about his marriage and how he really wants to leave. He talks about the disappearing chamber he has spent many weeks building and painting. "The job's still yours if you want it," he says. "My loyal assistant and disappearing girl."

"I *was* the disappearing girl for way too long," she says, and against her better judgment, hands the bottle back to him when he reaches for it. "And I did disappear, remember? I disappeared for a very long time."

"Glad you reappeared."

"Thanks."

"Sorry I haven't been much of a friend."

"Understandable."

"She hates you."

"I gathered."

"But she hates everyone." He pauses. "Unless of course they have something she needs." He laughs and rubs his hand on Joanna's head the way you might a child or a dog. "People really do say you've been married too many times to count."

"I know."

"So what's the real story?"

"Does it matter?" She turns to look at him and he leans in to kiss her but she pushes him back.

"I'm sorry," he says. "Really. I'm just trying to figure out how I got where I am. How did I get here?"

"You're asking me?" she asks, and moves away. "The physical *here* in the hammock on my front porch or the abstract *here*?"

"Yes, I'm asking you and the latter."

"Oh, I see. Now I get it. Because I've been there so many times before. Thanks so much, speaking of people who only show up when they need something from you." She goes inside and lifts Kurt from his carrier and then brings him back out with her. He wakes and stirs as she lifts him but then settles right back in against her chest as soon as she sits in one of the rockers.

"So, then, why don't you tell me how *you* got here." He stretches full length in the hammock and closes his eyes. "Tell me about the life that didn't work. The one with the kids you left behind. Tell me why you didn't live happily ever after."

"He was grieving when we met and for a while I filled up the empty space and then he fell in love with someone else."

"Ouch."

"He couldn't help that. It was just what happened."

"And the gay husband?"

"He taught me how to love. He's the best friend I've ever had."

"Ouch again."

"Grown-up friend. You're someone from childhood."

"You make it sound like another planet," he says. "I'm still your friend. I've always been your friend." He opens his eyes, but she doesn't say anything, just breathes in the smell of Kurt's damp sticky neck. "I am your friend. Why are you being this way?"

"We haven't seen each other in years, Ben. I don't know anything about your life. I know a boy who wanted to be the next Houdini—David Copperfield his distant second choice. We were friends—the best of friends. We even had sex once, remember that?"

Ben's cell phone rings and he can't find it to turn it off. She stands when Kurt starts to cry and jiggles him on her hip. Seconds pass and it starts ringing again, the shrill sound like an alarm sounding, breaking the strange dark silence.

"Of course I remember that," he says, and stares into the lit face of his phone. "How could I forget that? And you may not be lonely, but I am." He slams the phone shut and stuffs it in his pocket. "I've got to go. Looks like Abby has run away and Kendra is hysterical. I'm sure she's next door with Sadie Randolph like she always is, but I have to go before every cop in town is called."

"I'm sorry, Ben," she says. "I really am. I hope everything's okay."

"Yeah. Me, too." He hands her the bottle and she puts it down on the table by the hammock. "Can we try this again some time?"

"Okay," she says, and shifts Kurt up a little higher, presses his sleep dampened cheek against her own. "We can try it again."

"Don't go anywhere," he says. "Don't leave."

She watches until his taillights disappear down the road and then takes Kurt inside to change his diaper and give him a bottle and get him all settled in for the night. *The longest and most expensive journey you will ever take is the one to yourself.* She imagines Luke there in his black satin nightshirt, flipping through old albums and his stack of 45s, Tammy on the floor beside him, and she tells him he's right and that thanks to him, she is now miles and miles from where she began. *Gregory Luke Wishart* and *Willis Hall—keep us close, keep us alive—Mary Grace Robertson and Suzanne Sullivan. The pull, the pull. I am their mirror. You are my little girl.*

C.J.

S HE WALKS OUT INTO the cemetery, a small flashlight illuminating the ground around her feet, but Andy isn't there. She
shines the light all around to make sure he isn't hiding and about
to jump out at her. He has done that before and she cried for
over an hour, ashamed of her fear but still not able to stop. *Esther
Cohen devoted wife and mother.* She steps closer and there's a note
tucked into Esther's urn. *Go home. Dinner is waiting.* She turns
and looks all around once more and then starts making her way
back to her car, walking quickly now, feeling relieved by the note
she clutches, careful not to smudge her white silk blouse. This is
the kind of note he always left in the beginning. This is the promise of some kind of good take-out food and maybe like the time
he had a hot bubble bath waiting for her and all kinds of candles
and lotions. She gets in the car and drives through town as quickly
as she can. She could get mad at him for making her drive all the
way in and then all the way back out, but right now she is too
relieved to even care. She sees Abby's old magician dad, there at
the stoplight, but he doesn't see her, and if she weren't afraid of

waking Kurt, she would call Joanna to tell her that she passed him on the road from the beach, and that he probably *is* riding by her house all the time. But she's almost home. There's a light up in her window and Andy's car is parked where he always parks, across the street at the far back corner of the Texaco station.

She can't get there fast enough, running up the rickety steps and into the room where he is sitting and drinking a glass of champagne, one already poured and waiting for her. She puts Kurt's stuffed dog in the playpen and then throws her arms around him and breathes in, trying to smell what's for dinner, but all she smells is Andy, and for some reason, for just a second, she is reminded of the smell of Sam Lowe's shirt—nothing more than detergent and sweat—when he hugged her hello the last time she saw him.

"You scared me!" she says.

"What are you talking about sweetheart?" He kisses her and hands her the glass of champagne. "What's got you so frazzled?"

"What's got me frazzled?" She notices there is a little box all wrapped with a bow on the table. "Oh my God, you scared the shit out of me. You acted mad at me and then you sent me out to the cemetery."

"I see you're upset." He clinks glasses and motions for her to drink up. "But I wanted to surprise you. Where's Kurt?"

"Joanna's. He's there for the night."

"Perfect, even though I really can't stay long. I have to go out of town tomorrow. A conference in California."

"I wish I could go." She drains her glass and takes off her shoes, goes into the kitchen to see what's in the oven. Nothing. "Hey, you said dinner was waiting."

"Patience," he says, and motions for her to come sit beside him.

"Patience is a virtue." He fills her glass and tells her all about his day at the hospital, about the person who really should have died there on the operating table today but, thanks to him, is still alive. "You should have seen the look on his wife's face. Grateful doesn't even touch it." He keeps talking and filling their glasses. "It was nothing short of a miracle." He unbuttons her blouse and asks where she'd want to go if she could go anywhere in the world and what kind of house does she want to live in and how many kids and what kind of car. "Dream big," he says.

She carefully hangs the shirt on the back of a chair, telling him that she happens to know it is a *very* expensive item, and then she laughs and answers all the questions—Switzerland and a house like the big brick one on Main Street where Marge Walker used to live with lots of chimneys and a pool. She would love to have at least one more kid, maybe two, and a car that doesn't overheat all the time, one with air-conditioning and a CD player that works.

"And who is the person who keeps calling here? Last name Lowe on your caller ID."

"What?" She barely turns, head spinning, and he's there, leaning hard against her. "I've been watching you. And reading you." He pushes her toward the bedroom where he has all of her papers spread out on her bed. He has taken her journal apart, pages ripped and strewn. "You think somebody wouldn't figure out who I am? I can figure out all the other weirdos you've been with, except of course whoever this kid is you've started to mention all the time. The one you can always talk to," he mimics, "always count on."

"He's just a friend," she says, and he pushes her down in the chair by the window, the only thing in this whole apartment that her mother had owned. Her mother loved that overstuffed chair and Joanna had it reupholstered for C.J.s birthday in a soft blue velvet. She knows he knows that. She knows she told him. "This has all gotten out of hand," he says. "I'm the one in charge. I call the shots. I leave the notes. I decide how much money when. You're a risk." Her head feels heavy and she leans back to catch her breath; her heart is racing. The light from the Dog House sign is still lit even though they closed at eight and in the distance there is heat lightning—flashes of silent light.

Joanna

S HE KNOWS AS SOON as she gets to C.J.'s apartment, even before she resorts to using her spare key and cautiously stepping inside. The air is so still. She leaves Kurt in his carrier and turns it so that he is facing outward in the square of sunlight in the open door and then she moves to the bedroom and finds her there, half dressed, a needle in her arm. Her skin is cold, eyes closed. Joanna sinks to her knees beside the chair. Her impulse is to pull the needle from her arm, to dress and cover her, but she knows better and instead just reaches, smoothes back her hair, and lets her hand rest there, the skin of C.J.'s pale neck so cold. "Why?" she keeps asking. "*How* could this happen?" On the bed there is an uncapped pen that has bled into the rumpled sheet and a long handwritten page about her mother's death and another page with the heading: "If Anything Happens to Me." The flier about Abby's lost dog is on the floor beside her chair. *I was just minutes away,* Joanna says. *This never should have happened.* Her mind races, trying to reconstruct everything they said last night. C.J. *was* upset; she *was* worried. But she wouldn't have done *this*.

Joanna goes once more and kneels beside her, closes her eyes as she tries to trace back through everything. She said she had a date to drive Rachel Silverman around town this morning. She said, *I do trust you, I do want to tell you.* She said, she always has something up her sleeve, but not *this.* She couldn't have meant this. Minutes pass and Joanna just stays there, waiting, breathing, until she hears Kurt stirring and then she gets up and calls 911. She goes to the bathroom to retrieve the journal C.J. had told her about but there's very little there, loose pages and a silver coil that once had held many more pages. Burned matches are in the toilet and traces of paper ripped from the notebook litter the floor like confetti. Joanna crams what's there into her purse and then steps into the main room to wait. The white blouse is carefully hung on the back of a chair and the dog she had just given Kurt is placed in the center of his playpen in the corner. She reaches for the dog and when she does finds another scrap of paper: *Go home. Dinner is waiting.* She studies the square neat print, slips it into her purse with the other scraps and goes back once more and kisses the top of her head. "None of this makes sense," she tells her. "You said you'd never do this." As soon as she hears the siren, she picks up Kurt and goes downstairs to wait. He's awake now and babbling, laughing when one of the many stray cats that hang around the Dog House sidles up begging.

IT MAKES NO SENSE. Joanna has played through it all again and again, studied the fragments of notes left behind, but there's nothing there beyond the knowledge that Abby's dog might in fact be alive and that Ben once hit on C.J., and yet Joanna is absolutely certain that C.J. did not choose this. The note telling her or someone to *go home* is what she keeps coming back to. *Dinner is waiting.* But there was no trace of food having been cooked or eaten. And there was no job at Macy's. They had held no recent interviews and there was no application with C.J.'s name on it. When she called the number C.J. had written in the corner of the missing dog flyer, she got the voice mail for Sam Lowe and asked that he call her back as soon as possible. He was in a class that night and then home with his parents; C.J. was supposed to call him the next day. Joanna checked it all out, determined in her thinking that she will never stop trying to figure it all out. *Suicide* is what they're choosing to call it even as Joanna works hard to squelch that. "It was an accident," she hears herself saying again and again. "She would never have left Kurt. She never even did drugs." And she imagines all the ways she will try to spin it as he gets older, all the ways she will try to convince him, and the ways she will keep his mother alive in his memory.

C.J.'s death is one of those that comes and goes quietly—a murmur of *oh dear, so sad* and then on to other events. She gets lost in the funeral of Sadie Randolph, a woman loved and treasured by the whole town. People said there had not been a funeral that big since Judge Walker died. Ben was asked to be a pallbearer and stood there with Sadie's children who Joanna recognized from all the photographs and stories told. She spoke to Ben quickly afterward, Abby there with him as they all walked away from the grave and before Kendra could make her way up to the front. Everyone knew that Abby was in the room with Sadie and had fallen asleep on the couch; when Ben went to find her, he found Sadie, saying that he knew immediately that she was gone. He was the one who called 911 and he was the one who stood beside her bed and waited. Joanna wanted to say how they had both had the same experience within twelve hours of each other—one discovering the natural ending of a long and beautiful life and the other the tragic loss of someone barely getting started, but by then Kendra was back with them, looping her arm through his and giving Joanna a dismissive nod.

Everyone at Pine Haven has talked constantly about Sadie's death and how much they miss her. Several have mentioned *the hair and foot girl* and how awful that was as well. They miss the way she fixed their hair and the way she gave long foot massages when doing their feet. They say what a terrible shame that she chose to do that. They say things like: *Her legacy. Fulfilled prophecy. Downright selfish but pitiful, too.* They talk about how fond poor Harley was of both of them and how somebody needs to get rid of him. Joanna is thinking she should give him a good home before something happens.

"Could you have seen that one coming?" Abby asked Ben after Joanna mentioned C.J.'s death. He had trouble placing who C.J. was, which bothered Joanna even more, but then Kendra was there and so Joanna remained silent. "You didn't see Sadie's death coming," Abby said, and twisted away from Ben. "You didn't see Dollbaby's coming. You wouldn't see a train wreck either. You don't see anything. Nothing." Ben nodded at Joanna and she turned to leave, the volume and pitch of Abby's voice unbearable to hear and even more unbearable was Kendra's attempt at shushing her, which made it even worse. Joanna heard Ben tell Abby that things would get better. He talked about her birthday party, which had been postponed a week. "Saturday is going to a great day," he said, "a brand-new start, you'll see," and that got Kendra going about who all would be there and what they were going to do. *Sadie would like that,* Ben said. *Sadie would want that. Really, honey, she would.* Joanna turned and looked back and he was watching her; he held his gaze a little too long, which meant he would probably show up at her door as he had done again two nights ago.

JOANNA HAS A quiet gathering for C.J. there in the little chapel of Pine Haven and still hasn't decided what to do with her ashes. C.J. was afraid of the cemetery and said she didn't like it out there and now it bothers Joanna that she doesn't even know where she *did* want to be. They talked about so many things but never *that.* "I still find it so hard to believe," Rachel Silverman says after the service. She says that C.J. was supposed to drive her all over town, that they had made a financial agreement and that Rachel had looked forward to the time with her. "I liked that girl," she says, "I really did. Now Stanley is taking me." She holds on to Mr. Stone's arm and he nods and pats her hand. His sudden improvement and desire to shave and dress nicely has shocked everyone in the Pine Haven community as has the newfound friendship between Toby Tyler and Marge Walker; Toby has promised Marge yoga classes and health advice so she can live as long as possible and in exchange Marge will let Toby read and study all the true crime she has collected in her scrapbook especially that one horrible case and conviction her husband was famous for.

"We're all trying to do what Sadie would like," Toby says, and laughs. "Who the hell knows how long it'll last."

It is a small group, but Sam Lowe shows up and afterward when Joanna hands him the rumpled flyer of Dollbaby she had found on C.J.'s bed, he nods yes. "That's her all right," he said.

And now it is Saturday and Joanna has her own field trip. She takes Kurt to day care and then drives to the Ferris Beach shelter. Sam Lowe is out front and has Dollbaby all bathed and brushed with a pink bandanna around her neck. "What do I owe you?" Joanna asks, but he shakes his head, shrugs, and looks away. She hands him an envelope with the pages C.J. had written about him, how she hoped she could be the kind of person he might deserve. "Her death was a big mistake," she tells him, and takes the leash. "She never would have chosen to leave." He nods and they promise to keep in touch, but Joanna knows better. He will be like all the others who come in and out of her life, their association so tied up in loss and grieving that it will be best to move on.

It is later that afternoon when she drives and parks at the far end of the Pine Haven parking lot. She knows from her conversation with Ben that the birthday party will be over soon so she walks Dollbaby through the cemetery to where they can see Abby's house and then she sits there, the very place where she and Ben had played as children. There is the statue of Lydia and there is where the little girl's playhouse had been. She stays back in the shade of the hedge of myrtle and canopy of oaks and waits, Dollbaby already straining to get loose, whining and pulling, and as soon as Joanna sees Ben's car turn into the drive, she unclips the leash and lets her go. She doesn't wait but heads back down the path; she hears Abby screaming—*I wished for this, I wished for this*—and she can only imagine the shock of Abby's parents, especially her mother, to witness this miracle, this resurrection, this reason to believe.

She moves quickly now, over the gnarled surfaced roots and past darkened stones, the names of those she once knew. Pooles and Burnses and Carlyles and Bishops. Kurt will need a lot of things in this life. He will need an education and nice clothes and a good dog, but most of all he will need his mother and Joanna plans to give him all that she can. *Your mother loved you more than anything on earth,* she will say when the time is right. *Your mother was smart and good and kind and funny.* And she will save all the music C.J. was listening to—Neutral Milk Hotel and Nirvana and, weirdly enough, The Jackson 5 and Supremes. There is so much Joanna wants to know and understand and she is not ever going to stop looking and questioning. She wants to be able to tell Kurt that his mother did *not* kill herself. His mother *never* would have chosen to leave him. She has the books that were on C.J.'s shelf—mostly children's books that she had saved from her own childhood, *Carolina Jessamine* scrawled in crayon in the front. And then there are books about reflexology, palm reading, tarot and Switzerland, how-to books about making quilts and curtains and homemade jams, a strange assortment that Joanna has incorporated into her daily reading habits—flip one open and see what is there. In one of the books was a list of C.J.'s ideas for tattoos she might get. *I am listening to hear where you are,* she had written and so now Joanna is listening. She is always looking and listening. Carolina Jessamine Loomis. Luke Wishart and Martha Stone and Curtis Lamb and Suzanne Sullivan. Lois Flowers and Sadie Randolph.

Keep us alive. Keep us with you.

Do you believe in ghosts? Do you believe in the power of magic? Do you believe that a normal ordinary girl can disappear right before your eyes? There is an inner box and there is an outer box and they turn and turn and turn. Now you see her, now you don't. It's an easy trick, all about making the right turns, standing in the right place at the right time. If you look closely enough you can see the opening; you can see what's coming, but there's the real trick—because you don't look; for whatever reason, you don't look, you look up or off to the side, your mind is elsewhere—a flap of red silk, the sudden flight of a dove, bouquets of flowers pulled from a sleeve. Now you see her, now you don't. Then poof—abracadabra! She's right before your eyes.

Acknowledgments

I have many people to thank, as the writing of this novel has spanned quite a few years with life changes and a major move at the center of the interrupted process. At both ends are places I love and think of as home, both filled with wonderful friends and colleagues who have made significant impacts on my life. My love and appreciation run back and forth between Massachusetts and North Carolina with side trips to Bennington, Vermont, and Sewanee, Tennessee. Thank you one and all. A grateful thanks in memory of Jean Seiden and Liam Rector, two close and deeply missed friends who invited me into treasured communities; without them, I would not know so many of the people I hold dear. A big thanks to my earliest and long-trusted readers: Cathy Stanley, Betsy Cox, and Lee Smith. To the one and only Louis D. Rubin Jr.—friend, teacher, and publisher—who provided me a literary home and placed me in the amazing editorial hands of Shannon Ravenel twenty-seven years ago. I will always be grateful for that placement as well as the one of thirty years with my agent, Liz Darhansoff. Thanks to Brunson Hoole and Jude Grant for their careful and precise reading of the manuscript and to all at Algonquin who see a manuscript to the end of its journey.

Thanks to my sister, Jan Gane, and to all the memories that only a sibling can share, and to my mom, Melba McCorkle, whose love and wit and incredible stamina will always inspire me. My greatest love and thanks to my husband, Tom Rankin, for all the wonderful joys to come from joining our lives. I remain amazed. A big thanks to Julian and Alexander whom I am proud to call family. And to Claudia and Rob who will always top the list of my most important contributions to the world. Thanks to you both for your love and patience as well as suggestions for various characters and their music choices. Thanks to Claudia for invaluable insight and advice about the inner workings of a twelve-year-old girl and to Rob for the birth of the character Stanley.

Life After Life

Writing *Life After Life*

A Note from the Author

My writing process often involves a lot of note taking, every day jotting down thoughts and ideas and in the evening putting the scraps away for later perusal. Eventually, there are enough pieces that a whole begins to come into view. I think we all are like those old antenna contraptions that used to perch on rooftops, turning and turning to pick up signals in hopes of making a connection and finding clarity. The pieces that led me to *Life After Life* began accumulating long before I was ready to write it. The first being when my dad died twenty years ago; I wrote how strange it was that I was able to sit and pay bills and feed my children and do all sorts of everyday tasks in the midst of that sorrow. How odd that even as I was heartbroken, I was equally amazed and enthralled by the process of death and how the body does everything it can to protect the heart and keep it beating as long as possible, the color and life leaving the extremities like someone going through a house and turning out the lights. I was aware of how I had dreaded and had been waiting for this moment my whole life. My dad had suffered severe depression and was hospitalized several times during my childhood, and I think I had always been preparing myself to lose him again. And then it happened, and there I was, still there with my bills to pay and my children to care for and students I would see back in class the next week. In those last days, my dad said many things. He asked my sister and me to help him get to the corner where *they* (he wasn't sure who) were waiting for him. He said he wished he had a train and could go and pick up everyone he had ever loved in his whole life. He told me he was sorry that there were things he hadn't been able to do in life and hoped he hadn't let us down, and that he was sorry that he wouldn't be there to see his grandchildren grow. And then he said, *You*—meaning my mom, my sister, and me—*are my heart. That's all that there is.*

When I began writing this novel, it was with the desire to capture such moments of realization in a character's life, to reduce a whole life to the purest form, like a kind of distillation process. Who was this person and what is left? But I didn't see that so clearly then. It took many more scraps thrown into the mix: years of raising children and then realizing how much I missed bedtime stories and Little League games and snow days. My mother diagnosed with dementia and slowly losing touch with the present. One friend desperately fighting to stay alive and another choosing to leave.

I dreamed of my dad for a whole year after he died, and in the dream he would often say to me, *I'm not dead.* I had dreamed of my grandmother years earlier, and she had said the same thing. I have a photo of her I took with a little box camera when I was eight years old. Really, it's a photo of her screen door as she stepped in and hid from my camera. I have carried it around for years, loving that I knew that she was standing there behind the dark screen even though I couldn't see her—my picture of faith. I kept it with other photos slipped into the frame of my window over my desk and had done so for years. But when I moved to a new place, the light different, I looked up one morning and I could see her there, her image clear as a bell. I knew I would find a home for this in fiction, this image of faith revealed.

Not too long after, I was riding in the car with my then fourteen-year-old son, who asked me how often I thought we passed a car with someone in it who had committed murder. I looked at the long lines of traffic surrounding us and started reaching for a pen to make a note, knowing that the answer to his question was probably one we would really hate to know; it was a chilling thought, and of course it was an easy step from that to the consideration of all dark secrets. I was already attempting to work out a part of that equation for various characters populating my work. Where is the weak spot? What is it that no one else knows about this human?

The moment of death, faith, darkness. It began to come together, and in the bits and pieces, I began studying the ideas for various characters and where each might fit. I would resurrect my fictional town: here's the cemetery and here's the retirement home and here's the road to the beach. There is a man who is faking dementia to escape life with his son, a woman from Boston who has come to this place to retire because it's the hometown of a long-ago lover no one knew about; there is a hospice volunteer committed to collecting the most important details about those she sits with while also making amends with her own life, a young woman trying to survive the legacy of her own sad upbringing, a kid witnessing her parents' volatile marriage, and a senile third-grade teacher who believes we are all eight years old in the heart and who takes photographs and makes things happen that never did, most important, memories of herself with her mother, who died young.

I have always loved composite pieces, each character introduced like an instrument, their voices blending until there is a communal symphony of a particular place. I greatly admire the novel *The Heart Is a Lonely Hunter* for this reason, and for the way McCullers managed to highlight every walk of society and longing. In the same way, I have long been inspired by Thornton Wilder's *Our Town,* especially it's use of time and the way it gives voice to the dead. *That's all that there is.*

I am very interested in that fine line between fiction and reality and between comedy and tragedy—and pushing the line as much as possible. In this novel, I was also interested in pushing the line between life and death in hopes of finding that split moment when the reader is aware of both places—what those left on earth are recalling and what the one leaving is thinking, that brief spark of connection and recognition before the paths continue in different directions.

This novel is a love song to memory and life. It's a love song to the ocean and elementary school, Boston and the Lumber River and Meadowbrook Cemetery, where I went to bike all through childhood and still visit frequently, one of those places where you're surrounded by history and if you stare upward and no planes pass over, you could easily imagine yourself in another time. It's a love song to all those scraps of sensory memories that leave us feeling timesick: the way the light hits a wall, a piece of clothing or fabric you long forgot, the smell of a house you once visited, a strain of music—all those bits that come together to form your interior life and to mark one life as different from all others. It's an acknowledgment of the fragility of it all. It's nothing new, obviously, just my attempt at it.

Somewhere in the box of notes, I had written thoughts about how life is often like a magic trick—years and years of sleight of hand and lots of smoke and mirrors and doves and scarves and wands and words when so often the result is very simple, right before your eyes. I recently spoke to my mother, who at the end of the call asked, "Would you like to speak to your daddy?" and I said of course I would. After a few moments of fumbling she came back to tell me that he was in there on the bed taking a nap and she hated to wake him, that she would just tell him that I had called. And I could see him there. For several hours, I thought of him there. Sometimes she tells me they're at the beach and sometimes she's waiting for him to get home from work, and my mind leaps to the kitchen of the house where I grew up, and there's the dog from forty years ago, and there's that Chevrolet Caprice station wagon in the drive and the dogwood tree my mother named for her Aunt Lottie, and there's that antenna on the roof that turns and turns as it attempts to find a clear channel. My hope is that *Life After Life* will entertain but also will leave the reader to connect to his or her own signals and memories. After all, *That's all that there is.*

A Conversation with Jill McCorkle

What was the inspiration behind *Life After Life*?
My earliest idea for this novel came twenty years ago when I sat with my dad as he was dying. The idea was completely abstract, and I didn't even begin to know how to pursue it. But I knew that I was interested in capturing and highlighting that moment when a person leaves. One minute you are in the room with someone who has a life filled with detailed history and memories, and in the next minute, the person is gone, and those details and memories (those that have been told to someone) are all that remain. For me, it was a life-changing experience.

What was the biggest challenge in writing this novel?
The biggest challenge came when it was time to put it all together. The novel was in hundreds of tiny pieces and fragments for years. I knew I was working on a novel heavily based on memory—specifically on the memories that compose the substance of an individual's life—so it was easy to collect the bits and pieces without knowing exactly how they would ultimately fit together. Then came the day when it was time to stop collecting

and get organized. Though much changed over the course of the writing, what I did know up front was that the present timeline was fairly short and that if I could successfully ground that plotline, the other elements would surely fall into place. And yet, even then, there was something missing from my original idea for the novel. It was when I decided to use the notebook I had given to Joanna that the novel's scope became closer to my original intention, and the natural move into the points of view of those individuals at the moment of death brought it full circle.

The novel introduces a lot of very different characters. Did you know in the beginning that there would be so many?

I knew there would be a lot of characters because I felt it was important to create the sense of a whole community and, thus, a kind of microcosm of our society. This has been an interest of mine from my earliest writings and something I tackled in my novels *July 7th* and *Carolina Moon*. I am interested in how the town itself becomes a character in that it is the sole witness to the many ways lives crisscross and affect one another. I love Wilder's play *Our Town* for this reason and have long admired what Carson McCullers accomplished in her brilliant novel *The Heart Is a Lonely Hunter*. And so I set out to populate (or give the impression of) a whole community. What I hadn't counted on in the beginning were all of the voices of those dying, and it was exciting to discover how some of them overlapped with the present-day plot.

How does one even go about populating a whole society?

I think first in the broadest strokes. There needs to be a child and there needs to be someone at the other end of life. Of course, when I look back over the body of my work, I see that I have almost always provided myself with the mouth of a child and the mouth of someone elderly. Though there are certainly honest voices elsewhere, I find childhood and the end of life to be the clearest and purest. The child is untainted by the opinions of others, and the person nearing the end is likely focusing on what is most important and able to push back from much of the clutter that might have occupied life. A child, an old person, a conservative hell-bent on what's "right," a free spirit hell-bent on busting loose, someone who grew up with nice things, someone who grew up with nothing. The person who is going to offer a seat on the lifeboat and the one who will push others overboard to get in. And of course everyone has a secret. Everyone has a regret. I find as a writer that if I can tap into what this person loves more than anything and what he or she fears more than anything, then I know what I need to know.

Is there a particular character with whom you identify most closely?

They all feel close in one way or another—well, all but two. One of them I found completely unredeemable, and if you've read the novel, you know who I mean. And the other is someone you hope might smell the coffee and make some changes but could easily go either way. I was drawn to Abby's character because as a child I spent a lot of time with older relatives and going with my grandmother to visit people. I loved the connection to this older generation. And, as I hope my characters show, it ain't over 'til it's over. Even people in the throes of dementia often have glimpses and moments of clarity when some connection is made. I told someone recently that just because we can see the finish line up ahead doesn't mean we should stop running the race. In fact, that's when we need to give it all we've got. I like to imagine my elderly characters doing just that. I think that some of our society's greatest riches are housed in the two ends of life's spectrum—the very young and the very old. The two places have a lot in common, too, especially the very direct honesty and lack of pretense. Too much attention goes to the fat, selfish center of life. Staying in touch with the very young and the very old makes for a more balanced existence. That said, I think I would find myself in many ways housed somewhere between Abby and Sadie, who is the person I would aspire to be. This blend would probably come out looking like Joanna—someone listening and still moving toward the ideal of someone like Sadie. And of course I gave all the love I have of Boston—and the way I miss so much about it—to Rachel. I gave Toby my weariness of vampires and shape shifters and zombies. I am nothing like Marge (I hope), and yet I wanted to respect her, and so I did what I often do with a difficult character, I gave her something I myself would find interesting. She has the much coveted true crime scrapbook.

For a book that focuses on old age and death, there is a lot of humor within. Could you talk about that aspect of the novel?

We are used to seeing the most despairing portraits of old age and we are also used to the more slapstick caricature. I knew I wanted a realistic portrait that left room for a sense of joy and for the comic ways that humans often speak and act. It was important that it never seem I was laughing at these people. The humor I am most interested in grows out of the darkest places. You have to first know the people and understand them and their situations before you can begin to unearth and mine the humor there. I think Toby's rant provides a kind of humor that might stand on its own, and yet, for me, it's all the more meaningful knowing the conflicts and intricacies of her life. Likewise, my character Stanley, faking his dementia. The idea is funny, but the reasons behind it are not. I am drawn to those moments in life when you can't decide if you want to laugh or cry. Many of these characters had me feeling that way. And yes, it grew out of a full understanding of who they are and what they want.

There are a lot of different relationships discussed within this novel. Could you imagine calling it a love story?
In many ways, yes. There are expressions of all kinds of love— there is romantic love and familial love and love between friends. There is love for time—both past and present—as well as places, some long gone. And there is for many, I think, the discovery of a kind of love of self that allows acceptance and, by way of that, compassion for a much larger world—or such is my hope.

Did anything surprise you in the writing of this novel?
Yes. My idea is almost always twice as dark as what eventually happens. This has happened before—I get to the end and see that what I originally thought needed to happen is no longer necessary. My original idea was much more dramatic than the way it played out. The revision process is all about taking those bold dark lines of what might otherwise be caricature or stereotype and smudging

and blending them into a realistic portrait. I'm betting this is a surprising answer since apparently a lot of people have found my ending shocking.

And was that ending something you had always had in mind?

No, or at least not exactly. SPOILER ALERT! I always knew that C.J. would not live. She is my sacrificial lamb. She is the character who represents those members of our society easily overlooked and uncounted. She is someone whose heart is in the right place and who is doing all she can to fight the bad hand she was dealt. She makes a tragic mistake in judgment, and worse, she hasn't been able to confide in her best friend. Bad judgment, lack of trust. It's not a good situation. I believe that a novel operates in a way that's similar to what I believe about the universe. We all have free will, and these choices and decisions form all kinds of wild and crazy patterns; but there is also a system of logic. Now, yes, I could have had something in this universe intervene so that C.J. did not return home to meet Andy that night, but as I said, I knew from the beginning that she was the sacrifice, and as heartbreaking as I found it, I felt I needed the juxtaposition of her tragic and non-sensical death to that of someone like Sadie who has lived long and well—not without loss and heartbreak, but still long and well with many joys. The reaction to death is so often one of sadness and tragedy even when it comes at the end of a long and satisfying life. I wanted to distinguish between the natural and unnatural; I wanted to show the fragility of it all. And, I'm hoping that Joanna will continue to hold firm to her beliefs and perhaps someday gain the wisdom that will see her through.

You write a lot about magic in this novel. How did that come to be?

It was a simple note jotted down about how we are at risk of spending so much time distracted by this or that—that we lose sight of what matters. I think that may be the most common mistake we share. As soon as something nears its close, we begin to miss and regret all that we won't do again. The writer Barry Hannah said that Southern children are nostalgic by the age of nine, and I would tend to agree, adding perhaps that this applies to all children. So, I was thinking of the situation of Abby's parents not paying attention to her the way that they needed to, and I was also thinking of our inner and outer lives and how as we get older more and more time is spent within. The attention to the inner life is not unlike what we knew as children—then it was likely centered on imagination and fantasy instead of reliving memories—and yet, the awareness of this other dimension is a big part of our lives. The inner life resembles the mechanisms of a disappearing chamber—one box housed within another. And of course, from the very beginning, I had in mind the many ways a person might disappear—and there are many. I knew the final lines of the ending years ago—the "now you see her now you don't" lines—but then had to settle in and figure out how to get there.

Could you imagine writing another book about the citizens of Fulton, North Carolina?

My fictional hometown is in place, and it has been fun weaving characters from earlier works into the sidelines so that readers of other novels might find out what happened to so and so. Several characters from *Ferris Beach* make cameos in *Life After Life*, and

C.J.'s friend Sam Lowe is the son of a couple from my novel *Carolina Moon.* So yes, I definitely think there will be future glimpses. Abby lives in the house that was used in *Ferris Beach,* so who knows who will live there next. The town of Fulton, North Carolina, is very real in my mind; the seasons change and years pass; the river rises and falls, and it's an easy ride to the beach, where the shoreline is always shifting and changing. The cemetery will continue to grow out beyond the old shady parts, and babies will continue to be born, and those babies will be told about all the things they weren't present to witness, inherited memories that they will claim as their own.

Cast of Characters

Joanna Lamb—Hospice volunteer at Pine Haven Retirement
Facility, Fulton, North Carolina

Curtis Edward Lamb (1920–2008)—Joanna's father

C.J. (Carolina Jessamine) Loomis—Beautician at Pine Haven

Kurt Loomis—C.J.'s little boy

Sam Lowe—C.J.'s friend, manager of the Fulton Animal Shelter

Abby Palmer—Age twelve, frequent visitor at Pine Haven

Ben and Kendra Palmer—Abby's parents

Andrew Porter—Fulton surgeon

Sadie Randolph—Retired Fulton third-grade teacher, resident of
Pine Haven

Rachel Silverman—Retired Boston lawyer, resident of Pine
Haven

Stanley Stone—Retired Fulton lawyer, resident of Pine Haven

Ned Stone—Stanley's son

Toby Tyler—Retired Columbia, South Carolina, schoolteacher,
resident of Pine Haven

Marge Walker—Fulton socialite, resident of Pine Haven

Luke Whisnant (1957–2007)—Joanna's fourth husband

Hospice recipients

Jeremiah Mason Bass (1932–2004)

Rosemary Swell Carlyle (1933–2008)

Lois Elizabeth Flowers (1929–2010)

Willis Morgan Hall (1921–2007)

Mary Grace Robertson (1912–2007)

Martha Marie Anderson Stone (1935–2008)

Suzanne O'Toole Sullivan (1966–2009)

Judge Henry Morton Walker (1922–2008)

Animals

Dollbaby—Abby's dog

Harley—Pine Haven's cat

Tammy—Luke's dog

Questions for Discussion

1. The structure of this novel is unusual, with its many voices and viewpoints. Why do you think the author chose to narrate the story this way?

2. If you were asked to name the novel's most central character, which would you choose? Why?

3. The last-moment-of-life monologues are interesting strokes of authorial imagination. How did you respond to them?

4. What does this novel imply about how people face death?

5. What are the societal consequences of remaining far removed from the process of dying?

6. How accurately do you think McCorkle portrays life in a continuing care retirement community?

7. How would you describe Sadie's influence on her fellow Pine Haven residents?

8. How do you respond to Toby's reasons for choosing Pine Haven? What about Rachel's reasons?

9. How did your perception of Stanley change throughout the novel? Did you approve or disapprove of the way he dealt with his son's involvement in his life? Why?

10. What about Marge? Does her characterization allow any room for the reader's empathy?

11. What is your perception of Abby's role in the novel?

12. Did you find any redeeming features in Kendra's characterization? What about in Ben's?

13. What do you imagine will become of Abby? What will become of Joanna? What about Sam Lowe?

14. Did the novel's ending surprise you? What ending might you have preferred?

TOM RANKIN

Jill McCorkle is the author of nine previous books—four story collections and five novels—five of which have been selected as *New York Times* Notable Books. The recipient of the New England Book Award, the John Dos Passos Prize for Excellence in Literature, and the North Carolina Prize for Literature, she teaches writing at North Carolina State University and lives in Hillsborough, North Carolina.

Other Algonquin Readers Round Table Novels

The Art Forger, a novel by B. A. Shapiro

In this *New York Times* bestseller about art, authenticity, love, and betrayal, a long-missing Degas painting—stolen during the still-unsolved heist at the Isabella Stewart Gardner Museum—is delivered to the studio of a young artist who has entered into a Faustian bargain with a powerful gallery owner.

"[A] highly entertaining literary thriller about fine art and foolish choices." —*Parade*

AN ALGONQUIN READERS ROUND TABLE EDITION WITH READING GROUP GUIDE AND OTHER SPECIAL FEATURES • FICTION • ISBN 978-1-61620-316-0

The Watery Part of the World, a novel by Michael Parker

This vast and haunting novel spans more than a century of liaisons that develop on a tiny windblown island battered by storms and cut off from the world—beginning in 1813 with the disappearance of a ship off the North Carolina coast and ending 150 years later when the last three inhabitants are forced to abandon their beloved, beautiful island.

"A lush feat of historical speculation . . . A vivid tale about the tenacity of habit and the odd relationships that form in very small, difficult places." —*The Washington Post*

AN ALGONQUIN READERS ROUND TABLE EDITION WITH READING GROUP GUIDE AND OTHER SPECIAL FEATURES • FICTION • ISBN 978-1-61620-143-2

Heading Out to Wonderful, a novel by Robert Goolrick

In the summer of 1948, a handsome, charismatic stranger shows up in the sleepy town of Brownsburg, Virginia. All he has with him are two suitcases: one contains his few possessions, including a fine set of butcher knives; the other is full of money. From the author of the #1 *New York Times* bestselling novel *A Reliable Wife* comes a heart-stopping story of love gone terribly wrong.

"A suspenseful tale of obsessive love." —*People*

AN ALGONQUIN READERS ROUND TABLE EDITION WITH READING GROUP GUIDE AND OTHER SPECIAL FEATURES • FICTION • ISBN 978-1-61620-279-8

When She Woke, a novel by Hillary Jordan

Bellwether Prize winner Hillary Jordan's provocative novel is the fiercely imagined story of a woman struggling to navigate an America of a not-too-distant future, where the line between church and state has been eradicated, and a terrifying new way of delivering justice has been introduced.

"Chillingly credible . . . Holds its own alongside the dark inventions of Margaret Atwood and Ray Bradbury."
—*The New York Times Book Review*

AN ALGONQUIN READERS ROUND TABLE EDITION WITH READING GROUP GUIDE AND OTHER SPECIAL FEATURES • FICTION • ISBN 978-1-61620-193-7